DAYS OF HOPE, MILES OF MISERY

Love and Loss on the Oregon Trail

FRED DICKEY

Carved crudely on a rock is the fading inscription on the gravestone of Rachel E. Pattison. It is a testament to the danger and grief of the way west. She was eighteen, from Illinois, and a bride of two months. She died of cholera in one day while camped at Ash Hollow, which is now in western Nebraska.

To Kathy the wise:
scientist, naturalist,
and expert on me.

Available through Amazon, Ingram, e-books,
audio books, and wholesalers, and retailers.

For comments or reprint permission
contact Fred Dickey at freddickey1@gmail.com
Published by Lost River Books
lostriverbooks@gmail.com

Cover design by Lionel Talaro, La Mesa, Calif.
Design by Pamela Trush, Delaney-Designs.
Cover oxen art courtesy of Nat'l. Oregon Trail
museum, Baker City, Ore.

Kathy Dickey, editor

ISBNs: paperback, 978-1-7358341-0-8;
hardcover, 978-1-7358341-1-5;
e-book, 978-1-7358341-2-2.

HISTORICAL INDIVIDUALS
IN THE BOOK

Jim Bridger

Jim Beckwourth

Kit Carson

Lansford Hastings

Chief Truckee

John Sutter

KEY CHARACTERS

- Andrew **Banks** & Martin **Carter**
- Jim **Beckwourth**, mountain man
- Dr. Abel **Blanc**, Hannah's deceased husband
- Hannah **Blanc** (Spencer), Sarah & Billy
- Benny **Bogle**, pimp
- Jim **Bridger**, mountain man
- John **Burns**, drunken traveler
- Malachi & Ruth **Cohen,** committeeman
- Flora **Dickens**, Florence & Tom
- Henry **Griswold**, ailing man
- Lansford W. **Hastings**, promoter of dangerous route
- Maude, Earl & Roger **Horner**, mentally ill woman
- Abraham **Jackman** & Susan, committeeman
- **Johnny**, aka, Johnnythree
- Nimrod **Lee**
- **Magpie**, Nimrod's Crow wife
- Ezra **Mansfield,** committeeman
- **Many Horses**, Magpie's father
- Uriah **Meister**, slaver
- Zack **Monroe**, bully
- Billy **Owens**, Susan's paramour
- Jasper and Agnes **Patterson**, aged members
- Shadrach & Clara **Penney**, wagon train captain
- **Preacher** (Rev. Mather Poe)
- Aaron **Proctor** & Gertie
- **Red**, prostitute
- Ed **Spencer**, Hannah's abusive husband
- John **Sutter**, California land baron
- Simon **Tester**, troublemaker

CHAPTER ONE

November 1845

The evening sun sent its fading light across the mountain pass and onto the face of a granite peak. As though opening a shade, gray rock was transformed into glowing pink as nature served up a work of art called alpenglow. Hannah Blanc watched the Sierra lightshow with awe, but her admiration was beclouded by her whisper to the sky— "What a taunt, that hell should be so beautiful."

As the sun retired behind forested mountains, it gave way to a black sky under a spray of stars. Hannah knew cold was coming. Bitter cold. Cold without pity.

Late in the night, Hannah rose from where she lay to adjust thin blankets covering her sleeping two children and brush away drifted snow. Their whimpering was sandpaper on her heart. She laid more wood on the campfire that was both warmth and life. Clustered as lumps just feet away were the surviving pioneers she had cared for across months of bleak land and empty horizons.

Nearby and alert, as he had been for two thousand miles, was Nimrod Lee, their enigmatic mountain-man guide. As he had led their way, he also sought to find a man he needed to kill. When their eyes would meet, she hoped nothing was evident.

The other pioneers hugged each other for warmth. They shivered in ragged, smelly clothes, and endured the wind as it moaned through fir branches and gave teeth to the cold. Hannah hoped that when dawn came, and it was time to rise, every one of them would.

For those companions, it was a night of misery of a terrible kind. There was no defense and no escape. Stupor was their refuge. The mountains' intent was to break their spirits so they would quit the survival struggle and slide into death. Faint above the wind, sobs, moans, and prayers pleaded for deliverance. But nothing profane. Even the irreverent wouldn't chance that. Eternity was too close.

They blamed themselves for joining a caravan that brought them to this place where death awaited. All the people back home who had urged them on did not realize what they were urging. The pioneers had learned an adventurer's grim truth: It is better to die back home in one's own bed, and among one's own people, than to die where only crows and coyotes are interested.

Curse California for its beckoning.

Hannah looked down on her children lying entwined to share body heat. Guilt surged to her throat like vomit. She spoke aloud her agony: "Dear God, how did I let this happen?"

CHAPTER TWO

June 1840

Old Man Coyote, the creator and god of the Crow Nation, spoke to Grandmother Earth and decreed that the land should once again come alive.

Thus, summer gently returned to the high valley beneath Grand Teton Mountain. In its path, soft winds rustled through the leaves of reborn aspens, and crowns of snow melted on hovering peaks. Pronghorn fawns bounded in the joy of discovered life, and fireweed and bluebells splashed glory amidst buffalo grass and flitting magpies.

Nimrod Lee rejoiced in the beauty of the Rocky Mountains, but he wasn't beguiled by the dangers they hid. Nimrod was a mountain man and trapper of thirty-three; whipcord lean, and an even six feet, rather tall for the day. His wind-scoured face and straight-ahead manner underscored Scots-Irish grit. Alert, dark eyes hinted a touch of Cherokee, but it went unspoken in the family. Pockmark traces on his face evidenced a close call with smallpox. He had a short, uneven beard because using scissors in a quick clip was easier than shaving with a straight-edge razor in icy creek water. His dark hair was long and tangled. He had traded his metal comb to an Arapahoe for a mink pelt. It was a deal too good to pass up.

He was a mix of ornery and sentimental: the first when it was needed, the second when the situation allowed. The sum of his bearing warned he could be a dangerous man.

Nimrod smiled down on what made him a happy man, his young Crow wife, his *bia*, by the name of Magpie, or Maggie, as he often called her. Magpie was not a companion on loan from the tribe to warm a winter teepee, as were many trappers' "spouses." To

Nimrod, she was a regular wife, like the women back home.

Magpie's proud bearing and sassiness befitted the favorite daughter of a chief. She was used to getting her way. Magpie was an inch above five feet with a stout body of little fat. She had grown strong by living in a society where most of the heavy and tedious work was done by women. Men were occupied by horses, hunting, war, and telling stories. That left plenty of time for watching women work.

The hue of Magpie's skin was bronze with a blush of rose. Her onyx eyes were Asiatic, and her cheekbones were high. In Boston, she would be an exotic curiosity, but certainly not beautiful. However, snooty society was a long way from this camp where she was considered a great catch. And to Nimrod's great pleasure, he was the one who made the catch.

For her travel ensemble, Magpie was dressed in a plain brown deerskin dress with no ornaments. On the back of a packhorse, though, was a "party" outfit of a pullover dress decorated with elk teeth. It was worked to tissue softness and was of a creamy white color because it had not been smoke-treated. It was decorated by buttons of brass and a creative array of colored beads, all acquired from traders for furs. The leggings were of deerskin, complemented by moccasins of dyed vermillion enhanced with trade beads.

She had also packed a peach-colored, satin bonnet with a frilly trim that Nimrod had brought back from St. Louis, and which she had fingered with oohs and ahhs. It was the envy of the camp when she walked about with it covering her straight black hair, which she kept short in the Crow tradition.

In Boston, an outfit of comparable dress would draw scornful or amused looks. Here in the mountains, it was a fashionable ensemble proclaiming, "I am the daughter of a chief."

As Magpie stood below Nimrod, head-high to Bub's withers, in her arms was their infant daughter, a cherry-cheeked, plump little gurgler named Wildflower. She was a rare Indian child with cobalt blue eyes beneath raven hair.

Lying across Nimrod's pommel was another love of his life, one that had saved it more than once. It was a fifty-four caliber, thirty-three-inch barrel, percussion-cap rifle set to a hair trigger.

It was made by the brothers Hawken of St. Louis, Jake and Sam. Nimrod had paid eight beaver pelts when the pelt was worth five dollars. On this day, however, the gun's price would be at least fifteen pelts in a collapsing fur market. A few trappers clung to the flintlock rifle, saying it had kept them alive thus far. Nimrod didn't argue. A man should follow his own lights.

The Hawken was expensive, but it had proved its worth to the brief dismay of enemies who saw the puff of powder smoke an eye blink before the bullet struck.

Implied in Nimrod's bearing was the inheritance of the Big Moccasin Gap trek made from Virginia to Kaintuck by his father, and of the King's Mountain Revolutionary War battle fought by his grandfather. He came from folk who could make sweet music to Jesus, and then fight over a lazy hound, both on the same Sabbath. He was of that blood. For one otherwise amiable, Nimrod could be a testy man.

The name Nimrod was chosen by his Bible-reading mother. She came across it in the tenth chapter of the book of Genesis, where it read in her King James Bible, "And Cush begat Nimrod: he began to be a mighty one in the earth. He was a mighty hunter before the Lord."

His mother liked the sound of it, given that Nimrod was begat by Cush, who seemed to be related to Noah, but as to how, she got lost as the begats piled up. Biblical genealogy meant nothing to her son. He wasn't much of a prayerful man.

Nimrod's dress reflected the culture mix of what his life had become: a beat-up felt hat and wool pants tucked into St. Louis-bought leather boots. But also a belted and fringed deerskin blouse that reached just short of his knees. The fringe was more than ornamental; it provided useful strings. The blouse was a gift from Magpie, who had scraped the skin, tanned the hide, and sewed the thick leather. She had lacked trade beads to decorate the shirt, so Nimrod rode two hours in winter to barter for them at a neighboring camp. When he returned, he noticed the dress she made for herself was plain, so he insisted the beads be for her.

Apart from faith in Andy Jackson, aged Kentucky bourbon, and an occasional claim of being a Baptist, he didn't put stock in much except staying alive. He lacked time or inclination to put much store by anything else.

His English was not the outgrowth of a grammar book. It was a spotty mix of backwoods parlance, combined with usage picked up from book-learned folks. His six years of schooling enabled him to read, write, and do his figures enough to get by. In Nimrod's actions, regardless of his words, fellow mountain men would consider him an intellectual. Yet, amid educated folk, he tried his best to copy their speech and manners with checkered results. As the saying went, the quality of his speechifying waxed and waned. He was touchy about it. He might say "if'n" in one sentence and "if" in the next, or perhaps in the next clause, and be oblivious to both.

If he were in Tidewater Virginia, he would be uncouth. If those same gentrified folks were in the Rocky Mountains, they would be dead.

Bask though he did in the early summer breeze, Nimrod wasn't fooled by it. In those mountains, death was always waiting down the trail, every trail. Death was a willful thing with mood, purpose, and even whim. It was a hatchet in the head or being swept away in a whitewater river. It was the fangs of a rattler or the claws of a grizzly. It was waking up with cholera and in a grave by evening. It was a shallow, unmarked grave that wolves or Indians would dig up for meat or clothing before the worms could go to work. It was starvation in a winter camp, maybe staved off by a boiled leather moccasin, but maybe not.

An unfortunate trapper's folks back east would sigh and refuse to give up waiting for word that would never come— "Why don't he come home?" a mother in her farm kitchen might ask…and ask…and ask.

Nimrod stayed alive by a survival skill of trip-wire alertness. His thoughts were never far from danger, and his swivel scan missed little. An Arikaree hunting party once almost ran him down. But when he steadied his Hawken against a cottonwood and killed their leader from a hundred yards, the remaining Rees decided they were hunting the wrong game.

Five years earlier, a trapper from the Hudson's Bay Company stole a pack of his furs at a Pierre's Hole camp. Nimrod chased him for two days, but then the thief chose to fight rather than surrender the furs, though Nimrod would have been content to retrieve his furs and be on his way.

The late thief made the wrong decision. Nimrod returned alone with his furs, and also with the thief's.

It was the Blackfeet, though, who convinced many trappers that returning to St. Louis might be a boring life, but a breathing one. There was no dealing with Blackfeet. They did not yearn for beads and mirrors. They wanted scalps. Fighting the Sioux and other tribes was their birthright and their business. Killing every one of the hairy face interlopers who were taking furs they figured belonged to the tribe was their pleasure.

They were discouragingly good at it.

Danger made Nimrod wary of every move, his own and others'. However, he didn't obsess over it. He accepted the risk of death as a fair trade for being there.

Picturesque mountains were not on Nimrod's mind as he sat atop Bub in the Crow village he had called home the past two years. Surrounded by barking dogs, whooping children, and chattering women, he could relax and feel accepted.

Sun-bleached white buffalo skins were draped over lodge poles to make the tipis that gave Nimrod the comfort of home. It was where he returned after clearing his beaver traps.

The Crows were nomadic and followed the buffalo to wherever the beasts meandered in the northern mountains and plains. The tribe had been pushed out of the Ohio country by the Cheyenne and Sioux almost two centuries earlier, but this was where they would remain. They were closest to friendship with whites of all the surrounding tribes.

On a balmy spring day a year ago, Nimrod and pregnant Magpie stood on a cliff viewing the profusion of wildflowers covering the meadow below. They decided to name their baby after the most beautiful flower if it were a girl. Magpie singled out a yellow one as her choice. Nimrod laughed and said it might not be appreciated when she grew up to carry the name the white people gave to that particular flower— mule's ear. He suggested instead, they honor all the beautiful blooms and name her Wildflower.

Magpie handed the infant up to Nimrod. He held the baby high in the air and blew on her fat tummy. Wildflower squealed as he smiled and returned her to Magpie. A few feet away were the proud grandparents, Many Horses and Quiet Woman.

Many Horses sat above his world on a mount, which at sixteen hands was towering for an Indian pony. It befitted his status as chief of the White Calf band of the Crows, called *Apsáalooke* in their own language, or Absaroka, in the Anglicized version. His hair fell to below his waist and was slicked down with bear grease. The buffalo horn headdress he wore made him look towering and fierce, which he intended, and could become in a heartbeat.

In the Crow culture, women could occupy high positions, and Quiet Woman projected the confidence expected of her as *akbaalia*, or shaman, of the tribe. Her fringed white dress with spangles of bright beadwork bespoke her status. She put her hand on Bub's neck and spoke to Nimrod in Crow. "You must not take Magpie to the trading place. Bad men go there. They abuse Indian women. Magpie has only seen twenty summers. She does not know these things."

Nimrod knew she was right. The Fur Rendezvous was an annual drunken circus held after the snowmelt in the passes, and as the wildflowers came back to the meadows of the northern Rockies. Dozens of mountain men and a couple hundred Indians gathered to trade, drink, fight, gamble, and occasionally kill each other.

The stated reason for the get-together was the arrival of pack trains from St. Louis from which sober traders separated drunken trappers and Indians from the products of their hard and dangerous labor. Valuable beaver pelts, or "plews," as the trappers called skins with the fur left on, were exchanged for traps, guns, wool shirts, and tobacco plugs, all at balloon prices. After a long winter holed up in snow-bound cabins, most of the men lusted for rotgut whiskey, often leavened with tobacco, turpentine, and ingredients unknown. It was said a rattlesnake's head was discovered in one barrel, but no one died of poison— venom, that is. Lots of whiskey, all of it bad, resulted in trappers ending up as skinned as any beaver. A drunken trapper was not a shrewd bargainer.

The greater magnet, though, was the one chance each year for the men to socialize by more than a happenstance meeting on the trail offered. Even then, if a trapper had packhorses carrying a season's catch of pelts, any unfamiliar trapper he met would be regarded with wariness. Not the best beginning for a friendship.

Mountain men preferred a solitary life, or so the myth said. The reality was their work required it. However, they were also starved for all the vices city men could find around the corner. The Fur Rondy was a fire sale for sin.

Nimrod knew that if whiskey made mountain men mean, well, it made Indians crazy. The mix was volatile, and the inevitable blow-ups could be cruel to Indian women ill-advised to be present.

Nimrod nodded reassurance to Quiet Woman. He understood the native language better than he spoke it. He replied in Crow using the cartoonish word pattern often attributed to Indians trying to speak English. "I go alone," he said. "I leave Magpie Running Bull village."

"Swear it," Quiet Woman insisted.

"I give word to Quiet Woman. I give word to Many Horses."

Magpie handed the baby to Quiet Woman and mounted her pony. Nimrod wheeled Bub and led his string of three packhorses away from the village. Two were loaded with bundled beaver pelts, along with a few fox, skunk, and lynx. Five years before, three horses would have been required to carry Nimrod's winter's catch. The remaining horse carried food, utensils, tools, and clothing, everything a savvy mountain man and Indian woman knew was required to survive in that wilderness.

Just before he made the loud kissing sound to start Bub on the trail, Nimrod looked over at Magpie squinting in the blissful sun. He contrasted that moment with the days when the streams ran icy, and his fingers groped without feeling as he struggled with the cold iron of his traps. On those days, Nimrod yearned to be back in Kentucky plowing fields and sitting around a pot-belly stove swapping stories and spitting tobacco with neighbors. Kentucky had the tug of home, but he could never return and face what he had left behind. Best not to think about it.

From a chance encounter in St. Louis with a friend from back home two years previous, he learned things were well with his mother. She still had the farm. It was being worked in shares by Lloyd Cooksey and his sons. Mr. Faircloth had kept his word.

His favorite sister, Elsie, was married to William Johnson from town. As he heard it, they opened a prosperous dry goods store. She birthed a baby boy a while back. He didn't catch the name. The news made him happy, but he blocked an impulse toward nostalgia for his peace of mind. It was a resolve that had hardened over time. The wheels of his life had rolled forward to this place, in what would become western Wyoming.

As they headed for the Rendezvous, with jagged peaks framing Magpie's slim shoulders and snow-fed streams rippling past his mule's feet, Nimrod was aware of why he became a mountain man.

Magpie, of course, knew no other way. Magpie read the meadows the way a hack driver would read city streets. But at the moment, she was not thinking of the scenery.

Nimrod pointed into a grove of trees where a pack of wolves watched them. "Maggie, over there! See the big gray?" he said in English as they looked down a spongy swale. "He's a beauty."

Magpie ignored the wolves. "My life is always the same— boring. Running Bull's village is nothing but old people," she responded in Crow. They juggled languages between them like balls in the air, each learning from the other.

"I gave word parent," he said in stumbling Crow syntax.

"You treat me like a child," she said in an accusing voice.

" Trading place bad for women: Much whiskey, much fighting, many rough men."

"Other women will be there," Magpie argued in a pout.

"Different kind. Not like you," Nimrod said, trying to be conciliatory, and end the discussion. Her aggrieved look, however, made no such promise.

At the end of their second day, Nimrod and Magpie camped along a stream running swift from the snowmelt. They had a quick meal of fried meat, and the Indian "fast food," of vegetables and fat pressed into a cake, then roasted. From his last buffalo kill, Nimrod had prepared boudins, which were buffalo small intestines with ends tied into sausages, then roasted with the original contents intact. It was considered a delicacy.

After the tin plates were washed and packed, the animals were fed, watered, curried and hobbled. The two settled down in the night chill under buffalo robes. Nimrod looked tenderly at Magpie with her head resting on a saddle for a pillow. The small fire cast a soft, flickering reflection on her face. The cicadas were in full mating song as Nimrod reached for her, but she turned away and sobbed.

Nimrod ran his fingers through his hair in frustration. His chatter bounced around, looking for a way to lighten her mood. "Cicadas are the bad luck bug. It takes them seventeen year to get born, then they die in a month." His chuckle was unaccompanied. "I'd shore git riled up, it was me." Magpie's gloom was evident as he moved closer to her. "What's the matter?"

"I'll miss you, and I want to see the pretty cloth and the jewelry."

He tried again to make her understand. "It's not what you think. You have much to learn about rough men and their danger to women."

Magpie ignored his words. "I'll be a prisoner of old people. ... Maybe you want a new wife." Big tears rolled out of her black eyes and made furrows in the trail dust on her bronze face.

"That's not true," he said, torn at her sadness. He reached for her.

She angrily rebuffed him, but she sensed him wavering and flipped to a coaxing smile. "I promise to stay at your side and be careful," she pleaded while stroking his face. "You are my fearless warrior. You will protect me."

"Well, I..." His promise to her parents passed through his mind, but her smile was like the gravity pull of the moon, subtle and irresistible. "Uh..." he muttered, weakening.

"Oh, thank you, thank you." She chose to take his stumbling words as surrender, and he no longer argued. She kissed him from forehead to neck and whispered, "You're my dogface," a common Indian name for bewhiskered trappers.

"And you're my little redskin." They giggled at their happiness, and he slipped beneath her robe as she lifted it.

Later, she told him in Crow, "I like when you love me, it's like I'm special, like a, uh, a prize pony, with your gentle stroking and whispering in my ear."

"A pony?" he said, raising his eyebrows.

His amusement peeved her. "Oh, you know what I mean. Horses are of great value. Men in our tribe treat them better. They don't treat women the way you do. I like it."

"I would never kiss a pony."

"Oh, be quiet," she said with mock anger, then snuggled close and dozed off to dream of the exciting days ahead. They laughed together. Hers was happy. His was hollow.

She was warm and soft under his arm. Her breath was sweet as a baby's. He drew her head close to his chest. I love this little rascal, he thought fondly. But the blissful moment aside, sleep eluded Nimrod because he couldn't shake the foreboding over the promise he had just committed to break, and the price it might exact. He stared into the small fire looking for something. But when it died to coals, there was nothing. As the trees lost their shape in the deepening night, he continued to stare into the dark. He knew he had reason to worry.

CHAPTER THREE

March 1832

H annah Vogel smelled the man as he came up behind her. She heard the heavy clomp of his boots closing fast on the board sidewalk. As he drew even, he moved to her street side as a buffer against splashed mud, as polite men in St. Louis always made a point of doing. She shifted her eyes sideways, not wanting to be mistaken for a forward woman. She saw he carried a rifle and wore a long knife at his belt. He turned full face to her, which was daring in proper society. His beard was uncombed; his buckskin shirt had a smoked odor, but not the equal of his body smell. In the moment of his passing, he grinned and touched his battered slouch hat. "Good day, miss."

She nodded. "Sir."

The man moved on, but not before thinking—There ain't no woman like her upriver.

Trappers came down the Missouri to deliver the beaver pelts which would be shipped out to make hats to decorate the heads of dandies in far-off places. They were the original mountain men: violent, grimy, greasy, unkempt, and obstreperous; men who teased death from warriors and grizzlies to travel a thousand miles back to civilization lusting for saloon whiskey and soiled doves.

Trappers were a combination of adventurer and businessman and were common in St. Louis. They injected energy into the clamorous, crusty, river city of fifteen thousand, and gave it a zest of optimism, and also of greed. St. Louis was on the make. It fancied itself the gateway to the blank map called the Far West with its two thousand mysterious miles to the Pacific Ocean.

Hannah was the only child of Rudolph and Greta Vogel, second generation German immigrant traders who made a lot of money trafficking in the skins of those harmless, hard-working rodents trapped between steel serrated jaws. It was not a pretty business, but it was a profitable business, and created great wealth in St. Louis, and the moral trickery that followed fast money.

Though not a head-turner, Hannah was considered comely by those who judged such things, which was most people. 'Comely' is a polite way to say she was attractive enough, which was fine by her. She was medium in almost all the ways a person is judged at first glance: height, form, face, and voice. Hannah was pleasant and laughed at the right things without being giddy. She had light brown hair, a round face, dark eyes, and a sturdy body, which the harsh environment could not victimize as frail. But brains and determination? Ah, nothing medium about those. However, they weren't as valued as the skill to bake a tasty pie and to know her place.

Hannah was among the most looked-up-to of the young women of St. Louis. She had the money to dress in the Regency and French styles. Eastern dress alone made her a bit provocative because, in St. Louis, there were few to afford, or dare to wear, the latest fashions. European styles had turned a bit risqué with high-waist, free-flowing gowns emphasizing the bust line.

The Vogel home was one of the finest of the rustic city. Its tasteful decor would have been admired even in the drawing rooms of Cincinnati. The house also had a library with many books, and it was among those shelves that Hannah's mind flowered. Books consumed her, which caused her parents to be concerned she wasn't "well rounded."

She was enamored of *Charlotte Temple,* a bestselling American novel written fifty years earlier about a young woman ill-used by an older man, and her fall to a tragic end because of it. Hannah was impressed with the woman author, Susanna Rowson, who achieved fame and success without using a male pseudonym. Also, though the thought was subliminal, she relished the idea that a female character could fall into a sinful life, meet a bad ending, and yet be sympathetic to readers. In other words, people who read books were willing to see a woman protagonist as a whole and complicated person, even as men were. That's the way Hannah saw herself.

Hannah outwardly fit the mold of a young lady as genteel as the frontier allowed. However, she was the prim and proper young lady only from the neck down. Above the lace collar, Hannah's brain agitated for knowledge, and her parents were wise enough to recognize it despite misgivings. To her bountiful good fortune, they enrolled her among the first students to attend Lindenwood School for Girls. It was one of the country's first women's colleges, and located oddly enough on the edge of that frontier outpost.

Hannah made the most of it. She was cum laude over the entire curricula but was at her best in the sciences. Hannah sometimes wondered how she would perform back east at, say, Harvard College. ... She would have done fine.

The human body entranced Hannah, especially the vicissitudes visited upon it by disease and poor health. In her mind, she was a healer. She often told friends her goal was to become a physician. Of course, such a declaration made patronizing listeners smile and dismiss her as a dreamer. Her parents hoped such brashness would not discourage desirable suitors.

Sadly, for her ambition, society's purpose in educating women in 1830 was to create silk-dressed paragons of the social graces, adept at setting a table, witty small talk, and tutoring young sons for a life more important than hers. That she was well-read in poetry and literature had no market value.

One afternoon, during a break from classes, Hannah was dutifully taking part in a knitting circle with several other single young women. One friend broke into the chatter to comment, "Hannah, I do declare, what you did was so—so frightening, going to college. I would never have even thought of that. Whatever are you going to do with so much book learning?"

Hannah thought for a moment and looked around at the clicking needles. "I'm going to be a doctor."

The clicking stopped. An amazed woman said, "You mean a *doctor* doctor? That's not what a lady does."

" I could be a good one," Hannah said with a small pout. "I already know more about medicine than a lot of men doctors."

The first woman stared at her. "Gracious!" The needles resumed but clicked faster.

Hannah continued knitting herself, but her smile suppressed determination—Knitting is not what I want my life to be about.

Hannah finished Lindenwood with a brain abuzz for knowledge. Education had stuffed her head with all manner of ambitious ideas, but job opportunities were limited to tutoring other people's children. In disappointment, she turned down job after job, which made gossips tsk-tsk about her as uppity.

Hannah should have been considered a marriage prize. However, despite her status, she was handicapped in the betrothal sweepstakes of St. Louis society. Gossips buzzed to each other and into the ears of eligible bachelors that too much education was not a good thing for a girl and could be distracting to a wife. An obsession with book-learning could cause her to be inattentive to domestic, maternal, and less-mentionable marital duties.

For a year, Hannah went from one "girl's" job to another, and she quit all of them. Family money gave her an easy fall-back, but "failure" did nothing for her ego or social standing. Instead, she went back to her first love and read everything she could find on medicine. Some of it was accurate, but much was quackery. She had a knack for separating the two. But while she read, she was acutely aware of the passing of time.

The calendar showed 1831, her twentieth year. Hannah was closing in on dreaded old maid status. She pretended it didn't bother her much that most men seemed frightened of a smart woman.

The serendipity of good fortune seldom favors the unprepared. Hannah was both prepared and primed.

Her life turned around on a slice of ham.

On a Sunday evening after choir practice and before retiring, Hannah went to the cupboard and removed the remainder of a ham from Saturday dinner. She smelled it and detected nothing of concern. She cut a piece and nibbled on it as she climbed the stairs. Then, off to bed.

The ham's attack in the pre-dawn hours was a nasty surprise. Hannah felt the tell-tale sensation of a tightness rushing up to her throat from the stomach. She rushed to the chamber pot in time to purge the contents of the tainted snack, or most of it. Groaning, she lay on the floor next to the chamber pot, reluctant to move from it. She dragged herself back into bed and laid for hours, shivering and waiting for the next attack from either the stomach or the colon, whichever had the greater grievance.

When Hannah didn't come down for breakfast, her mother went up to check and discovered a moaning, sick daughter. She sent the maid with a message to Dr. Abel Blanc, an immigrant Frenchman from back east who had made a good impression on friends.

Blanc was an unremarkable man a dozen years older than Hannah, of small stature, balding, and with a boyish smile and kind eyes. He could have taught the bedside manner.

"*Docteur Blanc, je suis tellement malade.*" [I'm so sick.] Hannah said, at long last able to use her three years of French.

"*Je peux voir ca mademoiselle.*" [I can see that, miss.] He smiled, impressed at her fluid French. "However, let's make English our language of diagnosis. I have an idea of what we have here."

After listening to her description, he asked for the offending ham, and then smelled it. "Ah, ha! Here is the gastric villain." In an instant, he diagnosed early-onset food poisoning.

"Do you suggest an emetic, perhaps calomel?" she asked. "I hope not. I don't trust mercury as a drug."

"Well, well!" He raised his eyebrows in surprise and drew the words out. "I think I have a patient who has done some medical reading. What do you base your opinion on, Miss Vogel?"

"A chemistry professor who had misgivings. He said mercury had been shown to ravage the organs." She blushed. "I don't mean to suggest I know more than I do."

"*Au contraire.*" It's refreshing to talk to an educated person on this side of the Mississippi. Now, to answer your question: Your body is fighting back. You have but a small fever, and, as you tell me, vomiting and diarrhea are doing their jobs well. They are cleaning out your system. To assist them, drink all the water you can hold."

Hannah recovered in three days, but Abel Blanc saw the need to keep checking on her—just to make sure, he said. He was a bachelor who had yet to make many friends. He told her he had studied medicine at the University of Bordeaux, France.

"Ah, fine wine," she said with a sigh.

"I see your education has not neglected the finer things," he said, laughing.

He had come to St. Louis because he had heard the western frontier could mean bountiful fees.

Hannah's science acumen was apparent, and he thought maybe he could develop her as a nurse, and would be of great use in his practice. He had known many bright women and thought it idiotic of society not to make use of such a vast pool of intelligence.

When Abel offered the job, Hannah's excited smile was his answer. Her intuition told her his interest went beyond employment, which was of no concern because her interest was the same.

CHAPTER FOUR

Nimrod and Magpie crested a rise above where Horse Creek flowed into Green River, a week's ride northeast of the smelly salt lake and beneath the distant silhouette of the Wind River Mountains. Green River was a narrow but deep and dangerous water path that began in those mountains. It meandered down to join what became the Colorado River. The Green was known as the *Seeds-kee-dee-Agie* [Prairie Hen River] to the Shoshones in whose territory were the headwaters.

Spread out below was a lush valley normally featuring the songs and chatter of a dozen bird species, but the birds were drowned out by a boisterous carnival. Scores of traders, mountain men, and Indian braves and squaws were an undulating crowd spread among tents, tipis, lean-tos, and peddler's tables. They were haggling, drinking, fighting, target-shooting, urinating, gambling, arguing, and racing horses.

It was the annual Fur Rendezvous, and no one there knew it would be the last.

Many of the Indians who were rubbing shoulders and wandering around the gathering would, in any other place and time, be trying to lift each others' scalps. Although the tribes were neighbors in the mountain valleys and plains, they could have come from different continents. They were a dress combination of full feather tribal finery, and bizarre mixes of trader items, such as dresses of mismatched cloth, top hats, and even one fellow with spats over his moccasins. The whites they dealt with were indifferent dressers. They wore whatever was handy, warm, and not too ragged, although the definition of ragged was generously broad.

Warriors included Arapahos, Bannocks, Northern Cheyennes, Utes, Gros Ventres [Big Bellies], Crows, and from other of the seven Sioux nations. Each eyed the others as potential assassins and wondered if they would be waylaid on the trail home.

As Nimrod and Magpie rode into the camp, his face was a broad smile at anticipated reunions, nodding to some and waving to others. Looking around, he realized there were far fewer trappers than in the previous fifteen rendezvous. However, no one could have predicted this would be the last, because the beavers had made as big a sacrifice to fashion as their numbers allowed. The scarcity of animals was crippling the fur market and helped incentivize a fashion change to silk hats back east and in Europe. Over the last decade, the price trappers received for pelts dropped by more than half, down to three dollars.

Trappers were tough people, often mean, living in a time when mean wasn't shocking. They were not philosophers mulling the stars at night, or poets writing odes to the sublimity of nature. There was little romance in their grueling lives. Those men were prickly at a time when defending honor was worth dying for. They lived close to the ground and were encrusted with its dirt. There were many reasons why they weren't bankers in Boston. Most would be flabbergasted if told they would one day be the romanticized lore of the mountains.

Nimrod recognized a tall man nearby with a gray-laced beard astride a big horse; a man dressed as he was, dressed as they all were. Nimrod hailed him.

"Hey, Bridger. Jim Bridger!"

Bridger was a patriarch of mountain men. He was aloof to many who hailed him, but he responded to Nimrod with delight and rode over.

Nimrod and Bridger had first hooked up when Nimrod joined the Rocky Mountain Fur Company in 1830. Bridger had been his boss, or "boosway," a corruption of the French bourgeois. Nimrod worked alongside about one hundred other trappers in that brigade, including Jim Beckwourth, Joe Meek, Hugh Glass, and the legendary Jedediah Smith.

The company would take half the trappers' pelts in exchange for outfitting and providing the strength of numbers as protection from Indians. However, when the outfit got taken over by Astor's

American Fur Company in 1834, Nimrod got all entrepreneurial and struck out on his own as a free trapper. The lure of more fur profit made the greater danger of losing his scalp a risk worth taking.

Bridger was a robust man, and the hand he extended to Nimrod was calloused and meaty. "Well, I'll be go to hell, Nimrod Lee. I ain't seen you since we wintered up on Rosebud Creek—what, six year ago? Damn near starved and froze to death, we did. I didn't die on account of I feared you'd feast on me."

Bridger was an elder statesman of mountain men. The sole blot on his record happened in 1823 when young Jim and an older trapper were left as a death watch on Hugh Glass who had been mauled by a bear.

Glass refused to cooperate, taking his own sweet time to die. The two men got spooked by Indian sign, and figured Glass could die on his own time and left. Glass, however, crossed them up and crawled out of the wilderness and into mountain history.

No one talked about the incident around Jim Bridger.

Bridger offered a jug, and Nimrod took a swig. "Obliged," Nimrod said, wiping his mouth, and handing the jug back.

"You can wager that's the last decent likker you're going to get around here, lessen the Hudson's Bay Company blackguards over yonder stumble into an honesty trap and stop selling rotgut."

"Things be well with you?" Nimrod asked.

Bridger winced as he twisted in the saddle. "I got the trapper's disease, rheumatism, from standing hip-deep in freezing water for too many years. But no new holes in my hide. How 'bout you? How fare you?"

Nimrod gestured toward Magpie. "May I present Mrs. Lee."

Bridger removed his hat and swept it with a flourish toward Magpie. He turned to Nimrod and grinned in appreciation. "You doin' fine."

Nimrod nodded with a small smile. He was there when Bridger went broke with the Rocky Mountain Fur Company, but he didn't mention it. "The story is you fixing to open a trading post."

"You heard right. On Black's Fork, two days down the Green. Hang on to them plews you got there a mite longer, and I'll be pleased to cheat you out of them," he said with a laugh.

Looking over Bridger's shoulder, Nimrod recognized a trapper cinching his horse, Jim Beckwourth, a sinewy, light-skinned black man.

"Hello, Jim Beckwourth," Nimrod hailed.

Beckwourth turned and grinned as he recognized Nimrod. The child of a slave mother and white slaver, he had been freed by his father and wandered west. He found acceptance and made a reputation as a successful trapper. He also earned the name "Bloody Arm" for his ferocity as an Indian fighter.

He was also the best liar in the Rockies. Both skills reaped considerable esteem. One of his stories was about escaping on foot from a pack of howling savages. He capped the story by saying, "And on that day I did run fifty-two miles."

He was the Michelangelo of lying, except, as such, he painted a dozen Sistine Chapels, not just one. Lying was esteemed in mountain culture. It helped the trappers avoid cabin fever on long winter nights when holed-up with no other entertainment.

Beckwourth walked his horse over. The men shook hands.

"Good to set eyes on you," Nimrod said. "Last I heard, the Cheyenne scalped you."

"Howdy, Lee.…The Cheyenne? They adopted this child. That's a sight more agreeable." Beckwourth grinned at Magpie and lifted his hat. "Looks like the Crows been kind to you."

Nimrod dismounted, and Magpie did the same. Nimrod slapped his hand on the rump on one of his pack horses. "Riding in, the packs I seen were pretty thin, like this one. Don't seem like beavers want to get caught anymore."

Bridger laughed. "Either they're getting smarter, or we're getting dumber."

"Fact is," Beckwourth said, "they're getting scarcer. We've gone and done killed the gold goose."

With a final handshake, Nimrod left the men and led Magpie in search of a camp. "We'll get together later and do some work on that jug of Bridger's," Beckwourth called after him.

Nimrod and Magpie chose a secluded spot in the trees beyond the edge of the encampment to shield them from the din of the carousers. It was close to the swift creek, but distant enough to avoid most mosquitoes. Nimrod set up their deerskin tent and tended the animals.

For their mid-day meal, Magpie prepared a skunk Nimrod had shot, skinned, and removed the scent glands. She made a batter of quail eggs, water, and flour, then fried the meat, which tasted like rabbit, but resembled turkey dark meat. They ate it with boiled wild onions Nimrod had gathered from the stream.

As Nimrod set his plate aside, Magpie noticed his restlessness, so she smiled and said, in Crow, "I think you want to be with your friends."

Hand-in-hand they walked the quarter mile to the center of the sound where a group of mountain men that included Bridger and Beckwourth had gathered. Nimrod joined them, and they sat in a circle with other trappers. Magpie sat observing at his side. The trappers passed jugs, argued about any subject thrown up, and laughed at old stories that could have been recited from memory by the audience.

About a hundred yards distant, amidst a cluster of American elms, a group of trappers and a few Indians knelt before a man dressed in black and holding a cross aloft.

"What's those strange doings over there?" Nimrod asked.

An old trapper said, "That black robe fella is called by the frog name of Father Pierre De Smet. Came west to give religion to the Indians. That's the first mass in these mountains, I heard tell."

"A priest?" Nimrod mused on it. "I never met one. Back home, Catholics is frowned on. If the gentleman's going to make Christians out of Indians, he best not use trappers as saints."

The old trapper said, "If'n he goes amongst them, he shouldn't hurry to visit the Blackfeet. Them heathen might send him off to test his religion."

Beckwourth walked over and handed Nimrod and Magpie each a cup of lumpy dick, a pudding made by stirring dry flour into boiling water, or milk, preferably, then mixed with molasses.

Bridger slapped Nimrod on the shoulder and smiled at Magpie. "I hope this pretty woman ain't making you soft, Lee. I seen the time you'd fight a rattlesnake and give him first bite. You was a curly wolf, you was." Bridger turned to bystanders and raised his voice, "This old boy, Nimrod here, when he gets riled, he'll make an ordinary fight look like a prayer meeting."

Nimrod waited for the laughter to subside, then turned to Bridger: "Jim, you been to the Pacific Ocean any time recent?"

The laughter rose louder. The jibe went back to 1824 when Bridger led a group that came upon the Great Salt Lake, and thought it was the Pacific Ocean. Upon hearing the old joke, Bridger smiled. He knew he couldn't deny it, and besides, after a hundred prior recitations, he also knew the subject would soon change. It always did.

Several Indians on the outskirts looked on, baffled, wondering what was funny.

"It's a matter of time afore the U.S. of A. runs the greasers out of California and the lime eaters out of Oregon. Mark my words," Beckwourth said.

Another trapper said, "That'll mean more people. I like it the way it is."

"Why? What with the beaver 'bout killed off, a body can't make money without people around to take it from," Bridger said. The men nodded. Over-trapping of the beaver was a fact painful to all.

"The beaver's had his revenge," another trapper said. "We've gone from eating steak to scraps."

A man reclining against a tree, said, "Hear tell the next big thing is buffalo robes." He nodded. "Might be a way to keep a full belly."

Nimrod scoffed. "Ain't my idea of doing manly work, sitting on a hill and taking potshots at dumb animals, and then leaving the meat to rot. Least we ate the beaver tail."

Nimrod spat tobacco juice from a plug Beckwourth gave him, his first in over a year. Magpie found tobacco breath repulsive. He had never chewed as a habit, but now he realized he had lost his taste for it. However, among mountain men, a Kentuckian who abstained would have gotten attention for the oddity.

Magpie noticed a man watching them from a distance. "Who's that devil, and why is he looking at me?" she asked Nimrod. The man she noticed was ordinary appearing except for a single eye fixed on Magpie and a face hideously scarred by deep furrows, like a washboard. One eye had been gouged out of his head leaving a hole covered by scar tissue. The side of his mouth was contorted into a permanent grimace.

Nimrod turned to Beckwourth and motioned with his head. "Who's over yonder looking this way?"

The trapper twisted around to look. "That be Rake Face Marcel. He's so mean he'd steal a fly from a blind spider. Got on the wrong side of a griz while back, he did. Old Ephraim tore his face up; mistook it for his ass, Ephraim did. Best I can figure, everyone wanted to buy the bear a drink."

Nimrod looked back at the man looking at Magpie. Beckwourth completed his description. "Marcel's as ugly inside as out. He's so ugly he makes your eyes sore."

Another trapper nodded. "He's so mean snakes won't bite him; afeared of getting poisoned."

They turned to Bridger, who said, "People back east gonna be traveling west, you can bet, at least that's my wager. My trading post will be directly in their path. I'll sell them at my prices what they forgot to pack or run out of."

"They gonna need guides," a man resting on an elbow said.

"I'd rather slop hogs than be a shepherd for belly-aching pilgrims," Nimrod said with a grimace.

"It could be a living," the man said, nodding his head and looking around for agreement.

Across the circle, a weasel named Cy Perkins goaded Nimrod. "Hey, Lee, is that-there flop-ear you're riding good for anything 'cept pulling a plow?"

Beckwourth chuckled. "Perkins, hard as you try, you ain't never got the best of Lee yet."

Nimrod's devilish smile told the others their amusement was at hand. "That mule is sired by a thirteen-hands jack donkey out of a thoroughbred mare. The main thing he's good for is to run circles around the swayback what dragged your bony ass in here."

The other men guffawed, hoping for a contest.

"I reckon you've got five beaver plews to back up your brag," Perkins said, his weak jaw jutting.

"Yes, sir, I do. Truth is, I got ten."

Beckwourth whooped, and said, "Lordy, maybe brother Lee does have some bristle left on his hide."

Nimrod jumped to his feet to fetch Bub for the race, but Magpie tugged at his sleeve. "This is boring," she said in Crow. "These men smell. Do they ever bathe?"

Nimrod nodded. "Shore, afore winter sets in—some years."

They returned leading Bub, and Magpie started to walk away. "I'm going to look at the trade goods," she said in Crow.

Nimrod's mind was on Perkins' challenge. "Stay real close. These men are not to be trusted," he replied in English.

"I will," she promised.

Both men saddled their mounts and brought them to a starting line. The Indians edged forward. They understood a horse race.

Nimrod mounted Bub. The mule was excited, and eager for the race. Perkins was atop a small sorrel, a full hand shorter than Bub. The animals danced as the men sized each other up.

"How 'bout to the big oak down the way?" Perkins asked, pointing to a tree a half-mile across the meadow.

Nimrod knew the sorrel would be fast but didn't have Bub's staying power. "How 'bout to the oak and back?" he countered.

Perkins hesitated, so Nimrod goaded him. "What you got to worry about agin a plow-pulling mule? I'm thinking you be more feathers than rooster, Perkins."

Perkins nodded sullenly. He was aware of the greater stamina of the mule but was trapped by his own brag. The two men hunched in their saddles and waited. Bridger gave a shout to start, and the sorrel jumped out to a full-length lead, which widened to two lengths as it nimbly rounded the oak. As the race headed toward the finish, however, Bub gained on the small horse until at the finish he was pulling away, a half-length ahead.

Nimrod jumped down amid the cheers and back-slapping of the trappers. A pouting Perkins handed over the beaver skins. "You're damned lucky," he said.

"You want we should target-shoot, double or nothing?" Nimrod challenged.

Perkins walked away and sat nursing a jug beneath a tree. The others also broke out the whiskey and resumed their boisterous reunion. The drinking continued for a couple of hours, as it always did during Rendezvous. Finally, Nimrod passed up the circulating jug, and his head slowed its spinning, and the slur lifted from his words. But clearing the whiskey fumes from his brain would take a little longer. He fell into a snoring slumber. Two hours later, when dark had pushed the sun away, the shadows deepened, and the ground stopped pitching, Nimrod stumbled to his feet and looked around for Magpie.

"Maggie!" he called, repeating her name twice as he walked in circles. Then, louder: "Magpie!" He weaved over to where the trade goods were displayed—no Magpie. Then, assuming she was at the tent, he led Bub in that direction. Nothing indicated he should be apprehensive, but for some reason, he was. Perhaps it was the guilt of getting drunk and ignoring her. When he saw the tent with her pony tied nearby, he relaxed. She must be inside, waiting for him.

As Nimrod reached for the tent flap, he was stunned and knocked backward by the shoulder of a man holding a knife rushing to get out. Still woozy from the whiskey, Nimrod spun and fell. He looked up into the face of the man he had noticed staring earlier in the day—Rake Face Marcel. Nimrod struggled to stand up, but Marcel kicked him in the face and ran away.

Nimrod shook his head to clear it. He knew something was wrong, gut-grinding wrong, and he forced himself to pull back the flap. Inside, sprawled on her back with a gag in her mouth was Magpie, staring toward him with dead eyes. Blood covered her face and chest. A darker line ran across her throat where it had been cut. Her clothes were torn and half off. Nimrod cradled her head in his arms and wiped the blood from her face. The satin bonnet lay nearby. He knew nothing could be done.

From all around the meadow, Indians, traders and mountain men ran to the sound of Nimrod's voice and gathered around the tent. All except one. Marcel had disappeared into the trees, riding hard.

The onlookers were stunned and looked at each other with blank faces. They could accept this in the aftermath of a war party, or on the banks of a contested beaver stream, but not now, not here. The murdering of Magpie was not how people were supposed to die.

In a low, trembling voice, Nimrod started the Crow death chant, then as the shock wore off and grief built, the song grew louder, and his anguish became a wail.

"*Watseckya.' t,*" [My heart is broken.] he cried as he recited a Crow prayer of mourning. Pausing, he unsheathed his heavy skinning knife, placed his open hand on a rock, and chopped off the first joint on his left-hand little finger, then lifted it to the setting sun. Watching whites gasped, but the Indians understood. Nimrod was saying—Let my blood of grief and guilt flow as hers did and make this a pledge that her killer's will also.

As blood dripped down his wrist, he rocked back and forth as the crowd returned to the camp. All night he knelt in the mountain chill and prayed. "Old, Old Man of the Sun," he chanted, "forbid the wind to blow from my direction as I hunt my enemy."

Except for Nimrod's chants, the valley was still. A great horned owl high in an evergreen looked on with severe eyes and hooted mournfully. The Rendezvous was quiet as the stunned campers spoke in low voices or stared into the trees and got drunk.

With the first gray light of morning, Nimrod filled a basin with water and, with reverence, washed his wife's corpse, then took her clothes to the stream to remove the blood and dirt. He dressed her, and wrapped her in a bright red blanket, then gathered the few possessions she had brought and tied them and her body to a board discarded from a trader's wagon. With the help of several of the trappers and Indians, he carried it to a nearby cottonwood, and all together, they lifted it seven feet and lashed it to a platform made by a large fork in the tree.

Nimrod gathered his pack horses and Magpie's pony and walked them to Jim Beckwourth's camp. The trapper saw Nimrod coming and walked out to meet him, but offered no greeting. What was there to say?

"Jim, I'd be obliged for you to do me a service," Nimrod said in a flat voice.

"What be that, Nimrod?"

Nimrod swept his arm toward the group of horses. "Take these here animals and plews and sell 'em for me. First, cut out the best horse for yourself for the trouble I'm set to ask of you."

"What's on your mind?"

"Take the money—gold coin, no script—go to her father, Many Horses, and give him the money. Tell him to take the money to Jim Bridger's trading post at Black's Fork down on the Green. He can buy a whole mess of cloth, and knives, and such for his people. Many Horses knows money. He won't be cheated. This time of year, his band will be on Grassy Creek at the foot of Wolf's Head Mountain. It's in the Wind River Moun—"

"I know where it is," Beckwourth interrupted. "What do I say?"

"Don't rightly know. Haven't figured things out. Tell Many Horses what happened. Tell him I'm on the hunt."

Beckwourth understood and nodded. "Watch your scalp."

CHAPTER FIVE

D ay after day, week after week, patient after patient, Hannah watched everything Abel did and had questions about most of it. He welcomed her curiosity; it was an opportunity to share. He was a brilliant man, but when he didn't have answers, for example, about the cause of infection, he didn't hesitate to admit ignorance. For her part, she washed bloody rags and mopped up vomit. Everything had a reason and a purpose. She grew used to death but welcomed life.

One day, he took out a small brown bottle and showed it to her. "You should know about this," he said.

"What's in it?" she asked.

"Mercy."

"Excuse me?"

Abel turned the bottle in his hand. "It's tincture of opium, a compound of opium and alcohol called laudanum. It dulls pain. It'll save lives by permitting surgery that's no longer medieval torture. It'll also ease the last days of the death watch. As Satan gave us pain, God gave us this."

Hannah had a vague awareness there was such a thing. She took the bottle and studied it, marveling how a miracle could be captured in so small a bottle.

Myrtle Simpson, a childhood friend, and her husband, Arthur, came into the office a few days later. She was bending over and holding her side. Hannah helped her lie on the examination table where Abel poked her abdomen with care and observed her wincing reaction when he touched the lower right of her midsection. After a minute, he backed away, and Hannah helped her sit up.

"What is it, doc?" her worried husband asked.

"I'm certain it's appendicitis. I could be wrong, but I don't know what else it could be. It's a well-known condition."

The husband and wife looked at the doctor, then at each other, mystified. Abel explained where the "vermiform appendix" was located, using the old name, vermiform, meaning worm-like. He told them the organ seemed to have no purpose except to endanger people in whom it became infected.

"What does it mean?" Myrtle asked.

Abel hesitated, then faced them. "There's a chance it'll heal itself, and you'll be fine." The couple smiled at each other and exhaled with relief.

Abel was angry with himself. He had given false hope. He said, "I need to be more clear: It's a remote chance, remote like I've never heard of." He watched their smiles turn to doubt. "There's more, and I regret saying this: The stronger—much stronger— likelihood is Myrtle will get worse, and the infected appendix will burst."

"And then?" Arthur asked, afraid of the answer.

"God help me for saying this—she will die."

"You're a liar!" Arthur shouted, but then became shamefaced and regained control. "I beg your pardon, Doctor."

"I've got a child at home," Myrtle said, her throat catching. "She needs me."

Abel nodded his sympathy. He rubbed his hands to relieve his tension. "There's an alternative; actually, only one—surgery. It's a new procedure. I've read extensively how it could be done. I've been well instructed in the procedure."

The couple stared at him, anxious for any kind of hope. "You *read* about it? You haven't done it yourself?" Arthur asked.

Abel hesitated for a brief but noticeable moment. "Ah, the appendix is easy to locate. It's at the beginning of the large intestine. It's a matter of snipping it off and thus removing the corrupted tissue. The greater danger is infection after the wound has been closed."

Arthur noticed Abel's indecision. "What are the chances of success?"

"I can't say, but they are much, much better than doing nothing."

Arthur put his arm around his wife's shoulder. "We have concerns about modesty."

Abel said, "There is more at stake here than modesty. I assure you, my interest will not deviate from healing your wife."

Myrtle's eyes revealed her fright. "The pain would be terrible."

"I have something that should make the pain manageable."

Arthur took control of the questioning. "How do you know it's this append—thing?"

Abel said, "It's well known to every doctor."

"Have you ever seen one?"

Abel was taken aback by the question. "Not in a living person."

Arthur's questioning became more hard-edged. "You want to cut my wife open trying to find something you've not seen in a live person? Maybe what's ailing her is only indigestion, something she had for breakfast that gave her a sour stomach?"

Myrtle interrupted. "Art, this is more than a stomach ache, a whole lot more. I've never hurt like this."

Arthur said, "Can you promise she won't die for cutting on her?"

Abel's voice was quaking. This was conflict he didn't have the constitution for. "I can almost promise she will die without it."

"Almost," Arthur repeated the word, drawing it out. "What you want, is to cut into her stomach, something you've never done, looking for something you've never seen, trying to cure an ailment that might not exist." He shook his head in disgust at the audacity.

Hannah felt she had no choice but to intercede. "Arthur," she said gently, "I've been friends with Myrtle my whole life. I'd never be a party to putting her at risk if there was an alternative." She made a small gesture toward Abel. "This is a good man. He is a skilled physician. Myrtle will be in good hands."

Arthur was calmed by Hannah's gentle manner. "But…"

Hannah tilted her head and smiled in sympathy. "I understand and respect your doubts, Arthur. Keep in mind a human body is not a machine that you can repair, and then know how it will run. The body is mysterious and complicated. It takes a man of skill and knowledge to minister to it. A man such as Dr. Blanc. However, God is the ultimate healer. To make promises on such things would be to play God, and that would be the sin of arrogance. God expects us to do our best, and then he decides." She took a deep breath. "I'm not a doctor but I've done considerable reading about medicine, and much about this very ailment. And I will tell you what Dr. Blanc stops short of saying out of consideration for your feelings." She turned to the seated Myrtle and touched her friend's shoulder. "Myrtle, without this surgery your daughter will not have a mother."

Myrtle gasped, and tears flooded her eyes. She reached up and covered Hannah's hand with her own. Myrtle then took the decision out of Arthur's hands. "When do we do it?"

"Tomorrow morning, on your kitchen table. Don't eat breakfast," Abel said. "And pray to God he will bless our healing."

The next day, mid-morning, Myrtle walked into the kitchen on her husband's arm, wincing at every step. Hannah helped her onto a three-foot by six-foot board atop the table swathed in bedsheets. Myrtle stretched out, and Abel saw she had made a cut in her gown where he had instructed. He asked Arthur and her mother to wait in a nearby room and stay there.

"Why can't I be here with my wife?" he asked.

"I have no idea how you would react. I want no chance of being distracted."

Arthur nodded, then walked out with shoulders slumped after kissing his wife.

Abel placed a pillow under her head and patted her shoulder. "I'm going to put you to sleep, my dear. When you awake, it'll all be over."

He moved to a kitchen counter behind Myrtle's head. He spread a towel and laid out his scalpel, clean sheets, a needle and thread, and clamps of different sizes that resembled scissors except the surface was flat for gripping, not sharp for cutting. He reached for a water pitcher and washed his hands, then indicated for Hannah to do the same. "I don't know if this does any good, but we don't want to transfer dirt or impurities to the body cavity," he said in a low voice so Myrtle wouldn't hear. He didn't realize the "impurities" he feared were bacteria that could cause his efforts to fail.

Abel explained to Hannah what he intended to do and what

her role would be. He opened the laudanum bottle and, using an eyedropper, transferred thirty drops of the brown liquid to a small water glass. With Hannah observing his every move, he stood over Myrtle, and said, "I'm going to put this under your tongue to make it work faster. It'll be bitter for a moment. You'll soon go to sleep, and when you awake, the cause of your distress will be gone." Myrtle looked at him with both hope and fear, but nodded, then raised her head and opened her mouth.

While waiting for the laudanum to take effect, Hannah chatted with Myrtle about her child and everyday things. The opium solution took effect in thirty minutes as Myrtle's breathing evened out in induced slumber. To make sure the laudanum had taken effect, he pinched her hard on the tender skin inside the upper arm. There was no reaction. Abel started his incision on the lower right side of the abdomen and sliced through the skin and the yellow fat beneath. Blood seeped out and over her body and spilled onto the floor. He then, with exquisite care, cut the peritoneum, the thin protective membrane covering the cavity, and stepped back as a clear fluid that lubricates abdominal organs oozed out.

With every step, the image of textbook drawings told him where everything was, and how to maneuver in the complex abdomen. First, he located the cecum, a three-inch bag-like bump at the base of the large intestine connected to the four-inch tube-like appendix. The appendix was not punctured but was angry-red with infection.

Abel stepped back, took a deep breath, and wiped the sweat from his face. The next step had to be done with exquisite care. He had to tie-off both the cecum and the appendix to prevent spillage into the gut. He then would sever the appendix by cutting the tiny connection between the two ties. He cut a length of sewing thread more than a foot long and doubled it over, then, using his smallest clamp, he lifted the appendix and, with the other hand, tried to slip the thread loop under the appendix to clear space. He tried once, twice, three times to get the loop under the appendix, but each time, he couldn't get the thread to cooperate.

Time was passing. He looked with apprehension at Myrtle's eyelids. No flutter, thank God. Her breathing was regular.

With blessed finality, the thread made it all the way under the appendix. He then cut it at the apex of the loop so he had two threads. He positioned one thread at the base of the cecum, and had Hannah move the other to about a half-inch down the appendix. He tied a square knot right at the edge of the cecum, then backed off as Hannah tied off the appendix. She was more skilled at nimble-finger procedures. The final step was to sever the appendix between the two knotted threads.

Holding the scalpel like a pencil stub for maximum control, he maneuvered it to where he could make the cut, aware if the razor-sharp knife even nicked the large intestine, the patient would with great likelihood die of peritonitis.

He held his breath and made the cut. Done!

He cut the extra length on the thread remaining in the body and removed the appendix. After forty-five minutes of sweaty tension, he held it up like a tiny red sausage and laughed with nervous relief. "A lot of work for this little thing." He cut off his laughter, not wanting the close-by husband to think he was amused.

Hannah's arms were aching, but it was a good pain as she shared his elation. She removed the clamps to close the incision. He used a household needle to suture the cut. It wouldn't be a pretty scar, but if she lived, no one would complain.

Myrtle's eyes were fluttering, so Abel summoned Arthur who brought his father and brother into the kitchen. After recoiling from seeing so much blood, the four men carried the board and Myrtle into the front room where a narrow bed had been prepared close to the fire. The four men with great care shifted her off the board to the bed.

As the men thanked him, Abel proudly said, "She'll have to fight off infection. It's in God's hands now. I'll be back morning and night for a few days to give her more laudanum for the pain; opium can be addictive as all get out." He noticed Arthur's confusion. "'Addictive,' means like drinking whiskey until you can't do without it." Arthur's nod of comprehension allowed him to go on. "Keep her warm. Give her nothing but water and broth for two days, then soft foods for a week." A month later Myrtle's incision would be healed with no sign of infection.

With Myrtle resting comfortably in her bed by the fireplace, Abel gathered his instruments and accepted the thanks of the family. He was pleased to notice the pride on Hannah's face. From that day on, he would consider himself a surgeon, a successful surgeon.

As Hannah and Abel walked from the home, she slipped her arm into his. He stopped and faced her. "I love you. Will you marry me?"

"Yes."

They walked on, wanting the same things—each other, and to cause healing.

Hannah and Abel were married in 1832. A daughter, Rachel, was born in 1833 and a son, William, the following year. Abel's practice grew, and Hannah became a fixture in it, a combination of nurse and medical student. After a time, patients accepted her as a person with skills independent of her husband. The couple had a goal to prepare Hannah for a medical license. They knew the testing would be severe for a woman. There would be skeptics among the examining doctors, but Abel had no doubt she would make it. "With banners aloft," he boasted. The plan was, in time, to go together to the capital, Jefferson City for her test. Then their shingle would read, "Blanc & Blanc, Physicians and Surgeons." Her husband teased her by saying her biggest obstacle would be if she embarrassed the testers with her knowledge.

Over the next few years, Hannah studied every scrap of paper that offered information on the practice of medicine. She borrowed books from other doctors in the city and peppered them with questions until they ran out of answers, and sometimes patience. She observed every procedure and consultation of her husband except for the few who were not comfortable with her presence.

In time, Hannah gleaned a first class medical education, the equal of almost all doctors of the day, and exceeding most.

Life was a blessing. They shared a love for medicine, a love for their children, and a love for each other. Hannah proved an adept student by observing Abel and participating with him. After eight years of learning as his assistant and nurse, he said, "It's time to go to Jeff City, and for you to flummox the smug peacocks on the board of examiners. When you answer all their questions and puncture their doubts, you shall be Hannah Blanc, Physician and Surgeon."

"Are you sure?" Hannah said, her brow knitting with doubt.

He took her hand with a kind smile. "I'm as sure as I love you."

The three professorial men sat in upholstered chairs with arms and covered in red velvet. Hannah sat facing them in a straight back chair with wooden slats digging into her back. The men could have stepped out of the Old Testament, she thought, with their flowing white beards and piercing eyes. They sat and looked her over with hands clasped across rotund middles. She sensed no encouragement, which made her sad, not angry. She said to herself: They are supposed to be men of healing, men of compassion. Why do I see coldness in their eyes when I want to be the same?

She had been told by other doctors to expect a grueling two hours of interrogation. However, her examination ended after one hour and consisted of questions she answered correctly without hesitation. Almost too easy, she thought. At the end, the chairman, a self-important elf of a man, thanked her and said she would have their decision on the morrow. She thanked them and walked from the room, knowing their eyes followed her.

The next morning, a messenger called for her at their hotel and handed her a sealed envelope. With shaking hands, she tore the end off it and removed a single sheet of paper. With Abel trying to see over her shoulder, she read the blunt verdict of the august deliberators of her fate.

When she turned to Abel with tears in her eyes, nothing needed to be said.

The long coach ride back from Jefferson City took three days of slogging along a muddy track in the chill of gloomy November. Abel and Hannah mulled their thoughts as the seat across in the knee-to-knee small coach was filled by a man who managed to stay drunk the entire first day. The drunk had a marathon encounter with flatulence. Hannah passed the time by counting the seconds between farts. The game did not end quickly. On the second day, the space was shared by a colicky baby and a traveling evangelist passionately practicing his "altar call" appeal which capped each sermon.

On each of the two nights, an unwashed innkeeper led them to a dark, drafty room with a lumpy bed on which they could see bed bugs jumping with anticipation at the approach of a fresh meal. Both nights, they tried to sleep in misery on hard chairs. Neither night was conducive to a dispassionate discussion of her summary rejection by the medical board.

On the final day, they had the coach to themselves, and that allowed Hannah to let her tears flow. "It was wrong and cruel," she said. "I answered all of their questions. Those evil old men were against me from the start, I could see it. Why were they afraid of me?"

"If you can believe this, Hannah, I would guess they admired you but were afraid of what others might think. They know their lofty positions depend on fitting in, not seeming to be radical. They don't want to rock the boat that has given them smooth sailing." He sighed. "We'll try again."

She looked at the bleak scenery out the window. "Eight years… Eight years of study and learning, of emptying slop buckets and mopping up blood." Her voice hardened. "No. Nothing will change. If they wouldn't pass me this time, they won't a second time, either. I won't give them that satisfaction."

They passed the rest of the trip in silence, she in anger, he in sorrow.

A month later, Abel said, off-handedly, "We're stepping out tonight. I'm taking you and the children to dinner at the Missouri Hotel."

"Why? What are we celebrating?"

"You."

"Enough of your riddles, you sawbones," she said in a mock scold.

He removed his glasses and turned serious. "You might not know it, Hannah, but you have greater skills at birthing than I, and also for childcare, for that matter. You're skilled with the forceps; I've seen it often. Besides, many couples don't care for a male doctor, anyway."

Hannah looked at him and waited.

"I'm changing the sign out front. Right below my name, I'm putting, 'Hannah Blanc, Midwife.' Pregnant women and new mothers will become your patients. Lord knows we have enough of them." He took both her hands. "You have good hands in delivery. I've seen it. You have a kind heart and a keen mind. Mothers and newborns need such as you."

Each time Hannah lost a mother or child, she walked home grieving. Her rate of losing mothers was much lower than average for the simple reason she washed her hands. She had no idea of bacteria, but she believed in cleanliness.

Life was a blessing in the Blanc house. For ten years they shared a love for medicine, a love for their children, and a love for each other.

Then life broke its promise, as life tends to do.

It started with a limp. Hannah noticed Abel favoring his left hip as he walked from room to room.

"Are you injured, darling?"

He rubbed the hip. "I must have slept wrong or perhaps made an awkward movement."

"An old man at forty-two, such a shame," she teased, and they both laughed.

The limp did not go away. It got worse, until one day Hannah noticed the laudanum bottle left on his desk. Odd, she thought, and put it away. She noticed Abel acting unusually distant and listless. The diminishing level of the laudanum became impossible for her to ignore. Over several months, his condition advanced in her mind from concern to worry, even though he dismissed it as the weather or routine muscle or joint aches and pains.

It was a pretense he could no longer shrug off. He had difficulty holding instruments, and Hannah often heard his grunting with pain as he tried. He no longer played with the children or even gave them much attention. Moving was painful. Sitting afforded little relief. It would get worse, as he knew it would.

In effect, Hannah was the doctor in the office. Patients soon grew to trust her. She was afraid Abel would be unnerved by her enhanced role, but he showed his pride in what she had learned. She considered it a priceless gift of love.

Abel explained to friends who asked, "I've got a touch of the rheumatism." In reality, what he had was acute, progressive rheumatoid arthritis. He did not know it by that name but knew he was becoming an invalid. It was pathetic for Hannah to watch him attempt to treat patients, and then to watch the patients realize that he was sicker than they. One at a time, patients drifted away. Their income was declining toward the poverty level, and there was no way to stop the drain.

Hannah kept an eye on the levels of their laudanum bottles and noticed the opium painkiller continued to diminish at a far faster pace than patient needs required. She reminded him of the risk of opium, but he became irritated at her "badgering."

The worst was the cruel twisting of his hands. There were many things vital to his practice he could not grip or manage. He dropped much of what he could pick up. His fingers became so twisted they turned into a claw as one finger would not touch another. His nights were filled by thrashing and groaning.

Because of his agony, he sometimes lashed out in anger at Hannah and even the children. He was quick to apologize and implore forgiveness, but words spoken cannot be recalled.

Hannah urged him to seek treatment from other doctors.

"What's the point?" he replied. "I know as much as any of them, which is nothing."

The cruelest pain is that for which there is no end. More than once, Hannah heard him ironically recite that verse from the Book of Luke: "Physician, heal thyself." Once, he muttered, "Oh, dear God, if only I could."

It was poet's weather, a sunny, bird-chirping afternoon on the pillow of a soft breeze. The memory of the day would remain strong to Hannah, and she always wondered why.

The house was empty when she went into Abel's small office off the exam room to get something. She didn't remember what. He was seated and leaning askew to one side in his tilt-back chair staring at her. Except, he wasn't staring. His eyes were hooded and unfocused. He was dead. On a side table was an overturned brown laudanum bottle. In shock, Hannah turned it upright. It was empty. She closed his eyes and then used her fingers to straighten his hair. She sat close to him and took his hand in her one hand, using the other to brush away her tears. Hannah sat and looked at him. For a moment, she wondered if this were his thought-out decision or if the opium sneaked up on him in an overdose. She would never know.

She had grown to know pain among patients, to understand it. She had observed it in her husband. She knew pain could be a warning to heed, or an irritation, or a twisting rage of the nerves, or medieval torture. Abel had the piled-on curse of the psychic pain of knowing it would never end, and his career would never resume.

Since the children were not at home, she held a normal conversation as though he were alive. Her voice was controlled and quiet, though her eyes were pooled in tears. "Abel, I know your pain is gone, and I'm glad for that, but why didn't you let me take care of you? You didn't trust me enough. Why didn't you let the love the children and I have for you help you manage the pain and find a way to live with it? Oh, I know, it's so complicated. I feel so empty, sitting here looking at you, knowing you're not here, and never will be again. I can feel your hand growing cold and stiff as I hold it, but even so, I don't want to release it.

"I've always been honest with you, and I say to you that you shouldn't have done this or allowed it to happen. But I promise you I won't spend time thinking about that, because it would lessen the time I have to remember how we loved each other."

Patting his hand, she thanked him for loving her, for believing in her. She was glad she had also said that at breakfast, hours ago. He had kissed her and said, "Never forget: you're a healer." She had wondered why he said it the way he did, and at that particular time, but it made her proud.

"I can't stay here too long; the children will be home soon, and I'll have things to do. Painful things: arrangements to make, questions to answer, children to console and try to help them understand this. I'll protect your good name and tell your children often how much you loved them and remind them of what a good man you were."

She heard the door open and her children's boisterous entrance. Life was thrusting her grief aside and forcing her into a wilderness of loneliness, duty, and insecurity.

She spoke faster to the body in the chair. A horrible, hard job awaited in another room. "The children are here, dear, your children. It was a blessing for everyone you touched that you were here. You put value into my life, and I'll always honor your name. I loved you from the start, and it was good to do so. Goodbye, good doctor, my sweet prince. Rest."

She reached down and kissed his gnarled hand and slipped away.

In its issue of March 29, 1843, the *Daily Missouri Republican* newspaper ran an obituary for Abel Gaspard Blanc, M.D., who died of a heart attack on Wednesday, March 15. The article mentioned the eulogies offered to his memory and condolences to his family by many mourners. Services were at the Wesley Methodist Church, the Reverend Homer Kline officiating.

The passing of a spouse hits hardest twice: the death itself, then on the funeral day after the last guest departs an empty house. Alone with the ticking of the hall clock....

The money jar hidden in the woodshed counted out as three-hundred-ten dollars. The money would support them perhaps four or five months, but no longer. She had learned a midwife earns small fees because hers is regarded as a public service. However, in St. Louis, many expectant mothers turned to midwives in the pay of other doctors. She no longer had such a sponsoring doctor. Her father's fur business was a victim of the declining fur market, and of the Panic of 1837, so he couldn't help. Poverty loomed, with its red eyes and hot breath. Widows, in her circumstance, were usually driven to get married again as soon as possible. Hannah closed her eyes and tried to blot out the likelihood. However, she had children to feed, and with little means to do it.

For a year, Hannah struggled to survive as a single mother in a society that did not intend for her to do so. Her savings were exhausted, and her fees declined to a dribble. The wolf was at the door, but what the wolf wanted was the house. Driven to desperation, Hannah had to turn to reality.

It was the fate of needy widowhood that any single man interested in her would hold the upper hand. It was a "buyer's market." If a widow were in her thirties with few children and no resources, she was "available," which left her no leverage. And if she were well educated? Well, that could be overlooked if it hadn't gone to her head.

In the sociology of the 1844 frontier, a "widda woman" was in dire need of God's mercy. If the man who "claimed" her was not a gentleman, God's mercy would remain a forlorn hope.

Ed Spencer was no gentleman.

In the twelfth month of her widowhood, he made his flourish of an entrance into Hannah's life. He showed up unannounced with a heavy scent of cologne, a bouquet, and holding gifts for the children and leading a spotted pony.

He touched the bill of his hat. "Good afternoon, ma'am. My name is Ed Spencer. I live down the road a piece. I've come to pay my respects."

That was how it was done. One day, a prospective husband would appear, leading a pony for the children. He would dote on the children and boast of his means of providing, which in his case was as a breeder of thoroughbred horses. After that, in Spencer's courtship, it was all downhill. Hannah had become desperate. She knew little about Spencer because he volunteered little. Intuitively, she feared to know what she could not control.

She and Spencer were married two months later by the Baptist preacher. It was not a marriage of love, but love was a luxury she couldn't afford. The wedding was on a Saturday which Hannah completed with a closed heart. Saturday night, she endured. Sunday morning, Ed Spencer revealed himself. He was not yesterday's smiling man at the altar.

Hannah was now his. No need to continue the tiresome game.

One morning she saw him tying a pink ribbon to his horse's saddle. "That's pretty," she said. "Where did you get that?"

"A fella down river gave it to me," he said, and snapped his words.

She said nothing, but had never known a man in those parts that would risk the scorn of owning a pink ribbon.

On a cold day in November 1844, with no warning, he announced they were moving.

"To where?"

"California."

She didn't know what to say. California could have been China. All she could ask was, "Why?"

"I figure I can make a killing breeding and selling fine horseflesh to those Mexicans out there, but you don't understand business."

She had an urge to fling open the door and run for her life, but she couldn't. She was a captive of needing to care for her children. If she were to leave him, she would be a social pariah in the rigid mores of her community, and maybe even be seen as a loose woman. She had no place to go and without the means to get there. She tried to console herself by imagining California might be an improvement.... No! She corrected herself. Life with Ed Spencer could never improve, no matter the location.

They spent the following months preparing for the trip. For Hannah, her saddest task was to pack up and close the medical office she had shared with Abel. She carefully put his instruments in their black leather case, and then turned to the medicines. She had to choose carefully, because her new husband severely limited the amount she could take. Every item Hannah packed was a stab of pain to her because she was turning away from the happiest years of her life. Tears drenched her apron as she boxed up medicines from the shelves. She looked at the bottles one by one. Most valuable, and first to go in the box was a large jar of quinine, the magical drug that could combat the effects of malaria. Right behind it was castor oil to treat most everything else. Then, she looked at the other medicines. She packed some drugs she trusted, but they were few.

She turned to others that the medical establishment swore by. The first was calomel, an ancient mercury compound made popular by the nonpareil physician of an earlier day, Dr. Benjamin Rush. It was used for a wide variety of ills, including constipation, syphilis, gout, and even teething. The faddist, go-along medical profession of the time ignored that it resulted in hair loss, teeth falling out, and, too often, an early death. It was a poison. To reject this "miracle" drug was to invite scorn from the establishment. Hannah had been taught the evils of calomel by a wise chemistry professor, and her own observations confirmed the education. She discarded the bottle.

She examined a bottle with the claim on the label, "Sure cure for diarrhea and dysentery." It was a compound of "eleven powerful vegetable astringents which are soothing and innocent in their effects." She put it in the box, though she was suspicious of anything labeled "sure cure."

Next was a bottle named "Fahnestock's Vermifuge" which promised to rid children of intestinal worms. Hannah put that in the box also. She knew of no other treatments for worms. The other bottles she swept into the trash.

She had to restrict her reference books to only a few, but the first she packed was "The Family Nurse," by an author known as "Mrs. Child" and published in 1837. The binding was ripping because of Hannah's constant seeking of practical advice that she trusted and used.

The most important medicine she didn't have was Laudanum, the pain-killing opium-alcohol compound. Abel had consumed all they had in his self-treatment, and suicide, and she had not been able to replace it.

Finally, the dreaded day approached at the beginning of March 1845 when they would drive the wagon onto a steamer for the upriver trip to Independence, Missouri to join a wagon train.

It was time to say goodbye to her parents, and with agonizing finality. Hannah stood with a befuddled child on either side. They knew this was a poignant moment, but not the full seriousness of it. Tears flowed down Hannah's cheeks and moistened her dress. Standing close were her parents, Rudolf and Greta. She concentrated with all her might to memorize every feature of their faces, every mannerism, and the sounds of their voices. She couldn't remember noticing before, but they had grown old, almost seventy, and appeared to be smaller. She needed to store away every detail about them because she knew she would never see them again. The children didn't realize their beloved grandparents were about to disappear from their lives and soon become featureless memories.

Greta cradled Hannah's face between her hands. "I'll never see my little girl again." Hannah wanted to say something reassuring, but she knew her mother was correct.

Her father stood close, red-eyed, not knowing what to say, except, "God be with you, child."

She was desperate for them to demand of her not to leave, to plead with her to stay. But they didn't because they believed it was her duty to follow her husband.

Oh, dear God! Abel, why did you have to leave?

Hannah felt she was losing her life. She was a captive dragged to a place where she didn't belong and didn't want to go. She hugged her mother, desperate to feel the same comforting warmth of her childhood. Maybe there was still time to say no. He couldn't force her into that horrible wagon, could he? She prayed in her mind—Oh, please, dear Jesus, let this cup pass from me.

Hannah heard an irritated voice from the wagon out in the road. She felt her mother's hands slip from her shoulders.

"Finish up. Let's go."

CHAPTER SIX

May 1845

For five years Nimrod wandered from St. Louis to the adobes of Taos, to Yerba Buena on the banks of San Francisco Bay. He served with explorers, and worked as a teamster in expeditions to trade with tribes to whom white men were novelties. He hung around trading posts at Bent's Fort and Santa Fe. He got drunk in settlement saloons and picked up money cutting wood for Missouri River steamboats. He let the wind carry him, hoping to outrun his grinding grief and guilt. He traveled throughout the West; most everywhere, except among the Crows.

All the time, every day, he looked for the man he would kill without hesitation, and with no rush: Rake Face Marcel.

He asked strangers about Marcel right after saying hello. It didn't take long for word of his pursuit to spread through the frontier. Gossip was as common there as in Victoria's palace court. Sometimes, he thought he was close, but he always came up frustrated. Marcel was a mystery, a dark one. No, a black one. Even his given name had been forgotten. Nimrod learned he was once a voyageur, a French-Canadian human pack-mule that true mountain men looked down on. Marcel, however, found even such a servile position too lofty and abandoned it to become human scum, a man who would kill and steal as other men eat breakfast. Marcel was without virtue, and his sole skill was staying alive against the wishes of men he had wronged and would also have rejoiced to have him in their gunsights. However, his habits and haunts were a mystery to his enemies. He survived because he was a weasel who hid in the dens of fellow criminals.

Nimrod awoke with a start and looked around at the dirt-floor, lean-to shelter he'd been sleeping in. A dozen men were sprawled nearby, snoring, coughing, farting, and turning in sleep. Close by were the animals of the men, none of whom would allow them out of sight or hearing. Nimrod put on his boots, grabbed his saddle, rifle, and possibles bag. He fed and watered Bub, then saddled-up and rode toward town.

Independence, Missouri, on that blustery May day in early 1845 was a young, makeshift town located on the south bank at the bend of the Missouri River where it flowed down from the north and then made a turn east toward St. Louis and the Mississippi. It had a permanent population of a few dozen and several hundred transients. Independence served as the steamboat terminal for goods coming in by wagon from Santa Fe in the southwest. It was the jumping-off place for the new Oregon-California emigrant trail that meandered off west by northwest.

Riding along the riverbank, Nimrod watched as a steamboat from St. Louis emptied its cargo. Men on the bank waited with apprehension as their frightened oxen jostled down the shaky gangplank in a herd of about one hundred, their dangerous horns waving with their twisting, wide-eyed heads. The mules acted ornery, looking for someone to kick or bite.

Parked along the deck were the wagons the emigrants hoped, and wanted to believe, would take them to the edge of the continent, to a new place they could call home. It was a trail they knew could either kill or deliver.

Watching with trepidation and waiting along the railing were the wives and the children. They would go ashore last because, in this expedition, that's where they ranked. This trip, this whole idea, was a man thing. The children were frightened, but this was still a breathtaking adventure. The women, however, didn't want to be here, hadn't wanted to come, and with survival intuition, knew the following months would be the polar opposite of the warm, secure homes they had worked so hard to build.

Nimrod rode Bub at a walk through Independence along the crowded main street that had turned into a soup of mud, water, and dung. The atmosphere was of excitement and purpose: people haggling with merchants, the clanging of blacksmiths' hammers, the lowing of cattle, and Indians window-shopping at the wondrous merchandise they could not afford but might be able to trade for or steal out on the trail.

Drunken laughter carried out the open doors of bars and brothels as teamsters stored-up sociability before again hitting the Santa Fe Trail to the southwest. Their destination was *Santa Fe de Nuevo México*, in a territory of the new country of Mexico, which was a mere quarter-century independent of Spain.

Children peeked through the white canvas of wagon covers while their mothers sat with hands folded in laps atop the driver's seat as their husbands walked alongside lumbering oxen.

There were strong rumors throughout the country that the new president, James K. Polk, was kicking up a fuss and about to agitate a war with Mexico and annex the Republic of Texas, and maybe California. He also was spoiling for a fight with Britain over ownership of significant parts of the Oregon Territory. That's what they talked about in the livery barns, the churches, and the saloons. It was a vital conversation because the emigrants were bound for the Willamette Valley in Oregon or for Sutter's Fort in California. The goal of most of the California-bound was to get a Mexican land grant, as John Sutter had done.

To the teamsters and emigrants, a war with Mexico would be just fine. And they could also throw the Limeys into the mix. Didn't Andy Jackson give them what-for at New Orleans?

Nimrod saw a sign, HIRAM YOUNG, WAINWRIGHT, and guided Bub into a yard filled with busy black men who were sawing, pounding and shaping to provide the vehicles to carry families and their baggage west into the unknown.

Contrary to what some easterners believed, the typical "schooner" out on the trail was not the cumbersome Conestoga wagon used for freighting on the level, graded roads of the east. It was the humble farm wagon, reinforced by men such as Hiram Young, to withstand the pounding of the rocks and rivers on the trail.

The typical wagon was about four-by-twelve-feet with sides two-feet high and topped by a white canvas cover soaked in linseed oil or white paint for waterproofing and stretched over ribs of thin oak bows. It had drawstrings front and back for privacy and to protect from the weather. Boxes attached to the sides contained tools and cooking utensils and a small platform on which a water barrel would be strapped. The front wheels were of smaller circumference than the rear to shorten the turning radius. The springs were of leather strapping, which provided little comfort to sore bottoms. It carried about a ton of household goods, tools, and food. Any greater weight would wear down the draft animals, and many miles down the road would result in a path strewn with discarded furniture.

The wagon was best pulled by three yoke of six oxen. Some started with horses or mules, but those were the foolish ones. At two miles per hour, oxen were slow, but they were more disease resistant and could survive on the grasses and even sagebrush found along the way. Mules, and especially horses, could not pull a heavy load day after day without grain.

Nimrod dismounted when he recognized a short, middle-aged black man preoccupied with pounding a sideboard into a tight fit. Hiram Young looked up as Nimrod hailed him.

"Mornin', Mr. Young. Think we've seen the end of this rain?"

Young nodded a greeting and lowered his mallet. "Good morning to you, Mr. Lee."

Nimrod lightly punched the sideboard of a completed wagon. "I tell folks you make the best wagons, and I surely ain't lying."

Young was an ex-slave who had purchased his freedom by making ax handles and oxen yokes in his off hours and had become the leading wagon maker of Independence.

He glanced at the sky. "I reckon it won't rain again, at least not for another ten minutes, Mr. Lee. It's been raining like a cow pissing on a rock." He resumed his work and spoke without looking up. "We heard talk about the manhunt you're on. You have any luck tracking your man?"

"Everthing I hear, Marcel is still out there," Nimrod said.

"Renegades like him don't make it their custom to retire back east to write books," Young said as he finished the job and put down his tool. "Maybe he's already dead. Lots of men would pay to claim his scalp. You never can tell."

Nimrod removed his hat and raked fingers through his hair. "I trust the good Lord above not to let anyone get to him afore I do."

Young patted Bub on the muzzle, and the mule angrily tossed his head. "I see your mule still ain't learned manners."

Nimrod laughed. "The bastard was born mean."

Young said, "Feller from down Santa Fe way said he heard Rake Face and his boys ambushed a small wagon train on a feeder creek of the Vermillion a month or so ago. Robbed and abused the people bad." Young paused, and then said, "Who knows the truth of such stories, but, uh-huh, I would wager he's still out there."

"I heard tell he's been around," Nimrod said, nodding.

Young scratched his ragged beard. "Pilgrims go on the trail with their life savings hidden in a stocking and guns more dangerous to them than to enemies. They make easy pickings."

"Know of any trains going out that way might make a spot for a feller who knows the country?"

Young paused to think. "It's getting late. Most are all set to go, or already gone." He took another moment, then said, "Well, some pilgrims come in here for repairs from a camp over where the river takes an elbow to the north."

"They drop any names?"

Young chuckled. "Didn't ask, wasn't offered. You go over there, and if you see some pilgrims wandering around like they's lost, I reckon you've found your customers." Young started to return to his labors but then hesitated, debating whether to speak further. The code of the frontier was to speak seldom, avoid emotion, and mind your own business. Young fumbled for words: "Uh, Nimrod. You doin' all right?" He repeated the question to show concern. "I mean, you doin' all right?"

Nimrod understood the question under the question. Young could have been asking: Do you have nightmares reliving the murder of Magpie? Does your gut churn with guilt? Do you crowd out the good memories of your life and obsess on the image of Rake Face as he ran from the tent? Is killing him all you have left? Can you survive this, my friend?

Nimrod knew the answers were all "yes," but said nothing. He pulled himself up into the saddle and reached down to shake hands. "I'm obliged for the help, friend."

Young stepped back to let Nimrod ride out. "Mind your scalp."

Nimrod took in the hectic pioneer goings-on from a hillside overlooking the Missouri. The thought that came to him was—If these good people knew what was in store, they'd high-tail it right back to where they came from.

He then edged Bub down a steep, muddy path to where the swollen river rushed past wagons clustered on the bank. Nimrod weaved Bub through playful children, wives going from wagon to wagon seeking to commiserate with other women, and men muttering oaths while making repairs they often could not accomplish. He continued along the water's edge, then stopped to watch a small, crude ferry fighting the current in mid-channel, trying to make its way across the river. Such sights were familiar as inexperienced entrepreneurs tried to cash in on the traffic by hammering together boards into a raft, thus putting customers at the mercy of the swirling high water.

The twenty- by thirty-foot deck was crowded with a boy and girl, their father and mother, two crewmen, a lashed-down wagon, and four oxen. The ferry was pulled across by a team of mules on a rope with a capstan on either bank, and stretched across the river. A crew on the departing shore payed out the rope, then the process was reversed. The raft was unstable, and the deck was a foot above water and slightly tilted by current pressure. By its lack of stability, Nimrod guessed it had no keel.

Nimrod looked at the struggle and frowned at the danger of the current as it rampaged in the spring flood. The muddy water leaping into erratic whitecaps seemed to be grasping for something to kill. Though Nimrod had seen the river flood many times, there was a murky evil about its eagerness to destroy.

He muttered to Bub, whose big ears were often the only ones within the sound of his voice. "Damned fools are overloaded. I'd bet a stack of Liberty Gold Eagles those pilgrims didn't have the two dollars for a second trip." Bub snorted as a coincidence, but Nimrod chose to take it as a rebuke. "All right, you overgrown jackass, you know I don't have them."

Nimrod turned away but quickly wheeled Bub when he heard screams. He saw an ox slip on the deck, which tipped the ferry and caused people and animals to spill into the river. The animals struggled for the shore, but the people were being swept downstream, their heads bobbing above and then below the brown, furious water. Nimrod could see their eyes wide with fright and their desperate gulps for air.

He spurred Bub to a gallop along the shore for about two hundred yards to get ahead of their downstream sweep, limbering a rope and tying it to his saddle horn as he went. He plunged Bub into the water, slipped off the saddle, looped the rope over his hand, and held tight to the horn to let the mule carry him to midstream. Nimrod managed to intersect the boy who reached out choking and coughing but clung to Bub's tail. The mother was swept near and grabbed Bub's stirrup. The father and the two ferry crew had disappeared. Nimrod saw the girl near the shore and turned Bub hard. When he was within a few feet, he half lunged, half tossed the rope to the girl who was about twelve. A pretty towhead with blue eyes wild with fright. She grabbed at the line, but it slipped through her hand. Her mother cried and prayed piteously in a thin voice above the roar of the water as she watched from her grip on Bub's saddle.

"Hold on! Hold on! Almost there. Almost! Almost!" Nimrod pleaded to the girl. He prodded Bub to swim faster and again threw the rope that landed right next to her. She grabbed the line with both hands and struggled to hold on, screaming and crying in panic.

The girl dipped beneath the chop, choking and swallowing water. Her hands were slipping. Nimrod saw the look of frozen panic as her face emerged, then he watched with a falling heart as her hands surrendered their grip on the rope.

"Mama!" It was a scream of desperation and perhaps of reproach.

The rope fell free as the water washed over her head. She disappeared under the surface, leaving Nimrod with the image of her eyes filled with terror. A final reach of a small white hand above the water, then she was gone.

Her mother cried to heaven. "Noooo!"

The girl's last plea and the look in her eyes attacked Nimrod's conscience like a claw hammer for many years. It crept up and surprised him in the heat of the day; it sprang into the middle of a pleasant dream late at night. In an accusing voice, he heard an imaginary scream again and again—Why won't you save me?

The next day, Nimrod rode toward an isolated group of a couple dozen wagons sitting in disorder near the river. He approached the first wagon where a man was examining a horse's hoof.

"How-do. Obliged if you could direct me to your captain."

The man pointed with his tool to a nearby tent. "Shadrach Penney."

Nimrod dismounted and led Bub to the tent. "Hello, in the tent," he announced.

The flap pushed back, and Shadrach Penney emerged. He was a man in his mid-sixties, short, about five-six, scraggly gray beard, dressed in farmer clothes, of cordial demeanor, but forgettable appearance. You would expect to find him of a winter's afternoon sitting with other men of the soil around a pot-bellied stove in the general store moaning about crop prospects, spitting in the general direction of the spittoon, and watching it sizzle against the stove. Nimrod thought the old man was a little uncomfortable in the strange environment surrounding him. Even so, he had a command presence about him.

"What can I do for you, sir?"

Nimrod extended his hand. "Nimrod Lee, sir."

"Shadrach Penney." He laughed as he grasped the extended hand. "You an Old Testament man, too, I see."

Nimrod was stumped for a moment, then said, "Nimrod, book of Genesis."

Penney said, "Shadrach, book of Daniel. I reckon both our mamas studied the good book. I'm lucky she chose Shadrach stead of his partners, Meshach, or Abednego. They got cast in the fire with him. How'd you like to walk into a saloon, or even a church, with the name Abednego?"

Nimrod was at ease with the folksy leader. "I reckon they call you Shad."

"Ain't a shad a little bitty fish? I set my mind on being something bigger in the pond." Penney let his own laughter wind down. "You the feller saved those people from the river yesterday?"

Nimrod looked away. "Not all of them, I didn't."

"That was a brave thing," Penney said with an affirming nod.

"Out there, water's a big danger," Nimrod said, tipping his head toward the west. "People who can't swim a lick will step into a fast river like it was a Saturday night bath." He paused. "Where you headed, friend?"

"California. The land of milk and honey," Penney said with a chuckle. "I'm too old to swallow such flimflam, but it excites the young people."

Bub dumped a load where he stood, and Nimrod kicked the dung away from the tent entrance. "California's a far piece and a confusing road. I know the way. I'm looking to join an outfit."

"You hiring out as a guide? We got no money for one," Penney said.

"I'm not looking for your money because I maybe won't go all the way. I'm looking for a man I know, and if I see him, I might leave."

Penney became stern. "Everyone here has to shift for himself. You got money and supplies?"

"I carry my own weight. I put aside lean-time money."

Penney thought it over. "You strike me as honest, but I been fooled before. We could use some know-how. We're awful late. We should have pushed off the first of May. We've had a little trouble getting organized. Now, late May is the best we can do."

Nimrod tilted his head thoughtfully. "It's for the best you missed that getaway date. You'd have left too early. The ground would've been too soft, the grass too short, and the rivers too high. It takes time for things to dry out."

Penney was skeptical. "Many's the train already left."

"I wish them luck."

Penney started to protest, but Nimrod held up his hand. "Pardon me, sir, but I know what words are coming: You want to beat the snow to those mountains."

Penney's slow head shake was of worry. "We're all skittish of the California mountains. We been warned."

Nimrod nodded agreement. "If you start too late, you won't make it over the mountains before the snows hit. Start too soon, and mud or high water can trap or drown you. Start unprepared, you can die out there."

He suggested the group wait another two weeks. "I looked around coming in. You're not ready. Another two weeks is what you need. Getting there depends on getting prepared the right way."

Penney said, "Our folks are busting a gut to get going; waiting won't set well with them."

"With good reason," Nimrod said. "It's a fearsome business you're commencing." First of June should give you time to get ready."

Penney conceded the point with a somber nod. "It's been one thing, then another." He scrutinized Nimrod. "You related to the Lees of Virginia, if you don't mind my asking?"

"Who?"

"A well-known military clan."

Nimrod was amused. "I'm from the Lees of Kentucky, near Virginny, up on a place called Hogback Mountain. The onliest fighting we done was with the McKees down the road. We was well known to the sheriff, the tax collector, and the bootlegger. The preacher didn't even come around."

The two men walked to a nearby patch of grass where Nimrod let Bub graze while he busied himself with his saddle cinch. "I don't mean to puff like that steamboat out yonder, but I spent many a year trapping from the Bighorns to down Taos way. I rode with Captain Bonneville and Joe Walker in thirty-two when we explored much of the same land you want to cross. I rode most of the way with the Bidwell-Bartleson party of forty-one to just short of the Sierra. Old Broken Hand Fitzpatrick was the guide. He's an old trapper friend. I know the trail. I know how to manage in the country you're going to travel. I reckon I could ride from here to Sutter's fort without going a mile out of the way." His boast was an exaggeration; that's how mountain men often drove their point home, but it was not a time to quibble.

"You didn't finish with Bidwell? Why not?"

I wasn't signed on. I was traveling to look for a man I know. I just missed him."

We got books to tell us the way."

Nimrod smiled. "I wouldn't bet my life on a book. Writers are a sight better at making tall tales than good maps."

Penney paused and squinted at Nimrod in appraisal. "I'm fearful of buying a pig in a poke. No offense, but there be highbinders saying the same as you. The fact is, though, I got a good feel for you. I might be inclined to gamble on you and trust I'm not wrong. If my committee thinks you be the man to guide us for the few dollars we have, it would be a blessing."

"Every day I'm with you, I'll do my gol-durned best."

"What payment would you seek?"

"Trip like this, five-six months or thereabouts." He pondered a moment. "Five hundred dollars gold, plus my meals."

"Half would tax our purse," Penney said with a forlorn shake of his head.

"Two-fifty, then," Nimrod said.

Penney countered, "You accept paper money?" He assumed Nimrod would say no. Paper money, as often as not, was discounted far below its face value. Holding it was a gamble with the odds against the holder.

Nimrod nodded. "Paper money. I won't have time to cook, so I need to eat my meals with the families; spread it around, wagon to wagon. I won't be a burden; I'm not a fancy eater."

"I can't help asking: How could you work for so little?"

"My reasons are honest. If I have to leave at some point, I'll give you back your money."

"Leave? I'm suspecting you mean to find the same feller you left Bidwell for."

"I got that in mind."

"Well, we'd still be ahead. Right now, we got no guide, and naught other prospects." Penney pursed his lips in thought and studied Nimrod. "You could be a hard dog to keep on the porch, that's clear. But, if that's your bargain, we can't lose."

Penney scanned the people clustered around the wagons. He

saw what he was looking for, and said, "Mr. Lee, would you bide your time for a spell?" Penney walked over to the wagons and was joined one at a time by four other men. They talked for several minutes, each casting glances toward Nimrod. Finally, Penney motioned him over. "Mr. Nimrod Lee, I'd like to introduce the committee I serve on. I talked about you to them. They're chomping at the bit to meet you."

The members of the wagon train had chosen men to lead them they considered either distinguished or distinctive. The sole exception was farmer Shadrach Penney, but his obvious command-presence made him a reassuring choice.

Penney led Nimrod to each of the men. "Meet Malachi Cohen, he's an artist. This here is Abraham Jackman, he's a lawyer. Then there's Ezra Masterson. He's a schoolteacher." Penney paused. "Uh, I mean college professor." Masterson laughed, giving Nimrod the impression he was not a stuffed shirt. Lastly, Penney said, "Over here is Reverend Mather Poe. He prefers to be called Preacher, 'cause it's more biblical. If you're not a Baptist, the Lord might forgive you, but the good reverend won't."

Poe could have passed for an average man. He was three or four inches shy of six feet, about average for the period. He was a balding and middle age with judgmental eyes, and a prophet's beard displaying a sprinkling of gray. Poe was a bachelor who it seemed took no pleasure in laughter, including his own, seldom though it was. Neither did he take pleasure in anything not backed by a chapter and verse.

Malachi Cohen was a good artist who somehow put emotion into his images. He was full-bearded, and as biblical looking as his name sounded. He was a burly man with a lingering trace of German in his speech which came from his origin in the Prussian city of Berlin. As with so many of his Jewish faith, he was a survivalist who assumed things would eventually end badly. Based on centuries of history, and the challenges of the months ahead, the expectation was a reasonable caution.

There was nothing unusual in the appearances or accomplishments of Jackman and Masterson. They were well-regarded, successful men from the American mainstream. They impressed, but not memorably.

For several minutes the men quizzed Nimrod. They also had heard of men who looked the part of a guide, but the best part of their service was bragging the role, often with disastrous consequences. More than one wagon train was left stranded in the wilderness with no idea where they were.

The men were aware they were making what could be a life-and-death decision, and their questions were sharp and persistent.

When the questions wound down, Penney called the four apart to huddle in animated talk. Finally, Penney grinned, beckoned to Nimrod and extended his hand. "We have high hopes for your leadership, Mr. Lee—Nimrod."

"I'm beholden to you, Captain."

Penney chuckled. "I appreciate the title, but I ain't nothing but Shadrach."

"No disrespect, sir, and I don't mean to be forward, but on this train, you have to be 'Captain.' These people been cut out of their harness. They need someone who can jerk the bit. They need a captain. They need the title."

Cohen teased Penney. "Hell, Shadrach, if I was elected, I'd be a major at least; maybe a general."

Penney shook his head in exaggerated chagrin. "Captain is enough weight for these bony shoulders to tote."

The others nodded. From then on, it would be "captain."

Cohen said, "I see you've a feel for human nature, Nimrod."

"Thank you, sir. Sometimes I should bite my words. Not everyone smiles when they hear 'em."

Nimrod turned to Abraham Jackman who shook his hand, then swept his arm to encompass the wagon train. "Any trouble we have will not be with these good people. They appear to get along just fine, Mr. Lee."

Nimrod smiled and said, "Nimrod. I don't know a Mr. Lee." But he was thinking: Do you believe that, truly? However, he said, "That's wonderful to hear. It leaves the weather, rivers, mountains, desert, sickness, and, of course, the Indians, to deal with." What he also thought was that after the train left Independence, the members would be fellow prisoners of chance. The metaphorical prison would be the hostile environment, and natives with no reason to give friendship to uninvited strangers. The emigrants' protection would be the safety of numbers with others whom they might had come to loathe.

A sudden awkwardness came over the men, the way it sometimes does when people are out of things to say. They studied Bub grazing as though they'd never seen a mule. Finally, Penney said, "You're exceptional easy to do business with, Mr. Lee. Have a look-see around the camp, and then we'll call the folks together in the morning."

CHAPTER SEVEN

N imrod wandered among the wagons, tents, and livestock. Every few steps, he had to sidestep a puddle or a pile of manure. Children laughed, mothers scolded, and animals bellowed. They all ignored him.

The company numbered some seventy or eighty, spread among men, women, and children, and distributed over twenty-eight wagons. The people were obviously unaccustomed to rough living in tents and on the open ground. The men were unkempt with dirty clothes and tangled, long hair. The women wore coarse, long dresses appropriate for the farmhouse, but not for the wilderness. The children wore patched clothes and were barefoot.

Most were farmers from Midwestern states, but among them were merchants, scholars, adventurers, screw-ups, and maybe a fugitive or two. About half the women and men were in their thirties, along with some younger, some older. The few old people tried to be spry and help where they could. Nimrod saw no more than two children in each family. He knew that was because a single wagon could not carry enough food to feed a large family for five months.

The children were as young as toddlers, and Nimrod patted Bub on the withers and studied the scene. As he rode away, he lowered his head and shook it slowly. It would be a long way to California.

Nimrod tied Bub to the hitching post of a saloon named "The Starting Point" and headed inside toward the sound of a tinny piano and the raucous laughter of rough men relaxing. The smell of unwashed bodies at the door was a wall he easily burst through.

The saloon had all the charm of a building erected in a week, which was likely. The floorboards were uneven and warped from having been cut from wet lumber. The bar was a slapdash attempt at frontier respectability. Though made of raw pine, it at least had been sanded and didn't wobble, no doubt a passing effort by an itinerant carpenter to display his skill hurriedly. The bar mirror was cracked, either from a thrown bottle, or in transportation on the bumpy trip from Cincinnati. There were a couple of whores working, but their shopworn charms were weak competition for the whiskey, or perhaps an appreciation of those charms first required a copious dose of it.

Nimrod checked his weapons with the bartender as the house required and looked for a spot along the bar. It was lined by grizzly men in slouch hats and an assortment of frontier clothing. Laughter was a guffaw, never a chuckle. He recognized two mountain men, nodded to one, and spoke to the other. He was hailed by a third at the end of the bar, Elihu Walker, a rough-cut, loud man he had known for years in the high country. Nimrod smiled, took a space next to Walker, shook his hand, and ordered a drink.

"Well, howdy, Elihu. I heard the Blackfeet turned you into Sunday dinner for a buzzard family."

Walker grinned and snorted. "The heathen surely did try. Yes, they surely did, but the buzzards took one taste and spit me out."

The two men clinked glasses, and Walker looked around, and said, "This dump's as busy as a whorehouse on payday." Nimrod sipped, then looked at the glass in appreciation. "This'll be my last chance for fast living for six months. I figger to get corned up enough to keep me hungover 'til Sutter's Fort."

"Sounds like you're about to do some guiding," Walker said.

"It's honest work. Beaver's about as scarce as an honest trader, so we're stuck with pilgrims."

Walker frowned. "It's come to that, haint it."

They were interrupted by a jostling from behind. Nimrod turned to be face-to-face with Cy Perkins, the man he bested at the rendezvous five years earlier. Perkins moved close. His rancid breath made Nimrod blink. He was drunk and looking for trouble.

"Well, if it ain't squaw man Lee."

"You still riding slow horses, Perkins?" "Last I saw you, you was staring at a mule's ass."

"You can kiss my ass." Perkins hesitated, trying to think of something meaner. "Maybe I should call you squaw killer."

Nimrod roared and grabbed him by the shirt. He hit Perkins square in the face. His nose spurted blood like a squashed tomato, and he collapsed a nearby table, scattering protesting poker players. Nimrod rubbed his knuckles and glared at Perkins, but a friend of the downed man who was standing at Nimrod's blindside sucker-punched him in the face, knocking him down, also. Before Nimrod could regain his feet, Walker smashed a bottle over the man's head, and he, too, collapsed. Drinkers nearby either ignored the fight or laughed.

Walker extended a hand to Nimrod to help him up. "Now, can we get back to drinking?"

Nimrod rode Bub up to Penney's tent where the older man waited. The jar of dismounting made him wince and hold his head. His eye was puffed and closed and surrounded by a rainbow of discoloration.

Penney looked at his face. "My lord, what happened to you?"

"Oh, some fellers was saying Missouri mules are better'n Kentucky mules. One thing led to 'nother."

Penney chuckled.

Nimrod said, "Maybe I should talk to your pilgrims. I reckon they have a lot on their minds."

Penney frowned. "Well, they're all fired-up to meet you, but—"

"But what, Captain?"

"'Pilgrim' is not a name that'll please them. The members of this company don't see it as respectful; too many jokes. 'Emigrant' makes them sound like foreigners. Let's call these folks what they think of themselves as, what their grandpappies and grandmaws were—pioneers."

Nimrod offered an apologetic smile. "Let's go see the pioneers."

The wagon train company had prepared for everything they could think of to make their journey safe. Check-off lists had included a well-built wagon, plenty of the right food, firearms, and healthy animals to pull them along. What they could not prepare for was what they didn't know.

A sizable majority of the twenty-five hundred or so travelers of that early year were Midwesterners who had lived a comfortable distance from other people with whom they had developed life-long familiarity. Often, the nearest neighbor was out of sight in a farmhouse "over the hill," or, "down the road a piece." Their encounters would be at church or infrequent shopping trips to the local village: visit for a short while, then go home. "See you Sunday."

Coming in to also join the train, however, were strangers from places like Arkansas, Kentucky, and Missouri. They talked with accents and had different thoughts on the issue of slavery, in defense of which they were often willing to fight.

There were also wide variances of personality that easily led to disdain and disrespect, which with only a small nudge, could spill over into antagonism or even violence. Trouble would not have to look far for a reason.

They were headed for the middle of nowhere. There would be no going home. Five months was plenty of time for things to go dreadfully wrong.

Penney and Nimrod walked to a clearing where about forty milling adults perked up when they saw their approach. The pioneers were eager to meet the new hire who might guide them. But they also had a sense of uncertainty; it added another new thing to their situation already cluttered with the unknown. They had scanned the empty land to the west the way mariners of old confronted an unknown ocean, and they saw no safe anchorage.

An older woman with a limp came over to Penney's side. He introduced her as his wife, Clara. Nimrod tipped his hat and said hello. Clara smiled but said nothing.

Penney faced the crowd and held up his hand for silence. "Folks, I want you to meet a man y'all heard about by now." He paused and became solemn. "First, let me just say with my few years of country schooling, I don't know many big words, but I know the plain truth of this undertaking. We're setting out to make history, to make our lives better, and to extend Christian civilization into the land of the Papists and the heathen. God will surely look kindly on our work."

"Amen," a man said with feeling.

"Now, I'd like to introduce the man you're all het up to meet." He guided Nimrod forward with a hand on his arm. "This here's Mr. Nimrod Lee, late of the Rocky Mountain Fur Company. He's trapped and scouted the route we're taking for many a year, he says. He claims to know where we need to go, which is a heap sight more than we for sure know. From the way he talks, the committee has a feel that he can do as he speaks." The crowd murmured as Penney turned to Nimrod, and said, "Mr. Lee, talk to these pioneers. All we know about California are words on a page, but your eyes have seen it."

Nimrod looked at the faces and was not surprised at what he saw. The men appeared fit in the way of men who worked with hands and lifted with backs. They wore farmer clothing of baggy wool pants, and a waistcoat, or vest, not for style, but for warmth. Rather than shirts, they commonly wore waist-length smocks belted at the waist. Their shoes were calf-height rawhide boots. Headgear was slouch hats.

He noticed the men and women were paired as couples except for one woman who stood alone off to the side. She was something of a looker, not great, but more than passable. However, what stood out was something many women had, but had been taught not to display: the way she stood was strong and her manner self-assured, almost defiant. He liked that; many men didn't. He heard someone call her Hannah.

The men were pensive, but eager to begin their grand adventure. However, most women were nursing the long-suffering look of people overlooked or disregarded. The men wanted to explore beyond the mountain; the women wanted to be back home, safe, with their children. The men wanted a pot of gold; the women wanted a pot of oatmeal.

The women were dressed for going to the henhouse to gather eggs, or to fix dinner in the familiar surroundings of their own kitchen. Their dresses were long and draped straight down with a petticoat underneath. No bustles, hoops, or crinolines could be found. In the cold, women would wear long underwear, the same as men. Usually, a knit shawl or cape was around their shoulders and buttoned at the neck. They wore aprons all day, and on their feet were lace-up or high-button shoes ill-suited for walking on uneven ground. The women were soon to adopt rawhide calf-high boots for rough walking, the same as the men. They wore bonnets for protection from the sun. Common fabric for both sexes was linsey-woolsey, a coarse weave of wool and either linen or cotton. Otherwise, it was wool or cotton.

Little attention was given to Nimrod's black eye; everyday frontier violence was something they had almost come to expect. However, a stern man said, "You've been in an altercation. We don't want a common brawler."

"It weren't like that, sir," Nimrod said. "Some teamster was beating an ox, and I called him to account."

The crowd buzzed its approval. Penney turned away to hide his grin.

A man in the crowd called out, "No offense to your guide, Shadrach, but how do we know he's not selling us some horsefeathers?"

Penney nodded in a way to say the question was reasonable. "We don't know for sure, but if that's the case, we'll find out soon enough." He turned an unsmiling face to Nimrod. "Then we'll deal with it." Then, back to the man who had spoken: "Malachi talked to a wagon maker in town, a colored fella name of Young. Over the years, he's met most ever mountain man who passed through these parts, which means near all of them. Young said to Malachi, 'Mr. Lee is solid as a ten dollar gold piece.'" Penney gestured toward Nimrod. "Anyway, Sam, we're plumb out of options. If you know any, we'd for certain like to hear 'em."

A woman changed the subject. "What's California like?"

Nimrod waited until the talk subsided, then raised his own voice. "California has the tallest trees, the bluest rivers, and the highest mountains God ever saw fit to raise on the face of the earth."

"Were you there, for real?" a voice with a cynical edge called out.

Everyone quieted to hear his answer. "In thirty-three, twelve year ago, I was with Capt. Bonneville at the salt lake. He sent the great Joe Walker with a brigade to find a trail over the mountains to California. I was one of them he chose. We went a route south of the one we'll be taking, which is the shortest one to Sutter's Fort.

"We made it over mountains the Mexicans call Sierra Nevada, and into solid green meadows that stretch a long piece. A few days south, there's a valley where the cliffs reach the sky. The Indians call it *Ahwahnee*, which we heard means place of a gaping mouth." He shook his head in wonder of the memory. "If'n God wanted a summer home, he'd make it there."

An angry voice called out, "Blasphemy!" which was ignored.

There are trees there a feller could build a house out of and throw in a barn—just one tree!" He saw the disbelief. "That's true."

His words were quietly accepted as mountain man brag. Another voice called, "How about getting there?"

Nimrod grinned and nodded. "Getting there takes a bit of doing. We'll have lots of talk about that."

"How long on the road, and how far?" someone shouted.

"There ain't no road," he said to a couple of sniggers in the group. "But there are rivers we'll follow." He calculated mentally for a moment. "Figger five months, thereabouts, if we move slow, maybe a bit more. The distance everybody seems to have settled on is about two thousand miles, but I can't vouch for that. What's important is travel time."

A small, willowy young man spoke up, standing in the front next to a petite and pretty wife with the radiance of pregnancy on her face, and whom he indicated with an extended hand. "My name's Aaron Proctor. This here's my wife, Gertie." He chuckled and glanced at her swollen belly. "And either Caleb or Amelia."

Nimrod touched his hat. "Ma'am."

The Proctors had been hardscrabble sharecroppers in Arkansas who, for three years, had saved their egg money and what Aaron could earn hiring out to neighbors in the hope of transplanting to a golden, mysterious place called California. They knew that, back home in Arkansas, those who started out as sharecroppers ended up as sharecroppers. Aaron had built their wagon by himself; after two starts he got it right. They sold a barrow hog which sacrificed their winter meat; a gamble for people living close to the bone. Their two families contributed six oxen, though they had to stretch to afford it. Aaron and Gertie said they would pay them back—someday.

Against the wishes of their families, but with their prayers, they set off for Independence on the first day of March 1845.

When they sought to join the train, Penney said a purse of two hundred dollars was required so they wouldn't become dependent on others. Aaron replied they had but fifty-seven dollars. Penney was close to saying no, but the earnest looks on the faces of the young couple compelled him to nod yes and extend a hand of welcome.

When Gertie discovered she was pregnant, Aaron asked if she wanted to return to Arkansas. "Heavens, no," she said. "Twenty years from now, how would we explain to Caleb or Amelia that they're stuck in Arkansas because we didn't have the gumption to go on?"

Aaron was nervous to speak in public for the first time, but he was apprehensive for his wife and unborn child. "We're not blind to the dangers," Aaron said to Nimrod. "What are our chances of making it?" Aaron put his arm around Gertie as he said it.

"Most will. Not all," Nimrod said matter-of-factly.

"Are the Indians dangerous?"

Nimrod looked around and saw Indian danger preying on their minds. "Most Indians are regular people you'd be happy to invite home to Sunday dinner. Others'll cheat you when you let them, and maybe kill you if you seem helpless and have something they want bad enough. They's like a few bad apples you knew back home. Indians are most times content to watch us go away after they collect payment for us passing through."

"Damned if I'll pay some heathen for going through what's ours," a man in the back called out.

Nimrod smiled and scuffed the dirt with his boot. "Well, sir, I don't reckon they accept our ownership, seeing how they ain't sold it to us. They consider it like a toll road, and by-gum we ain't no strangers to those." He paused for their laughter. "That's fair, so long as they bargain reasonable."

"What should we not do?" Ezra Masterson asked.

"Don't go tricking them out of their horses or close-eyeing their women, in that order. Also, don't give them likker, even if they push or plead for it. They've lived content without it since Adam and Eve, and it unsettles their mind."

"How about trade goods," someone in back asked.

"Well, a buck Indian will ask for whiskey and guns, but we ain't gonna give 'em to him."

"What then?"

"Just like us, he's got to please his lady." He waited for the chuckles to die down. "We best give something cheap and light, things easy for us to carry and what his little woman wants: needles, thread, thimbles, knives and hatchets; above all, a yard or two of cloth, the brighter the better. So, if her husband says, 'I got a mind to go over and scalp them strangers,' she'll say, 'No, you're not.'"

An ill-at-ease woman in a long dress and apron stood up and said, "I have three children, and I'm afraid to trust their safety to anyone I don't know. So, forgive me for asking what your experience with a wagon train is."

Nimrod met her eyes and nodded. "I honor your question, ma'am. I rode most all the way alongside Tom Fitzgerald, old Broken Hand hisself, when he guided the Bidwell-Bartleson party to California four year ago. And if you was in a tight spot in those mountains in a party led by old Tom, you'd be able to sleep safe at night."

A woman in her mid-thirties stepped forward. She was the one standing alone who had earlier caught his eye. Her brown hair was bleached by the sun and swept back into a bun. Her clean dress was covered by a white apron. Her skin was ruddy, her smile sparkled, and her solid shape was unbowed by the hard work of a woman of the day. She was confident, and her voice rang clear. "I'm Hannah Spencer. I speak for my husband who couldn't be here."

Someone snickered in the crowd, which she ignored. Hannah was an easy target for snide comments. A few people, including some women, felt defensively jealous of this woman who was far better educated than their husbands. She was cordial enough, and helpful enough, but her lack of deference to her husband, and her discernible lack of affection toward him, was counter to the way they had been brought up and were trained to consider proper.

"Does she think she's better'n us?" had asked one woman who was married to a man who bullied her and their children.

Hannah knew nothing of those feelings, but wouldn't have much cared anyway. "There's been a lot of brave talk," Hannah said to Nimrod and the group. "But the truth is, we're children in this wilderness. We're farmers, and shopkeepers, and mothers. Tell us what to expect, Mr. Lee."

"The worst."

Hannah's head snapped back in surprise. "That's a frightful thing to hear."

Nimrod said, sympathetically, "You asked me what to expect, ma'am. There's always more things to go wrong than right."

He smiled. She didn't. He looked at her and wanted what he saw. She returned the look and feared what she saw. They held the glance a little too long, but neither blinked. It didn't mean anything, but it meant a lot. The look promised nothing, but it threatened everything.

Hannah turned away, and said, "Abel Blanc, my late husband back in St. Louis, was a physician. I served as his nurse and as a midwife. He was a good teacher." She looked around to gauge the reaction. People listened and waited for more. "I'm mindful of the sicknesses out there, especially the cholera they say came from Asia. It's out there. Be careful."

"Careful of what, exactly, Hannah?" asked a wife named Jennie in a nervous voice with three small children surrounding her.

"I don't rightly know. And that's the truth of it, so be careful of everything."

"And pray," Preacher added.

"And stay in bed all day," a man said to laughter.

Hannah watched Jennie's family walk back to their wagon and felt sad for what they might face. She also had foreboding because she knew disease and sickness. She knew in the coming months, grief would come courting. These fine people were putting themselves at the mercy of dangers they didn't even know existed.

Hannah knew their medical care would fall on her; there was no one else, and the thought made her feel small and inadequate. "Help me, Abel," she whispered.

✻

The conversation wound down, so the audience wandered away, busy with a thousand preparations for departure. Curious, Nimrod strolled among the wagons, until he heard frustrated shouts from near the riverbank. He turned and saw a young man dancing around two yoke of oxen pulling a wagon in a line toward the water despite his loud pleas to stop. A second man stood by and watched.

Nimrod trotted over, grabbing a long stick as he went. He ran to the ox on the front left and tapped the animal atop its head with the stick, and commanded, "Whoa!" The oxen took not a step farther.

The man rushed over and pumped Nimrod's hand. "Thank you, sir, thank you," he said, still agitated. "I feared the beasts would take our wagon right into the water. They're uncontrollable. Dangerous."

Nimrod slapped an ox on the flank and laughed, but not sarcastically. "The onliest way these old boys would hurt you is to step on your toes."

The man was too relieved to care. "I'm Andrew Banks," and as the other man walked over, he said, "this is Martin Carter."

They shook hands. Nimrod recognized the men as homosexual, but he was unfazed despite the severe public disapproval, even criminality, of that lifestyle in the public mind. He also noticed Martin had a dull, vacant stare in his eyes, and his movements were slow and listless. The man didn't seem to care, unusual for such an exciting time in his life.

"If'n I was you, I'd hire a boy to drive this team until you get the hang of it," Nimrod advised Andrew, who nodded and said, "If you know a boy, it'd get us over the rough beginning."

✻

Oxen did the heavy hauling of the Oregon Trail. They were the quiet heroes of the drive. They suffered from heat and had no defense against maddening insects. They ate scrub vegetation horses wouldn't touch. Their tongues hung out, and their eyes rolled in a desperate need for water. But though they suffered, they kept working. And even as they strained to haul a ton-and-a-half wagon up a steep hill, some senseless brute might take a bullwhip to them. They wouldn't hurt a soul, except by accident. They were harmless, and the oath, "dumb as an ox," was as wrong as it was stupid.

A working ox was an intelligent animal. He came of age at four when his muscles had matured, and he had the needed bulk. He was a steer, and because he had been neutered and would never be a bull, aggressiveness had given way to a gentle nature. Most weighed sixteen to eighteen hundred pounds, but a ton was not uncommon. He sometimes made the ultimate sacrifice by being slaughtered so his owners could survive on his flesh.

He was pokey, about two miles per hour, but the turtle would have understood, not so the rabbit, or the horse. He had been trained for many months to heed five basic voice commands: Giddup, whoa, right, left, and back. The leader was called the nigh ox. He was positioned in the front left. Excellent drovers used a stick to touch the nigh ox on the head or shoulder to reinforce each command. The other oxen would follow. Bad drovers would punish with a whip. However, a whip cut could fester and become infected. Skilled drovers would crack a bullwhip, but not touch the oxen. The oxen would respond to the noise the whip made.

Penney walked up to the three men, excused himself, then told Nimrod a man named Uriah Meister, down at the north end, needed help with his wagon. "He's over there with his darky, Johnnythree," Penney said.

"Johnny who?"

Penney explained that Meister said he always gave slaves a number to help tell them apart. Penney frowned and shook his head as he said it. "I don't hold with slavery. No, sir, I do not." The "do not" was ardent, almost angry. "Where I hail from, we're too poor to own ourselves, save another person."

Nimrod shook Penney's hand and walked over to a wagon where a dour middle-aged man was fumbling a repair attempt on his wagon, swearing and banging tools around. Standing ill at ease at his shoulder was a young black man who was very dark and strongly built, but small. He was wide-eyed, but with wariness, not curiosity. He was as skittish as a dog kicked too many times. Nimrod guessed him to be about twenty.

"Howdy, sir. Captain Penney tells me you could use a hand."

Meister grunted. "Damned wagon tongue's got a crack in it already."

Meister kicked the wagon tongue, and Nimrod bent down to examine it. "Thisuns made out of pine. Has to be hardwood, and it needs iron reinforcement."

Meister studied him. Your manner of speaking tells me you're from God's country. Did you ever own a bondsman?"

Nimrod looked up, bemused. "Own a slave? What would I do with one on a hardscrabble twenty-acre farm?" Nimrod brushed his hands as he stood. "Here's what to do: Take this wagon into town to Hiram Young the wagon maker. He'll fix you up."

Nimrod started to walk away when Meister decided to take his ire out on Johnnythree who was trying to be helpful by straightening out the wagon tongue. Meister kicked him hard in the rear and continued to rant and kick at him as Johnnythree scrambled away.

"You move things when I tell you, and only then, you black bastard," he screamed.

Nimrod stepped between them. "This ain't my affair, but them children down the way shouldn't see this violence."

Meister stopped and looked at Nimrod. The fierce glare he saw on Nimrod's face said something more potent than his words. Nimrod's eyes made him lower his own look. Meister muttered and turned away, but he stopped beating Johnnythree.

Nimrod mounted Bub and moved through the camp until he saw Hannah Spencer at her campfire. Next to her was a girl of about twelve and a boy maybe a year younger. A distance away, fussing with a team of horses, was her husband, Ed Spencer, in whom Nimrod sensed a character darkness. Nimrod dismounted.

"Morning, Miz Spencer."

Hannah straightened up, putting hands on hips to stretch out a sore back. "Well, good morning again to you, Mr. Lee. I trust you're finding things to your liking."

Nimrod allowed a small grin and looked at her, but not too daringly. "Better all the time, ma'am. From here to California is a long way to be a mister. I'm who my mama named me—Nimrod." He then related to her the need for oxen help by Andrew Banks. She listened, and then told him Billy was very good working with oxen, even at his young age. She also said she would welcome him helping the two men. Nimrod did not mention her husband's permission, assuming that was between them.

Hannah called her children over. "Mr. Nimrod, meet Billy, and this is Rachel." She indicated the man Nimrod had already noted. "Yonder is my husband, Mr. Ed Spencer."

Nimrod touched Rachel on the top of her head. "My, but you're as pretty as a peach." Rather than the anticipated smile, Rachel lowered her head without response. Billy seemed an ordinary boy, but when he moved, Nimrod noticed a hitch in his walk caused by a club foot.

"Billy, them two gentlemen over by the river are in need of a drover," Nimrod said. "You figger you might be the man for the job?"

"He's good with animals," Hannah said.

"There'd be a lot of walking," Nimrod cautioned.

Billy was excited, but he detected Nimrod's concern. "You mean my foot? I can't run fast, but I can walk to kingdom come. And Mr. Spencer's going to drive horses, so he won't need me."

Nimrod tousled the boy's hair. "You're one for duty, you are. Like a soldier. Like an old cavalry trooper I once camped alongside. I reckon I'll call you that—Trooper, that's who you are."

Billy smiled with pride at his new man-sounding name. Hannah said, gently, "You've got chores, Billy."

He turned and walked-ran with his burdensome hitch that he hated first thing in the morning, and last thing at night.

Nimrod and Hannah watched him go. Nimrod chuckled. "He's as happy as a pup with two tails."

"You have a nice way with children," she said.

"He's a good boy. I hope I weren't out of line, telling him about the job without first clearing it with you."

"Never be sorry for making a child feel valued."

As Hannah and Nimrod turned away from the departed Billy, their eyes settled on each other. There were no words, no smiles, no gestures. Their eyes locked for a moment in a reach-out of attraction. It happens between men and women when the moment triggers it. The encounter passes or is pushed away, but it can't be hidden from the chamber of the mind that stores such things. There was no reason for such a reaction to happen, except that it did happen, and it wouldn't easily go away.

Desire is impatient, but it can also be willed to wait.

Nimrod tipped his hat to Hannah and walked over to her husband who was combing the mane of a palomino with a pink satin ribbon tied to the saddle. A large bull-fighting breed of dog sat at his heel. Nimrod eyed the dog, and the dog eyed Nimrod and growled. Slobber dripped out of its mouth.

Nimrod didn't know what was in the dog's mind, but he did in his—If that son of a bitch makes one move on me, the buzzards'll be pecking up his remains.

"How-do, Mr. Spencer. I'm Nimrod Lee."

Spencer took his hand with reluctance.

Nimrod kept his eye on the dog. "That dog a biter, is he?"

"Sometimes, Brutus is."

"Fine young son you got there, young Billy," Nimrod said, undeterred. "I suspect a couple of men might want to hire him for a drover."

Spencer concentrated on his horse, not looking at Nimrod. "He's a stepson. Why would they hire a gimp? Maybe think they can get him cheap?"

Nimrod slapped one of the six horses on the rump. "Mighty fine team you got here. Blooded. You gonna sell them in town?"

Spencer scoffed. "Sell? I'm taking them to California. I'm told those Mexicans appreciate good horseflesh. Should bring top dollar."

Nimrod appraised the horses. "Yes, sir. Mighty fine, them horses. They might show some interest, the Californios—that's what the Mexicans call themselves. They're expert horsemen. As good as the best. Problem might be, they got horses like a barn's got mice." Nimrod noticed Spencer's angry reaction and changed the subject. He asked if Spencer were going to tie the horses to the back of his wagon.

"Hell, no. These beauties are going to pull the wagon."

Nimrod didn't want the conversation to turn unpleasant, but it was his new job to speak out. "Horses on this trail are for riding, sir, they ain't for hauling. Ox can get along on 'bout whatever grows and keep going. Horses, they can't. For the first few hundred miles, there'll be grass aplenty, but when we hit sparse grass, they can't work and survive on those slim pickings. They'll need grain to keep going." He patted the rump of one of the horses. "These here'll never make the Rocky Mountains without grain."

Spencer said, "I've got a brace of oxen to pull a wagon of corn," pointing to two oxen grazing near a small wagon. Nimrod didn't argue the point, but he had another objection. "Every Indian along the way will risk his life to steal these beauties—and they'll get it done, rest your mind on that. Long as they got plenty buffalo, they don't much want ox."

Spencer's limited patience with the nosy stranger had come to an end. "What would a man who rides a mule know about thoroughbred stock?"

Nimrod looked at Bub and smiled. "Ol' Bub here is a saddle mule. After a day's work on those plains, he'll be looking for a dance to go to, while any horse is taking to his rocking chair."

"You best tend to your guiding, Mr. Ah—"

"Lee. And that's what I'm a-doin'."

Nimrod walked away and grunted his scorn for such a man. Spencer was the sort of bully who would be dangerous if he figured you weren't. Intuitively, Nimrod knew a clash was inevitable, somewhere, sometime before they reached Sutter's Fort. He thought of Hannah, the woman Spencer was married to. She was as desirable as cream gravy. How, he wondered, does such a sorry excuse of a man appeal to such a woman?

CHAPTER EIGHT

Nimrod planned to assemble the company to discuss the supplies they would need. It would be a long list. Mindful of his own needs, Nimrod rode into Independence to shop. Because he had spent years as a traveling man, he needed little. He stocked up on coffee, sugar, a whetstone for knife sharpening, gunpowder, two bars of lead, and percussion caps.

Outside the storekeeper's shack, Nimrod was approached by a middle-aged man in patched farmer clothing. He also wore a downcast look and had the slumping shoulders of a defeated man.

"Asking your pardon, sir," the man said, "could that be your scattergun I see on this here mule?"

"It is, sir," Nimrod said. "How can I help you?"

"Well, sir, I'm looking to barter this here revolving pistol for such a firearm as that. Some call it a shotgun." He removed the revolver from his pocket and held it up for Nimrod to see.

Nimrod was curious. "I've heard about such a revolving gun. They say Indian fighters down Texas way done well with them."

The man said, "It's called a Colt Paterson from back east; made by a man named Sam Colt if I heard right."

"Seems to me, that'd be a keeper," Nimrod said. "If'n it works, why would you want to rid yourself of it?" He made no effort to hide his doubt.

"Oh, you betcha. It works, yes, sir." He then said, wistfully, "My needs have changed. A man's got no need for such a pistol on a farm; a scattergun, he does. You can shoot an Indian with this pistol, but you can't eat him. You shoot a rabbit with a scattergun, you got yourself a meal." He polished the revolver with his sleeve. "I paid thirty-two dollars for this back in Memphis," he said, glancing to see if the sum impressed Nimrod. It did.

The man, who introduced himself as Ellsworth Partridge, said his wife threatened to take the children and walk back to Arkansas, and if he wanted to join them, fine. Otherwise, he could go to hell or California, whichever came first. "So, you see, sometimes a man has to choose between his dream and his family. I'll do my duty, but I ain't happy about it."

The men walked to a nearby creek where Nimrod examined the pistol while Partridge looked closely at the scattergun. Partridge explained the pistol as holding five shots in a cylinder that advanced as the hammer was pulled back, thus putting the next round in-line with the rifled barrel. The same action caused a fold-up trigger to descend. Each slot in the cylinder had a nipple to hold a percussion cap which fired a barrel-loaded ball of thirty-six caliber.

"Thirty-six don't have much stopping power," Nimrod said as he hefted the unfamiliar handgun.

"You don't use it to hunt bear," Partridge said. "It's a man-killer; that's what it's good for. It shoots true about thirty-forty yards. Beyond that, it hits a target only after vigorous prayer." He lifted the hammer and rotated the cylinder. "If a man thinks he's riding into trouble, he best carry a loaded spare cylinder he can slip in."

The men tried out both weapons by shooting at driftwood floating by. Between shots, Partridge had an outlet for his frustrations.

"My daddy left me sixty acres I been farming for nigh on twenty year; beans and corn mainly; hogs for cash money. I got satisfaction out of selling hogs but not out of smelling 'em. Raising cattle is what gives me pleasure, but there's no money-making market for beeves back home, and not enough pastureland except for a couple milk cows, and maybe to feed a steer or two for winter. So, when I started hearing about California, how the Mexicans run hundreds of head in great spaces with no fences, and how they be offering free land for settlers to come, I thought: Well, if I don't answer that call, I'll never hear another one.

"Well, sir, Lizzie—that's my wife, Lizzie—She's not a woman who dreams a lot; leastways, not the same things as a man. From the start, she was agin' going on the trail to California. The Methodist church down the road was as far west as she wanted to travel. Then, when we sold the farm and got on the road, the spirit of the thing just wasn't in her…riding the wagon all day, cooking on the ground, mosquitoes like a cloud, putting up with rain and mud…No sir-ee, Bob. So, we're going back to Arkansas, tails between our legs—my tail, at least." He sighed and shrugged. "That's where I 'spect they'll bury me, between the hog lot and the chicken shack."

Nimrod listened without comment and took another shot at a log bobbing by. As the smoke from black powder curled around their heads, the men shook hands on the trade.

Nimrod walked away examining his new pistol. He felt like a man to be reckoned with. He already owned a gutta-percha poncho he used as a ground cover or blanket. Gutta-percha was a primitive latex rubber-like substance from Malaysia new to American markets. It was painted onto fabric to make it waterproof. Nimrod knew there were men in Independence who would kill him to steal it, and they'd have to do just that.

Nimrod had obtained his poncho in a St. Louis card game from a drunken peddler who had insulted him as a backwoods buffoon during a marathon poker game. Onlookers who knew Nimrod wondered at his calm reaction to the peddler's insults. However, Nimrod didn't mind. He was busy cheating the man out of his money and the curious poncho that shed water like a duck's back. Having made the hapless salesman almost a pauper, he declined the man's pocket watch in a burst of generosity.

Johnnythree drove the Meister wagon into Hiram Young's wainwright business. He halted the oxen and looked around, studying the busy work lot. To his surprise, he saw nothing but black workers who seemed to be their own bosses. He hailed a nearby worker. "Hey, boy! I got important business with your master, Mr. Hiram Young."

The man stopped his work and leaned on his ax. "'Boy' yourself. I ain't got no master, and if'n you be wanting Mr. Young, you'll find him right over there, if'n he has time for the likes of you." The worker indicated Hiram Young who was occupied a few yards distant.

Johnnythree looked over toward Young, then back to the worker. "Who you funnin', nigger? I don't want no slave. I got business with the boss."

Young overheard the squabble and walked over. He smiled at Johnnythree. "What can I do for you, my young friend?"

Johnny was stunned. He didn't understand a black man taking on the airs of a boss. "I done come here to get this here wagon fixed, what is owned by my master, Mr. Uriah Meister. I needs to see Mr. Hiram Young."

"I'm Hiram Young."

Johnnythree was perplexed and then suspicious. "You?"

Young nodded. "And you are?"

"Johnnythree."

"Three what?"

"Number three slave," Johnnythree said.

Young shook his head wearily." Lord, lord, lord." He then smiled at Johnnythree. "Not here. There are no slave names here. Now, what can I do for you, Johnny?"

"My master need a new wagon tongue."

"Let's take a look," Young said, examining the damaged tongue. "Simple fix. You can have it by evening."

Johnnythree indicated the half-dozen black workers. "Who these people be?"

"My workers," Young said.

"Your slaves?" Johnnythree had heard of free black men owning slaves, also.

"They used to be other people's slaves, but now they belong to themselves, the way God intended."

"They's no different than me," Johnnythree said in amazement.

"When a man's eyes get opened, the world's a different place," Young said with a kind smile. "By the way, how old are you?"

Johnnythree thought hard on the puzzle. "Well, I don't rightly know, but I heard a girl in the big house say she was born twenty year ago, 'bout the same time as me. I guess that's what I am, 'bout twenty."

"Where are your folks?"

"I don't know. I ain't never had none."

Johnnythree studied Young and wondered if he dared speak freely to a free man, black or white. "Boss Hiram," he started awkwardly, "how does a slave like me get some of that freedom?"

Young looked at Johnnythree with surprise. "You mean you don't know? You ain't been told?"

"Told what, sir?"

"When you leave the state of Missouri and go west, you'll be a free man."

"Me?"

Young nodded with a smile. "Free by law. You'll be in what they call unorganized territory. There ain't any slaves there."

"What do I got to do?"

"Your master, as you call him, must give you a paper called a manumission saying you're free. Otherwise, without proof of freedom, some bad men called slave catchers can grab you and bring you back to Missouri and say you're a runaway slave. They'd likely send you down river to the Mississippi plantations. Those are bad places.

"You're going into a place where slavery ain't allowed; then when you get to California, Mexicans don't allow slavery, either. That's what they say. But Mexican are like a lot of other white folks, they say one thing and mean another." Young thought of Nimrod. "Look for white people who'll help you."

"How is I to do all that? My master say I'm stupid as a hog in the sour mash."

Young's voice softened. "You ain't stupid, Johnny. A man kept all his life in the dark don't know what to make of the sun."

Young was hailed by a worker struggling with a job, but before he left, he appraised Johnnythree for a long moment, then asked, "Is your guide a man name of Nimrod Lee?"

Johnnythree nodded. "I seen him around camp, but he don't pay no attention to the likes of me."

Young took out a tablet and pencil and wrote a message, which he folded into a small square. Young placed the paper in Johnnythree's hand. "Put this in your pocket and hand it to Nimrod Lee when no one is watching. And don't tell anyone—anyone—about this piece of paper."

"Yes, sir."

He shook hands with Johnnythree. No free person had ever done that. "Good luck, son."

Young walked away as Johnnythree watched the free workers and imagined himself one of them.

Maude Horner dreaded going, which made waiting infinitely worse. She wanted to be almost anywhere but in a covered wagon. She wanted to be back in Terre Haute, Indiana, where familiarity brought her as close as she could get to calm living.

Peace of mind was not a normal state for Maude. There was only a small window in her mind open to happiness. She might briefly feel its breeze, but then the window would slam shut before it could gentle her. There were few smiles in her life. She did minimal housework. When she did become animated, it was often to berate her husband, Earl, for an imagined slight or for a matter of no consequence.

Neighbors and townspeople said she was crazy; not to Earl's face, but he knew it was being said.

Earl had no idea what could help his wife. Over time, he realized the answer was not much. In despair, he sometimes wondered what he had done to cause her condition.

Maude's condition worsened, bringing her closer to insanity. She was bedeviled by hallucinations and manic-depressive episodes. Of course, no one understood those were symptoms of a schizoaffective disorder. To keep her mind somewhat level, Maude was treated like a bottle of nitroglycerin wrapped in cotton. The cotton in her life was being surrounded by a familiar home, her extended family, the few friends she trusted, and by church parishioners who nervously tried to help her. Quiet routine calmed the seas threatening to drown her.

The solitary joy in Maude's life was their only child, Roger, a rambunctious, willful boy of twelve who resented a mother who humiliated him in front of his friends. He didn't know why he couldn't have a normal mother like his schoolmates. He acted out his anger in a hundred ways and was building a bad-boy reputation.

Earl had grown to hate neighbors' prying and gossip, and the shame he felt in his community. He decided new surroundings were what Maude needed: Maybe California, which was gaining a reputation-cum-myth for warmth and sunshine. He realized a change of location might not change anything, but he had to try something.

Maude didn't approve or disapprove, so the farm was sold. Within months, the Horners found themselves waiting for Shadrach Penney and Nimrod Lee to deliver them to California.

Living in a covered wagon on the banks of the Missouri, everything changed—except Maude.

Waiting was the toughest job left. Following Nimrod's advice, the train didn't move from the camp on the river as early as planned. It's not dry enough yet, he kept telling them. He urged June first as the departure date, still two weeks away. So, as the days passed, there they sat and watched the few remaining trains wend their way past and begin the trip west. A week later, a few trains were yet to depart. Then, there was but one—them.

Nimrod told the anxious pioneers: "If'n you start too soon, you'll get there too late."

Night after night, people had to listen to the boisterous din from Independence as trappers, teamsters, assorted rowdies drank, fought, and whored to celebrate the many sins of this frontier Babylon.

One morning before departure, Nimrod was in Independence when a long train of freight wagons lumbered into town from Santa Fe. One look at the shouting, cursing men with their unkempt beards and filthy clothes told him these trail-weary men could become trouble about an hour after draining the first bottle of whiskey.

He was not surprised when, close to midnight, he saw the silhouettes of about half a dozen revelers stumbling and wrestling their way toward his wagons, hooting and laughing. A celebration for men like these often rested on the thin ice covering the rage and violence below. He could see trouble coming down the path.

Nimrod walked a short distance to place himself between the oncoming men and the wagons. In his side vision, he saw several people leave their tents and watch from a distance.

"Evening, gents. I reckon you're in from Santa Fe. That's a far piece, so you boys deserve a good time. But our folks are bedded down, so I'd be grateful if you'd go on down the road a bit."

The men stopped and grew quiet and stared at Nimrod about ten feet in front. The man in front had a hairy face and beady eyes. His clothes were filthy, and he smelled of mule. His hat pulled low cast an ominous shadow over his face. He was heavy without being fat. He stared at Nimrod, then looked back and laughed at his fellows who were spectators at whatever might happen. One hanger-on nearby shouted, "Show him what for, Gomer." Thus encouraged, he turned back to Nimrod. "Who the hell are you, sodbuster? Get out of the way of real men."

Nimrod kept his voice calm and said, "We don't want trouble. Why don't you boys go back to town and have a real shindig? Ain't nothing to celebrate down here. There's children needing to sleep," Nimrod said in his unfamiliar version of a placating voice. He felt at his side for the pistol he was not yet used to wearing. It was not there.

Again, Gomer turned to the others and guffawed, whether for approval or support. Then, he turned back to Nimrod, but he was no longer laughing. "Ain't no plowboy be telling me to go nowhere!" he said with a snarl.

Nimrod raised both hands in supplication. "We got no quarrel here, fellers. I'd be obliged if'n y'all would take your carryings-on down the road a piece and leave us be."

"You whine like a pansy, hog raiser," Gomer said. He again turned back to his group and pulled a butcher knife from his boot and waved it while holding a whiskey bottle in the other hand. "You boys want to see something funny? Watch me make old corn pone here squirm." He started to turn back toward Nimrod when his world turned unfunny. Nimrod leaped forward and swept his booted foot against the side of the man's knee, which bent hard in a direction never intended by the designer.

The man screamed in surprise and pain and collapsed. He tried to lift himself up, but Nimrod kicked him in the face. He fell backward, and Nimrod stomped on the hand still holding the knife. He picked up the knife and threw it far into the river.

All was silent except the moaning of the man, as the festive mood of his friends turned ugly.

"You had no call to do that," one of the men said. "Gomer was funning. He's new to these parts."

Nimrod stepped backward. "Your friend can thank me, 'cause he's going to live to sober up. You pull a knife on a man out here, most times one of you be headed for a bone box."

The men started to fan out and move forward. "You ought'n done that to Gomer," one said in a low voice.

Nimrod sensed a presence next to him and glanced over to see Penney with a scattergun pointed at the men.

"You boys keep coming this way, I'll blow your guts out," Penney said through clenched teeth. He motioned the gun toward Gomer. "Now, you pick up that bag of wind moaning in the dirt over there and get out of here."

Nimrod stepped toward the huddle of men. "Keep your friend away from here. If I see him trying to walk heavy around these people again, I'll kill him." Nimrod was referring to Gomer, but everyone knew they were included.

Nimrod and Penney watched in silence as the men stole away lugging the moaning Gomer. Penney looked at Nimrod with a grin, and said, "You was like a terrier on a rat. I have it in mind to stay on your good side."

Nimrod shook his head. "Fighting's easy. It's talking that wears you out."

Walking back to the wagons, Nimrod passed Cohen sitting on a wagon tongue sketching on a pad of paper on his lap.

"What you drawing, Malachi?" Nimrod asked, leaning over the artist's shoulder. He spoke as though just coming from the barber shop, and not a live-or-die confrontation.

The older man raised his head. "I'm preserving the scene I saw you go through with those ruffians."

"Twernt a pretty picture."

"Not much of what humans do is beautiful," Cohen said.

"The most dangerous animals ain't in the mountains." Nimrod walked away shaking his head.

CHAPTER NINE

Penney saw Preacher approaching at a fast walk, looking like a bank teller whose accounts didn't add up. Penney said, "You got a snake chasing you? You're sure in an all-fired hurry."

Preacher shook his head with disgust. "I'm afraid we've got some discord among our flock," he said.

Penney lost his grin. "Oh, how's that?"

Preacher rubbed his cheek and studied the ground, looking for a place to begin. "Well, Shadrach, I'm not comfortable talking about this, but my duty demands it." He raised his eyes to Penney's. "That couple that joined us last week, the ones from Wisconsin; freshly married they are, I believe. I've had some complaints—"

"The Hibbard couple, you mean. What is it?"

"I'm not comfortable talking about it, Shadrach."

"What is it?"

"Well, sir, every night, at an hour when the rest of us are trying to bed down to refresh ourselves for the oncoming day—"

"What *is* it?"

"Don't rush me, Shadrach. This is not easy." He started over. "Every night, they commence carrying-ons in a—May I say?— in a Sodom-and-Gomorrah manner. I liken it unto a Roman orgy. There's a lot of laughter, and—I'm embarrassed to say this—there's a lot of moaning, squealing, and who knows what else is going on in that wagon. Disconcerting, I believe is a word I can use. It has caused talk among others, and not favorable. The sacred marriage bed is not intended for such, such frolicking."

"Have you mentioned it to those young people?"

"I consider that your job, Shadrach."

"Who else has complained?"

"I am not at liberty to say."

Thinking aloud, Penney mused, "Yours is the onliest wagon close to them that comes to mind, other than the Pattersons. I saw them this morning, and nary a word was said."

Preacher looked away. "I'd appreciate your stepping forward on this, Shadrach."

That afternoon, Penney called Herman Hibbard aside. "Herman, it's wonderful to see you and Mrs. Hibbard off to such a blissful start on your life together. I'm told your young bride is the envy of all the women. He laughed, and added, "I'm sure the men are jealous of you, but they ain't saying so."

"Thank you for those words, Mr. Penney," Hibbard said, but he knew something else was coming.

"The best advice I can offer, and I reckon I can speak with some knowledge on this, is to maybe be a little more private in your nighttime affections. Those wagon bonnets ain't walls. I say that with all respect for you and Mrs. Hibbard."

Hibbard reddened with embarrassment. "Has anyone complained?"

Penney shrugged. "Oh, no, no, not a complaint. Just a casual comment, nothing unkind. You both are held in high regards, you can bet."

The next day, the Hibbard wagon pulled out to join another train. Penney watched them go with some regret, and muttered to himself, "You're doing a good job, Herman. Don't listen to reverends about the bedroom."

Johnnythree finally worked up enough courage to approach Meister. "Uh, master," he said. When Meister turned to face him, Johnnythree swallowed hard and stuttered, but finally told him of the conversation with Hiram Young, and asked that when they drove out of Missouri, could he please have his freedom?

Meister smiled broadly. He had prepared for this moment. He beckoned Johnnythree to a camp chair, and said, "You've been a good worker, Johnny, and I apologize for being unkind at times. I'm under a lot of stress myself. You're a good Christian young man. You deserve your freedom. I'll have the papers written up giving you your freedom."

The newly christened Johnny just stared at the cruel man who suddenly had turned into his friend.

Meister said, "Now, my young friend, what do you plan to do with your freedom?"

Johnny looked at him blankly. "What am I supposed to do with it, master?"

Meister kneaded his hands together and looked troubled. "I have to warn you, Johnny, you're going to have to earn your own keep, and find your own place to sleep. A lot of people don't like freed slaves, and some of them will try to grab you and send you down river to the plantations. You'd have to find a job, and I don't where you could."

Johnny listened to Meister and closed his eyes where he could visualize a life of starvation and danger. Meister was watching him and slapped his own thigh as having just decided something momentous. "Tell you what, Johnny: I'll hire you as a free worker, and I'll pay you cash money. You can continue living out of this wagon. You'll have vittles and a warm place to sleep, just as always....Tell you what," he said, as though about to say something momentous. "I'll pay you two dollars script each month, cash money." He reached into his pocket and removed an official-looking bill and handed it to Johnny. "Here's an official five dollar bill issued by the Merchant's Bank of St. Louis. That's a good-faith payment in advance from me to you." He extended his hand. "Have we got a deal?"

Johnny looked at the hand mysteriously outstretched. A white man had never offered to shake hands with him before. He grasped Meister's hand and thought—Now, I'm a real man.

A week before departure, people crowded around Nimrod as he readied them for the beginning of the adventure they both hoped and feared would change their lives forever. Nimrod recited his check list of what was needed: For each adult and child: one-hundred-fifty pounds of flour, twenty pounds of corn meal, fifty pounds of bacon, fifty pounds each of beans and rice, thirty pounds of sugar, and ten pounds of coffee.

"Pack 'em in tight boxes and caulk the seams and caulk every seam in your wagon boxes to make them watertight for river crossings. "Flour soaked in dirty river water ain't my idea for the makings of a birthday cake," he said to the nods and laughter of the women.

"By the way, I saw a big stack of desiccated vegetables in that general store on the edge of town," he said. "Since most trains have left, you can bargain a good price, I'm thinking."

"What are those?" a voice called out.

"Different kinds of vegetables dried and pressed into a loaf. It'll last a long time. Just make sure you cut into one in the store to make sure sawdust ain't been added."

"We had some of those back in the army," a man said. We called them "desecrated" vegetables. A body wouldn't touch them unless he was starving."

"And if he was starving?" Nimrod asked.

"Well, then," the man said, "he'd be happy to have them for Christmas dinner." He waited for the laughter to die down, then said, "I'm told covering your face and arms with mud will keep mosquitoes away."

Nimrod nodded. "I've seen that work. It does for pigs." He told them to carry tobacco and pipes, for both men and women. "Mosquitoes hate smoke more'n they love your blood. Tobacco smoke'll send them home hungry."

"Most ladies don't smoke," a woman said.

"They can learn. Another thing," Nimrod said, "shoes. Pack all the shoes you can and borrow or buy some. Your bug crushers won't feel good on sharp rocks or snow."

A man in the back asked about guns.

Nimrod stepped with care around the subject. "Ever man seems to think he knows all about them, but that leaves me a little out of sorts. Man-pride can be a waltz to disaster.

"Some men start out on this trail thinking they'll just step out of the wagon and shoot a buffler for breakfast. Maybe you won't see a single buffler 'tween here and California. No telling. What you're sure to see are jackrabbits, prairie dogs, quail, and prairie chickens aplenty. If'n you was to shoot at any of those with a rifle, the good lord above would have to direct your aim to keep those varmints from laughing at you, and even then you might miss."

A couple of men muttered a protest. "Don't get your britches too tight," Nimrod said, nodding to the grumblers. "I'm sure there be men here whose aim is true. We'll need their rifles. But to hit those jumpy little critters, you need a scattergun."

"There are prairie dogs are all over out there. They should be easy pickings," a man said.

Nimrod smiled. "Out there, they die of old age. They's smarter'n us. You blink, and poof!—gone. They regular get away from more dangerous beasts than us."

A man spoke in a challenging tone. "Can you yourself rifle-shoot these little animals?"

Nimrod smiled. "Half the time, with a little luck. But I've been doing it a long time. Shooting for defense is the same, the targets just be bigger. I ain't heard of any Indians on the warpath; most times, they'll just want to beg or steal from you. But if'n they turn nasty, an ordinary feller with a rifle ain't going to hit a brave riding fast on his pony. Not in a month of Sundays, unless you can hit his horse. But you take a scattergun, and for sure, that'll make a believer out of any warrior with any sense. He won't come in range. He'll say, 'Excuse me, I'll just be on my way,' to a man holding a scattergun loaded with double-aught shot. He paused, then added, "While I'm talking about guns, you should teach your womenfolk how to load and shoot....You never know."

An aghast older woman raised her voice. "Heavens to Betsy, sir! It ain't fitting for a lady to learn such things."

"Begging your pardon, ma'am. Back home, that might be true. But out here, when a woman's child is threatened, she ain't no lady. She'd fight a cougar." He looked at the woman with a soft smile. "Not meaning to alarm you, ma'am, but I ain't sugar-coating it, neither. Where we're headed can be a bit troublesome at times."

I'd wager that with practice, some of you ladies could make your husbands sweat in a shooting contest. Fact is, every man woman and child big enough to hoist one should know how to shoot and how to handle a firearm."

"What's the value of all that?" a skeptical husband asked.

"Well, sir. Indians ain't dumb. They count, people and guns. And when them with mischief on their minds come into a camp and count twenty guns, that makes them happy. But when they count forty guns, they start thinking about where they might find easier pickings. Another thing, if'n you know how a gun works, you'll know enough to be afeared of it, 'cause it would welcome the chance to kill you if'n you mishandle it."

Nimrod kept talking because he knew this would be a rare time to have everyone's attention. "Speaking of aggravating things, if'n you see a rattlesnake, keep clean away. He don't want to be your pet. And when your wagon is moving, make your children settle down and don't jump around. To them wheels, a child is just another bump."

Nimrod recommended not bringing pet dogs along because they eat food that can't be spared, and they spook the livestock.

An older woman who identified herself as Agnes Patterson clutched a small terrier in her arms. "My little Benjamin just eats scraps," she pleaded.

"Ma'am, on this trail, scraps can be mighty scarce." He thought to himself, that dog looks like a barker to me, a bad sign.

"My thinking is, if'n you got a dog, give it away or shoot it. On the trail, it'll eat food you can't spare, it'll spook the livestock, or sure-as-shooting, it'll be a meal for a wolf."

People with dogs protested with anger or sobs, but since most did not have dogs, they voted to get rid of them. Agnes Patterson's Benjamin stayed hidden.

Nimrod convinced the committee to require four extra trained oxen for each wagon "If'n I was you, and I had an extra fifty dollars or so," he told them, "I'd also go into town and buy me a milk cow. You can tie her to the back of your wagon. The milk will be appreciated, and she can be yoked to the wagon, if'n that's necessary.

Nimrod could see his audience was drowning in details, but thinking about details now might mean they'd live to see California. "You need to know what skills are among you. Find out who can fix things and settle on what they're going to charge for their services."

A farmer from Pennsylvania stepped forward and said, "Mr. Lee, I know where we want to end up, but I'm not clear how we get there. I'd be obliged if you could tell us."

"We ain't got nothing but a general idea where this trip is going," another man complained.

Nimrod was surprised at the question, though he knew he shouldn't be. Pilgrims are pilgrims. Nimrod pondered an answer. He was used to thinking in terms of a day's ride between beaver streams.

"We're here at the bend in the Missouri," he said, tracing in the dirt. "We head west a short ways, and turn north at the Kansas River, named for the Kansa tribe. We got easy traveling—level ground, water, and grass a-plenty—all the way to the Platte River. We follow the Platte about two hundred miles to where it splits. Then we travel the North Platte northwest up to Fort Laramie; then we stay on the North Platte as it loops around to meet the Sweetwater, another two-hundred mile thereabouts. Then we follow the Sweetwater to its end. Then we dip southwest over South Pass, then follow the Green River south awhile to Fort Bridger. Then we head northwest to Fort Hall, then south to the Mary's River. Then cross the desert, get over high mountains, then down to Fort Sutter."

"What's the worst part?" a man asked.

"Ever step can be dangerous, but the last half will have you wishing you stayed home: sickness, deserts, thirst, mountains that reach the clouds, rain and lightning like you never seen, maybe snow if we lollygag."

He spared them the details of the back-breaking labor of clearing trail, the danger of flooded rivers, the anguish of the sick and dying, and the suffocating dust. They would learn all that soon enough.

As the audience broke up and walked away murmuring to each other, Nimrod caught up with Cohen and they started for a committee meeting. As they walked, Nimrod glanced at the edge of the camp and saw an old man next to a cut-down wagon off to himself with three oxen grazing nearby. He stopped and looked. "Who's the old man?" he asked with surprise.

Cohen shook his head doubtfully. "His name is Henry Griswold. He came into camp last evening. We almost turned him down, but none of us had the heart. Judging from his appearance and his rig, we probably made a mistake."

Nimrod frowned, "He's got no business going out there." He resumed walking. "Ever time I see something like that…"

Johnnythree fingered the arms of the chair. It was the first he had sat in with armrests. Meister looked over at his new-found black "friend" and smiled. They both turned to the big man in the frock coat and a gray beard who walked in with heavy steps. Meister said, "Judge Nichols, this is, uh, John—" Not saying the name without adding the "three" sounded strange to him.

John asked in awe, "Judge? You a real judge?"

Meister and Nichols assumed Johnny was stupid. He was not. He had been kept in ignorance to make him more manageable. But the time would come when his "master" would discover ignorance was a remedial condition.

"John what?" Nichols said in a gruff voice.

Meister and Johnny looked at each other? Finally, Johnny said the only name that came to mind, the name of his benefactor, the man who was freeing him—"Meister," Johnny pronounced proudly. Meister reacted with a stunned look. Then he shrugged, and said, "Okay." Thus, the soon to be "freeman" assumed a surname with the same value as his promised freedom.

Nichols had obviously been prepped. He added the new name to two duplicate documents on the table, reversed one for Johnny to read, which, of course, he could not. "Here, Johnny. This is the document that makes you a free man. It is also an employment contract that assures you of having a job. This is your copy." The heading on the contract, which Johnny could not read, said: "Manumission from slavery and agreement for servitude."

Nichols used his pen to point out conditions to Johnny that meant almost nothing to him. Nichols explained that Johnny would earn two dollars a month in script for his labor, payable when they reached Sutter's Fort. In return, he would receive food and shelter. The contract was binding for the term of ten years of legal. If he ran, he could be caught and returned to slavery Nichols summed it up, by saying, "This is a good day for you, Johnny. Mr. Meister thinks highly enough of you to guarantee you work at a fair salary for ten years, subject to his abrogation, of course. In return, you have to keep your promise not to run off. If you do, he can send the law after you." Nichols stopped and smiled reassuringly at Johnny, "Of course, we know you won't do that." He waited for Johnny 's reply.

"Uh, no sir. I mean, yes sir."

Nichols stood and shook Johnny's hand. "Congratulations, young man. Now, if you will sign your mark on the line at the bottom, I will sign as a witness and attach my seal as a justice of the peace for the great state of Missouri."

John signed an X, and the judge gave a final admonition. "Just remember, Johnny, if you break the terms of this contract, the law will track you down wherever you go. They can even use hounds."

Meister gathered up the documents and shook hands with the judge. "Thank you, your honor," he said as he slipped a ten-dollar gold coin to Nichols.

The committee members stood by Penney's wagon in a circle because there was no place to sit, at least not in a way that would preserve their dignity. They all had concern on their faces.

"Going back to the meeting we had a short time ago, Nimrod, your strong words spread some worry among the company," Penney said.

"Good," Nimrod replied. "There's cause for it. I'd rather tell them the truth before we start instead of them finding it out a thousand miles from nowhere."

Cohen said, "I have a different concern. I was taken aback when you told the captain here that we shouldn't start until the first of June. That's ten days of wasted time, and we don't even know how far California is. Hell, most trains have already left."

Nimrod nodded to Cohen. "Well, then, good luck to them. It'll come in handy." He let that sink in, then said, "The spring rains have slacked off, but we have to wait until the ground dries enough, and the rivers go down, and for the grass to come up to give the animals feed. Every day we can wait helps. Soft ground will tucker the oxen out afore we even get going, and high rivers will drown you before you even get wet."

Masterson waited for Nimrod to finish, then said, "Maybe I can help on Malachi's concern, because he's right: It all comes down to distance. Before I left Pennsylvania, I did considerable reading on that.

"A few years ago, an American frigate was anchored in San Francisco Bay equipped for navigation measurements. Their reading in the bay was latitude 122- degrees west. Then, when Captain John Fremont passed through Missouri three years ago on his surveying trip, he measured Independence at latitude 94-degrees west. Well, navigators know that each degree is sixty-nine miles."

Nimrod was impressed. "The things they don't learn you in country schools…"

"What does that come down to, miles-wise?" Cohen asked.

"So, that figures out to—"

"One thousand, nine hundred, thirty-two miles," Nimrod said in a moment.

Jackman looked at him, amazed.

Masterson nodded agreement. "Since San Francisco Bay is a ways west of Sutter's Fort, and also considering, travelers don't move in a straight line, I'm at ease to say that two thousand miles is a number I'll stake my reputation on."

Nimrod said, with a bit of pout, "That's what I said the other day."

Masterson agreed. "Indeed, you did. And impressive that was."

Nimrod added, "That means we have to travel a full thirteen miles each day to get to the mountains afore the snow does—if old man winter's acting reasonable and normal." He looked around. "That's what I told y'all."

Masterson looked for a way to compliment Nimrod, to let him know it would be his knowledge that would deliver them to California. "You're a mighty fast man with figures, Nimrod."

Nimrod grinned and looked at the others. "I can cipher to a fare-thee-well, my momma always said."

Jackman said, "I'm not worried about numbers. All I know is, we got to get over those mountains before the snow falls."

Nimrod returned to Jackman's concern. "We got to outrun the snow by traveling fast and smart and hope the good Lord thinks we're deserving. I don't worry about counting miles. I worry about covering them. If'n we have enough get-up-and-go, we can make the foot of the Sierra mountains 'bout the first of October. That should get us over them by the time the snow comes." He noticed the relieved looks. "Should, I say," he added.

"And if we don't travel fast enough, we could die in those mountains, won't we? That's a frightful thought," Preacher said.

Before the men broke up, Penney held up his hand. "Something else on my mind. Most every family has considerable dollars in gold coin. Script won't spend in a trading post, at least not without being discounted way down. Along the way, ferries and the few trading posts will charge as heavy as they think they can get away with."

"We know that, Captain," Cohen said.

Jackman said, "Money can make good people turn bad, and bad people turn worse. How can we trust other people, us having all that money in our wagon?"

"Then don't. Trust no one and be prepared to defend your property. Start by not lip-flapping about how much you have, and hide it good," Nimrod said.

Masterson looked at Nimrod. "We could have some criminality, I suppose."

Nimrod said, "We may be waylaid by drygulchers. They ain't stupid. They know wagon trains have money, and they think we're all a bunch of sodbusters who can't stand up to them." Nimrod waved his arm to the west. "Out there, there ain't no jails. There ain't no judges. You'll be the law."

Penney said, "Now, Nimrod wants to say something about defending ourselves."

Nimrod nodded. "Every man reckons he's Dan'l Boone, so we need to give them a chance to prove it. We'll shoot some targets and find out who can use their weapons. Women, too."

Jackman said, "If my wife learns to shoot, I'll have to mend my ways." He laughed as he said it, but the mirth was gone from his humor which had turned sad at mention of Susan.

"That reminds me, Nimrod said. "Tell folks to keep a dry load in their guns, but don't leave a percussion cap on the nipple. That's how people kill themselves without meaning to."

Jackman said, "How do you mean—'Without meaning to?'"

"There are hard days ahead that'll seem to have no end. Keep your eyes open for folks who grow quiet and seem whipped."

"Suicide is a mortal sin," Preacher said.

Nimrod looked at him with no expression. "What these folks'll be facing might cause God to allow some leeway." He cleared his throat and changed the subject before Preacher could retort. "I ain't a know-it-all, but I learned a few things you're paying me for. First, trade goods need to be purchased to keep squaws happy; beads and trinkets, knives, roll cloth, pots, and blankets, the brighter the better. No guns or liquor."

"How about what we need?" Penney asked.

"I's getting to that. You need two well-built crosscut saws, a good-sized fishing net, and fifty feet of stout rope for each wagon."

"We got axes," Masterson said.

"We'll be clearing a lot of brush. A crosscut will do ten times what you can chop with an ax, and it won't cleave any feet off. We'll also need an adze."

"What's that?" Jackman asked.

"A shipbuilder's tool," Masterson said.

"We ain't going sailing," Penney said.

Nimrod chuckled. "You're gonna see so much water you won't take a bath this side of California."

"That means Shadrach'll miss one bath," Cohen said to laughter.

Penney said, "Come to think of it, nothing in the guidebooks we've read said anything about saws or fishing nets. Why would that be?"

"You'd have to ask the fellers who wrote them books," Nimrod said. "You'll find them in rocking chairs back east."

"Most of our group brought chains. They're stronger than rope," Masterson said.

"And a whole lot heavier, a whole lot. Except, for the ox rigging, sell 'em in town." Nimrod said. He wasn't through. "Each wagon should have a spare wagon tongue, a rear wheel and front wheel. Build racks tight under the wagon bed to carry them. Hiram Young in town'll give you fair prices."

"That's extra weight," Jackman said in a worried voice.

"Better than sitting in the middle of the desert with three wheels."

"It's also extra money we didn't count on."

"You can't eat money if you're starving in the desert," Nimrod said.

"Oh, that makes me feel better," Cohen said to laughter.

As the men started to walk away, Nimrod said to Cohen,

"I saw one wagon with a big chest of drawers in the back."

"That's the Patterson wagon. Mrs. Patterson couldn't bring herself to leave it behind. That chest was her grandmother's."

"She can sell it here or dump it in the desert, but they pay more here."

Jackman studied Nimrod's face. "You're a demanding man, Nimrod."

"I have a reason to get where we're going."

"Why don't you talk to Mrs. Patterson? We've tried," Jackman said with a shrug.

"Ain't a guide's job. I'm afeared of meddling."

"I appreciate that thought, but your experience is much needed."

Agnes Patterson and her husband, Jasper, were standing near the front of their wagon when the men walked up and Jackman introduced Nimrod. "I listened to what you had to say to us travelers," Jasper said. "I'm obliged for it."

Nimrod nodded his thanks, and Jackman said they came calling to talk about the Patterson wagon load.

Jasper sighed, and said, "I'll call Agnes over. I can't get anywhere on that damned chest."

In moments, Agnes appeared without her husband. She had a grandmotherly presence, and Nimrod was sure she made a wonderful neighbor in the life she left behind. The look on her face said she sensed negativity was coming. Jackman introduced Nimrod who suggested in his country manner that carting a heavy piece of furniture two thousand miles might not be a good idea.

"That chest was my grandmother's. It came with her from Wales. I feel it would be a betrayal to just cast it aside."

Nimrod nodded. "Ma'am, I respect your feelings, I surely do. I wish my kin had a lady like you. However, on the trip we're about to commence, you're gonna see enough furniture to outfit a hotel strewn about the trail. None of it'll fit in a tipi, so the Indians will use it for kindling." He gestured toward the grazing oxen. "You know, these ox have a big job to do, so an extra hundred-fifty pounds to tote all across the country, well, they might resent it. I reckon that there chest of drawers would fetch a pretty penny in town here, and some nice folks would enjoy it, 'stead of it starting a fire in an Indian camp."

Agnes thought hard for a moment, then tightened her jaw and said, "I'm being taken to God knows where. I have to leave everyone and most everything behind. Now, first you want to kill my dog, then you want my family heirloom." Her mouth set firm, and she was in foot-stomping mode. "The chest goes with *me*." She defiantly put her hand on the chest at the back of the wagon.

Nimrod touched his hat brim. "I wish you well, ma'am."

The women of the company spent time practicing loading and shooting at targets in the river. They had been advised to lighten the powder charge slightly to reduce the kick. Anything they had occasion to shoot would be close. The activity brought an audience of men, several of whom hooted in glee.

One woman, Flora Dickens, seemed most assured with her rifle. She loaded it in less than one minute and handled it with the dexterity of a farmer with a pitchfork, and seemed to hit what she aimed at. She was a strong-looking, tall woman. Few men would call her attractive, but women would. Of course, they looked for different things.

Flora put the butt of her rifle on the ground and turned to the loudest of the taunting men. "Sir, care for a contest? Perhaps a wager?"

The man looked around embarrassed. The other men started laughing and hooting. The man muttered "Ahh—" He gave a disgusted wave and walked away.

Hannah went to Flora's side and laughed as they walked back to the wagons. "I barely know you, Flora, but you're already my best friend on this God forsaken ride. That was a knee slapper, the thing you just did. Some might say brash."

Flora grinned at her victory. "If they say 'brash,' then I say 'good.' My folks had no boys, so I had to do the work of one. Put me in a pair of trousers and I'll plow as many rows in a day as most any man."

The two women formed an instant bond. Flora was a similar

age and also the mother of a boy and girl. They had good education in common, plus Flora was the daughter of a physician from Tennessee. Similarities aside, the two women shared the chemistry of a strong bond: they could talk together, laugh together, and, if need be, cry together.

CHAPTER TEN

No one said anything. The children looked at their nervous parents and were aware something big was about to happen. The fathers stood next to their oxen; the mothers sat on the wagon seats. The women would not occupy that position for long, because the jarring and swaying of the wagon's leather-strap suspension made walking seem pleasurable by comparison.

The children were mystified by a kaleidoscope of emotions: fear, doubt, excitement, and determination rippled over them in waves of emotion. Among their parents, lips moved in silent prayer. A father reached up to his wife with a grimy, calloused hand and clasped her red, chapped one. Their grip tightened into a belief—actually, a hope—that all would be well.

Over the prior few days, their number had been reduced to twenty-six wagons. Four families, one at a time, had pulled out and headed back east. They were going home, having seen all of the trail they cared to without having even started. Those who remained watched their wagons disappear with an unspoken touch of envy. There were no goodbyes, no waves, and no calls of good luck. The friends they made in the camp had been strangers only weeks ago, and to that they would return, soon to be forgotten. Those who left were not proud of giving up, but pride exacts a price, and those four families had decided the price was too high. They would return home, the men embarrassed, and the women grateful.

❧

All eyes were on Penny. He raised his arm, a bit theatrically, then swung it forward and shouted, "Ho-ooo," in a drawn-out voice.

The line of wagons crept past the bend of the river and out into a sea of grass. Nimrod rode up and down the line to reassure that he was leading them.

Nimrod noticed the woman and boy he rescued from the river standing alongside the road watching without expression, but with shock still on their faces. He trotted Bub over to the front of them, then removed his hat and held it over his heart as a sign of respect and sorrow. They looked up at him without recognition. He understood, and as he rode back to the wagon train, he thought how the death of the mother's little girl, or any child, is the twisting of a knife in the soul of a parent. And if that parent had put the child in danger, the knife becomes serrated. Realizing that, Nimrod's thoughts turned to his own daughter, Wildflower, wherever she might be. If she were in danger, it would be his actions that put her there—Will I someday be the faceless man she hates, the man whose negligence killed her mother? The thought was a blister on his brain.

He put Bub's reins in one hand so he could rub his eyes.

The first day's travel ended as they camped on the edge of four two-story brick buildings behind a groomed yard, but otherwise in an empty prairie. A sign identified it as the Shawnee church mission to educate young plains Indians.

After setting up overnight camp, several of the pioneers stood around looking at the young Indians doing chores, carrying schoolbooks, dressed like white youth going about the business of living and learning. They speculated on the meaning of an Indian community in the prairie that could just as easily be in the middle of Baltimore.

Ruth Cohen said, "Landsakes! Doesn't that beat all. Maybe soon all Indians will be civilized like that."

"Not soon enough," someone said.

A man named Johnson who was superintendent of the mission, said, "What news from back east? Drovers who come by here from Santa Fe say the Mexicans are kicking up a fuss about going to war if the United States takes in Texas as a state."

"Back in Independence, the talk was all about making it to California and Oregon, not about some ruckus stirred up by politicians," Masterson said.

"This country is stumbling into something that's going to cause graves to be dug," the superintendent said. "The signs are there. Don't think your trail will take you away from trouble. Remember, California is Mexico's."

The first morning after breakfast, Nimrod was walking Bub to water when he heard a child weeping. He looked around until he saw an Indian girl of eight or nine standing frozen and looking at something. Nimrod followed her gaze and saw a snake about five feet from the girl. It was small and dark gray with a white pattern. Nimrod recognized it as a massasauga rattlesnake, coiled and rattling. Its black eyes and flicking tongue were directed at the girl.

A woman from the train was heading toward the girl. Nimrod called out, "Stand back." He moved within the vision of the girl and gestured to stay where she was.

Nimrod crept to the side of the snake about seven feet away. He got down to his hands and knees and started pounding the earth. The snake was distracted from the girl and swung toward the new threat. Nimrod jumped to his feet and motioned to the girl to run, which she did in a panic. The snake turned and disappeared into high weeds.

A knot of people had gathered and applauded Nimrod. "How'd you do that?" a stranger asked.

"A snake hears through the ground. I just got his attention."

"How'd you know that?" the same man asked.

"These old boys and me, we been sharing this country a long time."

Penney moved to his side, and said, "Why didn't you shoot the critter? It aimed to bite that girl. You just let the damned thing crawl away."

"Indians say you rile up a bad spirit if you kill just to be killing. It stayed coiled because that's how they protect theyselves. If it stretches out to crawl, it's got no defense. When he crawled away, he was leaving peaceful. Anyway, Captain, you got to respect a rattlesnake's honesty. He is who he is, and he don't lie about it. He don't want trouble, but if called on, he's sure to give it. If you make him nervous, he'll make you sorry."

A man asked, "Surely you don't believe that bad spirit business?"

Nimrod tipped his head in thought. "Until I see it proved wrong, I'm going to walk soft around it."

"You think like an Indian, don't you?"

Nimrod smiled, not offended. "They got some right smart ideas."

The following days lapsed into lazy routine as the train made good time over the prairie, outlined against the blue sky while rolling over rises and fording shallow creeks.

Nimrod happened to be riding alongside the Abraham Jackman wagon, where Jackman walked alongside, and his young wife, Susan, sat on the seat.

"Pleasant day, Abraham."

"And to you, Nimrod. This is my wife, Susan. Susan, this here is Nimrod Lee."

"I've not yet had the pleasure, ma'am." Nimrod tipped his hat to acknowledge her smile.

"Down there is my hired hand, Davy Owens."

Nimrod nodded to Owens, but noticed the eye-locks between Jackman's young wife and the young hired hand. He also saw the grim expression of Jackman as his eyes switched back and forth between his wife and the hired hand.

"That bull moose on the bay there is my nephew, Zack Monroe."

Jackman gestured toward a surly brute who didn't acknowledge Nimrod's nod.

Jackman lowered his voice. "Zack's not high on manners. I promised my sister I'd see him to California. That's why I don't send him packing."

Nimrod departed and was riding alongside the Spencer wagon when Ed Spencer hailed him. "Hey, trail guide, any way of speeding up these damned cows? My horses are chomping at the bit."

"It's a long way to California," Nimrod called back.

Nimrod squinted into the lowering sun as he rode along the wagons, shouting, "We got water and good grass here. Let's circle up for the night."

The wagons started their improved circling with Nimrod directing traffic, sending one peeling off to the right, the next to the left, and coming back around until the circle was complete. The difficulty of the task was judging the proper circumference of the circle, but the pioneers had learned quickly. The purpose was to form a corral for the animals if that proved necessary. It also provided a defensive position in the event of attack.

The animals had been herded into a grassy meadow close by with guards scheduled to rotate through the night. The folks set up their overnight camp, then relaxed after supper in the soft spring evening air. They laughed, told jokes, uncorked bottles, and watched Willis and Mazie Patrick unlimber musical instruments, which they employed skillfully. They were an older couple from Arkansas with perpetual smiles who loved to entertain. Back home, they had spent many evenings and Sunday afternoons entertaining friends, church members, and themselves with church or bouncy popular music, and sentimental ballads. Each had learned from others who taught them to play by feel and by ear. She played the banjo, and he the fiddle.

Leaning against a nearby wagon, they struck up well-known songs of the day, "Little Topsy's Song," "Kathleen Mavourneen," "Dan Tucker," "Am I to Blame?" and a popular minstrel song of the previous decade, "Jim Crow."

Boisterous children wore off pent-up energy by weaving in and out of adults relaxing close to the big campfire. As Willis and Mazie settled into a harmony groove, couples edged into a bare area in the middle of the group and began to dance. Three couples returned to their wagons for lanterns which they place at the edge of the impromptu dance area.

As Nimrod, Penney, and Masterson talked on the edge of the clearing, Nimrod watched Davy Owens and Susan Jackman dancing close together and laughing as though sharing a secret. They would bear watching.

Masterson said, "If I'd known it would be this easy, I'd have gone west long before."

Nimrod smiled. "If'n it was this easy the whole way, then

bankers and their ladies would make the trip in their Sunday finery in carriages pulled by ponies with plumes on their heads. No, this part is just old mother nature funning with us."

Masterson examined Nimrod's face. "I do declare, you surely are a man of dark outlook."

"I reckon it comes down to what I see ahead, sir."

Nimrod walked away a little disgusted, but not so it showed. He didn't tell them that nature doesn't give up without a fight, and that trials and tests would be swooping down on them like berserk bats.

A young couple named Ignacio and Narcissa Lopez walked by with eyes for no one but themselves. Ignacio bumped into Nimrod.

"Sorry, sir. I wasn't watching my step," Lopez said.

Nimrod smiled, then tipped his hat toward the young woman. "I think you had good reason. *BuAaron noches*, Señor Lopez. My respects, young lady," he said. He extended his hand to Ignacio.

Ignacio shook his hand vigorously. "Mr. Lee, we're greatly pleased a man of your experience is leading us; a man who knows the trail. And I'm pleased to hear Spanish words in this train, even just a few."

Nimrod shook his head modestly. "Ah, I've traded some in Taos and Santa Fe. My *Español* well ain't that deep, and it's mostly dry. I picked up enough to order me some mezcal and say *hola* to the young ladies."

Ignacio was tall and self-assured. He had an aquiline nose and light complexion that by itself marked him as a member of the Mexican ruling class. His happy manner was of a young man in love. Narcissa was pretty with dark curls visible beneath her bonnet. She had bovine eyes, but with an appeal that no cow could match. Her unchanging smile could have been painted-on. The whole world belonged to her, and it was promising to get bigger.

Nimrod nodded pleasure at Ignacio's compliment. He looked from one young face to the other but directed his question to the woman. "Are you the young folks who jumped the broomstick just in time to join this outfit?"

Narcissa nodded, pleased to be asked to speak. "Yes, sir. We were married two days after my seventeenth birthday in Alton,

Illinois, my hometown, just across from St. Louis. I was a Sanders."

Nimrod wanted to say something about young love, but he figured it would be out of place for a trail guide to speak of such. "And what is your destination, if I may be bold?" When in the company of gentry, Nimrod's church-social manners of earlier days returned to his speech.

Ignacio smiled proudly that the trail guide was interested in them. He explained that his father was Mexican consul in St. Louis and had been since independence from Spain in 1821.

"You speak American real good," Nimrod said.

Ignacio laughed. "Well, I've had about a quarter century living among Yankees. I didn't have much choice." He reached for Narcissa's hand. "Now, I'm teaching my señora *Español*."

Hola, mi nombre es Narcissa, she said, beaming.

Ignacio patted her hand, and said, "Two years ago, I read a book called *Two Years Before The Mast* by a writer named Dana, as I recall. I shared it with Narcissa. Mr. Dana's adventures in California inspired us to start our lives there. It's a fresh place, and it's Mexican, so it'll be a homecoming." As he spoke, the faces of both shone with their dream, and he looked west toward a place he knew was at the end of the trail; their own empire of fair skies, vast spaces, and year-round warmth. "We decided we'd like to give that gift to our children." He looked again at Narcissa, and each smiled.

Narcissa said, "I read a lot of poetry, and it lifts my spirits to go yonder where our lives can sing a hallelujah."

Nimrod bit his lip to keep a straight face. He would not mock a young lady's poetic vision. Instead, he nodded. "Those are beautiful words. I'm set to do my best to get you there." He touched his hat. "I bid you a good evening."

Nimrod walked a short distance away, and Narcissa wandered over to listen to the music. Ignacio took the opportunity to follow Nimrod.

"Pardon me, sir. But may I ask if you've heard any news from Washington?"

Nimrod was bemused. "Me and Washington, we don't talk much."

Ignacio looked around and lowered his voice out of caution. "I see you as a fair man, so, if I may talk freely…" He looked around again, then paused, as though deciding if he wanted to continue. "I don't want Narcissa to hear what I'm thinking; she's too young to worry about such things. However, the outcome of the election last fall between Clay and Polk is a cause of great concern."

"We don't hear much about that out here. I heard tell Andy Jackson was for Mr. James K. Polk. That's enough for me."

"That's the real reason I'm headed for Mexican territory."

"Sir?" Nimrod tilted his head.

"Things are headed in a bad way for Mexico. Back east, they talk about "manifest destiny," which is something we're starting to see in all the newspapers. It seems to have caught on."

"What's that mean?"

"It means that the United States sees it as a God-given right to conquer part of my country."

Nimrod rubbed his cheek. "Well, I haven't given much thought to that either, but it seems to me it's big enough for everyone."

Ignacio sighed. "I wish it were that simple. We'll have to fight, you know."

Nimrod also looked around. "It won't benefit a soul to make this a campfire conversation. Some people from back home get testy about politics." They shook hands again, and parted.

Nimrod wandered back over to join others watching the dancing. He noticed a man drinking from his jug with conspicuous enthusiasm. He was John Burns, a loudmouth Nimrod had marked for watching on day one. "John Burns over there sure is a dear friend to that jug," he said.

"I'll wager he's provided rent money for many a bartender," Masterson said.

"He's been sucking on that thing since he joined up. His wife does all his work," Penney added with a frown.

"That's trouble, sure as we're standing here." Nimrod knew that hard boozing on the trail was a giant step toward disaster. Close living with strangers can create tense relationships that can be inflamed by drunkenness. Also, a man in his cups can't put in a good day's work, though he'll claim he can.

Meister walked up and addressed Nimrod. His manner was

cocky as he held up his rifle. "Mr. Lee, I noticed you have a Hawken rifle, just as I do. What say we have a target contest sometime? It'd be interesting to see who makes best use of this fine firearm."

"You know anything worth wasting powder on?" Nimrod answered, not eager to be cordial to a slaver.

"Afraid of a little competition?" Meister said with a smirk.

"This trail is going to give us all the competition we want," Nimrod said and walked away.

On the edge of the crowd, he noticed a man dressed in a black suit with a string tie and black hat. Nimrod had quickly recognized his dress as the uniform of a saloon sharpster. He knew the type. With him were three women. One appeared to be in her teens, and the other two were at least mid-thirties. The man claimed his name was Benny Bogle, but probably not on police blotters. The women had not given names.

Penney had said Bogle was allowed to join the train just before departure. It was a hasty decision he admitted.

Penney said, "Look at that strumpet in the calico dress. She's ugly enough to scare a buzzard off a dead rabbit."

Nimrod looked, and said, "It's a hard way for a woman to earn her keep—so long as she has suitable wares to sell."

Nimrod noticed the pioneer men looking with interest at the women, and their wives glaring in the same direction. Not good, he thought.

As the musicians broke into the vigorous "Sans Souci" galop, Nimrod noticed Hannah and Ed Spencer sitting near the dance area. Rachel was clinging to her mother's side, solemn as usual. Nimrod watched them and argued with himself—Don't, do, don't, do—then, though he knew it wasn't wise, he nonchalantly walked over. "Mr. Spencer, may I ask your wife to dance?"

Spencer acted bored and indifferent. "That's up to her."

Nimrod turned to Hannah, bowed slightly, and touched his hat brim. "By your leave, ma'am."

They walked to the center of the clearing, then joined hands for a country version of a drawing-room slow dance. It was apparent that Nimrod had a flair for dancing. When the song ended, the musicians stepped-up to the livelier "Crystal Schottische," a variation of the polka, a dance craze imported from Paris the previous year. The couple took a second to capture the beat, then twirled around the improvised dirt dance floor.

"You cut quite a figure, Nimrod Lee. I doubt you learned to dance so fine in the mountains."

"No, ma'am. In saloons."

As she stepped to the music, Hannah pondered how to broach a delicate subject. "No offense meant, but I can't help but notice you have a most interesting smell about your body; ah…not altogether unpleasant. May I ask its origin?"

He pondered for a moment what she was referring to. Then, he took his hand and touched something around his neck on a rawhide string beneath his shirt. "Ah, you mean my acifidity bag. You carry it around your neck. Back home, most do. It blocks disease and illness, at least that's what I heard tell."

"I've heard some about that. I'm told many country folk carry them. Does it work?"

"Well, Aunt Hazel swore by it, said it cured Uncle Earl of the rheumatism, at least made it better. After that, all the kinfolk started carrying one. Most people do, down home."

"Whatever is in it? As you know, I'm interested in medicine."

"Uh, different plants and herbs all ground up." He thought for a moment. "Let's see: pokeweed, mustard seed, ginseng, yellow root, lots of garlic, and a couple of things the Cheyenne swear by which I put in 'cause it came from a medicine woman. I've carried it for some time."

"Yes, I guessed as much," she said, laughing gently, so as not to offend, then said, "I hope it gives you a long life."

"It don't protect against bullets or Old Ephraim."

"Old who?"

"A griz—grizzly bear."

"Interesting life you have, sir.…May I assume you're not married?" she asked, as he eased her into a swing.

"I was. Four times. One took."

"Whatever does that mean?" she asked, her brow knitting.

"With Indians, if a marriage takes, it's for life. If'n it don't, it becomes a thing of convenience until it ain't convenient no more."

"How quaint; rather barbaric, I should think."

Nimrod chuckled. "When the Indians move to Boston, I'm sure they'll do things right proper."

"Tell me about the one who 'took.' You use the past tense."

"Past what?" he asked.

"Where is she?"

"She passed on," he said flatly.

"Was it one of those sicknesses that seem to afflict Indians?"

"No, ma'am."

"I'm sorry for your loss. I'm familiar with the feeling."

"Her name was Magpie. I called her Maggie. She was daughter to a Crow chief."

The musicians swung into a slow waltz, and Nimrod slipped his arm around her waist in another new dance seen by some as naughty.

"What was she like?"

"A magpie."

"Excuse me?"

"She was just like the bird—she could make you laugh, but she was saucy, you can bet. Magpie most always got what she wanted, or she'd drive you crazy."

"Do you have any children, Nimrod?"

"A daughter. Somewhere. My aim is to find her someday."

"Please pardon my prying."

He was aware of a faint scent. Was it perfume, or was it just something natural, a part of citified women he was unfamiliar with? "Nothing to pardon, ma'am....How about you? Your husband said your boy was his stepson."

"My first husband, Dr. Blanc, died. Mr. Spencer was our neighbor; he's taken good care of us."

"That sounds like one of my Indian marriages."

Hannah stopped dancing and stepped back, glaring up at him with eyes flashing. "Mr. Lee! I consider that impertinent."

At that moment, Ed Spencer walked up, ignored Nimrod, and took Hannah's arm. "Time to get back to the wagon." He started to walk away, then paused and turned around. "By the by, sir, I think you took liberties with the closeness of your dancing just then."

Nimrod stood mouth agape. "Sir, no offense intended. That was a modern dance called a waltz. It's the rage in St. Louis."

"The rage you'll find out here is from an insulted husband."

Hannah pulled back from her husband and looked up at him. "Ed!" she said softly but with an edge.

Nimrod noticed several people watching them out of the corner of their eyes. "I ask your pardon, sir."

The couple walked away as Nimrod stared after them. He started back to the edge of the circle and swore at himself with gritted teeth. He scolded himself—Stay away, far away, from other men's wives.

Even from yards away, Penney noticed the tension between Nimrod and Spencer. He shook his head apprehensively, then as started toward his wagon, he caught up to Jackman and matched his steps. "Abraham, you doing all right? The last few days you seem fretful."

Jackman looked to the distance. "Just trying to deal with a personal matter. Nothing serious." He started to walk away, then turned back to Penney. "I've been feeling out of sorts, Shadrach. My spirits are in down in a trough. I've hired an extra hand. I've asked him to pay a call on you to introduce himself. Name is Tester, Simon Tester."

Jackman shook his head in disgust. "Zack's as worthless as tits on a bull. And that Owens fellow, I plan to fire him when we reach Fort Laramie." Jackman was breathing heavily with tension lines frozen in his face. He angrily turned to leave.

Penney studied him with concern on his face and foreboding in his thoughts. "Take care of yourself, Abraham."

Penney reached his own wagon, but watched Jackman for a long moment, then went to tend his oxen. Later, he was about to turn in when a stranger approached. He was a heavy man about thirty with a bushy black beard and piercing eyes. The way he walked made Penney think of a rooster that had once lorded it over his barnyard.

"You Shadrach Penney?" he almost demanded.

"At your service, Mr. —"

"Tester, Simon Tester, out of Evansville, Indiana. I hired on with Mr. Jackman. I came to introduce myself. I'm prepared to be of value to your company."

Penney was put off by Tester's arrogance. Strange for a hired man, he thought. However, he prided himself on accepting people until he learned otherwise. He said, "That's the best promise I've had today. I'll enjoy seeing it happen."

It was Tester's turn to be vexed, which is just short of irritated. "You'll find I more than pull my weight."

"I'll tell you what, Mr.—?"

"Tester, Simon."

Penney had heard it the first time; he just wanted to get under the man's skin a bit. He wanted to say no to this jackanapes, but he didn't have that right. "Go over and see Mr. Cohen, he's the third wagon down. He'll read you the rules and requirements."

Tester was introduced around to the other people the next morning. He was one more pair of eyes to stand guard, and one more gun. His mouth was not considered an asset. As Masterson said, "Every time he speaks, I think he's going to lift his leg on me."

CHAPTER ELEVEN

"Indians! Indians!" Nimrod heard the panicky shout from the front of the train and rode hard toward the commotion. He got there in time to see Masterson, who had been scouting ahead for water, shouting and reining his galloping horse in hard. Masterson shouted again, and the train boiled into turmoil as the company scrambled like confused sheep. The menfolk ran for their guns, and the women gathered the children and disappeared into the wagons.

In the distance, a small group of Indians on horseback approached. Nimrod studied them for a long moment, then shouted to the people, "Hold on! Hold on! They're Wyandottes. Lower your guns."

"Are they friendlies?" Masterson asked.

"Depends on their mood. Wyandottes is a small tribe, so their intentions are not well known. They'll want you to fear they're on a scalping raid, but that's just to soften you up for the gift-giving—maybe."

The Indians rode warily up to the wagons, examining the people and their goods. The men returned the stares with pinched faces, the women shrank back and children peered out from below the canvas.

Nimrod walked Bub up to the leader. With their mounts touching noses, Nimrod started a dialogue in sign language with the chief: "We welcome the Wyandottes."

"I know your face," the chief signed.

"I have traded at your villages."

"You have gifts?" the chief asked.

"We have shirts."

"Gunpowder?"

"No gunpowder," Nimrod signed with hand gestures. "We need for hunting. We travel far."

"You small group."

"But strong." Nimrod knew he was being sized-up.

"I take shirts."

Nimrod signaled to Penney, and the captain rode forward with four colorful calico shirts. The chief inspected them with satisfaction. For the next half hour, Nimrod kept a close eye on how the Indians and pioneers interacted; trepidation by the pioneers, assertiveness by the Indians. All Nimrod wanted was for the Indians to be gone. Even with friendly tribesmen, relations could turn violent in a flash. An instant of animosity or misunderstanding could leave the ground soaked in blood.

As he feared might happen, one brave had obtained whiskey and became boisterous, riding in circles, gulping at a jug with half of it running down his chin. He jumped into a wagon and started throwing things out, screaming and threatening the occupants. Nimrod rode over, trailed by the chief. He pulled the Indian off the wagon as he was attempting to tear a bolt of cloth out of a woman's hands.

The Indian fell to the dirt, more from inebriation than from Nimrod's yank. Rising unsteadily, he screamed a war cry, raised a hatchet and headed for Nimrod. He was just a few feet away, so there was no time for Nimrod to evade his onrush and let the chief handle it, as he would have preferred. In an instant, Nimrod pulled his revolver and shot the man in the head. With his small caliber, a body shot would not have stopped his momentum. The Indian's eyes went wide in disbelief before he fell back dead.

Distressed, Nimrod turned to the chief who watched without reaction. His braves, however, edged forward with angry undertones. Nimrod was quick to sign: "I regret."

The chief responded without emotion: "This one, bad man. Whiskey crazy. Not much mourning...You take scalp?"

"No." Nimrod waived the right of conquest to show his respect for the tribe.

The chief nodded. "Good...No one but squaw sad. Maybe."

Nimrod knew if the other Wyandottes became enraged, they

could still turn the chief against him. A politician was a politician. Furious, Nimrod turned to the Burns wagon, where the whiskey originated, and where Burns seemed oblivious to what was happening around him. He was self-absorbed in singing a drinking song off-key: "If the ocean was whiskey and I was a duck, I'd dive to the bottom and suck it all up."

Nimrod spotted a thick roll of cloth. He glared at John Burns who returned his look, but blankly. "Hand me that bolt of calico." Burns turned blustery and his voice slurred. "You can kiss my ass I wi—."

"Do it!" There was brittleness in Nimrod's voice, and the look on his face made Burns' thoughts clear enough to sense danger. He hesitated, then fumbled with the cloth and handed it down. Nimrod gave the cloth to the chief, a gift of rare magnificence. It was necessary, he knew, that the Indian leader come out of this with something to show for a brave's death.

"Cloth for chief's squaw."

The chief smiled as he fingered the cloth.

Burns moaned. "That calico was meant for trade. Cost me fifteen dollars!"

Nimrod looked the chief in the eyes, unblinking. "Go in peace."

The chief nodded, and two of his braves loaded the dead man on his horse. The Indians whooped and rode away.

Nimrod turned in surprise to a grim-faced Hannah who had been watching with others. She stepped forward. "Did you have to do that, kill him? Was there no other way?"

Nimrod was flustered by the unexpected accusation and anger. "Ma'am..." He shook his head in frustration. "I can't explain what you can't hope to understand."

"I heard your shot. I turned around and saw the man fall."

"You saw what happened. You didn't see what was about to happen."

Hannah stomped away, and Nimrod turned to Burns. "God damn you, sir. I warned against giving whiskey to Indians."

Burns shrugged in a self-pitying way. "He was a jolly fellow; gave me a fox skin for the jug."

Nimrod was tight-lipped. His voice was low and his voice hard as he turned his fury on Burns. "Give me the damned stuff. All of it."

Burns, drunk as he was, sensed the situation could turn dangerous for him. "Now?" It came out a whine.

"All of it, damn you. I won't see another man die because of your rotgut."

With red-rimmed eyes, Burns handed over many jugs of whiskey to Nimrod who, in a fury, smashed them against the rocks. Mrs. Burns was in the background watching, but gleefully approving. Nimrod gestured into the wagon. "That last one hidden in the corner, too."

"That one, too?" Burns asked as though pleading for mercy, which he was not given.

Watching Burns' jugs shatter, Penney knew he had an issue to deal with. Though Burns' situation was extreme, dealt with by Nimrod extremely, Penney knew that every wagon, including his, kept a jug or more. He had to turn the Burns incident into a teaching moment. He called everyone together.

"Folks, it was regrettable what happened here today, but it reminds us of what can go wrong on this-here trip. Drunkenness. Now, don't get me wrong, I appreciate a taste of the corn like every red-blooded American, but if it gets out of hand, it's a bushel of trouble for ever man-jack and woman of us. So, here's the rule the committee agrees on: Anyone who gets drunk and affects the safety or smooth travel of the train will be dealt with."

In an aside, Cohen said to Manchester, "Some of these old boys might get sick if they have to drink water. Their systems aren't accustomed to a foreign substance."

In camp that night, several people approached Nimrod as he curried Bub. One man stepped forward. He was someone Nimrod early-on had recognized as the type whose quiet strength could give glue to the company in a trying circumstance. In any situation with a ragged edge, Nimrod always sought out such men for back-up.

"Sir, my name's William Dickens. I'm just a dirt farmer from Tennessee. I don't know a lot about this here country, but I listened, and much of what I heard has got my hair on end. I've got a wife and two children with me. If you don't mind me saying so, I was jumpy as grease on a skillet when you shot the Indian." He half-turned to those nearby. "I'm hoping you won't think less of us if we tell you we're all a mite jittery and would like to ask you just how much danger we're in."

"No, sir," Nimrod said. "That's a fair question, but it ain't easy to answer on account of I can't speak for redskins who been known to have a mind of their own." He thought for a long moment. "Indians ain't inviting you into their backyard, and they ain't crazy about you being there. But if you offer them gifts, they'll let you be, mostly."

"Mostly, you say?" a man asked.

Nimrod nodded. "Mostly."

Zack asked, belligerently: "What is it they'll come begging for?"

"Begging?" Nimrod asked with an ironic twist. "A few shirts, such as you just saw; some gunpowder, or maybe a beef, if'n they be hungry."

Zack jutted his jaw. "Damned if I'll give any critter of mine to some dirty savage."

Nimrod looked hard at him. "If'n you look at a brave like he's something you swat against the wall, he's gonna think maybe you don't respect him, and that could settle on his dark side. He could become resentful, and it might not end well."

Dickens saw sparks building between the two men. "I think what Zack's saying is they would be demanding a bribe, which doesn't sit well with a white man."

"They see it as a fair toll for crossing their land. I'd rather give an Indian a steer I can replace than a scalp I can't."

"What are the chances of an attack?" Dickens asked.

"Indians ain't like white men. They won't charge into muskets to win a fancy piece of tin just so it can be pinned on them in the casket. They value their hides too much, and there ain't enough of them to spare. They'd just as soon pick your cattle off with arrows, then, when you're helpless on the trail, pick you off. But you can appreciate they got other things to do. Unless they're crazy riled, Indians ain't going to attack a train. If your scalp ends up on a lance, it's likely you got careless and was easy pickings."

"Can you protect us?" another man asked from the back.

"I can maybe teach you to protect yourselves."

"Are you a friend to them?" Gertie Proctor asked.

Nimrod thought about it. It was a question every mountain man often pondered for his own safety. "A friend? That question ain't never been settled. Most don't celebrate when they see me coming, but they know I won't cheat them. I won't steal their women or their horses. That's usually enough."

Abraham Jackman said, "I hear they're thieves."

"Their way is to share, and they don't see why we won't."

"What you're saying makes a body shiver," Gertie said, hugging herself without realizing it.

"Yes, ma'am."

After a few days, they established a routine. At four in the morning, Penney walked through the camp beating on a pan, and shouting, "Up and about. Time to start the day. Californey is just over the hill." Within a few minutes, people emerged from tents or tumbled out of wagons. The men shuffled off in one direction, the women in another, headed for morning ablutions. The men yoked the oxen, and the women roused their children. There was no time to cook, so breakfast and noon dinner had been prepared at supper the night before. It was important to be on trail at first light to take advantage of the cool of the day. Also, they learned to be rolling before the occasional other train got ahead of them. Their own dust was quite sufficient without having to endure choking and sneezing behind another wagon train.

They were on the easiest part of the trip as the wagons wound their way to the northwest through the lands of the Kansa tribe who chose not to make themselves visible. The undulating grassy plain was different from what it would become in later years after settlement. There were few trees except along riverbanks; whole groves would be planted later by settlers. The soft, tall grasses, such as bluestem, switchgrass, and Indian grass, waved a welcome to the pioneers. Spring rains often came in brief mid-day showers and made the grasses glisten.

Spread through the grasses was a colorful quilt patterned by spring flowers. Most splashy were yellow marsh marigold, purple wild garlic, and orange butterfly milkweed. The teasing scent of the garlic and wild ginger would waft through on the breeze for a moment and then be gone.

Perched on a fallen branch would be the meadowlark, the diva of the prairie, boasting a black necklace and yellow vest, singing with a warbling, flute-like sound. Bobolinks flitted among the grasses, and crows circled as squawking nuisances. Hawks, sharp-eyed and silent, swooped for rodent kills. On one occasion, Penney halted the train so the women could walk on the soft earth up a rise to pick flowers and let their hearts be gentled by the prairie Elysium.

Nimrod sat atop Bub at the head of the column and watched. "Enjoy it while you can, ladies," he muttered.

His reverie was broken by Penney and Willis Patrick who trotted up to him on foot. "Have you seen Hannah Spencer?" Penney said between gulps of air. "Missus Patrick is hurting bad. She needs help."

Nimrod said he'd seen her at the Masterson wagon. He followed the men as they hurried to find her.

Hannah pursed her lips as she studied the older woman who was stretched out in her wagon and breathing as asleep, but unresponsive. "It's a clear case of apoplexy, near as I can tell," she said.

Willis kneaded his hands. "Will she get better?" he asked with nervous hope spread across his face.

Hannah put her hand on his forearm. "Dear, Willis, if it is what I fear, it means the blood to her brain her been blocked in some way. That's well known, but not why. There's nothing to be done except wait and pray."

"Nothing?"

"I'm so sorry."

Hannah turned to the three men looking into the wagon. "Why don't you gentlemen let us keep her comfortable?"

When they were alone, and Hannah checked Mazie's tongue to make sure it was clear, then tried to make her comfortable. As she worked, Willis said, "We knew she was ailing. We wanted this trip to be our great adventure. We never thought it'd end like this."

"It's a blessing you shared your dream," Hannah said. "Many are denied that. The memory will be yours to keep."

"Tell me honest, Miz Hannah, will she live?"

"I don't know for how long, Willis. If she lives, I fear it'll be like we see here. Back in St. Louis, I saw two cases like this."

He nodded, accepting.

The next morning, Nimrod noticed Willis meeting with the committee. Curious, he drifted over as Willis was speaking.

"...There's no hope for it, sirs. My Mazie is not going to get better. I know that. We can't go on. You know that. We have to go home."

Penney said, "Willis, we are so sorry, we—"

Willis' smile was tired. "I thank you. But you've got your own job to do, which is to keep moving. We're not more'n a few days from Independence. We can take a steamer down to Memphis, close to home. Back home, I can tend to her." He stood. "I'll be stopping by that Indian school and donate her banjo. Maybe they'll have a youngster who can learn to play it." He glumly shook hands with all the men, then walked away.

They watched him until he disappeared into his wagon. "Well, that's the end of our music," Preacher said. "Sad. Their playing comforted people; made them forget the misery of our undertaking."

Masterson said, "Losing them is more important to the spirit of this company than I care to think."

Cohen said, "What was Shakespeare's line about music soothing the savage beast?"

Masterson said, "Breast. It was William Congreve: *Musick hath Charms to sooth a savage Breast, To soften Rocks, or Bend a knotted Oak.*"

Penney shook his head in amazement. "How the hell you know that?" He glanced at Preacher. "Sorry. A slip."

Cohen said, "I stand corrected. Well, we've got plenty of savage breasts. We better find another way to soothe them."

That evening, Willis was packed and ready to turn his wagon

around the following morning. After things had quieted down after supper, he sat on a stool outside the wagon, close enough to hear Mazie if he were needed. All was quiet except for the sawing of crickets. The children were asleep, and it was too early for the snoring. Willis was languidly playing a popular song of the day, "Consider the Lillies." His mood was calm as he stared beyond his violin as he played. His face was sad, and his mind was fixed on thoughts from deep within.

Hannah had come to see Mazie, but she stopped and put her hand on Willis' shoulder. She happened to know the song. In a soft, slow alto that further calmed the air, Hannah sang to his playing:

> *He clothes the lilies of the field.*
> *He feeds the birds in the sky.*
> *And He will feed those who trust Him,*
> *And guide them with His eye.*
> *Consider the sheep of His fold,*
> *How they follow where He leads.*
> *Though the path may lead across mountains,*
> *He knows the meadows where they feed.*

Atop a green hillside a day west of Independence, later travelers would come across a fresh grave with a simple wood marker and an epitaph written in charcoal that was already fading:

Mazie Patrick

Arkansas

1781—1845

She Made Music

Nights were still too chilly for mosquitoes to be in full force, so the after-supper hours were spent next to creeks with fish and firewood for the taking. In the softness of those evenings, romantic fantasies about this trek seemed genuine to the pioneers while also telling fond stories of what they had left behind. Then they fell silent for private memories under the moonlight in the soft red glow of a campfire, then ending with the winking lullaby of a sky of stars.

As it had a way of doing, the pastoral euphoria would vanish as nature changed moods.

Nimrod was seeking a ford to cross a creek with no name. He was looking for a crossing, but also for quicksand. He studied the creek bank and saw sand that extended into the stream. He knew that water-logged sand could turn into a jellied substance that offered little resistance to the weight of a human body. Contrary to common fears, there was no danger of a person sinking out of sight in quicksand, because after sinking to about the waist of an adult, the compression of the sand would support the lighter human. However, the greater danger would be if the quicksand were under water. In that case, a person could drop beneath the surface and drown. Nimrod didn't immediately see signs of quicksand, but he knew it was secretive. It liked to surprise and grab the unsuspecting. He quickly found the ford, but the quicksand was more elusive.

Nimrod was pointing out the gravel-bottom ford he had chosen. It was wide, slow, and no more than a couple of feet deep. He knew that the wider the crossing, the shallower the depth since width gave flowing water space to spread. However, he was not fooled by the placid surface. He turned to the others. "This creek looks like it's asleep, gents, but it's just waiting. I suspect we got some quicksand. It'll grab you like a bear trap, so stay in line when we cross."

Penney walked away with a beckoning motion. "Let's get 'er done, boys."

The men busied themselves moving the wagons and livestock across the river, while a group of children found amusement on the bank by throwing a ball back and forth. A boy of about eight missed the ball and watched it bounce into the water and drift toward the center on the current. Without hesitation, he waded in to retrieve it. But just as he grabbed the ball and attempted to return, he stepped into a hole and got stuck in quicksand. He started to settle in with the water armpit high. When he couldn't move, he cried out for his mother who was not nearby.

Hannah saw the boy and waded out to help. The others gathered to watch and shout and scream as Hannah, too, got stuck when she reached the child. The boy's father started to go to their aid, but Nimrod, who heard the shouting and hurried over, stopped him. "No point getting anyone else stuck."

Nimrod called for a long rope and, working fast, tied a stout stick on the end to give it heft. He waded into the water and cast it in Hannah's direction—once, twice she missed it as she and the boy slow sank lower, inch by inch. The boy was submerged to his neck, while the water was almost to Hannah's armpits.

Anxiety exploded among the group on the bank. They could see the panic in the boy's face and the fear in Hannah's eyes. "For God's sake, hurry!" the boy's mother screamed.

After several throws failed, Hannah was able to grab the rope.

"Wrap it around the boy and hold on," Nimrod shouted. As Hannah secured the boy with frantic hands, he tied the rope to Bub's saddle horn, and the big mule slowly pulled them out of the sucking sand and to safety. When the two reached shore, the boy's mother clutched him, and others congratulated Hannah.

As the people crowded around Hannah, Ed Spencer stood off to the side and glared. Then, as people returned to their tasks, he walked over to her. Nearby, Nimrod overheard what Spencer said to her. "You got children of your own. You were stupid, going out there."

Hannah returned the glare of her husband, then saw Nimrod standing beyond. In that instant, their eyes connected with a message that both pushed away. It was danger. Nimrod broke the spell by smiling and then touched his hat brim in silent salute.

Hannah and Spencer walked away, and Nimrod joined Penney at the creek bank.

"That there is one hell of a gal," Penney said while watching Nimrod's reaction, wondering if his hunch was correct. It sure seemed like something might be going on there.

Nimrod gazed at the departing Hannah. "She's got a hard row to hoe."

As Penney headed back to his wagon, Nimrod watched the last of the wagons roll across the river, followed by the livestock. He took steps to return to Bub. As he turned, he spotted a girl's doll in high grass at the water's edge and reached down to retrieve it, but he happened to put his hand into a patch of weeds where a female snapping turtle had just laid her eggs. Defending against the intruder, she grabbed hold of the flat of his left hand and bit hard.

Blood gushed, and Nimrod hollered in pain as he fell to a knee. Attached to his hand was a hissing thirty-pound, armor-plated prehistoric monster whose beak could snap a thick stick. Others gathered around in shock but stood frozen at the sight. Standing next to him, Penney gaped in astonishment.

"That's by God the biggest damned snapper I ever saw," Penney said.

Nimrod's face contorted in pain as he hissed between clenched teeth, "Get a knife. Quick! Cut its damned head off!"

Penney pulled his knife and sawed away at the turtle's neck.

Nimrod swore in pain. "Shit! Shit! Shit!"

Penney paused with a disapproving look. "Be more cautious of those words. Children got big ears."

When the turtle's body dropped away, the jaws still clung to Nimrod's hand. "Ain't the time to be polite…Pry its jaws apart," he said, speaking in a strained whisper.

Penney detached the head, and Nimrod sighed. "God does answer prayer."

Preacher, standing nearby, frowned, and said, "No need to blaspheme."

Nimrod was not in a mood to be corrected. "Blaspheme? I *was* praying."

Hannah heard the ruckus and rushed over. She efficiently cleaned his hand, put some ointment on it, and covered it with a tight bandage as he winced. "Oh, I hope I didn't make you hurt," she said.

"That devil critter didn't mean to do me any favors. I ain't smarted like that since my maw took a hickory branch to my hide." He laughed. "At least the whipping was deserved. I don't think the turtle had a good excuse."

That evening, after camp was set up, Nimrod rode a circuit around where the animals grazed. Seeing nothing, he returned to camp and stopped in the middle of the clearing where most of the folks were gathered in a festive mood.

"What's this, a chivaree? Someone get married?" he asked Penney, who was eating off a plate of food.

Penney paused with his mouth full. "We're having a turtle

bake." He motioned toward the fire. "There's plenty left. Have some."

Nimrod moaned, but he was also amused. "Enjoy your dinner, seeing as how me and my partner, the turtle, went to some trouble to provide it."

At the other end of the camp, there was a lantern flickering in the tent of the Spencers. Inside, Ed Spencer was raging against Hannah with flecks of spittle covering his chin. Billy and Rachel huddled in one corner, Brutus, the dog, sat on his haunches in the other. "I've seen you cozy up to that guide, don't think I haven't."

"Ed, we just danced. That's all. It was nothing but a dance."

Spencer pushed his face into hers. "He's a half-savage squaw-man. Maybe that's what you want in a man; maybe that's what you deserve."

"You told him he could dance with me," she said, trying to reason calmly.

"You were trash when I took you in. You couldn't even feed your brats."

Hannah's eyes flashed. "Don't call my children that."

Spencer reached over and grabbed her by the hair and twisted. Brutus started growling. The children started crying.

Hannah winced, and said, "Don't upset the children. Your dog frightens them."

"Brutus does what I want, remember that. You better do the same. You betray me, and it'll be the last thing you do," he hissed through his teeth.

"I'll talk to whoever I want." Her face radiated defiance as she locked eyes with him. "Now, let me go, or I'll scream and have every real man come running over here."

CHAPTER TWELVE

On a morning start-up, Zack was yoking oxen when Agnes Patterson's little dog, Benjamin, appeared from behind Zack's wagon barking and nipping at the heels of the nigh ox. The ox reared its head and slammed the heavy yoke into the Zack's forehead. He let go of the yoke and grabbed at the injury and wiped away the trickle of blood.

"You goddamn cur," he shouted and kicked Benjamin, who ran away yelping.

Penney was watching from a distance and shook his head in disgust. Benjamin had already irritated some people by barking in the middle of the night and sneaking unattended food.

During a stop to water the stock, Nimrod turned Bub to ride the length of the wagons to see if he were needed. When he reached the Cohen wagon, Malachi was standing at his tailgate and waved to him. Nimrod rode alongside and hailed with his hand, which was healing with a smaller bandage.

"You looking for some company, Malachi?"

"That would be just fine...This is beautiful country, but not enough trees to my taste." He started to put away what looked like a sword.

"Whatcha got there, if I ain't being too bold?"

Cohen pulled it out for Nimrod to see. It was a shiny saber in a brass scabbard with inlaid work. "This is a dress saber I took off the body of a French officer."

"How'd such a thing come about?"

"I was at a battle called Waterloo. I suppose you've heard of it."

"No idea."

"About...let's see. It was thirty years ago. I was a youngster conscripted into the Prussian army. I tried to hide, but they got me, but they didn't get much of a warrior. I didn't see much point in killing an English lad who probably had the same idea."

Nimrod hefted it. "Such a skinny blade wouldn't be much use out here."

"Well, it was of considerable use back there, but we can assume not for the fellow who owned it."

As the two men chatted, unknown to them, on a low rise in the distance, Rake Face Marcel was watching through a spyglass. The deep scars on his face were irritated and red, which did little to help his disposition. He lowered the scope as three men rode up to his side. They were as rough looking as him, but not as repulsive, which is not to say they weren't competitive. The dominant one of the three was named Esau Clink. He was comfortable with Marcel because he was a colleague in evil.

Nimrod swept his arm across the vista, pleased to be able to educate Malachi, the only artist he had ever known. "These are the Great Plains, or some call it the Great American Desert, although this ain't nothing of a desert compared to where we're headed. This'll never be good for farming, but it makes for easy traveling.... Mind if I ask you something?"

"Of course not."

"That little bitty hat you wear under your real hat. It don't seem good for anything. Why is that?"

Now it was Cohen's turn to educate. "It's called a yarmulke. It shows respect for the almighty. Many Jews wear one."

Nimrod looked at him in astonishment. "You a Jew? I've read about you people in the Bible; never thought I'd meet one."

Cohen laughed. "Well, I'm glad to be the source of your enlightenment. Notice I don't have horns and a tail."

Nimrod scoffed. "I ain't never paid no mind to that, but I did hear—yes, I did—that you people skin the end off a man's dobber."

Cohen was taken aback, then amused. "You don't think that's a good idea?"

Nimrod shook his head. "Woeee! Afore they take a knife to mine, I'll guarandamntee, it's gonna be a matter of INtense discussion." The men laughed together, while unseen in the distance, Marcel and his gang rode away.

The camp was jarred by a shot coming from among the wagons. Without a word, Nimrod turned and raced to the spot. Heads popped out from behind wagon bonnets and followed. When he got to the wagon, Hazel Grover, a woman who had kept to herself, was sprawled on the ground, dead. Asa Grover, her husband, was staring at the rifle he was holding like a foreign object, Next to him stood a boy and girl lost in confusion. People nearby exchanged looks of shock.

Penney came on the run, and as he struggled for breath, demanded, "What happened here?"

Grover stared at him, stunned. "I was just putting my gun back in the wagon, just putting it back...She was standing right here," He pointed with a shaky finger to a spot on the ground. "It just— went off." The man dropped the gun, fell to his knees, and covered his face. "My God! My God! What have I done?" he cried out.

The two young children started to wail. Nimrod reached into the wagon for a blanket, which he placed with care over the body. Penney turned to the gathering crowd. "Did anybody see this happen?" No one answered. Penney pondered for a moment and studied the grieving Grover. He led the man aside and asked, "No offense, Asa, but I got to ask—Did you mean to shoot your wife?"

Grover's eyes widened. "Huh? Oh, my god, no. We'll be married nineteen years come fall." Tears poured down his face. "I loved this woman, my Hazel."

Penney patted the man's arm, then returned to the crowd. "Well, I see no reason to doubt this." He turned to the man. "Mr. Grover. You have our deepest sympathy. Let us know how we can help." He looked around. "I'm confident the ladies will assist you."

Several women stepped forward to comfort the children and tend the body. Nimrod and Penney stepped aside, as the women began to prepare the body by lifting it to the wagon's tailgate. "All right, company, let's be about our business," Penney said in a loud but respectful voice. He turned to Nimrod as they walked from the crying. "A good woman's gone, and there's not a thing a body can say or do. Not a thing."

Nimrod half-way expected something like this somewhere along the trail. "They should keep their damned guns unloaded. Unless they're on guard duty, there's nothing they need to shoot that won't wait 'til they can load."

"A damned costly lesson," Penney said.

"There's lots of ways to die out here," Nimrod said. "I'm seeing children playing on wagons while they're moving. I mention it to parents, but it's not easy to keep track of children when you're on the move. They get restless, but mark my words, that could come to grief."

Penney was in a somber mood after what he had just seen. "Harnessing children is harder than mules."

"And they kick harder," Nimrod said absently, as he looked around and saw plenty of grass next to the spring they had stopped at. "We can camp here and get an early start, you think, Captain?"

Penney nodded. "We'll bury the woman after breakfast."

After a quick breakfast had been eaten by families hunched gloomily next to campfires, the people gathered on the side of the trail over an unmarked grave with heads bowed and hats off. Dirt formed into small dust devils around them, and long dresses flapped in the strong wind. Preacher finished with prayers for the dead woman's soul as her family wailed their grief. Penney patted the widower on his heaving shoulder. With the last amen, the men replaced their hats, pushing them far down on their heads and leaning forward against the wind. The entire group started to move toward the wagons, eager to get started, eager to put this unhappy scene behind them.

As the wagons were readying to move, Nimrod raised his voice. "All right now, run the animals over the grave. Let's get 'em moving."

The widower clutched at Nimrod's sleeve. "Do you have to do that? Hazel's grave will be lost."

Nimrod turned to him and put a sympathetic hand on his arm. "Sorry, sir, I know it's hurtful, but with wolves out there waiting, and Indians ready to dig up the grave for her clothes, it's best."

The oxen were driven up and milled over the grave, bawling at the unfamiliar task.

As the train awaited the start up signal, Ed Spencer went to his grain wagon and ripped open a bag of corn. He stared in shock, then cried out in anguish. Frantically, he ripped open bag after bag—all the same: loaded with fungus. "Nooo! God damn it!" he wailed. He put his head in his hands and moaned.

Nearby, people rushed over and stared in silence at the open corn bags. Instead of bright yellow corn, they were confronted by green mold. Every farmer looking on knew what it meant—aflatoxic fungus. William Dickens looked at it and shook his head. "Any animal eats that, it's as good as dead."

Nimrod and Penney stood off to the side, watching. Penney muttered to Nimrod, "Well, there goes the feed for his high-fallutin' horses."

Nimrod said, "Them horses need grain. They better get used to grass that'll be like a stew with no meat."

"They ain't going to like it," Penney said.

Nimrod spotted the line of trees before the others because he knew they were nearing the Big Blue River. It was the last significant stream before the train had a clear run of four or five days to the Platte River.

"Is yonder river the Big Blue you been telling us about?" Jackman asked.

"There she is," Nimrod said. "The name's the biggest thing about it. It's wide, but yay-high at the deepest." He held his hand at mid-thigh. "It has good fords with gravel bottoms."

Penney said, "It's 'bout four hours 'til sundown. We'll stop for the day at the bank, then cross in the morning." Unless overridden by the committee, choosing the campsite was his call.

"Beg pardon, Captain." When Nimrod used the "captain" title, Penney knew he was politely saying, listen to me on this. "My belief is to cross the river before night, if'n we can. Slow creeks can turn into fast rivers overnight, if'n a big rain sneaks in. When that happens, it's best to be looking back at the river, 'stead of facing it."

Penney studied Nimrod's face, aware of the guide's experience. "We're all tired. Crossing a river is hard work. It'd be better to have a good meal and a night's sleep and tackle it fresh in the morning."

Nimrod looked skyward. "I don't like the look of them wispy clouds. It might be nothing, but you never can tell."

Masterson said, "Maybe Nimrod's got a point, Captain."

Penney thought for a long moment, then slightly irritated, said, "All right. Let's get across this son of a bitch."

When Nimrod returned from scouting a crossing spot, he guided the wagon train up to the riverbank. He rode over to Penney, and said, "This is a good ford, but all along here, we've got these high banks." Both men looked at a bank a vertical three feet above the river.

Penney turned to his committee. "Well, boys, get your shovels out."

As they gazed at the brown water, they were jarred by a shrill scream from the rear of the column. Everyone raced toward the sound and came upon a barefoot girl of about six sitting on the ground holding her foot. She was screaming for her mother, her little face crumpled with tears and pain. Hannah ran up to the girl, then cradled her foot and looked for a wound.

"I don't see anything," she said, "massaging the girl's foot as she continued to scream. "No, here's a red bite mark on her big toe. It doesn't look dangerous." By then, the girl's panicky mother had come up and taken the girl from Hannah. She cooed to her sobbing daughter, and said in her despair for the world to hear, "I hate this place. I hate everything about this trip. This never would've happened back home." None of the women standing nearby chose to disagree.

Nimrod walked a couple of feet and nudged something with his boot. "Here's what happened." He pointed down. "This here's a tarantula spider, at least what once was. It's been killed by a tarantula hawk; that's a big wasp-like critter. It didn't have a chance to drag the spider away. This is pretty far north for both those boys. The girl must have stepped in his way when he was on the job killing this here spider."

The girl continued to scream. Nimrod said, "She's got reason to cry. Not many things hurt worse. I can vouch for that. She'll be okay in five minutes or so."

Hannah looked up at Nimrod and showed a flash of irritation. "You don't seem much sympathetic."

He shrugged an apology. "No offense. The little girl will forget this in an hour. Most people who get hurt in these parts would settle for that. There's a whole lot worse out here."

Several people listening did not smile.

Mansfield leaned over and studied the tarantula." That's one big arachnid."

Nimrod looked up. "No, that's a spider."

Mansfield grinned and resumed his inspection.

One by one, the pioneers broke up the circle around the girl and walked back to the immediate problem of getting across the Big Blue.

All the men and older boys were called together and told a ramp had to be excavated out of the bank on both sides so the wagons could be lowered and then raised without having to unload and then reload.

The men were organized into two crews, one to each side, and started digging. Penney noticed the ex-slave, Johnny was among the diggers, but not his "boss," Uriah Meister.

"Where's your boss, Johnny," Penney asked. He was happy not to use the word "master."

"Oh, he's yonder at the wagon," Johnny said, casting a veiled glance at Nimrod standing nearby. When Penney turned his back, Johnny passed Hiram Young's message to Nimrod who looked surprised, then slipped it into his pocket.

Penney walked over to Meister's wagon and found him puttering with some harness. "Why aren't you over there digging with the other men?" he asked.

Meister looked up. "Oh, I sent my man over to help out."

Penney took a couple of deep breaths. "I ain't going to argue about this. You get a shovel and get your ass over there and start digging."

Meister stood up. "How dare you talk to me like that," he said with a sputter.

Penney fought to keep his cool. "When you signed up, you agreed you would carry your own weight. Nothing was said about your bondsman doing your work, too." He looked over to where the men were working. "Best I can tell, he's doing his part. Now, goddamnit, you do yours."

"You insult me, sir."

"Look, Meister, I don't like your kind—people who use other humans like draught animals. And I wouldn't like you anyway, for damned certain." Penney gave a dismissive wave and turned to walk away. "I've got work to do, and, by God, so do you."

Later, Johnny looked to the end of the line and saw Meister sweating over a shovel. He turned back to his work with an at-peace look on his face.

Meister had shown kind concern for Johnny back when they were close enough to Independence for Johnny to walk away as a free man. However, the farther they got from his possible escape, the more abusive Meister became. The slaver's reservoir of compassion proved to be ankle deep. More than once he told Johnny that if he ran, the Indians would catch him and boil him alive, then feed his body to their dogs.

A half-dozen men on either side played-out the ropes while the oxen restrained the wagons from falling down the bank. As the wagons were being rigged to be sent across, Nimrod glanced up at the clouds he had noticed earlier to see they had disappeared. Relieved, now that the train was heading across the river, he put the weather out of his mind.

When each wagon reached the water level, the ropes were reversed and attached to the rigging of eight oxen, which pulled it across the shallow river and up the bank.

With so many men working, it took a mere ninety minutes to dig two ramps of gradual angles on the soft riverbanks on both sides. Then they backed up three yoke of oxen on the crossing side, then one at a time, attached two ropes to each wagon's frame, then through the iron ring on the oxen harness to lower them down to river level. A half-dozen men on played-out the ropes while the oxen restrained the wagons to ease them down the bank.

As the wagons were being rigged to be pulled to the other side by other oxen, Nimrod glanced up at the clouds he had noticed earlier to see they had disappeared. Relieved, now that the train was heading across the river, he put the weather out of his mind.

When each wagon reached the water level, the ropes were reversed and attached to the rigging of eight oxen, which pulled it across the shallow river and up the bank.

With the last wagon secured on the far bank, and the livestock herded across, the sun had turned to deep dusk. The men put away shovels and walked down the ramp to wash up, laughing and playfully shoving the way men do when a hard job has been accomplished by teamwork.

The camp was pitched in a grove of walnut trees. After supper, each woman gathered live coals from the cooking fire and put them in her Dutch oven. It would serve as a brazier, so they could be rekindled for breakfast the next morning. Otherwise, the fire had to be extinguished.

With the chores done, the people surrendered as one to the exhaustion of the day's labor. The soft lowing of cattle mixed with the harsher snoring coming from the tents.

Nimrod walked outside the circled wagons to check on the grazing livestock. Since there had been no Indian sign for several days, the animals were left overnight outside the circled wagons, but the guard had been increased to three.

Nimrod heard footsteps and looked over to see Hannah's son, Billy, fall in step with him. "Well, Trooper! How's our young drover? You taught them two fellers how to handle them evil oxen yet?"

"They don't need me no more. They're doing fine. Mr. Banks does almost all the ox driving. They're good fellers," Billy said with self-importance.

"How about Martin, the other feller?"

"Mr. Carter? Oh, he sleeps most of the time. He has this little bottle he takes sips out of. Or he just sits on the seat and stares, but it's like he's not seeing anything. It's spooky."

"Is he sick?"

"Naw. Sometimes, he's just normal."

Nimrod's eyes were on Billy, but his thoughts went beyond. "Interesting."

Nimrod was the hero of every boy in the train, and Billy was puffed-up at having a man-to-man talk with him. He hoped the other boys were watching.

Nimrod picked up a rock and threw it at a small tree. Billy did the same. Both missed. "Your sister sure is quiet. Does she ever laugh?"

"She used to."

"It's nice your father let you earn a little extra money," Nimrod said, and sensed Billy becoming tense at the words.

"He already took the money. And he ain't my father."

Nimrod stopped and faced Billy who tipped his face up to listen. "I know that, Trooper, but I was just showing respect, and so should you."

Billy clenched his jaw and stared at the ground. "I don't respect him, I hate him. I don't care if you tell him and I get a whipping."

Nimrod rustled Billy's hair. "Whoa. I'm not telling a single soul anything. It's just a shame for a nice young gentleman to have so much hot sauce in him."

"He hits my mother and calls her awful names," Billy said with a catch in his voice.

Nimrod was mindful of his duty, an essential part of which was to stay aloof from domestic problems among the company. "A man oughtn' to do that." Nimrod wanted to end that part of the conversation. "You best go back now. We're getting a bit far from camp."

Billy shuffled back, and Nimrod walked through the herd of grazing cattle, horses, and mules. The horses were held closer in because Indians valued them much higher, and thus would be primary targets of a raid.

Nimrod saw the shadow of a man ahead and called out, "Hello, the guard!" He wasn't about to surprise a jittery guard.

It was Andrew's watch, and upon hearing Nimrod's words, he advanced out of the shadows with his rifle at port arms. He was of slight build, and his body language was not threatening, but the look on his face said he was holding the rifle for a serious purpose. "That you, Nimrod?"

Nimrod stood with hands on hips. "You was maybe hoping it was a Pawnee brave?

"Not even a Pawnee papoose. Not even a Pawnee puppy."

Nimrod walked over and shook hands. "You fellers doing okay, you and Martin?"

"Uh—well, nothing we're not used to. We're not the most popular men in camp, if you know what I mean."

"Reckon I don't," Nimrod lied. The subject made him uneasy, and he fidgeted with his rifle.

"Well— there's been some comments about me being a dressmaker, or a play-actor, as Martin is."

Nimrod couldn't resist a grin, but Andrew didn't see it. He wiped his smile, and said, "We got all kinds of people thrown into the pot. But to get where we're going, we need to keep the peace, not court trouble."

Andrew smiled, but with doubt. "With me, you're preaching to a deacon. Others I can think of might need that sermon."

Morning broke dark and still. The clouds from the day before were back. This time, however, they were high and billowy.

He felt a drastic drop in barometric pressure, which he knew was not a good indication. The sky was filled with wispy, pearl-gray clouds that veiled the sun and made its light thin and milky. Within a half hour, the wind picked up and the temperature became twenty degrees colder. One word came to his mind—cloudburst.

It started to rain. And it rained. And it rained. As it got colder, the rain turned to hail; small pellets stung like little rocks and tore holes in the wagon bonnets that would take the women hours of grumbling to sew up.

The rain and hail came down in a howling sheet pushed sideways by a strong north wind. Lightning in the near distance speared into the ground time and again, and thunder cracked like cannon. The men walked among the animals with soothing words and pats on their flanks.

The company members had seen hard rain many times before, but not like this, not that left them huddling in thin tents or under wagons, naked in the sight of nature. There were no dry houses to peer out of, no barns to house the animals in. The full force of the storm shook them as a terrier does a rat. The cold wind expelled a deep breath and howled with a force that sent hats fluttering away, as well as anything else loose and light. Streams of water turned everything to muck. The livestock just beyond the wagon circle chewed the lush grass and gazed into the wall of water, nervous at the thunder, but grateful for the release of the yoke.

Nimrod knew his job was to force the pioneers to do what they dreaded. Because they were camped in a grove of trees, Nimrod knew the position was a magnet for lighting. They had to move. He ran from wagon to wagon, urging people to break camp, yoke up the oxen and move about five-hundred yards to a near-by hollow. The dip in the earth was deep enough to reduce their exposure to wind and lightning but would still leave them at the mercy of the rain.

Masterson shouted above the wind. "Why the hell should we move out of the only shelter in miles? Have you taken leave of your senses, man?"

"It's better to get soaked than fried. Trees draw lightning. I've seen it," Nimrod shouted back, then continued, "Blindfold the horses, 'cause they're more skittish and liable to run." He pointed to the shallow dip in the ground where they were headed. "When you get to yonder hollow, don't bother to circle-up, and keep the ox yoked-up; easier to control."

Grumbling, the men gathered their teams. The rain plastered clothing to the skin as they shivered, skidded and slipped, then managed to move the short distance to the hollow.

Nimrod yelled above the wind's howl for the men to blindfold all the livestock. "They won't run if they can't see where they're going," he shouted above the howl. He also urged people to protect food and gunpowder from the rain; anything else could be dried later by the sun. At one point, there was a loud crack and flash. People looked and saw lighting had split a large cottonwood amidst the grove they had just left.

For three hours, the people endured. Women and children stayed in the wagons and prevented bonnets from flying off and tried to keep the contents free of water that got through. The men hunkered under the lee of the wagons. Every few minutes they ran to check on the restless livestock standing alone under the beating rain.

Gradually, the downpour slacked off to a light rain, then stopped. People emerged from whatever cover they had found and looked at the sky as though they had never seen it clear. When people glanced back the way they had come, they saw the Big Blue had become a torrent of rain runoff.

CHAPTER THIRTEEN

As the miles stretched, the camp had settled into a familiar routine. If Indians were not seen in the area, the cattle, mules, and horses grazed and rested from evening to dawn with several guards working in shifts to keep them herded and as close to the camp as grass availability allowed.

The pioneers had come together as strangers and set about forming a village on the fly. Most were neighborly people who set about befriending other equally confused pilgrims, not knowing who they were, or where they all might end up. They were church-goers and debt-paying proud people who wore strong patriotism on their sleeves, though they might have stumbled if called to explain it. Not everyone was upstanding, but just like in their hometowns, those who were not would be found out. For the most part they had led complacent and happy lives back home, and they were determined to be that way again. They tried hard to reestablish life-long social routines. After eating supper and doing chores, families strolled, visited, mended harness and clothes, or erected tents. They gossiped, laughed, disapproved, and admired in their interactions. They got along. For a while.

Like any village, they quickly stratified into cliques of Michiganders, Indiana Hoosiers, or Illinois Suckers, although no one knew where that uninviting nickname came from. Also, slave staters, and abolitionists, though they tried to keep that under wraps. Everyone found a stratum according to their wealth, their assertiveness, their kindness, and those who had that ineffable "it" that others rallied to, especially when danger seemed afoot.

As happened often, Nimrod and Hannah encountered each other. Each sensed the need to remain aloof. Nimrod might touch his hat, then say, "Ma'am," and Hannah might say, "Good day, sir." Each would have denied, even to themselves, that there was an ulterior motive, or even a tacit understanding to avoid each other. Nothing was said, but each recognized the tension of the other's presence, and each knew what it meant. Each was aware something could happen one day. Each hoped for it, and each feared it.

A dozen pioneers were attracted to a musician named Enoch Brister making music on a strange instrument invented in Europe only a decade previous. Brister seemed as strange as his instrument. He was a gangly, scarecrow sort of man, who spoke with a stutter, but said little. No one knew anything about him, and he didn't offer to share. He had a small wagon only half full and pulled by two yoke of oxen. He had been a quiet, almost reclusive, member of the company who stayed to himself and no one knew much about. But when Willis and Mazie departed, he knew music was needed in the camp.

He sat playing familiar songs from home for a group of pioneers sitting around a fire kept high to ward off mosquitoes. One suggested "Buffalo Gals," a national favorite since the building of the Erie Canal, and Brister lost not a beat in starting the familiar tune as his audience started singing. They ignored, if they knew, that the song's lyrics were composed as an ode to the whores of the city of Buffalo from boatmen eager for a visit.

On the edge of the circle, Cohen sketched the happy singers as his pencil flew over his sketch pad. What emerged, almost magically to those peering over his shoulder, were the faces and emotions of his subjects who witnessed themselves being memorialized, if only by a lead pencil. He would often make a duplicate drawing and give to his subjects. Cohen would slip his finished drawings into a portfolio. When he reached California, he intended to transfer the best into paintings. With photography still an infant, Cohen saw himself as a storyteller of the people making the perilous trek. It was a role he considered sanctified by art history.

Penney was more prosaic. Sitting next to his tent, he held up a container of liquor and beckoned to Nimrod listening to the music nearby. "I got me a jar of 'family disturbance' here. Sit, and have a taste. At this very moment, I'm as content as a tick on a fat dog.

I doubt the feeling will last long, considering this job I got roped into."

Nimrod plopped down nearby. "It don't have to be good whiskey to gladden my heart."

"Then I reckon you came to the right place." Penney poured for both into tin cups after shaking out the dust. "Obliged," Nimrod said and winced as he rubbed his backside. "Ohhh, bouncing around on that bony mule pains my ass, and that strange music over at the fire don't soothe my spirit much."

The two men listened to the music for a few moments. "Folks need music, even though it's not Willis and Mazie," Penney said. "I don't know nothing about Brister's squawk box contraption, or about Enoch Brister, for that matter."

Nimrod watched the group of listeners. "You see plenty of toe-tapping. They just needed to get the hang of the music he's playing, I reckon."

Penney said, "He calls that thing a concertina, he does. Whatever the hell a concertina is."

"A concertina is something that screeches, but it's a good screech," Nimrod said."

"Well, it's something. If we're not grateful for what we got, it might irritate the Lord," Penney said.

Nimrod half-smiled. "Preacher find the door into your head, did he?"

Penney gave a snort-laugh. "I don't like to have to watch my language around him. It cuts my supply of useful words way down. He keeps agitating for Sunday services; you know, the Baptist ones that go on and on until the deacons do the altar call to be saved again, just so they can get home for Sunday dinner. Preacher needs to feel he put in a day's work." He growled at a thought. "Being upstanding can be a trial. Like you told him, we got to skedaddle to California. He can pray while walking the trail just as well as on his knees."

Penney sipped generously, then said, "I been sitting here thinking about my farm back home. The corn would just be passing ankle high."

"Why'd you leave?"

Penney kneaded his thigh. "My damned body wishes I hadn't." He drank, then looked at the cup and swirled the contents. "The sawbones back home told me if I didn't give up the skull varnish, it could ruin my heart which had been skipping around like a Saturday night square dance anyway. I figger my heart will do its job until it decides to quit, and no country doctor can change that. Penney paused, and his face became sad. "You seen my wife, Clara. Right?"

Nimrod nodded. "A nice lady. Don't say a lot."

"She don't say nothing. It happened year afore last. Doctor called it apoplexy, sort of like what you saw Mazie Patrick having, only not as bad. The doc said another word was stroke, but not a big one." Penney snorted a laugh. "I don't know about that. I reckon a 'small' stroke is one the other fella gets. It seemed like a stroke of bad luck to me. The upshot was that Clara got better but was left with a bad hitch in her walk, but worse, she was struck dumb. Couldn't get anything out but a squawk. Her friends dropped off; not being mean, just confused on how to deal with her. Couldn't blame them. Ain't nobody at ease giving pity, let alone be given it. What people didn't take the time to realize, she was the same good woman after she couldn't talk as when she could." He paused to nod his head emphatically. "Yes, sirree, Bob. We're a pair, me and her."

Penney sipped his liquor. "Well, sir, I up and said to her, I said, 'Let's get us a wagon, old gal, sell this farm and chase the sun, find out more about this world than central Illinois can tell us.' We talked about it—I did, she made hand signs. She never was taught her letters. But over time we learned to read each others' minds. Anyways, we decided the hell with it. We'd just find a new life. Me and her. The two of us, just like we started." He gave a that's-that nod.

Penney studied the amber liquid in his cup. "I should be pouring you French champagne 'stead of backwoods whiskey, what you did for me."

"You led me into the brambles on that one," Nimrod said.

"When you happened along back in Independence, I was about to drown myself in the Missoura. I was confused as a hog in the sour mash."

"You looked fine to me," Nimrod said, concentrating on his whiskey as it swirled in his cup.

"I learned to look fine. It's an art. I'm an old horse, good for nothing 'cept to pull a garden plow." He looked up at Nimrod, as though to say something amazing. "I was born before George Washington became president. You believe that?"

"Damned if I'da guessed that," Nimrod said, trying to sound amazed.

The jarring sound of moaning and screaming erupted a few wagons away. The singing stopped abruptly. Nimrod jumped up.

Penney chuckled and didn't move. "That's the Burns fella with the horrors; getting the whiskey out of his system. He's probably seeing snakes,"

The singing resumed as the others also realized it was Burns with the delirium tremens.

Nimrod grinned at the thought. "For his peace of mind, I hope they're garter snakes."

Penney resumed his reminiscence. "I was in the War of 1812. Fought with Andy Jackson, I did. I once held the general's horse. You believe that? He thanked me. Had a high voice. Crotchety old bastard, but the man could fight. Yes, sir, he could, he surely could fight. The boys called him Old Sharp Knife. Worst thing ever happened to the Creeks and the Red Sticks, not to mention the Redcoats."

"I'd like to have a story or two like that. Save me the trouble of thinking up lies," Nimrod said.

Nimrod said, "That's what I'm about down to, stories. Back in Independence, these folks made me a big frog in our puddle 'cause I was a county sheriff for one two-year term. Most dangerous thing I did was to tell drunk farmers to git on home on Saturday nights. No one else wanted the job. I was just a dirt farmer, is what I was; never anything else, and never anything special on the dirt farming."

Nimrod said, "Any farmer can hold his head up. It's hard work. I hold that calling in high regard, since I was shy of being any good at it. The Bible gives a heap more praise to farming than to trapping beaver. If I was behind a plow and you was in the same field, you'd best watch your toes." Nimrod added an emphatic "Yes, sir." Then he turned his face sideways toward Penney. "These people respect you, Captain."

"I appreciate your kind words, but I don't feel very captainish. I'm about as handy out here as a cow in the hen house."

Nimrod tapped the old man on the thigh. "You're a rooster in the hen house, that's what you be."

Penney shook his head in a doleful way. "I swear, I don't know. I just don't know.... I always figgered folks is folks wherever you set them down. I prided myself on being able to watch a man around his neighbors and know what he was made of. But being a part of this wagon train showed me how ignorant I am. When people change their lives, they change the way they act, and not always for the better.

"A feller can be a saint as a neighbor and a part-time Gospel preacher. His wife can sing in the choir and take soup to sick folks. However, they cut those ties and get out here, and there's a chance he turns into a bully, lording it over other folks, and she becomes a harpie and a gossip."

Nimrod said, "There's plenty of good folks in this wagon train."

Penney took a moment to rethink his sour judgment. "Well, that's true enough. I'm seeing black when the truth is gray. However, there's enough black to make me think I got this job because every sensible man was too smart to take it."

Nimrod said, "We've got a long way to go before we roll into Sutter's Fort."

Penney threw away the little remaining whiskey in his cup. "If, my friend, if. If we get there."

Nimrod finished his drink and got up. "Get a good night's sleep, Captain. You'll be ornery as ever in the morning."

Penney also rose on legs that didn't want to. "I'll be another day older is what I'll be."

The campfires died out, and the pioneers settled down in their tents and lean-tos next to the wagons. The night guards walked among the grazing animals, alert to dangers from wolves or Indians.

The cicadas claimed the night, and their humming set a slumber tone for the camp. Next to the Jackman wagon, Abraham's snore seemed to threaten his tent.

A quarter-mile distant, Zack Monroe stood in front of the bushes and urinated in a thick shrub. However, off to the side, the bushes rustled and a moaning could be heard, which made Zack button his pants and smile; actually, more of a leer. He crept closer and got a glimpse of Davy Owens and Susan Jackman having sex. They were trying to stifle their noise, but the intensity of the coupling could not suppress low moans. Zack watched with growing tension in his body. He turned and crept away. He was anxious to get off by himself to some private business of his own.

The train reached the Platte twenty-five days after leaving Independence. About thirty people stood in a cluster at the front and stared into the sluggish-muddy water about two hundred yards wide. There had been an eagerness to reach its banks because it represented a reassuring mark of progress that would mean the journey had turned almost due west. The miles to California could be eaten in gulps along its level banks.

It also represented the gravest threat to their wellbeing. The river was host to many killers that lay in waiting: cholera, dysentery, typhoid, malaria, and other diseases that preferred to work anonymously, but found their efforts easier because of the close contact in the wagon train. No ailments were more dreaded than diarrhea and dysentery. They were caused primarily by bad water and spoiled foods. Diarrhea could make life miserable, and if its big brother, dysentery took over, death could be the result.

All the diseases sprung their traps from hiding. However, in 1845 cholera was rather quiescent; perhaps awaiting the much larger throngs that would travel the trail in following years. The Platte, too, was the cleanest it would be for many years. The microbes in the river grew fat on the filth that hordes of travelers and animals would dump in the Platte.

One nasty customer was giardia, an intestinal parasite that wouldn't kill you, but for a couple of weeks could make you wish it had. There were no dependable medicines for these ailments. The only protection might be resistance built up over years of dealing with them in streams back home.

One woman's comment was the gist of the mood when she said, "This mud puddle? This is the famous Platte River we've been yearning to see?"

"I heard one feller say this river is too thin to plow and too thick to drink," Jackman said.

Penney nodded. "And as hard to read as a loose woman's heart." He happened to glance at Hannah who rolled her eyes.

Having reached a major landmark, the women staged a revolt of frowning. They made it clear they were tired of wearing clothes so dusty that whenever it rained they almost turned to mud. Rather than fight an unwinnable battle, Penney declared a full-day stopover to rest livestock and allow the women to do laundry along a clear feeder stream to the Platte.

The women had won, but it didn't diminish their joyless view of the entire undertaking. As Hannah, Gertie Proctor, Ruth Cohen, Clara Penney, and Millie Plum sat along the stream bank, their glumness was evident as they rubbed knuckles raw on corrugated washboards and their hands became chaffed and red from the harsh lye soap, which was an inexact blend of lye boiled out of hardwood ashes and rendered animal fat.

Millie had missed her second period just as her husband, Emory, was gathering supplies for the trip to California. She had first urged him not to go, then, on the trip to Independence, she constantly begged him to return to their Ohio farm. Once there, she surrendered her plea, but not her anger at being uprooted. Millie put down the shirt she was scrubbing and leaned backward to stretch. "My back feels like this washboard."

Ruth, with the patience of an older woman, said, "It'll all be worth it once we get to California."

Gertie said, sarcastically, "If and whenever that happens."

Mute Clara Penney contributed to the conversation in the only way she could, by smiles, frowns, or nods.

Millie shifted her heavily pregnant body and threw a sopping shirt down in disgust. "I'm sick of this: It's sleep on the wet ground, start the fire in the cold, and make breakfast over an open fire like a squaw." She sat upright to stretch her back. "Just after Christmas, I was elected head of our church Sunday school. They were counting on me, and…well, it was embarrassing."

Millie started quietly singing an old Scottish tune, what would in another day be called a protest song:

> When I was single, I went dressed so fine,
> Now I am married, go ragged all the time,
> Dishes to wash and spring to go to,
> Now I am married I've everything to do,
> Lord, I wish I was single again
> Two hungry children lyin' in the bed,
> Long comes the drunkard and calls them a fool,
> When I was single, marryin' was my crave,
> Now I am married, I'm troubled to my grave,
> Lord, I wish I was single again

The others smiled, and one giggled, but the floodgates had been opened, and the complaints poured through from all the women: "The children are sick…." "I miss my family, my church, my home…." "We had no say in the matter. We go where we're told…." "The babies have to re-use dirty diapers. Poor things…."

"It's the way it's always been. Women just have to help each other," Millie said, trying to gain a perspective. But Gertie provided a better one: "Men feast on big dreams, and it's left to us to wash their dirty dishes."

Hannah listened to the complaints and mused to herself: There are worse things.

Clara Penney smiled and kept working. No one asked for her opinion.

✲

The first aim of the day was to get a jump on the sun. At four a.m., men and women would drag themselves out of tents or wagons and resume their labors. The goal was to be on the trail by five a.m. The children would bring in the animals, the men would yoke up the oxen, and the woman would close the camp, and put away their belongings. If time allowed, rarely, she would make flapjacks and also cold meals for the midday stop; otherwise, they would eat leftovers from the previous night, saved for that purpose.

After breakfast, they would head for areas designated for ablutions the evening before. Women were assigned the most secluded area, and anyone violating the privacy of it would face harsh criticism, and maybe more from a husband or father. A few insisted on using a chamber pot, also indelicately called a slop bucket, inside the wagon, then emptying and rinsing it in a nearby river.

They used river water for whatever required to be wet, including their thirst. Clear, fast-moving streams were preferred when they were available. Many rivers and streams became cesspools, the Platte quickest of all.

They would travel until about noon, then stop for a cold dinner, rest for a half hour, water the animals, and put them out to graze. They would be back on the trail by two in the afternoon and until about five, depending on where Nimrod could find water and grazing. They would circle the wagons and set up camp. The evening would be spent by the men taking care of the animals and the equipment. The children would clear a cooking space large enough to avoid fire getting loose, and take containers to fill at the river. The women would bring out a Dutch oven, or skillet, and the kettle for coffee. The main meal, supper, would be a stew of whatever meat was ready to cook, bread, and vegetables, if any were available. That was repeated night after night.

The pioneers all along had expressed apprehension about the danger of Indian contacts. However, to their relief, most of the Indians who entered the camp were there to be fed. Flapjacks were the primary object of their begging. The women were kept busy mixing dough and frying little pancakes, which the Indians ate right off the griddle. Butter and syrup weren't asked for, because they were unaware of those condiments. If they had tasted syrup, the wagon train might never have broken camp. They kept asking for whiskey, but Penney made sure none of the pioneers repeated the mistake of John Burns and his "hospitality" with the Wyandottes.

It became clear the Indians made the rounds of every train that passed by. The tip-off was when one brave approached Penney and greeted him with a joyous, "You son of a bitch!" After blinking in surprise, Penney grinned as he realized the Indian had overheard a drover having a conversation with a balky ox.

Penney responded politely, "Hello, you son of a bitch."

Another Indian expressed gratitude for his flapjacks by exclaiming to the woman serving them, "goddamn!"

The guests were a U.N. of plains tribes with the same coherence of that body. They were a mixture of Oglala, Winnebago, Potawatomi, Omaha, Pawnee, and Arapaho. Some of the tribes were ancient enemies, but the camp seemed to be neutral ground. Nimrod had coached the men to be on their guard with their guests: be firm, but not aggressive; keep firearms at hand but not menacingly. Indians would sometimes test the pioneers. One Cheyenne grabbed a hammer from the boot of a wagon. The owner pointed his rifle at the man and demanded its return as the camp shrank back in tension. Nimrod stepped in and cajoled both men, and Penney gave the Cheyenne three feet of red ribbon. With the wisdom of experience, he assumed the man's squaw would prefer something pretty to an ugly hammer.

To the Indians, visiting a wagon train was akin to a county fair, a chance to do and see things that interrupted the humdrum of their lives. Because the wagon trains passed on through, they had not yet perceived the danger these white strangers posed to their way of life. It's difficult to become alarmed by a novelty.

Almost all the visitors were men because they had leisure time, and their women did not. The men had few duties around their own camp, leaving the grunt work to the women. In fact, the absence of women in those "come callings" was a source of concern to the pioneers. The presence of women would tend to forestall any mischief or violence by the men. Plains Indians were warlike to an extent equaled by few societies, unlike, say, peaceful West Coast Indians where natural resources were more plentiful and year-round.

The Plains Indians lived a feast or famine existence, depending on migrating herds of buffalo. They occupied ground inhospitable to agriculture, at least to their knowledge. As with any peoples in barebones circumstances, the property rights of richer strangers did not cause them much concern.

The grim life of the plains Indians was a surprise to many pioneers who had admired James Fennimore Cooper's series "Leatherstocking Tales," including *The Last of the Mohicans.* At that time back east, their Indians had been "tamed," so writers felt free to indulge the myth of the "noble savage." Nobility was, in fact, a quality of many Indians, as it was with all peoples, but pioneers, isolated and vulnerable out in the middle of nowhere, were not of a mood to bestow such a blessing.

One late afternoon as camp was being set up, a war party of Dakota Sioux appeared. They were not there for flapjacks. Their face paint, edged weaponry, and tight-lipped demeanor caused many gulps. They were on the warpath against Arapahos, who, by good fortune, had not appeared that day. When the Sioux departed, the sighs of relief in the camp could have caused a gust of breeze.

On a rainy late Saturday afternoon, the train stopped as Millie Plum's time came due. She gave birth to a son, her first. Hannah attended her, but quickly realized the baby was early, at least two months premature. There was nothing she could do as the baby boy took a few faltering breaths that faded to nothing, then stopped. Millie was awake and aware. Her cries alarmed children in nearby wagons until their mothers told them not to worry. However, the mothers recognized Millie's cries as those of grief, not of childbirth. The men were ill at ease and busied themselves with minor repairs.

The baby was unnamed and was buried alongside the trail. Millie cried for a day, then left her bed and went about her work, but in a cocoon of grief. She was bitter at leaving her baby's body in an unmarked hole in the desert. She kept her resentment away from the other pioneers, but not from her husband, oh, no.

The train moved west along the south bank of the Platte like a trail of sleep-walking ants. Nimrod had been riding out front a couple of miles, looking for game and grass, but also swales and rough spots in the trail to avoid as well as for a daunting list of other dangers. About noon, Penney's concern was alerted by seeing Nimrod riding back at a fast gallop. Penney held up his arm to stop the train, then rode out ahead to meet Nimrod about a quarter mile ahead. Nimrod's mule was lathered, and the man himself was breathing hard from what Penney recognized as stress. Nimrod kept looking over his shoulder toward distant hills.

"What're you staring at? See some ghosts over there?" Penney asked.

"Riders, but ghosts would be more welcome," Nimrod said as three horsemen emerged in the distance, first as dots, then taking form as white men riding in a tight cluster. They stopped about three hundred yards from Nimrod and Penney.

One man held up a white sheet as a peace signal. He waved it, and shouted, "Will you honor a parley flag?"

Penney shouted in reply, "I reckon so."

"Who are they?" Penney asked, his voice reflecting the concern he observed in Nimrod.

"Nobody you'd invite for dinner, you can bet."

Malachi Cohen and Aaron Proctor rode up to find out what was happening.

"The one in the lead is Esau Clink. I'd know him, even at this distance. The fact he's been allowed to live speaks ill of God's judgment," Nimrod said to the others.

Penney nodded toward the strangers who had not moved. "Well, I reckon they want to talk. I don't have a good feel for this, but it seems we got no choice."

The men from the wagon train urged their mounts at a trot toward the waiting three. All the men on both sides were armed, but no one was menacing. The men followed Nimrod and pulled up to about eight feet from Clink and his men and proceeded to look them over with a mixture of curiosity and dread. The strangers were dressed as ordinary mountain men and had a manner that seemed to find the encounter amusing. However, beneath the leering was menace.

Clink spoke first. He had broken, stained teeth, a week-old brown beard, and skin darkened by sun and ground-in dust and dirt. Cohen had the fleeting thought of wondering what the man's breath smelled like.

"Well, Mr. Lee. Fancy meeting you here," Clink said, finding his own words amusing.

Nimrod stared at him. "Where's Rake Face? You still ride with him?"

Clink frowned. "He don't like that name.... Ain't seen him in nine-ten months."

"What's your business?" Nimrod asked abruptly.

Clink's brown teeth bared in a mocking grin. "Ah, I knowed you was a smart man. You guessed we didn't just want the time of day or a cup of water." Clink laughed and looked back at his men for appreciation.

"Get on with it," Nimrod said flatly.

Clink's grin vanished. "We want your guns, your money, and your horses. Give us those, and then we'll return the guns so you can be on your way. A fair exchange: we get what we want, and you get peace of mind."

Aaron moved his horse closer to Nimrod. "What right do you have—"

Clink's voice turned mean. "We take the fucking right, sodbuster."

"We have your word you'll let us go?" Cohen asked.

Clink wasn't prepared for such a naive request. "Uh, uh, sure, absolutely. My word of honor." He seemed to be swallowing a laugh.

"And if we say no?" Penney asked.

Clink's horse became restless, so he took a moment to quiet it. Then, his look scanned all four men to drive his point home. "We got buffalo rifles. I got a Lancaster, bored to sixty-eight caliber. We can lay back and pick off your livestock just for target practice. Then we can start on you. We wouldn't shoot the women, you can bet." He chuckled at his own words. Then his humor vanished. "But if you—" Clink kept eyeing Nimrod's rifle lying across his saddle and pointed in the general direction of Clink. In irritation, he demanded, "Say, Lee, we're under a white flag. Can't you do something else with that rifle?"

Nimrod stared at him. "I'm fixin' to."

Nimrod cocked the rifle as Clink's eyes widened, and he knew he was about to die. Nimrod pulled the trigger and blew Clink from the saddle, the heavy slug hitting like a hammer. In the next motion, he pulled his revolver from its pommel holster and shot the second man in the head. The third man got off a shot at Nimrod that missed but killed Aaron's horse. Penney raised his rifle and shot him in the shoulder. The man recoiled at the wound but steadied his horse as it reared, then turned and fled. The second man's horse scattered in fright.

Nimrod holstered his pistol, jumped from the saddle, reloaded his rifle in half a minute, lowered to a knee, and took aim at the man who was by then about one hundred yards distant. His calculation for wind and distance was instant and accurate. He fired. The man fell with the dead-weight collapse of death. Nimrod again pulled the pistol and examined the fallen men. He walked toward Clink, who was struggling to one elbow. He stared at Nimrod, his face filled with fear, but also resignation. Nimrod pulled the hammer back, extended his arm, and with no hesitation shot him in the head.

Penney was watching this, but his thoughts were mired in self-disgust. "I just winged the son of a bitch. Can you believe it? That's embarrassing."

Cohen let his reins drop in shock. His lips moved in disbelieving outrage. "Murder! You killed in cold blood. They were under a white flag. They hadn't a chance. And the wounded man, he was no threat. Whatever—"

Nimrod went off. He clenched his fist and pointed an accusing finger at Cohen. "Murder? MURDER? What the hell you think was in store for you, Malachi? What was you going to do, take a damned drygulcher into your wagon and nurse him back to health? You think this is Philadelphia? He'd turn around and kill you like a rabbit." Nimrod nudged Clink with his foot. "Clink here was a real Sunday school teacher. While back, he raped and gutted an Osage woman just out collecting sticks."

Penney ignored the outburst, shaking his head in disbelief and disgust. "Can you believe it? I had the bastard centered. I've hit a running rabbit with this rifle at a hundred feet."

"Running?" Aaron asked, impressed.

Penney shrugged. "Well, he weren't sitting still."

Aaron had mounted Clink's horse, and after settling it down, shouted, "I'll chase down that other horse."

Nimrod gained a grip on his anger and grabbed Aaron's horse's bridle. "No. I saw sign up ahead. Pawnee be my guess. They'll get the horses. You don't want to be got, too."

Penney also reacted and directed Aaron to "Grab their guns and boots. Anything in their pockets is yours."

Nimrod prepared to ride away, but Cohen shouted, "How about burial? We can't leave them out here."

Nimrod reined in, and said, "It'll save the wolves the trouble of digging them up." But then, in exasperation, he added, "But if you want to bury them, Malachi, we got plenty of shovels. You go right the hell ahead."

The others returned to the train, leaving just Nimrod and Penney staring into the low hills from where Clink had come.

Penney said, "I near dropped my teeth. In a month of Sundays, I never'd thought you had *that* in you."

Nimrod was still agitated. "Neither did Clink, and you see the mistake he made."

Atop a rise in the plain, hidden by high brush, Rake Face watched everything. Without expression, he collapsed his telescope and rode away.

Later, as night fell, and the rest of the folks meandered off to their tents and wagons, Nimrod was looking desolate and sitting by himself on a log next to a banked fire. Andrew walked by on his way to retire when he noticed Nimrod and walked over. "I heard what happened. You all right?"

"Just watching my thoughts roll around in the dirt."

Andrew sat next to him. "I'm a good listener," he said.

"You can't understand," Nimrod said with a sigh.

"Try me."

Nimrod stared straight into the eyes of the soft-spoken greenhorn. "I killed three men today."

Andrew returned the stare as he thought of something to say but came up empty. He got up to leave, but stopped and patted Nimrod on the shoulder. "You're right. I can't. Sorry." He left Nimrod, staring into the fire.

CHAPTER FOURTEEN

O n a beautiful late spring morning, people readied to again
start west, a direction that stretched beyond sight above
a blanket of waving grass. The dew was fresh and the sun
was making even reluctant wives feel exuberant about being here.

Nimrod was tightening Bub's cinch, preparing to start his scout
for the day, when the mule decided to act up by tossing his head and
knocking Nimrod's hat off. Billy, leading an ox, approached from
behind.

Nimrod swatted the mule with his hat. "Don't you fight me, you
flop-eared son of a bitch!"

"Why're mules so cussed ornery, Mr. Lee?"

Nimrod replaced his hat and turned around, surprised to see
Billy. "You didn't hear them words, Trooper." He gave Bub a loving
pat. "He can be a bit too willful. I guess Bub's just afraid someone
will mistake him for a horse if he acts too polite."

Billy patted the ox he was leading. "Ox are nicer."

Nimrod smiled and patted the animal, too. He recognized Billy
as a sad boy who because of his handicap was teased because he
couldn't keep up with the other boys. He was left with the sadness
of the outsider. The boy felt betrayed by fate, was maybe resentful of
his father for dying too soon, and was mistreated by his stepfather.
Nimrod tousled the boy's hair. "Animals be like people: they can
be nice and they can be bad, all on the same day. But they always
end up being true to their nature. Take your ox here: If'n an ox
was a man, he'd be a helpful neighbor, pay his taxes, keep shoes on
his youngins' feet, and not get drunk on his wife. He's also sneaky
smart. He don't waste his time on cows—"

"Why's that?"

"We cut their balls off so they don't care."

"Yes, sir, I know about that," Billy said in his most grown-up manner.

"It gets complicated," Nimrod said, eager to move on. "Ox are also smart. People who say, 'Dumb as an ox,' are too stupid to know that. What an ox is, he's a steer that's gone to school."

He patted Bub's head. "But the mule now, he'd be like one of them army fellers. Like as not, he'd get in fights, get drunk, and land in jail. But treat him fair, and when the time comes, he'll do his duty."

Billy eyed Nimrod's rifle. "Can I hold your rifle gun?"

Nimrod reached for the gun, made sure the percussion cap was off, and handed it to Billy. "Handle it careful. Don't point it at nobody. Some would take offense."

"Yes, sir...Wow! This is a real Hawken. This must be the best gun in the whole world."

Nimrod laughed. "The best gun in the whole world is the one that hits what it's shooting at, which comes back to the man what's aiming it."

Billy took an imaginary shot at the horizon and then returned the heavy gun to Nimrod. "The other boys say your pistol will kill a whole war party."

Nimrod removed the sidearm. "This here is a revolving pistol made by a feller back east name of Samuel Colt. Not many around. This cost me a good scattergun. Now, I got to go buy another one."

Hannah walked up with Rachel at her side. Her eyes avoided Nimrod. "Billy, Mr. Spencer is looking for you."

Billy made a face and walked away, kicking dirt clods to show his displeasure. Nimrod watched him go. He was nervous about being alone with this fiery woman, but he turned and touched his hat brim. "How-do, Miz Spencer."

Hannah's smile was friendlier than he expected. "Hello to you."

Relieved, Nimrod leaned down to Rachel. "How are you this fine morning, missy?"

Rachel shrank back without responding.

Hannah patted her daughter on the shoulder. "Run along and scrub the pots, dear." She watched as Rachel walked back to the wagon, then she turned back to Nimrod. "I apologize for her.

Sometimes, the change from girl to woman sort of tangles our feelings."

Nimrod nodded as though he understood. "I've heard that."

Hannah's voice lowered in sincerity. "Nimrod, I owe you an apology. I was rude to you at the dance."

"No, ma'am. I spoke out of turn. Polite-talking to ladies ain't what you learn up in those hills." He cast a fleeting glance at the skyline. "Not many drawing rooms where you trap beaver." He laughed a little, then stopped when he saw her straight face.

Relieved at having crossed that barrier, Hannah shrugged her shoulders. "Yours was but a small slip of the tongue."

Nimrod, too, was eager to move on. "Earlier, I voiced some low opinions to your husband about driving horses on this trail. I hope he took no offense."

"Don't concern yourself. Sometimes he cares more for horses than people. She paused. "He knows more about them, too."

They fell in step and ambled towards the wagons, both staring at their feet. "That's a beautiful palomino he rides, what with the pink ribbon and all."

Hannah's chuckle was scornful. It did not go unnoticed. She said, "He claimed some man gave it to him, but I think he just believes it makes him look dashing."

"Well, a man can be pardoned for wanting to strut a bit," Nimrod said.

Hannah's wagon was off to the right, and she saw Rachel scrubbing the pots and her husband closely watching her. She turned to Nimrod. "Marriages aren't like you read in those flowery novel books. Sometimes a woman has to do for her children. A widow's lot is not an easy one."

Nimrod nodded. "My maw was a wida-woman."

Hannah sensed she had said too much. She looked over at her husband, and said defensively. "Mr. Spencer and I are quite happy."

Nimrod touched his hat brim. "Yes, ma'am."

Nimrod watched Hannah from behind as she walked back to her family. He noticed Ed Spencer glaring at him and averted his gaze.

The next morning, one of the company, Leebert Cooley, approached Penney, and said, with a touch of shame in his voice and on his face, "Captain, I'd like a private word, if you please."

Penney took one look at Cooley's uneasy expression, and thought—Oh-oh. "Yes, sir. What can I do for you?"

Cooley hemmed and hawed for a moment, "Well, Captain, we respect your leadership, and all—"

"I'm figuring you're about to pull out. Am I right?"

Cooley was relieved that Penney saved the need for a drawn-out explanation. "Well, Captain, here's the situation: Last evening, I saw my rear axle had a crack in it. I have a spare, but I figured, one more break—this is rough country—another such break, and my whole family will be stuck out in the middle of nowhere; up shit creek without a paddle, if you'll pardon the expression. So, the missus and I talked it over. This trip is taking a bit more than we figured, what with the killing, and all. We're set in our thinking to turn around whilst we still got four wheels and our scalps. She was strong in her opinion, my missus was."

"How about putting a bolt through the crack in the axle?"

"You're a farmer, same as me, Captain. It just don't work that way. No patch is as strong as the original." He paused and shifted his feet. "It ain't gonna be easy, showing up back in Big Mound Township after all my big talk about California and all. But we men gotta take care of family first."

Penney rubbed his hands. "Well, Leebert, my friend, it's clear your mind is set. I respect you and your decision. You have to do what's right for you and yours, but you'll be out there on the prairie alone for a far piece. Have you thought about that?"

Cooley looked away. "The Millards and the Osbornes are going, too."

Penney blinked in surprise. "I didn't know."

Nimrod and several of the men were standing at the bank of a rushing creek that fed into the Platte. It had to be crossed for them to continue west. Most times, it was a placid stream, but runoff water from a recent cloudburst had coursed into it from miles around, turning trickling into treacherous. It was about ten yards wide, but

Nimrod knew from experience that narrow streams are the deadliest because of the funnel effect in which water is forced into a tighter channel which makes the flow faster and deeper.

Earlier, Nimrod had guided Bub across it and found where the wagons could cross so long as they kept to a gravel ford upstream from the Platte. But he also knew that rising water could make any crossing impossible until the water receded, costing precious days. They needed to move fast. "I scouted this creek," Nimrod told the men. "It's fast, but it's fordable, even with high water. You might get your peckers wet. Pay a mind where you step. There are some deep holes. You can't trust it, so stay in the ford."

Aaron said, "Well, I'm game to go," and headed for his wagon as others followed.

As the wagons edged across, Andrew was wading through the creek alongside his oxen when he stepped into a hole in stronger current. With a choking cry and flailing arms, he was swept away from his wagon and into the current.

Johnny was adjusting the load in Meister's wagon on the near bank a short way downstream when he heard the shrieks of the bystanders who were witnessing Andrew's plight. Turning toward the water, he saw Andrew sweeping toward him, rolling over and over in the fast water, gasping and struggling, held in its grasp and at its mercy. Johnny jumped into the water, grabbing the end of a tree limb extending over the bank as he hit, and wrapping his arm around it. He reached out and grabbed Andrew's collar as he swept by. Holding onto Andrew with one hand and the limb with the other, Johnny cried out for help from the crowd rushing toward them. His arms shook with the strain of holding both Andrew and the limb as the rushing water tried to tear him from both.

One man took a rope and threw one end into the water, hoping it would float close enough for Johnny to reach it. On the third try, he was able to release the limb and grab the rope. Several men heaved on the other end, and both men were pulled to the bank, choking and coughing.

The entire company crowded around and cheered. It was a rebirth, as though Johnnythree the slave was a spectral figure on the edges of their awareness. This one, this Johnny, was a man. They clapped Johnny on the back as he rose exhausted from the muddy river's edge. Andrew was shaken and in shock but rose and embraced Johnny. "God bless you. You saved my life." Johnny smiled, not knowing how to respond to praise from a white man. A man who made no secret of his pro-slavery views stood next to them, and shouted, "Three cheers for Johnny, folks." Thus. His slave name was retired for all to hear. The crowd agreed: "Hip, hip, hurrah! Hip, hip, hurrah! Hip, hip, hurrah!"

Johnny grinned as he basked in the praise until he looked past the crowd and into the glaring eyes of Meister. Johnny looked away, but the smile had vanished from his face.

As the group broke up, Preacher approached Nimrod and leaned toward his face. "Did you see the Sodomite put his arms around the colored boy? I warned all of you."

Nimrod backed away from Preacher's stale breath, and said, "A man saved from drowning don't have nothing on his mind but spitting out enough water to say, "thank you."

Nimrod was walking toward Bub as he prepared the morning scout for the best route when Penney stopped him. "The committee wants to have a meeting. You best hear this." Without asking why, Nimrod followed him. Penney muttered as he walked along. "I swear, the things a man has to tend to..."

The two approached a small group waiting on the edge of camp. It was the committee along with Ed Spencer. The men nodded to Nimrod with blank faces. The mood was tense.

Penney said, "Nimrod, Spencer here is accusing you of putting his son amongst ungodly men, them two fellers with the strange ways, Andrew Banks and Martin Carter. He thinks they may lead him astray, what with driving their oxen." Penney seemed embarrassed by his words.

"Step-son," Nimrod corrected.

Preacher cleared his throat to intensify Penney's mildness. "Sodomites, the Bible calls them. We should cast them out," he said, his voice rising in pitch. "Mark my words. The lord will not bless this company unless we purify ourselves."

Nimrod said, "I 'spect the Lord will not bless us if'n we fight amongst ourselves about who he favors. We could be so busy bickering over such as this we could get to the mountains just in time to have a snowball fight."

Masterson said, "Captain, Nimrod, did you gentlemen know the type men they were before this?"

Penney shook his head. "I'd had no experience with such as that."

Nimrod said, "Passing judgment on members of this company ain't my role. But to answer your question, I didn't know for certain, but I figured they was most likely fancy boys. Likely, I say, because I didn't care enough to peek under their canvas at night."

Masterson nodded toward Preacher. "On the trail, those two're about as useful as a four-card straight."

Penney scoffed. "We ain't what you'd call royal flushes."

Cohen said, "In Prussia, great effort was made to cause hatred between people who were different. I don't want to see such a sickness among us. Let the men be."

Spencer happened to be standing toward the back. Though not a committee member, he blurted an angry rejoinder to Cohen. "That's foreigner bullshit!"

Cohen smiled faintly. "Thank you for making my point."

Penney turned to Spencer. "Thank you for coming, Mr. Spencer. We won't be keeping you."

Spencer had started to walk away when Masterson said, "A mother complained to me, said your big dog was growling at her children. We'd be obliged if you kept your dog close."

Spencer glared, but said nothing.

Nimrod returned to the issue of the two gay men and tried to reason it out with common sense. "Men such as them are in every group of people, near as I can tell."

"That's true," Cohen said, nodding.

"Indians call them women-men, and they're honored as medicine-makers and peacemakers. And I ain't never heard of an Indian buck getting that way for being decent to them," Nimrod said.

"What are we going to do?" Preacher challenged Penney.

The older man shook his head. "This goes beyond my bag of

tricks. But let me ask you: Why do them boys bother you so much? Seems to me, fretting about them ain't getting us one mile closer to the end of this foolish undertaking."

The men were at an impasse, so Nimrod moved in. "How about we get so busy trying to reach California we don't have time for such as this?"

Spencer also sensed his accusation was having no effect, so he stepped forward. "I'm also telling you, Lee, in front of this committee: Stay away from my family." Everyone knew he meant Hannah.

Nimrod's eyes turned hard. "Tread lightly, sir."

Penney turned to Cohen and said in a low voice, "Spencer best not push. He'd last as long with Lee as a pint of whiskey in a four-handed poker game." Penney then decided it had gone far enough. He laughed and held up his hands. "Gentlemen, gentlemen: I've got one more question— Who just farted?"

The men peered at each other. Cohen said, "With beans for most every meal, maybe everybody."

Laughter put a top on the meeting, and they started to leave. However, Preacher stopped Nimrod with a hand on his arm and concern on his face. "I'm also in prayer over our traveling on the Lord's Day. It should be a day of rest."

Nimrod thought about it, then said, "That's the captain's call, Preacher. However, until the Lord arranges camps with good grass and clean water on the seventh day, I'm going to urge us to keep moving. If'n God wants us to see California, he'll appreciate my good sense. Any other day of the week seems good for worship, seeing as how God made them all."

Leaving the meeting, Nimrod was in a dark mood and looking for something distracting. He noticed Simon Tester lounging with his back against his wagon wheel reading a small book. Nimrod had seen him around the train from time to time. He always seemed to be agitating about something or other—When to quit for the day, the choice of a camp site, having too much guard duty, or loud noise coming from the Maude Horner wagon. He often was seen in the company of Zack who had become his follower.

"Howdy, Mr. Tester," Nimrod said. "Good book?"

Tester looked up from the page. "A new one just printed. Picked it up in Cincinnati. *The Emigrants' Guide to Oregon and California.* Fellow named Lansford W. Hastings. He's from Ohio, same as me."

"That so? What advice does he give?"

Tester reverted to his waspish self. "How would I know? I'm just now reading it."

"Enjoy the evening, sir." Nimrod walked away. He wasn't in a mood for this surly man. Even so, his day was not finished with nastiness.

Walking through the middle of the camp, he overheard Zack Monroe speak to Narcissa Lopez in a loud, insulting voice. "Pretty lady like you coulda had a white man, stead of a greaser."

Narcissa broke into tears which was noticed by her husband, Ignacio, from where he was standing not far away. He hurried over to his wife and asked what had happened. When she told him, he turned and faced Zack who was standing nearby, grinning.

Ignacio glared. "You insulted my wife, blackguard."

Zack closed his fist and held it up for all to admire. He laughed and looked around for an audience. "Step right over here and I'll jump on you like a chicken on a cricket."

Ignacio scoffed. "I am Castilian Spanish. I do not brawl with a poltroon like a barroom drunk. I'll fight you as a gentleman." He paused to get Zack's full attention. "I challenge you."

Zack stared, perplexed. "What's a poltroon?"

"A coward," Lopez said with his lips curled in disgust. "You need to learn English." Lopez pressed home his challenge. "Pistols at twenty paces. Choose your second."

"What? What the hell you talking about?"

"I intend to kill you in a fair fight."

Nimrod was finding this delightful. "I seen him shoot, Zack," he lied in a solemn voice and shook his head at the thought of it. "It'd be better if you had, too."

By this time, a small crowd had gathered and waited, hoping Zack would get his come-uppance.

Zack looked around at the blank faces staring back at him. Looking for a way out, he muttered, "Oh, you ain't worth it," and walked away.

The crowd broke up; blank faces bloomed into grins.

"Look what I found!" Billy shouted as he walked back to camp. He had gone out to drive the livestock in for yoking, but instead he was leading what looked to be a big pony, except it had a watermelon head topped by big, erect ears. It was white with large golden-brown spots on its body, as though flicked on by a paint brush.

Billy led the animal to the center and was quickly surrounded by curious pioneers. Masterson laughed, and said, "What Billy brought home, folks, is an *Equus asinus.*" He answered questioning looks by adding, "A donkey, a burro. You can even call it an ass." A few people frowned at a word they thought inappropriate around children. Donkeys were rare in eastern America because they were mainly used in desert environments. Although all had heard of a donkey, most had never seen one.

One of the pioneers, a farmer from Louisiana, stepped forward and patted the animal which stood silently with a bored demeanor. "I had me a couple of these old boys on my farm on the lower Mississippi. What he got here is a standard size Jack; that means about four-feet at the withers, and five-hundred pounds." He examined the donkey more closely. "This donkey is what you call a paint, white with color splotches. They call it buckskin." He waited for the murmurs to die down, then said, "Interesting fellers, these. They're hard working, loyal, and don't cause any trouble— well, sometimes." He paused. "They hate dogs, and they're spiteful toward folks that don't treat them right. They got sharp hooves you don't want to have aimed at you. If they bite you, you'd prefer an alligator."

Nimrod said, "How 'bout it, Trooper? You thought of a name?"

Cohen said, "In the Bible, they're called asses. Some folks around here might not appreciate that. The Hebrew name for a male donkey is "Hamor." Is that a fit name?"

"Ham-o?" Billy asked.

Cohen smiled. "Close enough."

"That's who he'll be." Billy said the name solemnly. "Hambo."

"You got finder's rights, boy. He's all yours," Penney said.

"Gee, golly," Billy said, "I'll love him just like his mama did."

At that, Spencer walked up. At his heel was the dog Brutus. Spencer said, "Just a minute, here, I'm the boy's father. I demand a say in this." He looked around as though his rights had been trod upon. "We don't need another animal lurking around our wagon, eating food meant for valuable horses. I'm saying we got no room for such a worthless beast as that."

The farmer who first spoke, looked directly at Spencer, and said, "That ain't even close to the truth, what you said about being worthless. This donkey— Hambo, you call him?" Billy nodded, and the man continued, "Old Hambo ain't like a horse. He don't run away. He stays and fights. Hambo here will guard your herd at night. Any prairie wolf come around, this donkey will stomp and bite it to death, or send it home yelping. Donkeys hate dogs, the why of it, nobody can figger."

"We ain't seen any prairie wolves," a young bystander said.

The farmer laughed lightly. "Well, son, critters, they've seen you. What they'll do is sneak in among the cattle and hamstring one. They know it ain't going anywhere when the train moves on."

"What about wolves?"

The farmer said wolves are far fewer, and hunt in packs. They also shy away from herds where humans are around.

"One other thing," the farmer said. "You need to know this is a desert critter. He won't grow a deeper coat for the cold like a horse. If you mean to take him into mountain winter weather, he won't do well. No, sir, he won't do well. It'll be like you going for a winter walk bare chested."

At that moment, Brutus decided to make a move. He barked and advanced on the donkey growling. "Hambo bared his teeth, and uttered a bray that frightened everyone close by, especially Brutus, because the big dog yelped and ran under the nearest wagon.

A watching woman laughed. "That cur just decided he wanted to live to chase another rabbit."

Penney crossed his arms. "Well, I guess that cooks it. The donkey's going to be given a job, and speaking for the committee, which I'm sure they'll back me up, young Billy here is given the job of taking care of this valuable resource." He looked at Spencer, "I repeat— valuable resource."

Spencer started to protest, but Hambo must have picked up a hateful vibe, because he blared a bray directly at Spencer who quickly backtracked with Brutus at his heels.

Hambo might have been safe, but when Billy returned, Spencer grabbed him by the arm and took him out of sight behind the wagon. With Hannah not present, Spencer removed his belt, and said between his teeth, "I'll teach you to disobey me." He folded the belt and began to whip Billy around the legs and thighs without letting go of his arm. Billy refused to cry despite the repeated blows of the wide leather belt. He gritted his teeth and scrunched up his face, but he wouldn't give in, which infuriated Spencer all the more. When others happened to walk about nearby, Spencer let go of Billy who ran away, and went to his donkey and wrapped his arms about the big neck.

CHAPTER FIFTEEN

On a mild June day, Nimrod, Penney, and others were standing dismounted on the riverbank, holding their reins and feeling quite contented when Aaron and Gertie approached. Before them was the Platte being its shallow, muddy self, and pointing the way toward California in its meandering, listless way. The pioneers knew the south bank of the river was the highway to follow for hundreds of miles crossed what would become Nebraska.

Penney stared at the water. "I'm going to close my eyes when I drink this brown stuff."

"You don't seem to have no trouble with whiskey," Nimrod teased.

Gertie pointed to mounds of dirt, dug-up holes, and discarded crosses strewn along the bank. "Are those graves?" she asked.

Nimrod stared at the mounds and didn't look at Gertie. "Once were. Wolves ain't respectful. I shoveled some cover-up dirt this morning."

"What happened to those people?" Aaron asked.

"Indians, but unlikely. They don't show no signs of that," Nimrod said. "Cholera or smallpox, I'm inclined to think. No other disease kills in bunches. The onliest way to steer clear of sickness out here is to pray, and folks have seen mixed results with that."

Ruth Cohen walked up, looked, and put her hand to her mouth. "Oh, my God."

Nimrod nodded. "That's a start, ma'am."

The mild June weather continued for several days as the wagon train made good progress along the flat, straight riverbank. Most months, the Platte was not a candidate for a painter's landscape. However, during migration time, it became a stopover for some of the most entrancing birds of North America. The long river was a natural waystation in the middle of a vast, semi-arid plain.

The wagon train was at the end of the spring migration for birds heading north, but many thousands could still be seen along the weedy banks to the considerable discomfort of bugs, small snakes, fish, and seeds. Cranes, geese, mallards, and eagles shared the uninviting river with countless of their smaller avian fellows. The birds were happy to be there, and said so with honks, squawks, and tweets. The men were also happy, as they whooped with delight in shooting down numerous geese, ducks, and an eagle and crane, unfortunately. Even the worst shot among them became a sharpshooter.

The pioneers, accustomed to the lush greenery of back east, may for a moment have forgotten that the landscape they occupied was monotonous and dreary. However, after the birds flew away, they returned to reality.

Hannah was walking by Nimrod during the noon break when she stopped and pointed out into the prairie. "That must be a lost dog I see out there," she said.

Nimrod followed her point and saw a medium-size canine trotting along. It had the pointed ears, the long snout, and the bushy tail of a wolf. He chuckled. "That ain't no dog, Hannah, and he sure ain't lost. That's a prairie wolf. You don't hear much about them back east."

"I didn't know wolves could be so small."

"Well, that old boy ain't an actual wolf, but he's enough of a shirt-tail relative to get invited to wolf family reunions. Truth is, he's 'bout as thieving as a politician. You ain't careful, he'll eat your chickens and sell you the feathers. Mexicans call him a coyote." He used the Spanish pronunciation, "ko-YO-tay."

"What does that stand for in English, coyote?"

The question stumped him. "Just coyote, far as I know."

Hannah continued walking, but with a gratified smile. Nimrod had called her Hannah.

Many of the company grew irritated at Meister as he continued to abuse Johnny. Cohen grumbled to the other committeemen, "Something needs to be done about that Meister fellow."

Nimrod said, "He's as popular as a wet dog at a church social."

Penney sighed. "He might as well have the fellow back in slavery."

Jackman said, "Well, he has a legal servitude contract, so not much can be done. If we were to interfere, he could sue us when we get to California, although I don't know Mexican law on that. Or, if California becomes part of the U.S., like they're saying, he could sue everyone having a part of breaking that contract."

Masterson shrugged. "Let him sue."

Jackman grunted. "If you've ever been sued for a lot of money, you wouldn't say that. A lawsuit can grind your guts."

Preacher said, "I consider it a sin to break a lawful contract."

Cohen grimaced, and said, "Preacher!" He let his voice trail off with a slight what's-the-use shrug.

Masterson shook his head in disgust. "Meister can go to blazes. Let's just declare the young man free and be done with it."

Jackman looked at Masterson thoughtfully. "You must remember, we've got members of this train from the south. We could be inviting discord in our company if we deny Meister his rights. Is our purpose to get to California, or to fight the wrongs of the world?"

No one had an answer for Jackman, so the subject withered away in indecision.

Meister's abusive ways faded from attention as the heat and tedium acted as a drug on the pioneers, and the animals plodded on. But even the oxen slowed as the heat and burdens sapped strength from their hulking bodies.

Nimrod walked around the camp observing. As time passed, the human stresses became more irritating, and the men became angrier. What might be laughed at as a joke back home could become an insult in a tense situation. Oaths that would be embarrassing back home in the Victorian primness of their communities rolled off their tongues without a second thought. The kids overheard, and as they always do, began to mimic their fathers' oaths. However, that often ended with a painful reminder that bad words like bad habits were the exclusive domain of grownups.

Penney and Cohen joined Nimrod and they silently watched women prepare dinner over an open fire as the kids worked off stored-up energy.

As usual, straggling into camp about thirty minutes later was the Spencer horse-drawn wagon. A half-hour behind Spencer was Henry Griswold alongside his half-wagon, plodding along with a single yoke of oxen and a spare animal tied to the back.

Jackman pointed to Griswold struggling in the distance. "I do declare, that old man's having trouble keeping up with his team. Never knew a man who had to hurry to keep up with an ox. An old-timer such as Griswold needs to be on a horse."

Turning away from the cooking fire, Penney said, "A horse won't help him. A man's got to walk to work oxen. I told him, I said he should think on hiring a boy as a drover, then he could ride. He said he didn't have money to pay a boy fair all the way to California. Said he didn't set out on this trip to be nurse-maided."

"A strange duck, he's got to be. I ain't had the chance to visit with him since he joined up late," Nimrod said.

"We've all been too busy to pay much attention," Penney said. "I 'spect he's a lonely man. If a buzzard happened by and saw Griswold hobbling along, he'd pull up a chair and wait."

"It don't give comfort to a body who knows what's in store for Griswold out on these plains," Nimrod said. Penney nodded sadly.

Nimrod swung up into Bub's saddle. "Shadrach, can I have the loan of that bottle of who-hit-John you keep hidden?"

Penney walked a few yards to his wagon, reached in and pulled out a bottle. "If it comes back half-filled with creek water, I'll damn well know it."

Nimrod grinned. "You'd live longer drinking creek water."

He rode back until he came to Griswold, then dismounted and offered the bottle to the old man. "Need a little propping up, sir?" He introduced himself. "I beg your pardon for not giving you the courtesy of a how-do afore now."

"You're a busy man, Mr. Lee. I'm pleased not to have required your attention."

Griswold was a short man who looked on the doorstep of seventy. He had an uncombed gray thatch, a tangled beard, dirty clothing, and a wince on his face caused by pain from every step. The creases on his face were deep, and his fingers were gnarled with arthritis. He walked with a bow-legged, crabbed motion forced on him by knees that demanded sitting. He sighed and sat down on a rock, and smiled his thanks. He started to take a swig, but then went to his wagon and took out a cup and poured some and drank. "I didn't know a guide could also read minds."

He handed the bottle back to Nimrod who took it and wondered why Griswold felt the need to reach for a cup. Such fastidiousness was unusual on the trail.

Nimrod was drawn to something in the old man's face, the open, honest way he looked at a person. He sensed Griswold was a man with insights into human nature; not an everyday quality so far from civilization. Nimrod said, "Mind if I walk a spell with you?

"I'd welcome the company." Griswold wearily pushed against his knees to stand, and commanded his oxen forward with Nimrod at his side leading Bub. The two men set off in the direction of the wagons up ahead as the iron wheels scraped along on the graveled ground.

Nimrod's words were blunt but were softened by concern. "No offense, sir, but I'm not a man to dance around a subject—You can't keep this up. I don't even understand why you're out here."

Griswold kept moving. "A drover costs money, and riding in a wagon adds weight."

Nimrod stopped and looked at the horizon. "No, I mean, why you're out here—out here." He swept his arm over the vista. "You shouldn't be on this trail at all. I reckon you know my words are meant Christian."

Griswold also stopped walking, and his eyes met Nimrod's. "I know your intentions are good, and I'm obliged. Here's the cold truth: I've got no other place to go. My folks are all dead. My wife died of a tumor a year ago, a female thing. My son cut his leg with a scythe cutting weeds. Gangrene set in. I don't even like to think about that. My daughter died an infant, a beautiful little girl with a gurgling laugh. I'm not sure what sickness he had. My money disappeared when my bank went broke. My choice was to go west or to the poorhouse, so I took my last dollars and bought this rig. I'm poor as Job's turkey."

"Well, sir, you got sand in your gizzard, ain't no doubt there. But there's a lot easier ways to get by," Nimrod said.

"Not back in Springfield, not for me."

"Springfield?"

"Illinois; good farm country. I know two well-off farmers, named Donner, George and Jacob. George lived just down the road. They both have a bad case of California itch. They're all het up about making the trip. Said the Mexicans would give a good farmer all the land he wanted if he would work it. I told them no one knows what the Mexicans might do.

"They wouldn't listen. Rich as they are, both George and Jacob are used to having folks listen to *them*. They said they read that in California it never snows, and it rains just when you need it, and a man can harvest two crops a year with irrigation." Griswold walked over on stiff legs and adjusted the yoke on an ox. "I listened to those men describe their plans, I looked out the window at the snow and ice—it was January. Then I listened to their dreams and saw the glint in their eyes, and I said to myself, 'Old man, what you need before you die is a dream of your own and some sunshine in January.' So, with more gumption than common sense, here I am."

"What happened to those Donner men?"

"They're getting their affairs in order to travel next year. I hope to be at Sutter's Fort to welcome them." His voice dropped. "Lately, I don't know…"

Griswold started walking again. He soon winced at his bad knees and sat heavily on a rock. "Ten years ago, I could've danced this route, but no more, as you can see. I would like my final days to be spent trying to do something. I want to see California. I didn't figure on my knees giving out. They feel like I've got glass between the bones."

"We can maybe get you some kind of help."

Griswold again stood up and prepared to continue. "Every person in this train already has a purpose. That'd just cause resentment. It'd be charity, just like the poorhouse back home. If that's what I wanted, I wouldn't have to come this far."

Nimrod found the old man fascinating, but he had a gnawing fear in his mind he might end up like Henry Griswold someday. "You sound like an educated man. What was your work, if I don't offend?"

Griswold chuckled. "Educated? Ah, yes. Not very useful out here. I spent my life in a dim room with a narrow window with students who didn't want to be there, either. California has no narrow windows, I hope." With mock sincerity, Griswold asked Nimrod, "Would you care to join me in conjugating some Latin verbs?" He laughed and shook his head at the idiocy of Latin on the plains. "No? Well, someday, someone might find a useful purpose for it. None of the boys I taught did." Nimrod blinked and stared at him. Griswold smiled, and said, "Well, then, you can see I have no usefulness to offer this company."

Nimrod felt he could trust the old man. "Education's a thing I've always favored, but from a distance, I'm afeared to say. I ain't never had a chance to get close to it. Where I come from, lack of education was a club used to keep you in your place."

"You have a good head on your shoulders. It's easy to tell that."

Nimrod shook his head modestly, though he was flattered. "Ahh, I can read and write enough to get by; I'm good at ciphering, really good. I'm weak knowing about the world. I don't know anything about any place I ain't been to or heard about. When I hear educated people use highfalutin' words like you, and Masterson, and Cohen, I feel pretty low about myself. I'd like to use words the way smart people write them."

Griswold's face became a kind smile. "You belabor yourself. You make everyday sense, which is what words are supposed to help you have. A lot of men with fancy diplomas on their walls can't make sense."

Nimrod looked at the ground. "I had me five years of schooling, but my sisters just had four. I don't tell people all that."

Griswold reached for the bottle again. "Be thankful for what you have; don't mope about what you don't. The best way to learn words is to listen to those who use them well, and then train yourself to use them the same way." He paused to rub his sore knees, then continued. "If a man out here snickers at how you talk, I'd wager it's because he feels like a worm, because he's frightened of this wilderness, and depends on you to protect him like a parent does a child."

"I sometimes talk right, and other times I fall back on my old ways. It ain't easy to get it right if'n you ain't been schooled the right way."

"Do you worry people might laugh at you?"

Nimrod's eyes narrowed. "That ain't going to happen."

Griswold smiled and nodded. "I don't want to sound like a know-it-all, but, for example, I've heard you say 'if'n' instead of 'if.' That's a simple mistake, but it's easy to fix. If you listen real close to educated people, it's the same as being in school—well, not quite, but close."

Nimrod furrowed his brow. "I thought I said 'if.' I'm sure of it. I'll be more careful."

Griswold smiled. "I'll wager you will."

Nimrod remounted and prepared to ride away. "I wish you the best, sir. I'm at your service."

Hour after hour, day after day, they plodded on. The terrain became increasingly uninviting with gullies that had to be circled around, and hills of sand that had to be struggled over. Some days, they would see a wagon train or two, and then go two weeks without seeing any. The pioneers continuously scanned the landscape for threat and peril, but not certain if they would recognize either, or what they would do if they did. One mortal danger no scan could reveal had the name *Vibrio cholerae*, a bacterium from which emerged a toxin that caused diarrhea, massive dehydration, and vomiting. The bacteria's strike was more lethal than a rattlesnake's. In some cases, victims felt fine at breakfast, but were dead by dinner.

As the land became more flat and dry, the Platte River slowed, causing it to become even more shallow and brown with silt and microbes that the sluggish flow couldn't purify by current.

Summer wore on and clean feeder streams became rare, making use of the Platte for drinking, cooking, and bathing necessary. Slop buckets with human waste were emptied into it, and animals defecated in it as they watered. The water became a launch pad for disease, a comfortable home for a world-wide cholera outbreak, and also typhoid and other forms of dysentery. The three were the hungriest killers on the trail. Lacking knowledge of bacteria, Hannah and other caretakers were mainly helpless before the onslaught.

Rivers provided the routes west, and also water when pioneers were desperate for it. Without those benefits, emigration to the West Coast would have ceased, or slowed to a trickle. But the rivers demanded a toll, and they were paid it.

Nimrod, Masterson, Cohen, and Penney were standing around a small fire finishing morning coffee and watching the daily drama of the train preparing to move out.

Masterson said, "The Bible said there would be trials in our lives, but it could have warned us about these damned mosquitoes." The others laughed except for Preacher. The comment sounded suspiciously close to sacrilegious.

"Count your blessings, gents," Penney said. "He could have made them weigh five pounds."

Cohen said, "He did, a few. One pinned me down before it bit me. We can blame Noah. He could have swatted them before they got in the ark."

Their disrespect was answered by a fresh attack of the irritated mosquito army. The pioneers and mosquitoes shared a need to be near water, which was convenient for the insects.

All day and all night, the people were assaulted by waves of the tiny terrorists. It wasn't enough that they drove the people half-crazy, they brought along their wicked witch, the female anopheles mosquito. The grim lady had killed more humans than any predator in history by infecting her victims with the malaria, or ague, parasite. The pioneers dealt with mosquitoes in the same way as the Neanderthals. They suffered.

The pioneers were also cursed with unappealing hygiene. Hot

water for bathing was a rare luxury. The abrasive soap they used made it easy to put off bathing and laundry for another week, or maybe two.

The climate of the trail they were trudging on day after day made them feel miserable inside and out. The constant and swirling wind dried skin and turned eyes red, The sun and heat drained energy like a spigot. The sweat that poured off them plastered their bodies with dust and mud. Bacteria went to work in sweat and body secretions and hatched malodorous colonies in armpits, groins, and hair.

A short distance away, the men's attention was attracted to a familiar irritating voice as they watched Zack ride up to where Andrew and Martin were preparing their team. Zack began to mimic kisses and sucking sounds to the two. He made ridiculous faces and extended his arms in a fluttering motion and mocked in a high falsetto. "You-hoo, ladies, don't forget to put-on your sun bonnets." He threw back his head and laughed uproariously but stopped in mid-roar when Aaron grabbed his bridle.

"Damn it!" Aaron said, glaring at him. "It's work enough to make this trip without your stupid remarks. Keep this up and I'll haul you before the committee."

Zack was aware nearby heads were turning, so he pulled hard on his reins, forcing the horse up on his rear legs to make a show. "You threatening me?" he shouted. "I'll knock you so far it'll take a bloodhound a week to pick up your smell." He was enjoying his own voice. "I'll slap you naked and sell your clothes." He jerked his bridle and rode away.

Nimrod and the others exchanged glances, each was aware what they were watching would cause trouble down the line, guaranteed. However, there was nothing to be done until it happened.

"Half the company is ailing," Cohen said, changing the subject and shaking his head. "The loosest thing we have in this company are bowels. If you see something suspicious hiding behind a sage brush and fear it's an Indian or wolf, chances are it'll be one of our squatting pioneers."

Hannah tried to treat diarrhea and dysentery, but gastric problems were unfamiliar to her, so all she could do was go to one of her reference books. From that, she prescribed crushed wood charcoal in which she would put a drop or two of essence of peppermint. It didn't do much for the ailments, but it definitely helped the breath smell better.

Penney stopped abruptly when he heard a voice calling him and turned to see the stricken face of Flora Dickens as she hurried up holding a teenage girl's hand. Standing next to her, looking frightened and bewildered, was a boy of about twelve. Flora was thirty-two, or so, but her face at the moment conveyed the dread and weariness of a woman years older.

Penney said, "Good morning, Mrs. Dickens."

"Begging your pardon, sir, but I need your help. My William is terribly sick. Can you come?"

Without a word, the captain followed her. When they reached the Dickens tent, they heard the man moaning inside. Penney pulled the canvas back, and they could see he was in bad shape. The smell of diarrhea was extreme. Dickens' eyes were sunken, and fever coated his face with misery. He lay in a bed of vomit, holding his abdomen and groaning in pain. Penney reflexively held his nose.

He straightened up and turned to Flora. "Ma'am, would you take the children over to my wagon? Mrs. Penney has some fresh biscuits."

As Flora herded her reluctant children away, Masterson and Nimrod came up. Masterson started to enter the tent, but Nimrod took hold of his arm to restrain him, and then talked to Dickens from outside. "William, tell us how you feel."

The man groaned from within. "My stomach hurts bad. I'm burning up. I got the runs real bad."

"Sir, I'm no doctor, but I've seen this before. I think you've got the cholera. I've seen it before. I tell you that so you won't let your loved ones come near."

"Will I die?"

"Some do, some don't," Nimrod said bluntly. "I wish I could give you brighter words. We should know by tomorrow."

Penney said, "I'm sorry for your plight, sir. We can hold the train until tomorrow. You might want Preacher to attend you."

Word spread through the camp causing a fog of despair to settle over it, not just for Dickens, but because they knew cholera could spread through the entire camp, selecting victims as though drawn from a hat. The pioneers didn't know what caused the disease, and they had no idea how to cure it, except by prayer, which all victims tried, but with discouraging results.

Hannah heard about the situation and hurried over. She looked into the tent and saw the filth William was lying in. She hunched over, moved inside, and gathered up the vomit-soaked rags near his head. As she walked out with the rags and headed for the creek to wash them, Nimrod rushed up and knocked the rags out of her hand and kicked them into a nearby ravine.

"What are you doing, sir? How dare you," Hannah protested.

Nimrod walked in a small circle, breathing hard with agitation. "Don't... don't go near that tent! There's death there. You should know better."

She was offended and embarrassed. Her face got red, and she sputtered, "Well, I'll be!" However, she quickly realized he was right, and she was wrong, and backed off. "I was trying to help," she said in a level voice, though still a bit pouty. Then, as a way of apology, "I know little of this disease. I've never seen it close up."

Nimrod was still agitated. "Then help your children not become orphans by staying away from cholera. And wash your hands, fast."

"Who made you the camp doctor?" However, she went to the riverbank and rubbed her hands in the water.

He followed. "Hannah, you know St. Louis medicine, but you don't know much about cholera, I do. I've seen too much of it out here," he said, repentant for his outburst. "I don't know how it gets passed, but it damn sure does."

"Don't speak to me as you did back there." She sputtered in indignation and embarrassment. "I never..." She stomped her foot and stalked away, back to the Dickens tent.

"I'm sorry," he said, lamely, but to her back.

Penney had been watching. He walked up to Nimrod chuckling. "That woman has a fire burning water won't put out."

All through the day and night, the wife and children maintained vigilance at the entrance to the tent. Hannah stayed with them.

Following Hannah's advice, Flora edged inside to give William water and remove the dirty rags on the edge of a stick. She felt guilty at treating her husband like a leper, but she was fearful of catching the disease herself. It wouldn't help her husband to make their children orphans. From inside the tent, the family was tortured by cries of pain as cramps racked Dickens' body.

Cholera is water-borne and not passed by touch from person to person, but no one standing vigilance on William knew that. They only know it would kill you, and didn't worry about exactly how.

Dawn came, and Dickens was dying, and not easily. It started to rain, and Penney and Nimrod joined Hannah and the family standing outside in what was accepted as a death watch. The rain increased, but even so, both men had their hats off. Flora and the children huddled closer. They were all crying.

"Mr. Dickens, your wife and children are here," Hannah said gently.

Nothing but groaning was heard.

"Mr. Dickens?" she repeated.

"Flora...Alice...Tom?" Dickens said in a weak, raspy voice. The family's sobbing intensified. "Are you there?"

"We're all here, William," Flora said.

"I had so many years to say what was in my heart, but I did not. Now, I'm to die, and I have no voice...Please forgive my shortcomings."

"There's nothing to forgive, dear. You've been a good husband and father."

"Penney. Mr. Penney?" Dickens said.

"I'm here, sir."

"Promise me you'll see my wife and children safe in California."

Penney hesitated. "We'll do the best we can."

"Promise me."

"Your family will be helped," Penney said.

Dickens was racked by coughing. "My dear family...I leave you my love."

Flora stopped crying and wrapped her arms around the children. "Take our love with you, dear William."

Silence in the tent. Hannah put her arm around Flora and walked her and the children away from the scene.

Thirty minutes later the rain stopped. Nimrod volunteered to stay behind and attend to the burial. As the wagons disappeared over a rise, he took a rope he had ready for the purpose and threw a loop around the leg of Dickens' body. He dragged it out of the tent and maneuvered it to the edge of a grave dug by the men shortly before. He then set fire to the tent and picked up a shovel. He stood over the grave and looked down at the body, then tumbled it into the grave with his foot. "No disrespect, sir," he said, and then nothing was heard except the scraping of the shovel on the sandy dirt of the prairie next to the killer river.

CHAPTER SIXTEEN

The tabletop prairie began wrinkling into low hills; unchallenging to the gaze, but exhausting to man and beast in the climbing.

Their torments knew no limit. Angry nature came alive and greeted them as the wagons crept along. When the terrain allowed, the wagons spread out parallel to hold down the dust. Taking a rotated turn at the back of the column was a day everyone dreaded and was a duty sullenly accepted.

The few other wagon trains that crossed their path on the trail were sometimes viewed with apprehension, or even hostility. The reason was dust. Although only about twenty-five hundred emigrants were on the trail in 1845, they seemed to show up at unwelcome times. The issue was usually about dust, and who would eat it. The competition to get ahead could generate language the children ought not hear, or even fisticuffs.

Dust could not be escaped. It flew on the wind and swirled like a snowstorm in the dry air and invaded everyone's lungs. It was the leader of a conspiracy of the elements. It kicked up under wheels and into wagons, into water buckets, and into the soups bubbling in Dutch ovens.

Day after day, the wind never wearied. It worked dirt and sand into every crevice of their bodies, into beards, and babies' diapers. Eyes became red and irritated because no amount of blinking could shield the grit. Every bite of fried bacon included the sandy crunch of Platte River grime. The sun gave them no slack from mid-morning until late afternoon and bore down with a blanket of heat. It drained their bodies of the river water they drank, and which soon boiled into sweat and left them with a desperate thirst minutes after the last drink.

Dust drove women half crazy because their job was to keep family lives orderly, clean, and behaving civilly, impossible jobs all. Men walking alongside the oxen vented by stomping, grumbling, and erupting with curses they would not utter back home except in an empty barn.

Not one word of sympathy was said for the oxen. The huge beasts just plodded along pulling their heavy load with tongues out and heads down. Their misery was ignored except when it affected performance. Any slowdown was responded to with a lash or cursing.

Each day was a trial of Old Testament-level despair, like the Babylonian Captivity, something like that. Dust was the devil; sun, wind and heat were his demons.

The wagon train had reached the first major landmark of the trip, where the Platte had become one from the merger of two rivers, the South Platte and the North Platte. The accepted belief said it was the quarter mark to Sutter's Fort, about five hundred miles Both rivers meandered up from the south, springing from the mountain snowmelt of what would become Colorado. It was the North Platte they would follow in a bell-shape loop around eastern Wyoming-to-be.

They first had to cross the South Platte. To the relief of the tired travelers, the bank was low, and the water was slow and shallow. After Nimrod had crossed first, poking yard by yard for quicksand, they crossed without loss.

Scholar Masterson said to a group that the crossing was a blessing from Hecate, the Greek god of travel. His comparison drew blank looks from listeners and a nasty stare from Preacher, always on the lookout for heretics and worshipers of false gods, though they tended mainly to be Catholic saints.

Once across, the train had to ascend the plateau separating the two rivers. The first chore was to climb California Hill. As people looked up the slope, they were not intimidated. However, the oxen would have deferred judgment had they been consulted. It looked gentle until the climb was begun, and then gravity served a wake-up call. It rose two hundred forty feet over a mile and a half. To make the climb, they had to increase oxen teams from three yoke to five yoke on each wagon. Even so, it was a hard day's work for each animal. Spencer's horses, especially, labored and slowed. Penney directed Spencer to the rear of the column to not impede progress. Spencer protested, but he had no choice.

Once every wagon was atop the ridge, it was a drive of eighteen miles before the next test, which was even more challenging. Windlass Hill awaited.

The hill was a descent to the North Platte Valley of three hundred feet at a grade of twenty-five degrees. The men stood on the crest and looked down with discouraged grumbling. The descent resembled what later generations would recognize as a medium-grade ski slope. At the base, they saw Ash Hollow, a verdant, small valley nestled between the bottom of Windlass Hill and the North Platte. They greedily looked down on Ash Hollow with its clean water, green grass, and shade trees. It was a vision of bliss to people who had choked on dust for many days and miles. But first, they had to get down to it.

Various methods had been employed by others to slide the wagons to the bottom. The most common was to restrain a wagon with rope and lock the wheels with rods through the spokes, then gradually feed the rope out and let it slide down the hill, all the time hoping to prevent a run-away. The main problem was the pressure of the ton-plus wagon would sometimes break the wooden spokes, and the sliding over rough ground often damaged the wagon.

Penney walked to the front and looked down, then around at the men. "Gents, I been thinking on how to beat this damned grade. As I opine, we don't want to block wheels. That's a good way to destroy wheels. Maybe we can use a block and tackle rig."

"Ain't no trees around here stout enough to hold a block and tackle fast," Aaron said.

Penney smiled and raised a finger. "We've got the best gosh-darned brake right amongst us; our old partners, the oxen."

A man off to the side spoke up. "Ox can't take a wagon downhill. That's—"

Another man interrupted. "I don't think that's what he's saying. Let the captain finish."

Penney nodded his thanks. "By my way of thinking, we yoke up five brace of oxen here on top, then attach one block to the oxen and the other to an iron bar of the running gear under the box. We have about a half-dozen fellers feed the rope through the rig and lower the wagon down the hill backwards; a couple of drovers will steady the oxen to anchor it all."

"And if it all falls apart?" a skeptic asked.

Penney was expecting the question. "We have a second rope attached to the axle with about ten fellers on that rope. If something breaks, they can hold the wagon and let it down, gradual like, even if a little faster than we might like."

"We can do that," Aaron said, and the chatter of the men showed they agreed.

Penney raised his hand. "One more thing, and I can tell you this from my own sad experience: Any men on the rope should be wearing gloves to guard against rope burn....All righty, men, what say we go to work?"

The plan for descending the steep hill went according to Penney's design. The oxen held steady, the block and tackle rig worked as planned. Almost.

The last wagon belonged to the Horner family. Even after weeks on the trail, they were strangers to the others. They stayed to themselves, except the boy, Roger. He seemed to be everywhere and into everything, a general nuisance. Penney called him a "whippersnapper." He impressed others as an unhappy boy, and was even suspected of stealing small possessions of other children. When his mother, Maude, came looking for him, her manner was standoffish to other women. Earl, the husband, was quiet and seemed sad, though not unfriendly. When the other men would engage him, he would smile, give deflecting answers, and look for a way to get out of the conversation.

When the Horner wagon was half-way down the hill, the rope snapped, and the block and tackle fell to the ground. The men who had control of the safety rope didn't grab it soon enough, and when they did, it sped through their hands so fast even those wearing gloves had to release it to avoid burns.

The wagon slammed into the bottom of the hill and cartwheeled bottom-up with sideboards and contents spread over ten yards. The rest of the company ran for safety as the wagon rumbled down. When it lay in a heap, they converged on the scene.

Maude Horner ran to the wagon and started to rush around picking up unmentionables and keepsakes. She was sobbing and screaming. Her husband, Earl, went to her side and held her close.

Hannah watched and thought—This is odd. It's certainly bad, but not to the extent of her carryings-on. Hannah moved to the center and spoke in a commanding voice: "Back away, people. Let's have a few adults here to collect the Horners' belongings." Maude was standing nearby and still crying. Hannah put her arm around her. "Try to calm down, dear." She stroked Maude's hair. "It'll be all right. We'll gather up your goods, and the men'll fix your wagon. I'll bring some supper over for the three of you directly."

Maude's husband took her from Hannah and held her close. He faced Hannah with a haggard look. "Thank you, missus."

Penney skidded down the hill and looked over the damage, then said in a loud voice meant to be reassuring, "Ain't nothing here we can't fix. The axles are just fine, and the wheels ain't broken. We can fix this wagon good as new in a day or two. Meantime, like the lady said, let's make a pile of the Horners' goods. We'll cover it with the bonnet from the wagon." He looked skyward. "I don't see any rain coming, so everything's going to be jim-dandy." He looked across the meadow and saw another wagon train parked. "We'll post a guard tonight to safeguard these goods."

People started to walk away, but Penney said, "A moment, if you please. Me and the committee, we been discussing staying here for a spell, maybe two or three days, to rest the animals, and let them feed in this good grass." Preacher gestured for Penney's attention, which reminded him, "One more thing, friends, Preacher here is having a prayer meeting after supper at his wagon. Bring a blanket or a stool and praise the Lord for getting us this far." As they walked away, he said, "Bone appleteet." When people looked at him quizzically, he said, almost apologetically, "Oh, that's some French talk. Ezra Masterson's been teaching me a little. It means enjoy your supper."

As the pioneers separated, Penney and Cohen watched them go. Penney said, "Some things I don't understand, Malachi. I expected some peculiar things to happen on this-here trip that wouldn't happen back home. But this has been one thing after another. A half-year ago, most of these people would've been church leaders, and upstanding as all get-out. But out here…" He frowned. "It's all consternating for an old farmer."

Cohen busied himself picking up some of the Horner possessions. "What we have here, Shadrach, are ships lost on a stormy sea with no anchors. These folks are the ships, and their anchors were left back home. And the stormy sea? These mountains and deserts are their stormy sea. What's happening here is not a new story. It's the way people are."

The idyllic two days at Ash Hollow were only a few days in the past, but already they seemed a distant memory. The animals were holding up and no more sickness had struck, but an early summer heat wave continued to slow progress by draining energy from people and animals alike. Elevation snuck up on them in a subtle but continuous tilt upward, causing muscles to burn and breaths to heave. The effect was gradual enough not to be remarked on, but it was real, and it shortened people's fuses in dealing with each other.

Back in Independence, the elevation was one thousand feet above sea level; when they reached the Platte, it was two thousand. Ahead of them was Chimney Rock at four thousand; five thousand at Ft. Laramie; six thousand at Independence Rock; and seventy-five hundred at South Pass.

Tormenting rashes on inner thighs and groin crevices caused placid men to turn to furious scratching, which, of course, necessitated more scratching. Some would whip reluctant animals as they never would have back in their own fields. Women got tired of sweat-sticky clothes and worried about body odor and "looking a mess." In frustration, they threw things around in their wagons, searching for cooking utensils that would be at hand in back-home kitchens. Infants became fussier. Older children grew bored, and daring boys played too close to moving wagons.

Men found fault with each other over matters that back home would have been shrugged off. People were tempted to lash out in their misery. The available targets were family first, and then those in other wagons who were often primed by their own misery to give it right back.

Their lives had changed psychologically in ways they could not have prepared for. Religion went from being a cornerstone of their lives to secondary importance. Preacher's call to prayer became a plea. People who had faithfully occupied the same pew in their home church for years, either did not attend Preacher's services, or shifted restlessly as their minds wandered.

They were lonely in a crowd: Americans, by circumstance and by choice, were accustomed to lots of space and carefully selected associations. In the small group of pioneers, they had abruptly become hemmed-in by strangers whose habits and manners disgusted them. It was toxic claustrophobia.

A punishing affliction that couldn't be prepared for was homesickness. Pioneers walked around with far-away looks because their thoughts couldn't let loose of the dear things that had been left behind, almost certainly forever—family, friends, homes, goals, even pets; they were all gone, and nothing to replace them except dust, endless walking, and dangers of every description lurking at their elbows.

Frustration never slept, and many people did so only in fits and starts. At night, the dominant sounds from exhausted travelers within the circled wagons were the snores of a score of men sleeping in the confined space. They ranged from Preacher's basso profundo dish-rattler to a lilting soprano ending in a lip fluting accompanied by a moist vibration. That melodic snore might have come from a woman, but no lady stepped forward to claim it. A diet high in beans provided staccato counterpoint.

However, all that became background to the wild fantasies coming from Maude Horner: "Oh, this isn't real, is it Earl? We're back home, aren't we? There's my mother walking down the road bringing fresh eggs." She never seemed to tire.

One night, when she was especially loud, Meister came to Penney's wagon and hailed the captain. "Say, Captain, can't we shut her up? She's nuttier than a squirrel turd."

Penney held his hands out wide. "There's nothing to be done. The woman's entitled to her say, even though her voice is sandpaper on our brains."

"Well, I'm going to have something done, damnit."

Penney's voice was low and flat. "Probably not, Mister Meister, probably not. Now, you're disturbing my sleep, just like you say she is."

Just after dawn, Aaron rushed to the Spencer wagon and called for Hannah. She came from around the wagon, and the agitated young husband said between pants, "Hannah, you need to come quick. Gertie's time is now. She's in awful pain."

Without a word, Hannah reached into the back of the wagon and grabbed a small leather bag. She fell in beside Aaron and ignored Ed, who shouted, "Where you going?"

The attention of the pioneers was diverted from Maude's howls to the drama at the Proctor wagon. In the 1840s, childbirth was a time of both joy and peril. The outcome could be a healthy infant, or the death of the mother or child, or both. Dread always hovered until the event was safely concluded.

A stillness fell over the company as they waited to see which it would be. Each time a sob or muffled scream came from the wagon, the reaction was a nervous murmur. Gertie had been in labor for hours, the pain made worse by the jostling of the trail.

Hannah climbed into the Proctor wagon. In moments, she pushed back the canvas and asked Aaron to boil water on the noon fire to provide hot rags. After two or three minutes, she again emerged, and calmly said to Aaron, "The baby is in a breech. Feet first. I'll have to turn it. Gertie tells me her water's broken, and the labor pains are coming closer together. This is her first, so it takes some time."

The wind gradually picked-up to a stiff breeze. The farmers in the group sniffed the air and shielded their eyes as they stared at the sky. They were experienced with winds kicking up dust and tended to assume it would soon pass.

Nimrod said, "Dust storm coming. We need to be hunkered-down directly."

Penney said, "A dust storm ain't nothing to fret about."

Nimrod knew better. He snorted, and said, "You think you seen dust before? You ain't."

What he feared headed their way was not an Indiana dust blow that, once finished, would be cleaned up by sweeping the front porch. What he anticipated was what mule skinners in Taos called a Mexican blizzard, because it attacked with sand, not snow. The main difference was sand hits harder than snow.

Standing outside the wagon, Nimrod was joined by Penney and Masterson, and a small group hoping for drama that didn't affect them. Nimrod pointed to the west. "This here blow is going to get worse, I'll wager," he said. "There's a grove of cottonwoods yonder; see that dry creek bed? I reckon a mile, thereabouts. We better head for that. It'll protect the animals."

Hannah overheard, and said from behind the bonnet, "We're not going anywhere. Gertie can't tolerate the bouncing—I need a woman's help in here."

Clara Penney, standing next to her husband, tried to climb into the wagon, but her crippled leg wouldn't cooperate. Penney helped her up. When he turned back, Nimrod said, "She's a giving lady, I can see." Nimrod looked at Penney. "For sure, is Clara staying with Gertie?"

Penney shrugged. "I can't ask her to undo what she's set her mind to. She's quite the gal. She'll stay, which means I got to."

Nimrod smiled his admiration. "Quite a gal you got there."

Penney nodded, and said, "She's been of service to others her whole life." He paused, and a break came into his voice. "If people see any light in me at all, it's a reflection of the sunlight in her soul."

Cohen had walked up and was listening. He spread his hands in praise, and said, "Captain, that's poetry." Penney was embarrassed by the unfamiliar flattery, but he was touched by it.

He cleared the frog from his throat, turned away, and raised his voice. "Folks, we have to move to that grove a mile or so down the trail. Malachi's in charge. I'm staying here. Hurry some men back here when this is over. We'll be easy pickings out here." He shouted, "Get a move on," and waved them forward.

Penney smiled at Nimrod and shook his head in feigned disgust. "I swear, if you don't get me in trouble, my wife will."

Nimrod gestured to the oxen on the Proctor wagon. "Aaron, get towels and cover the eyes of these critters. It'll protect their eyes and keep them quiet."

Aaron nervously asked, "Have you seen any hostiles?"

"I seen a Cheyenne camp, fresh and not far. Indians is always around, and they ain't known to send notice they're coming," Nimrod said.

"Will you be okay here?" Masterson said.

Nimrod laughed. "I got no idea. Me, Aaron, and the captain will stay here to guard." He turned and looked up at Hannah. "Do you understand the situation, ma'am? I saw Cheyenne sign a ways back. Judging by their camp signs, I suspect a small war party. They ain't known to be friends of whites."

"I can't leave a patient in need. I'll stay."

Ed Spencer blurted out, "Like hell you will. You're not staying here alone. Not with him!" He pointed an accusing finger at Nimrod.

In front of a dozen onlookers, Hannah said, "Like hell I won't."

Nimrod had no time for Spencer. He head-gestured toward Aaron, and Penney. "Bring a couple of scatterguns."

As the wagon train moved off toward shelter, the incessant wind raked across the treeless plain with a sound that in a brief time grew from a whisper to a howl, to a groan. The wind blew in gusts, but steadily stronger, and with shortened intervals. The sun dimmed, and visibility through the swirling sand was in feet. Sagebrush became airborne, and the buffeting of the Proctor wagon's tightly closed bonnet sounded like tearing paper, but it held. The three men could hear the dim moans of Gertie and the bustling of Hannah and Clara.

The three men wrapped their faces in bandanas and covered their gun breeches. They turned into the wagon for protection from the sting of swirling sand and dirt surging like ocean waves. They could hear Gertie's moans grow louder over the wind's howl.

Aaron called out, "Is Gertie okay in there?" There was no answer.

The storm was as brief as it was violent. In less than an hour, the wind slacked off and visibility improved to a haze. As daylight struggled back, Nimrod saw what he most feared. Staring at them, silently and motionless, from about a quarter mile were twelve mounted Indians. Outlined against the sun's filtered glare, they were mounted specters from the Book of Revelation with spears pointing upward: a visitation of death.

Aaron half breathed his words. "Oh, my God."

Nimrod started checking his guns. He said, "God's got nothing to do with it. They're Cheyenne. A raiding party. They mean us no good. Spread out, fellers. If they circle, move with them. If they charge, don't shoot too soon, and aim for the man and horse. They're counting on you to panic. For the sake of the women in the wagon, don't!"

"Help is yonder, a mile away," Aaron said, and looked at Nimrod for confirmation.

"Might as well be a thousand mile for all the good they can do us right now. They can't see us from over that rise. They'll be expecting us to join them. Whatever happens, will happen quick."

The Indians, hunched to make a smaller target, circled the wagon at a languid trot over several minutes, tightening the circle a little as they went. It was a game of nerves. The three men walked around the wagon in synch with them. Nothing was said. Nothing happened except the constant circling.

Nimrod said, "The lead warrior is figuring out if they can take us without losing too many men. He's trying to get a fix on our grit. We might be worth losing two braves, but he's got to be asking himself if wiping us out might be worth losing maybe four or five. Right now, he's judging if we can do that."

The Cheyenne were in no hurry. They were waiting for a fatal mistake or a sign of panic. At last, they regrouped and spread out, preparing to charge. The men readied themselves. One brave made a dash toward Nimrod, testing him, then pulled up short when Nimrod trained his rifle on him.

Over the wind, an abrupt thin cry was heard from within the wagon. The Indian leader was caught off guard. He stared at the wagon for a long moment. Then, he smiled and raised his lance in a salute. Nimrod hesitated at first, then saluted in return. It was obvious the other warriors were not happy, but they fell in line behind the leader and rode away.

Nimrod, Penney, and Aaron shook hands with the glee of knowing they would live to see another morning.

Hannah looked out with a big smile on her face. "Both Gertie and young master Caleb are doing just fine. She's tired, and he's furious."

Aaron whooped and jumped onto the cabin seat and looked inside. Hannah said to Nimrod, "What's happening out there?"

"Everything's fine. It's been a good day."

As the train crept along the dry and treeless plain, they increasingly were forced to rely on "buffalo chips" for fuel, which were nothing more than dried animal feces. Hannah and the other women hated to cook with them. They burned hot, but too fast for sensible cooking. The very idea revolted them, compounded by the act of lifting them out of the dust in a sort of scavenger hunt, especially when they were not quite dry. For diversion, the women sometimes called them by the Sioux name, *nik-nik*, the comic "plains oak," or muttered "bull shit."

Hannah and Flora were walking together beside the lumbering wagons performing the duty of collecting buffalo chips and dropping them into burlap sacks they dragged along. Normally, children were assigned the task, if they could be found—children, that is, not chips. Both could be elusive. The women wore bonnets for sun protection; both could have passed for beggar women on the streets of Baltimore. Flora wore a woolen smock overdue for a washing. Her hair was in a bun, plainly pinned up without a mirror. Hannah's shapeless, patched gingham dress would never have been worn on a St. Louis street. Her high-button shoes were scuffed with a tear in one. They might have once been black.

From when they first met, they had formed that mystical bond of women who immediately sense a soul sister. In a short time, Hannah and Flora each knew she had a confidant, a confessor, a tower to lean on, and a judge of candor.

Hannah walked close to the other woman and said, "Flora, let me say again how sorry I am for your loss. I regret we couldn't do more to help your husband."

Flora dropped a chip in her bag, then turned to her friend. "I wish I could go to bed and mourn for a week, that's how much I miss him. But this train has got to keep moving, and so do I."

"You're a strong woman."

Flora put an arm out and hugged Hannah's shoulders. "You're very sweet, and much appreciated. William was a man better than many."

Hannah was startled to hear Flora refer to her late husband, barely cold in his grave, as "better than many." It seemed too limiting, too conditional.

Flora noticed Hannah's reaction, and said, "I'm not going to make him into a saint. That would be dishonest to the memory of who he really was. A man doesn't have to be perfect to love him. But what William was—faithful, kind, hard-working—was more than enough. I was blessed, even though he could drive me to distraction at times." She paused and smiled to herself. "And me him."

Just saying those words put a catch in Flora's voice. She swiped at her eyes and changed the subject. "I reckon we've both had strong marriages." Flora had noticed Ed Spencer's treatment of Hannah and wanted to give her a chance to vent. "How are things with you, my dear?" Flora paused, wondering if Hannah would unburden.

Hannah said nothing at first, then opened up. "My first husband, Abel, was a wonderful man—good doctor, loving husband, good father. But, in the end, he was not strong enough. I would've gladly done anything to help him. But he gave in to his physical misery. He left the children and me in a terrible bind without the means to support ourselves. We were forced into the grasp of—" Hannah wiped her eyes. "Oh, I do go on. I've no right to speak so. Ignore what I said."

Flora said, "You can regret your husband couldn't balance his pain with his responsibility, but you can't blame him. Weakness is not a sin."

Hannah said, "Mr. Spencer can be difficult, but he provided a home for us, the children and me."

The women continued to scan the ground for the dried buffalo scat. Flora shook her head forlornly at Hannah's tepid reference to her present husband. "I care not for Mr. Spencer," Flora said. "He trapped you. You're a struggling fly."

"That's harsh, Flora."

"Is it now?" Flora put down her sack, turned to Hannah and embraced her. "Oh, my dear. I have eyes. I know, I know…"

Hannah shook her head. "I've spoken too much."

Enough said on that, Flora realized. Her lip curled in a wisp of humor, unnoticed by Hannah. "Our guide, Nimrod Lee, now, there's an interesting fellow."

Hannah was instantly alert. Had Flora noticed the way she and Nimrod looked at each other? She tried to sound nonchalant. "Interesting? I would say curious. Yes, I would call him a curious man. He's a backwoods ruffian. He's a—" Hannah searched for the right word. "He's a quaint man. He's a violent man. Goodness knows how many men he's scalped. I think he's scary." Her voice became harsh. "I hate violence."

Flora said, "Well, maybe he does, too; hate violence, I mean. I think you have to allow for differences in the roles people are called on to play. You wouldn't ask a mountain man to dance the quadrille, but you would ask his help to survive in this wilderness. I don't know what Mr. Lee did in his mountain haunts, but from what I've seen here, he's gentlemanly." She looked directly at Hannah and smiled. "And a welcome feast for the eyes."

Hannah blushed. "I hadn't noticed."

CHAPTER SEVENTEEN

M aude pleaded for her torment to stop, to depart, but it wouldn't.

The fervent wish of everyone was for Maude to make peace with her demons and quiet down. They knew little of mental illness because back in their home communities, insanity was as concealed and denied as leprosy. It was considered the mark of the devil by many people. Those who said it was an illness were themselves looked on as somewhat strange. But out on the prairie, there was no hiding it, and having to face reality was maddening itself for those in neighboring wagons and tents with pillows over their heads.

Her husband, Earl, was a rock. He stood by her, reassured her, tried to comfort her, and didn't leave her side. He could sometimes be seen sitting on his wagon's driving bench, holding head in hands. He greeted everyone with eye contact and a smile. He tried to minimize the discomfort being pushed on them by his wife.

Their twelve-year-old boy, Roger, was a different story. He was rambunctious by nature, but he had cause, a kid's cause. However, the tumult at home, which he did not understand, resented, and assumed was somehow his fault, turned him into a camp mischief-maker. He was always underfoot, always into something where he had no business, always challenging other boys to fight. People tried to understand and sympathize, but culturally, they were ill-prepared for understanding, and not much for sympathy.

Preacher watched Roger's antics, and lectured to no one in particular, "Spare the rod and spoil the child."

Just weeks after William died, Flora Dickens was in her wagon sorting through shared memorabilia. She was enduring the wrenching project of deciding what to keep and what to throw away. She swiped at a tear when she opened the leather case protecting a daguerreotype the two of them had made on a trip to Chicago just six months before starting for California. The photograph was imprinted on a copper plate with a silver veneer. It was a new process by Frenchman Louis Daguerre and was the rage of fashionable people for the latest miracle of modern science. It was spur-of-the-moment and expensive, but it gave them a keepsake. When she studied the contented couple in the picture, they seemed to make eye contact with her. She saw happiness in their gaze. Her only regret was their stone-face pose, which they did at the insistence of the photographer for the sake of steadiness. She sighed and put the picture next to William's Bible in her memory chest.

She was interrupted by hearing her name softly called. She went to the front of the wagon and looked down to see Simon Tester. "Yes, sir. May I help you?"

He tipped his hat. "Good evening, Miss Flora. It's a pleasant evening, so I was thinking you might enjoy a stroll down by the river. Beings there are Indians about, I might escort you."

She was dumbfounded. "Your attention is unwelcome, sir. I'm not 'Miss Flora.' I'm Mrs. Dickens. You must hold me in low esteem to think I, a widowed mother whose husband is not cold in the grave, would respond to your lack of respect for my mourning. You're a cad and a bounder." She went back in the wagon and pulled the bonnet closed.

Tester looked around to see if his embarrassment had been observed. Seeing no one, he shrugged and moved off.

They had traveled a tedious six weeks along the Platte, and then the North Platte. The train finally arrived at landmarks they had heard about and which offered longed-for proof they were actually making progress toward California. Looming before them were Courthouse Rock and Jail Rock. They had read about the two monoliths of clay and sandstone close to each other, each rising two-hundred-fifty feet in massive dominance amidst sandy patches of weeds. After twenty more miles, they were able to crane their necks at Chimney Rock and gaze in awe at its solitary spire raising its finger into the sky.

Penney studied the freak of geography. "Well, how many more surprises does this old world have for me?" he muttered. He then halted the train so everyone could gather to ogle the strange rock formation. It was the highest remaining vestige of a vast plateau long since eroded away to a flat plain. At an apex of three-hundred-fifty feet, the needle atop the broad base was a visual affirmation of the things they had read they would see, and here it was, before their eyes.

Masterson gazed at it, then said to Aaron standing next to him, "That's something you won't see in Arkansas."

Aaron made a futile swipe at a squadron of mosquitoes. "Reckon so, but now I've seen it. I wish these damned mosquitoes was interested in scenery and not me."

Not long after she gave Tester the boot, Flora was struggling with a campfire that was being whipped by the wind. As she reached for a skillet, a loose fold on her ankle-length skirt was blown to the edge of the fire where it flared up. She frantically beat at it, but it wasn't extinguished until Cohen happened by and smothered it with his jacket.

"Are you all right? Are you burned?"

"Thank you. There's no damage to the dress. It's not fit to wear in this wilderness, anyway. The thing singed is my pride."

He laughed. "I don't think any little fire is going to burn out your spirit, Flora."

Two more families resigned from the company and joined a larger train camped nearby. The reason they gave Penney was Maude Horner's crazy screaming. "We can't take it no more," one man said. His wife nodded and said having a "touched" woman as a neighbor might be a bad omen.

Penney shook hands with the men and wished them well.

From their guidebooks, the pioneers realized Fort Laramie was fewer than one hundred miles to the west. Arriving there would be a needed respite from the trail. However, Nimrod advised to not stay more than a couple of days. He reminded the committee of the temptations of bad women and worse booze that could consume precious dollars and even more precious time. Places like the fort were not known as hotbeds of hymn-singing Methodists.

One evening after supper, Simon Tester, with Zack Monroe at his heels, approached Penney and asked for a word. Penney nodded and walked out of earshot of the others.

"What can I do for you, sir?" Penney asked. Nothing he had seen of Tester's nosiness and agitation among the company had told him he was not wrong about his first mistrustful impression of the man. He once told Masterson, "Anytime I talk to Tester, I fear he's going to lift his leg on me."

Tester first looked around for eavesdroppers, then said, "That Maude woman; you need to do something. She walks among the wagons late at night crying, and the things she says spook the children."

"That's right," Zack added with a vigorous nod.

Penney looked down for a moment to gather his composure. "Mr. Tester, the woman is sick. It behooves all of us to show some mercy for her and her son and husband. He's a good man."

"Some say she's possessed," Tester said.

"A lot of people," Zack said, then looked to Tester for approval.

Penney inhaled and held it for a moment. "Possessed by what? Maybe you should discuss your devils and demons ideas with witch doctors or shamen, or whatever they're called. You'll find them amongst these tribes all around us. They might have some ideas."

Tester huffed. "I must say: You have a strange attitude, considering people are talking."

Again, Zack said, "That's right."

"I'm sure you're deep into those conversations and started a few of your own, Mr. Tester. I don't appreciate the attitude I'm seeing from you. You're as cocky as a goat on a narrow ledge."

Tester huffed. "You use poor judgment for a man who's supposed to be the leader here. Something needs to be done."

Penney's eyes narrowed. "If so, it won't be done by the likes of you."

The captain watched Tester and Zack spin together and stalk off as though choreographed. Penney's silent lecture to himself was not a happy one— Shadrach, you damned fool! You didn't have to sign on for this idiot's job. Nothing will rise up and bite you in the ass sooner than a job you volunteer for.

Hannah was busy trying to clean her wagon when Flora fast-walked over with a wide grin. "What're you doing, Hannah?"

Hannah stoop-walked to the front of the wagon. She stood straight and stretched her back with a deep sigh of relief. "If you don't know by now, dear lady, I'll be happy to show you. It's called housework. 'Wagonwork,' if you prefer. If you want to know more, I'll give you a free lesson."

"I want you to come to my wagon. I'm having a ceremony."

"Excuse me?"

"I'm going to burn my corset. I'm through having that medieval torture thing squeeze me like a sausage. I won't put one of those on again unless the man I'm with wears one, too."

Hannah thought for a moment, then said, resolutely, "I can add some fuel to your fire." She went to their tent and was rummaging in her clothes when Spencer asked what she was doing. "I'm looking for my corset. I'm getting rid of it."

"You're what? You'll be walking around in polite company looking like a fat fish monger's wife. I won't have it."

Hannah stood up and faced him. "Ed, if you want me to wear this thing again, you'll have to put it on me. It'll be easier to put trousers on a cat."

Flora and Hannah fed a campfire until it was leaping knee high. Other women noticed the activity and walked over to investigate. They watched agog as Flora and Hannah made a defiant show of throwing their corsets on the fire. Ruth Cohen gave a supporting shout, and went to get hers, as did two other women, all desiring to feed the flames of discontent and of physical comfort. Not one woman looking on appeared to disapprove.

After a satisfying nineteen-mile day, the camp was settled down when three yoke of oxen lumbered into view pulling a wagon loaded high with buffalo skins. The man walking beside and driving the oxen was a type increasing seen on the plains. He was a likely ex-trapper adjusting to a new enterprise by slaughtering buffalo wholesale for skins, then leaving the meat to rot. Sitting up top on the seat was a man holding a rifle. A third man was herding a half-dozen reserve oxen bunched behind the wagon.

Nimrod hailed the driver who tapped the nigh ox and shouted, "Whoa." He walked toward Nimrod and was preceded by his rank smell. It was of dried buffalo blood and offal, also sweat and dirt from weeks of sleeping in his clothes, last washed when the man bathed, which was not recent. Closer, Nimrod saw a matted beard, teeth stained green and brown, and skin with grime impacted into the pores. His fingernails were long and black. His hands were hatched with nicks and scars from skinning animals. His appearance was not of a trapper who took at least some pride in looking the role. He had transitioned to a scavenger of the plains. Perhaps spending days and weeks elbow-deep in blood and gore had changed his self-image, if it changed at all. Closer still, the man's breath caused Nimrod to breathe through his mouth.

Nimrod wanted the man's rig to keep moving, but frontier courtesy had its demands. "How do, friend. You and your men are welcome to some coffee."

The men shook hands. "Name's Thessalonia Bone, out of Taos." He cackled. "And other places where the law would like to see me again."

"I beg your pardon, sir. I didn't catch your name." Nimrod could see Bone was a talkative man, common to many who had emerged from deep solitude.

"Thessalonia. It's a town in the Bible. Maw liked the sound of it, coming from the Gospels and all. She said it sounded like a lawyer or something high-falutin'." He again cackled and looked around to call attention to his cleverness. "It do make me stand out among the riff-raff. It's a burden for people to spell, so I goes by Thess. Most can spell that, at least close enough."

"Thessalonica," Preacher said from a few feet back.

"What?" Bone said.

"That's the name of the Greek city, Thessalonica, not Thessalonia. And it's not from the Gospels."

Nimrod looked at the ground and thought—Shut up, Preacher,

damn it!

Bone looked at the sky and half-laughed, incredulous at the insult he had just heard. He then squinted at Preacher. "You saying my maw didn't know her Bible?"

Preacher's face blanched. "I, well, no—"

Nimrod cut him off. "I'm Lee, the guide here. You Independence-bound?"

"As fast as these pokey bastards will get me there," Bone said. "I ran out of coffee near a week ago. I'm way behind on my whiskey and whores, too."

Nimrod pointed at the direction behind Bone. "What's up ahead on our trail?"

"The redskins be getting a bit quarrelsome about the buffalo we been taking. Ran into some a while back was downright unsociable. I bought them off with two old trade rifles."

"Not supposed to trade rifles to Indians."

Bone snorted. "I'd not waste a minute to trade them a cannon to save my hide. They was giving my outfit a hard eye to take us down. But we wouldn't go easy, for certain sure. I could see them calculating the price they'd pay would be too high for hides they didn't have much use for."

"What tribe?"

"Crows, I 'spect, the way my scalp was itching."

"Their leader have a black horse with a white star?"

"Can't say. I was worried about other things."

Nimrod couldn't say whether he was relieved or not. "You're in Pawnee country now."

"I got me a Pawnee wife. I'm a tribe member. She's ugly, but useful." He laughed. "I'm married all over these parts. Squaws favor me. My bed never gets cold." His eye caught Spencer grooming his horses alongside his wagon, and Bone laughed even harder. He pointed to Spencer's horses. "Them bonebags gonna have to be carried in the wagon if they ever gonna get past the Sweetwater."

Spencer glared at the man. "You're talking about thoroughbred stock."

Bone thought the entire scene was hilarious. "I'm talking about buzzard meat."

Spencer seethed. His animus was not lost on Bone. "I lost my grain, otherwise…Mister, you be willing to sell those extra oxen?"

Bone rubbed his jaw, recognizing the strength of his position. "Money won't get me to Missouri, but I might be talked into a trade."

"Are they yoke-trained?"

Bone almost shouted in his mirth. "Trained? They'll haul your wagon all day, then play a hand of poker after supper."

Spencer tried to look calculating. "One horse for your six spare oxen?"

Bone laughed and turned to his men so they could appreciate the slick deal he was about to make. He turned back to Spencer and became serious. "Six oxen for your six horses, except that pretty palomino you're riding. You can keep him. And I'll be generous; you can keep another one."

Spencer's lips thinned to a line, and the words came out under pressure. "You can go to hell."

Nimrod was quiet, but he thought—Careful, Spencer.

Bone expelled a long breath and walked around in a circle, then turned back. "Thems bad manners. Now, I want the palomino, too."

Spencer realized he was trapped. He almost choked on his words. "I keep the palomino and one other. I'll see them all as bleached bones before I give my riding horse up."

Bone gloated. "Well, I'll accept that. You can thank Jesus I'm strong on Christian charity, pilgrim. If'n this was a day I was feeling grouchy, I'd jump you like a chicken on a cricket."

Spencer wrote out a bill of sale and handed it to Bone. "I consider you a blackguard and a thief."

Nimrod's shoulders slumped, and he said under his breath. "Oh, shit!"

Bone's eyes grew wide, and he stepped forward and pulled a butcher knife with dried blood on the blade.

Masterson and Cohen had wandered over, then backed away.

Bone's face turned dark, and spittle dripped from his lips. "That'll cost you your liver, too, pilgrim. I'll be leaving with your horses and your hair on my belt."

Nimrod stepped in with his hand on the butt of his revolver. "Put the knife away, friend. You skinned him on the trade. You can be content with such for today. You best take your horses and be on your way."

Bone turned on Nimrod and waved the knife toward his face at ten feet distant. Nimrod took his pistol out and aimed it straight at Bone's face without a word. Bone lowered the blade and glared at Spencer who scrambled away. He turned to Nimrod and gestured with his head toward his man on the wagon with a rifle aimed at Nimrod. "Your fancy pimp's pistol won't help when my man Otis up top lets go with his Lancaster, sixty-nine caliber."

In response, Nimrod tipped his head toward newcomer Penney off to the side. "I think old Otis up top there is about to have his own concerns. One second after he does something rash, he'll fertilize the sagebrush for a mile around."

Bone and Otis turned to see Penney with a scattergun trained on Otis who licked his lips, flitted his eyes, and lowered the rifle.

Nimrod shrugged in sympathy. "Your man Otis is losing interest in defending your honor. I'd say he's a man who wants to stay alive to get drunk in Independence."

Bone replaced his knife with a strained laugh. "I was just gonna put the fear in your horse man there." He pointed at Spencer. "Looks like I got it done. He's shaking like a dog in a rainstorm."

Nimrod said, "You best worry about them up in the hills already eyeing your horses."

Bone shrugged. "Pawnees. I know their chief. I'll give him a horse. That'll keep him my friend." He looked again at Spencer and laughed in derision. "This been a mighty profitable transaction. Yes, sir. A pretty penny has been made here today, and I thank you for appreciating that I'm a greedy man."

Bone gathered his new horses. As he tied them behind his wagon, he started looking at Nimrod as though trying to think of something. Then, he hooted and pointed at him. "I figured it out. I've been puzzling on it, but now I know who you are. You're *that* Lee. You're the one the Crows gonna flay like a flopping trout."

Standing off to the side, Hannah was alone in hearing Bone's words. She stared at Nimrod, her face reflected curiosity, but also concern.

Bone continued laughing as he gave the command, and his rig faded over a low hill. The rumps of Spencer's horses were the last to disappear.

Nimrod turned to Spencer, and said, "The last lesson you learn will be the one that's too late."

Penney stood before Flora's wagon and softly called out, "Hello, inside." The bonnet slid open, and Flora stepped out and took a lithe jump to the ground.

"You're quite an at-e-lete, young lady," Penney said, grinning.

"A tom-boy is more apt," she said. "I never grew out of it."

"I came to ask how you're faring."

She smiled. "I'm grateful for your kindness." She crossed her arms and hugged herself. "I admit to being afeared of this strange, empty, endless country. I don't know where we're headed and what'll happen to my children."

"How's the youngins getting along?"

"Growing up faster than I would encourage. Tom is driving our oxen just fine, and Alice—" She noticed Penney's fatherly smile. "Alice, she's helpful and learning about life. She's nearing the point where a mother worries about you-know-what."

Penney looked down and gave his head a small, forlorn shake. "We all have scares in our heads, but most don't have your honesty to speak up." He looked her in the face and reached down and held her hand for a moment. "All you can do, mama tiger, is to keep going; same for all of us."

Hannah and her children were eating their evening meal when she looked over to notice Nimrod eating alone nearby in front of a small fire. She picked up her plate and stool and walked over to him. "May I join you for a moment?"

"Yes, ma'am."

"I'd like to ask you a question."

"Yes, ma'am."

Hannah placed her stool across from the fire. "When the hunter bought Ed's horses, I heard him say Indians want to kill you."

Nimrod used a stick to stir his fire. He knew if he didn't tell the truth, worse would be assumed. "There's a thing I got to work out with the Crows."

"But, your wife was a Crow."

"When men get together for trade out here, it ain't a gentle event. A few years ago, Maggie—Magpie—wanted to go with me to a get-together. Her parents made me promise not to take her."

Hannah pressed, though she could see it made Nimrod uncomfortable. "But you did anyway?"

"Magpie was willful. I weakened."

"What happened?"

"She wandered off. I found her murdered. It was a renegade trapper name of Rake Face Marcel."

"Well, surely, the Crows don't blame you for that."

"I was too ashamed to go back right away, and when I was fixing to, Marcel had spread the lie I got drunk and killed Magpie in a rage."

Hannah leaned toward him and nodded knowingly. "And it was the lie that took hold."

"The Crows didn't know otherwise. I learned that truth smolders, but a lie takes off like wildfire."

"You feel guilt, I can see."

"In the last hour of the last day of my life, I'll feel guilt."

Hannah looked at their surroundings. "I should think this would be the last place you'd come to."

Nimrod's food had grown cold. He put the tin plate down. "I've got a man to call to account, a daughter out here somewhere, and the truth to set straight."

Hannah's tone changed from sympathy to suspicion, and her voice sharpened. "Forgive me if I'm too blunt, but I can't help asking: Are we—I hope we're not the bait. Surely you wouldn't put all of us in danger just to clear your conscience?"

"No, ma'am. Many Horses—he's their chief—he ain't like that. This is between me and him. This ain't anyone else's affair. The Crows ain't enemies of the whites. I made my position clear to Mr. Penney when I signed on."

"How do you know that, about chief what's-his-name?"

"If I didn't know that for certain-sure, I'd have never joined this train. There ain't a mountain man in these hills don't have a hatchet sharpened for Marcel."

As Hannah rose to leave. Nimrod said one more thing. "Many Horses was Magpie's father." Hannah's eyes widened.

Not far away, Spencer was watching them with hate in his eyes. Hannah glanced at her husband, but ignored him. She said to Nimrod, "There are bad men in this train, but I don't believe you're one of them. I'd like to trust you. It would be nice to believe a man again."

"Yes, ma'am," he said, and touched his hat brim, but he saw doubt on her face, and that hurt.

Hannah noticed, and said, "I don't mean to impugn anything. A question is not an accusation."

"Yes, ma'am." He would ask Masterson what 'impugn' meant. But then, a question lingered in his mind that he pushed aside— Why did he care?

꧁꧂

Nimrod rode back to the train from a scout to find the wagons stopped. He rode up to Penney to ask why.

"Well, you know that Percival feller?"

Nimrod said, "Roy's his name. He don't have much to say, but I've spoken to him. It's just him and his boy."

Gertie standing nearby, said, "He lost his wife and daughter to typhoid back in Wisconsin Territory, I'm told."

"Well," Penney said, "We're having a birth in our midst." In response to Nimrod's blank look, Penney said, "Percival's cow's having a calf. Roy says he's been too busy to even notice she was coming due." He laughed. "It's our bell cow, the one named Bossie. What do you make of that?"

"Well, I'll be," Nimrod said. "A farmer who don't know his cow is carrying. That's a head-scratcher."

"Well, Roy's got his hands full now. The cow is down and trying to pass the calf. I reckon this is a good place to stop for the night. There's good grass down by the river."

The Percival cow was on the ground, struggling to birth her calf. The bell was still around her neck. A muted clang was heard whenever she moved her head. Roy was on his hands and knees, peering as closely as he could. "Its head is right close to coming out, but it's big, really big," he announced to the surrounding farmers. Then, turning back to the animal, "I don't want to lose this cow. She gives good milk."

He asked to be handed a nearby rope, then he reached into the birth canal and groped for the legs of the calf. "Easy there, Bossie," he said as the cow started to move. He managed to slip a loop over the front legs of the calf, asked bystanders to pull, but not yank. As they did, Percival guided the head past the opening, and the calf emerged. As the new-born heifer lay outside the cow, it was obvious something was different. The head was larger, rounder, and covered with matted, tight curls.

"Well, I'll be dipped in shit and rolled in bread crumbs," said one astonished man. "Looks like you got a half-breed on your hands, Roy." A chorus of mutterings and laughter followed his words as the men crowded around.

Percival stared down at the calf, stunned. Then, he said, "Well, if that don't beat all. Some randy buffalo bull snuck into the pasture. Stepping out on Mrs. Buffalo is what he was doing." He turned to the others. "In our part of Wisconsin there's still some buffs grazing there." He shook his head. "I've heard this can happen, but, in a month of Sundays, I never would of…go figger."

The men drifted away, and Percival looked the cow over. She was on her feet and seemed no worse for the ordeal. The calf was already moving and attempting to stand. "Go figger," Percival said again, shaking his head with amazement."

The heifer was on its feet in two hours, and soon was walking; unsteady, but stronger by the minute, and already nursing. People gathered around to see the strange hybrid and lost no time in naming it "Wooley."

A man lifted his small daughter and brought her next to Wooley. He took her hand and extended the index finger. "Watch this, dear," he said to her. He put the finger up to Wooley's mouth, and the calf started sucking on it. The little girl shrieked and giggled at the sandpapery tongue. Others laughed and applauded. One woman called out, "Looks like we got us a good luck charm, folks."

As the people surrounding the new calf chatted and laughed, Penney was talking off to the side with Roy Percival. He saw Nimrod and Masterson at the edge of the group and waved them over.

Penney said, "I been talking to Roy here, gents. We got us a problem. His new calf is the problem: It won't be able to keep up."

"Sounds like veal to me," Masterson said.

"Most times, you bet," Penney said, "but the children are already attached to it. I don't think eating little Wooley would sit well with them. Lord knows they need a little jubilation in their lives." He turned to Percival with a questioning look. Percival returned the look and raised his eyebrows.

As the children played with the new calf the next morning, Aaron galloped into the train, shouting, "Buffalo! Buffalo! A huge herd. Get your guns, fellers."

Several excited men gathered around Aaron, then raced for their horses and rifles and galloped in the direction he came from. Nimrod watched them go as Hannah came up to stand next to him.

"Why're they lathered up?"

Nimrod chuckled. "Aaron found himself some buffalo. I saw them last night. A small herd, a couple hundred. The boys is just itching for some excitement. They'll be back in a few hours, I 'spect a lot more tired than when they rode out. Bufflers ofttimes don't wait around to git shot," Nimrod said with a knowing smile.

Hannah tsk-tsked her lips. "I hate guns, and I hate the way men make playthings out of them."

Nimrod laughed. "Well, I suspect them buffalo are pretty safe."

By mid-day, Aaron and the men returned to camp, tired, dejected, and without a single buffalo to brag about. Aaron rode up to Penney and Nimrod.

Penney chuckled in sympathy. "Not the same as killing a chicken in the barnyard, I reckon."

Aaron took a deep breath of resignation. "Those animals are faster and shiftier than we figured."

Nimrod said, "Well, let's me and you ride out in the morning...."

Nimrod dropped Bub's reins and crested a rise cautiously. He tossed a few weeds into the air to watch the direction they were blown. He saw he was downwind of the small herd of buffalo about two hundred yards below in a grassy hollow. Nimrod grunted approval and turned to Aaron who was at his elbow. "They can't see worth a damn, but they can smell if'n you been eating beans."

A quarter mile off to the right, three Indian women also studied the herd, but without weapons, and looked nervously at the white hunters who had suddenly appeared. Nimrod and the women studied each other. He pointed to the herd, then to the women, and made an open-arm questioning gesture. The women were at first confused, then they understood and nodded, and he waved in return. Nimrod took out a stick tucked between Bub's saddle and blanket. It was a gun support shaped like a "Y" with a leg about two feet long. He spiked it into the ground, then knelt behind it and laid the Hawken in the cradle. He guessed the drift of the wind, gauged the distance to the herd, and made allowances for the bullet's drop. He chose a cow on the edge because their meat was the most tender. His rifle ball was not of a large caliber, so it had to hit a vital spot. He took slow aim at an area just behind the shoulder and two-thirds down the body where the heart and lungs were. He avoided a headshot because the thickness of the skull might block the ball. The rifle report rang in their ears as they watched the cow fall and not move. Neither did the herd. It grazed on, oblivious to the danger.

Nimrod stood up, faced the women, pointed to the cow, then at the women, and made a deep cavalier bow in their direction. They understood and waved their delight and thanks.

Nimrod went back to the business of providing meat for the wagon train. He took down another cow, all the time explaining what he was doing to Aaron. He then slid over and let Aaron take the rifle. He pointed out a yearling calf and walked Aaron through the steps to take the shot. Aaron hit the animal in the leg, so Nimrod reloaded and finished it. He saved face for Aaron by telling the young man his shot was off because he wasn't familiar with the Hawken.

The wagons were brought up so the men with butchering experience could carve up the animals. By dusk, the usable meat had been cut into thin strips and piled upon the skins of the slaughtered animals awaiting the dawn so the drying of the meat could begin. Two knife cuts were incurred by the butchers, which Hannah quickly bandaged.

After posting men to guard the meat from the teeth belonging to the glittering eyes in the darkness beyond, the company settled down to a feast of buffalo hump and tongue. Aaron carried his plate to where Nimrod sat eating a two-foot-long sausage.

"What you eating there, Nimrod?" Aaron asked.

Nimrod bit through the sausage, and talked as he chewed. "Buffler gut. Boudins is what we call it. Just cut it, cook it, and tie off the ends. Fresh, it's better'n steak."

"What's in it?"

Nimrod answered with his mouth full. "Gut."

"Gut? You mean—gut? Not sausage?"

Nimrod spoke over a mouthful. "It's sausage for me. I put it in the coals for about a half-hour, which turns it into a trapper's Sunday dinner." He saw the look of disgust on Aaron's face and laughed, the bloody juice running down his chin. "While back, I was in Memphis, and I went into an eye-tal-yan restaurant—I didn't even know such folks was around. Looking at what they was cooking up almost made me hop on Bub and run for the hills. But I ate it, and it was as good as my maw could rustle up. Just goes to show."

"Show what? Aaron asked.

Nimrod finished the boudin, reached for a thigh bone lying nearby. He cracked it on a rock and scooped out and ate the marrow, then leaned back content. "I ain't got all the particulars yet, but I've learned a feller don't have to be the same as me to be regular." He stopped and considered the downcast Aaron. "What's ailing you?"

"Ah, we go out and chase buffalos around most of the day, but then we come home with our tails between our legs." He fluted his lips in disappointment, then said, "I go out there all fired up for easy hunting and come back holding my—rifle in my hands. You go out as calm as you please, like you do it every day, and before sunset, you come back with all the buffalo we can eat. I can guarantee it don't make me feel like Daniel Boone.

Nimrod chuckled. "You're a good farmer, I'm going to guess. You'd get a belly-laugh if you saw me trying to plow a straight furrow. It's all in what a man knows and how hard he works at it."

CHAPTER EIGHTEEN

The company laid up for two days to slice and dry the buffalo meat. They hung the meat above a shallow ditch and kept a slow fire going beneath it. Since they also had strong sunlight and a stiff breeze, the meat dried fast, at least to the extent it would keep for a few weeks.

Roy Percival joined the men drying meat. He was accompanied by his teenage son, Wiley, a redhead with a face full of freckles and a perpetual smile.

"I swear," he said, that half-breed calf, that Wooley, could run for mayor of this wagon train and win in a walk."

"In a trot," Preacher said, chuckling, then looked around for appreciation of his quip.

"That gives us a problem, a diplomatic one, so to speak," Masterson said. "For certain, the animal has a following, but it can't keep up with the wagons. Problem is, if we butcher it, every child will declare a day of mourning, and then blame us."

Penney listened, then said, "Me and Roy will work something out."

The next morning, the calf was gone before breakfast. When the small children came around to play with it, Roy told them the calf died during the night, and he had already buried it. The kids listened in sadness and half-belief, but they knew better than to question too hard, and went back to their wagons. The cow, Bossie, was restless, so instead of leading the livestock as a bell cow, she was tied to the back of the Percival wagon, which happened to be positioned in the rear.

When they stopped for the noon break, Roy Percival approached a group of men and asked, "Anyone see my cow, Bossie? She broke free of her rope."

Those within hearing looked at each other and shook their heads. Penney walked over and quietly asked Percival where the calf had been taken. He said his son, Wiley, had been told to take the calf before dawn beyond the sound of a rifle shot and shoot it. Wiley was told to then take Bossie to the calf's body, and then bury it. The cow needed to know her calf was dead, otherwise she would chase its scent.

"Difficult thing for a youngster to do," Masterson said.

"A boy's got to learn life ain't easy, especially doing something merciful that seems cruel," Percival said. He called Wiley over and put his hand on the boy's shoulder. "Son, where'd you take the calf?"

Wiley's smile vanished, and he hung his head. "I, uh, I was fixin' to shoot it, and then I saw a small buffalo herd real close by— kinda close by, so I figured—" He looked up to see if anger were directed at him. "I figured maybe joining the herd might work. Maybe the calf could find a buffalo mother to nurse it, and the herd would accept her. I figured she should have a chance to live."

No one said anything. Wiley's father pursed his lips, squeezed his son's shoulder, and studied him before speaking. "Boy, doing something wrong for a good reason don't make it right. Now, the cow is off who knows where looking for her calf. We might lose both. When you're given a job to do, son, there's a reason for it."

Tears formed in Wiley's eyes. "I'm sorry, Dad. I was just trying to save the calf."

"You're forgiven, Wiley. Now, brush those tears aside. You're too old for that." His voice picked up, signaling he was back to business. "We're sure to lose that cow to wolves or Indians." He looked away. "Damn it! That's a good cow. She gives three gallon a day." Percival looked at Nimrod, hoping, but reluctant to ask.

Nimrod nodded and walked over to Bub nearby. "I'll go," he said.

The cow was easy to track. Nimrod retraced the morning route at a gallop. After four miles, he could see the cow in the distance and also running, but much slower. The bell could be heard faintly. As the distance closed, the cow stopped and put her nose to the ground. As Nimrod rode up, he could see she was standing over the carcass of the calf. On a rise a couple of hundred yards away, two coyotes paced, impatient to return to their kill, but restrained by Nimrod's approach. Nimrod dismounted and put a rope around the cow's neck.

"Nothing for you here, Bossie. Sorry, old girl." Nimrod led the mooing cow away as the coyotes returned to their kill. As they left at a walk, the bell clanging slowed to a knell.

At supper with the Cohens at the end of a satisfying seventeen-mile day, Nimrod had just finished running his tongue through a bite of catfish, trying to corner a small bone, when he heard frantic shouting from a wagon across the circle. He grabbed his rifle and ran for the sound, joined by Penney, who chased behind as fast as he could.

When they arrived at the Spencer wagon, Nimrod almost ran into Ed Spencer who was flailing his arms and shouting in a spitting rage. About a hundred yards out on the prairie, Spencer's dog was sprawled in the dirt with a lance protruding straight upward. An Indian brave on horseback had attached a line to the lance and was starting to tow the dead dog away.

"That barbarian son of a bitch killed my dog. Where's my rifle?" Spencer screamed. He reached into the wagon for his gun and swung it toward the Indian.

Nimrod shouted, "For God's sake, don't shoot! Stop him!" He was, however, too far away to grab Spencer who was about to fire. At the last second, Hannah pushed his arm up, and the gun fired into the air.

Spencer wheeled on her, almost hitting her with the gun barrel. "Damn you!" he screamed and raised his arm to strike her. Just as his arm was about to come down on her face, Penney wedged himself between them.

"You don't strike a woman in my presence, no sir," Penney said as he spread his arms between them.

Spencer shook his fist in Penney's face. "You interfere, old man, and you'll get it, too."

Penney didn't blink, and a devilish smile crossed his face. "For certain-sure, you'll work up a sweat doing that job."

Nimrod put his hand on Penney's chest and edged him back out of Spencer's face. He turned to Spencer. "You shoot that brave, and we'll all lose our scalps."

"The bastard killed my dog!"

"To you he did, but to hisself, he killed hisself a meal. To these people, if it's on the prairie with four legs, it's to be either rode or et."

"You talk like an ignoramus," Spencer scorned.

The insult stung Nimrod, considering it struck a sensitive nerve and was overheard by people whose respect he valued. He stared at Spencer with dead eyes. "There is things I do right well."

Spencer snorted in derision. "Talking's not one of them."

Nimrod stared.

The rage seeped out of Spencer's voice to be replaced by a whine. "I paid fifty dollars for that dog."

Nimrod was astonished. "You paid fifty dollars for a *dog?*" His question was followed by a titter from onlookers who hated Spencer more than they loved dogs. Nimrod glanced at the Indian disappearing in the distance dragging the dog. Seeing he was out of range, Nimrod turned and joined Penney, and they walked away from Spencer. Laughing, Penney said, "That Indian could've fed his whole tribe at Delmonico's for fifty dollars."

"That dog ain't nothing of the bastard's problems. Spencer best be worried about his horses. They're near played out," Nimrod said.

"He's blind to it," Penney said.

"Then, he'll pay."

Penney went to the edge of the camp one evening, wondering where the cattle were. In the distance, he saw the young herdsmen driving them back.

Penney asked the first boy what had happened. The boy told him Benjamin, the little white terrier, had upset the cattle by nipping at heels and barking. They trotted a couple of hundred yards away from the little pest, and that's where the boys found them.

Penney knew what he had to do. He walked to the Patterson wagon and helloed politely. Jasper Patterson looked out and climbed down. "Hello there, Shadrach," he said with a smile. "What can I do for you?"

Penney's look and muted voice erased Jasper's smile. "It's about your dog, Jasper. He chased the cattle again."

Jasper eased out a breath and looked skyward. "I been expecting something like this." He looked at Shadrach. "I don't suppose—"

Penney shook his head. "You're a farmer, Jasper. You know you can't let a dog spook cattle."

Jasper nodded and paused as though gathering himself. "Agnes?" he called out. "The captain here wants a word with you."

"What about?" an older woman's voice asked, already suspicious.

"Come on out, darling."

Reluctantly, Agnes climbed down from behind the bonnet. She held Benjamin in her arms and looked at Penney in fear.

"Evening, missus," Penney said, touching his hat brim. "I reckon you know why I'm here. Your dog, Benjamin here, has chased cattle again. It seems strange such a little feller can spook beeves, but that's the size of it."

Tears ran down Agnes' face, and she hugged the little dog and kissed it on the head.

Penney started over. "Miz Agnes, cattle are partial to things being regular and quiet. They take comfort in that. When your little dog stirs them up, it affects how they eat and sleep. I know it sounds strange, but your husband here can tell you it's true."

Jasper looked at the ground and said nothing, and Penney was sorry he dragged him into it. "It's a hard job, running this wagon train, ma'am. I hope you understand the committee is sorry for what has to be done."

Agnes was crying now and stroking the dog as it reached up and licked the tears on her cheeks. He reminded Penney of a dog he had years ago, and how sad he was to put it out of its misery from old age.

Agnes reached out and put her hand on Penney's arm. "Captain," she said through sobs, "I had to give up the home me and Jasper built with our hands in Wabash County. I left the graves of my children, Eddie, nine, and Eleanor, newborn, and named for my mother. All I have left is my good husband, Jasper, what's in this old wagon, and my best friend, little Benjamin." Her look was imploring. "Captain, I'm an old woman."

Penney reached for the dog and eased it out of her grasp. "I would spare this little animal if not for my duty." He walked away with the dog cuddled in his arm and licking his hand. Agnes' sobs grew fainter and then disappeared, but not their memory. He walked across the camp to where Nimrod was standing and motioned him aside. "Nimrod, can I have the loan of your revolving pistol?"

Nimrod understood and handed over the gun butt first without comment. Penney turned and walked away into the darkness.

Later, Penney stopped by Nimrod's tent and returned the pistol. Half asleep, Nimrod reached over, holstered it, and went back to sleep.

The next morning, Nimrod awoke, took his trip to the bushes, and then ate some cold buffalo hump. He saddled Bub and put a fresh load in his rifle, then reached for his pistol, which he knew now had an empty chamber. He opened it to reload and noticed all the chambers were full. He looked toward the tent of Jasper and Agnes Patterson. Tied to the wagon wheel with a long cord and red ribbon was Benjamin.

Starting out, the pioneers spent their worry time on catastrophes: fire, drowning, breakdowns, diseases, and Indian attacks. However, what quickly vexed them most were the daily irritants and sufferings that, as they accumulated, threatened to drive every one of them crazy.

The humorless joke was that Satan himself was tormenting them in the guise of the mosquito. But there was much more to that little bug than nasty bites. Malaria, for instance. They didn't know the little devils could give them that, too.

The pioneers were used to filling the portable tin tub in the kitchen every Saturday night for the weekly bath to prepare for Sunday meeting. On the trail, they could go many, many days before finding a clear stream in which they could bathe fully clothed for modesty without emerging from the water dirtier than when entered.

Clothes might be worn every day for two weeks before the women demanded loudly enough for a delay sufficient to do laundry.

Hemorrhoids? Keep walking, though wincing with every step…A cold or touch of the flu? Keep walking and coughing… Twisted ankle? Hobble along…The "trots"? Run for a clump of bushes, then keep walking…Yeast infection? Try to ignore… Broken leg? Endure the agony of a bouncing wagon…A hundred other maladies? Dread…

Death? Waiting, just over the next hill.

Gossips enjoy nothing more than watching youth discover romance. And on the trail, enjoyable distractions were in short supply. Eyes and smiles tracked Alice Dickens and young Wiley Percival as they blushed and smiled at each other around the campfires. They looked for excuses to walk together along the trail. Alice's mother, Flora, of course, didn't miss a thing. Wiley's father, Roy, was vaguely aware of the goings-on.

It almost blew up one evening when Aaron Proctor was walking along the riverbank and saw young Wiley Percival kissing Alice Dickens. Bad enough, but Alice's dress was lowered to her waist, and one bud-like breast was in his hand. Aaron backed away, and when he was some yards out of sight, he made some noise to let the kids know to cover up and move apart.

Aaron, of course, told Gertie with a promise not to repeat it. Gertie, of course, told another woman with a promise not to repeat it. And so on until the whole camp knew. They dutifully feigned shock, but also smiled.

Contact between the pair was, as expected, thenceforth forbidden. Still, the young couple couldn't be stopped from following each other with their eyes, and when those eyes met, a knowing smile at the beautiful discovery they had made.

One afternoon, a bigger boy teased Wiley about "puppy love," which, of course, caused a fight, and a bloody nose for Wiley. As he held a rag to his tipped-back face, he pledged to himself— I'll love her forever.

The deaths of Hazel Grover and William Dickens put a dark mood over the train because they were reminders that danger walked at their side every step, and also how families were without support and succor in such a wilderness. They were alone, and their only help had to come from people who had been strangers just weeks before, and who shared their fears.

Nimrod and Penney pondered the why of it all one evening as they sat relaxing on stools outside Penney's wagon.

"That poor Dickens woman, left with two younguns, and her daughter just starting to feel her boy oats," Penney said.

"Just why in hell do people put their families through this?" Nimrod said.

Penney pursed his lips in thought. "Some folks just want more than they've got, whatever it is. Others figure they can shed the life they've been saddled with, or already messed up, and they think distance will do the trick."

Nimrod shook his head. "These people are risking everthing for what might be a poor riverboat gamble."

Penney tossed a pebble aimlessly. "Since the Garden of Eden first opened for business, there's always been a California of a hundred different names to dream about and gamble on. Always will be. Some men are always in a hurry to lay down a bet, either on a horse race, or on their lives. I feel a little sorry for some of the women. They were dragged here by husbands chasing greener grass, men who had, when they courted them, promised a safe home in a civilized place. Most of these ladies just want to be back to the life they thought they were marrying into."

"How about your wife, Shadrach?" The question was one Nimrod would not ask of a man he felt less comfortable with.

Penney's face became a sad little smile. "She didn't like the life she had. She was all for California."

Nimrod was distracted by John Burns doing maintenance on his wagon. "Ain't it a sight how Burns over there hopped on the water wagon? I ain't seen him take a drink since he had those snakes in his head."

Penney nodded. "Cold turkey. More's the credit."

In another part of the camp, Spencer was tending to his tack when he noticed something. Curious, he stopped and watched. He glimpsed an Indian walking in the general direction of the livestock herd, and close to his horses. His pulse quickened. He moved to his wagon, grabbed a rifle, took aim, and fired, then grunted with satisfaction as he watched the person fall.

At the rifle report, Nimrod, Penney, and others ran to the Spencer wagon.

"What happened? Why'd you fire?" Nimrod shouted, holding his pistol in his hand.

Spencer gestured with contempt toward the prone Indian as people rushed to the body.

Spencer acted as though he had just fought off a war party. "The damned Indian was trying to steal my horses."

Nimrod stared at him then lunged for Spencer's throat. "You dumb son of a bitch. She was an old Indian woman. You've gotten us all killed."

Other men restrained Nimrod as Spencer twisted free. "She was a thief," he shouted. "You damned Indian lover."

Nimrod regained control and shook off the restraint. "Pawnee women don't steal horses. That's men's work."

"Then what was she doing here?" Spencer demanded.

Nimrod pointed to a bag next to the woman's body with brown discs spilling out. "They live here, you damned idiot. She was collecting buffalo chips."

Zack elbowed to the front. "Maybe they won't miss her," he said.

Nimrod gave Zack a withering glare, then ignored him. Turning away, he said, "I've got to think..."

For a long time, Nimrod walked around the camp and the covered body which lay just outside the camp. The men took turns guarding the body to prevent animals from disturbing it. He talked to no one except Penney, and then briefly, because what could any of these back-East tradesmen and farmers say to him about defusing a life-and-death crisis with the Pawnees?

When dawn broke, Nimrod called the men together and had half of them stand guard with guns loaded but held close-by and out of sight. The other half he put to work constructing a scaffold about a hundred yards from the camp. The four legs were made of wood about five-feet high taken from young cottonwoods from a nearby creek bank, and atop it they made a bed of willow branches laid on top of a lattice of rawhide and stout limbs. They took the wrapped body of the woman and placed it on the platform. Then Nimrod sent the men back to the camp to wait.

Nimrod stood alone by the scaffold, and in each direction used sign language in large gestures: WE TALK. He signaled that message in every direction under the glare of the rising sun. After doing it several times, he walked back to the camp where Penney met him.

"What now?" Penney asked.

Zack crowded close. "Nothing to stop us from just skedaddling down the trail."

Nimrod didn't even bother looking at him. "You go right ahead and climb your fool's hill. When we catch up, we'll bury what's left of you."

Abraham Jackman walked up in time to say, "Shut up, Zack."

Nimrod never took his eyes off the horizon. "We wait."

All day they waited, sweating in the heat, swatting flies, glancing with apprehension at the skyline in every direction, and trying to stay busy with chores and puttering. Every hour, Nimrod went back to the elevated bier and made the same sign-language message: WE TALK.

Just about when the women started their supper-time bustle, a group of warriors appeared a quarter-mile out. No one saw them approach. They were just there. The reaction in the camp was a fearful hum that Nimrod hushed. Several men rushed for their guns, but Nimrod stopped them. "If they wanted a fight, they wouldn't be standing out there," he said. "If they decide our scalps are what they want, they won't make such fine targets." He saddled Bub and prepared to ride out.

Penney rode up with his rifle in hand. "You can't go alone."

Nimrod said, "This shore ain't going to be a friend visit."

Penney was grim. "Then, I should be with you."

Nimrod put this hand on the older man's shoulder and smiled, just a little, though he didn't much feel like it. "Shadrach, you might have a mind to die with me, but I'll have too much on *my* mind to appreciate it." Nimrod handed his guns to Penney.

"You might need these."

"A couple of guns won't stop them if they want to kill me. If I go unarmed, I'm hoping they'll see me as a peace-seeker."

"You should be praying, not hoping," Preacher said.

"I'd be grateful for any help you can give me, Preacher," he said sincerely.

"Go with God, son," Penney said. It sounded like a benediction.

"I hope He comes along," Nimrod said in a light banner which sounded reassuring, but not what he felt. He rode at a slow canter out to the Indians while people watched with shallow breaths and wide eyes. Their mutterings merged into a buzz as the Indian leader rode out to meet Nimrod. His imposing carriage was enhanced by eagle feathers in his hair and clothes of fringed buckskin with intricate beadwork. Nimrod knew he was facing the chief, but also a man whose rigid posture and angry face made Nimrod tense.

Not knowing each other's speech, they relied on sign language, which over the years had become articulate in its own way among tribes.

Chief: We watch you many days but not attack. Why you kill woman?

Nimrod: We sorry. Deed of one bad man. We are friends of Pawnee. We treat body with respect.

Chief: Why you not kill him?

Nimrod: Would you believe if we did?

The chief thought about that, then said: My warriors want to kill all.

Nimrod: That not justice. Many warriors die.

Chief: We not afraid of dying.

Nimrod: Neither we. We offer blankets, shirts, many beautiful horses...

Chief: She my mother.

Nimrod: My heart grieves.

Chief: No gifts. Give us bad man who kill.

Nimrod: Not our way.

Chief: Then all die for your way.

Nimrod: I must talk with my chiefs.

The Pawnee chief abruptly wheeled his horse and galloped away. Nimrod turned Bub and trotted back toward the wagons. With every breath he expected an arrow in his back.

Penney grabbed Bub's harness. "Well, I'm pleased you're alive."

"For now." Nimrod dismounted, as people pressed around to hear their fate.

"What did he say? What do they want?" A woman asked.

Nimrod removed his hat and wiped the sweat from his brow. "I offered apologies. I offered them horses." He glared toward Spencer. "I offered them *his* horses."

Cohen edged close and asked with tension in his voice. "Was it enough?"

Nimrod shook his head. "They don't want horses, cattle, or any other goods we can offer."

"What, then?" Preacher asked.

Zack was mystified. "She weren't nothing but a squaw."

Nimrod glanced in Zack's direction, as though he didn't deserve a full look. "Why don't you go explain that to her son? He's the chief."

An anonymous voice said softly, "God help us."

Zack scoffed. "Wait'll they taste some of our lead."

Nimrod looked at him with distaste.

Jackman growled at his nephew." Shut up, Zack."

Penney interrupted a frightened cacophony of questions. "Folks, folks, this'll get us nowhere. We need some order on this. Let the committee figure something out, and then we'll call y'all together. Just give us a little time."

A man in the rear shouted, "All of us should decide about this."

Penney shook his head. "No, sir. We'd just argue in circles. I'm not going to shuffle this off on anyone else. This is our job."

The men of the committee walked some distance for privacy and stopped in the shade of a black locust tree. They chose seats on a protruding rock, on a dirt ledge, or stood with arms folded. The mood was glum, befitting men who had to choose between options, all of which seemed probable to end in death.

"Call Spencer over," Penney said. Cohen left, and returned with

Spencer a step behind. He extended his hand, but no one shook it. Spencer looked from one face to another and saw only grimness. Sweat beaded on his forehead, and his lower lip trembled. "So, what do they want?" he asked with a shaky voice.

Nimrod looked around the circle, then said in an even voice. "They don't want a thing, not a thing—except the man who killed her." He looked hard at Spencer, who blanched. "They want you."

"Oh, God," Spencer said in a quaking voice.

"And if we say no?" Cohen said.

"They attack. Which means we all die, or worse."

Jackman said. "We can make a case for manslaughter. He thought she was a thief."

"We ain't in court, Abraham" Masterson said.

Preacher said, "Is there an actual law against shooting wild Indians?"

"God has one. Apparently, the Indians do, too," Cohen said.

Penney paced in frustration, back and forth, then glared at Spencer. "I got no truck for you. You've been spoiling for trouble since the Indian speared your dog."

"Before that. From the moment he showed up," Cohen said, glaring at Spencer.

Jackman said, "We have to follow the law here. We can't just surrender a man to Indian justice."

Preacher looked surprised. "Indian justice? Is there such a thing?"

Penney frowned, and said, "The Indians seem to think so. Right now, it's their justice we got to deal with."

"We can fight them off," Masterson said with more hope than confidence.

Nimrod said. "Not the whole tribe, we can't. It would be a short fight. Anyway, they're warriors; we're farmers."

Jackman became angry and glared at Spencer. "I'm not going to see my wife scalped just to save this rat."

Penney turned to Nimrod. "Lee, how do you size this up?"

Nimrod spoke as though Spencer were not there. "Indians don't have long-winded court sessions or twisty lawyers. If we give up the killer, we go free. If not, we all die."

Preacher said, "As final as that?"

"The Pawnees will make it final."

Spencer buried his face in shaking hands. The other men exchanged long, silent looks. Cohen coughed. Preacher's lips moved in apparent prayer. Masterson rose off his rock and walked a few steps where he stared into the distance.

Penney said, "I guess we don't need no more words. I don't like this a bit."

"Spencer," Penney said in a sober tone, "we're in an impossible situation—put there by you. The Pawnees are demanding justice—or else."

Spencer said nothing; his lips moved, saying nothing.

"They want you," Penney said.

Preacher protested. "Mr. Penney, we're a God-fear—"

Penney cut him short. "I'll handle this." He turned back to Spencer. The two men locked eyes: Penney sad, Spencer frightened.

"What are you talking about?" Spencer asked. The bravado was stripped away, replaced by a frightened voice. The other men looked away or toward the ground. The darkening of their mood was not lost on Spencer. He turned to pleading. "Please, I thought she was stealing our horses.... I've got a wife and two children. I' ve—"

Penney interrupted him. "We've got to think about the welfare—"

Henry Griswold had been standing nearby, ignored by the men. To everyone's surprise, he walked forward and into their midst. "I've been listening—Send me."

Penney was mystified. "Send you where?"

Griswold said, without looking at Spencer, "He's a bad man, but he's got a family....Me? Not a mortal soul will miss me ten minutes after I'm gone."

"Go back with the others, old man," Penney said. He was in no mood for such nonsense.

"I'm a walking dead man. I've been keeping off to myself because I've got a touch of consumption."

Masterson interrupted, but with sympathy. "No one's got a *touch* of consumption, Henry."

Griswold nodded. "True." His nod turned to a sad head

shake. "Like an old fool, I thought maybe the sun and warmth of California, or so I've read, might give me a few more years. But…" He looked around for reaction; there was none. "I'll never make California, and you all know it. My knees are on fire every step I take. My lungs are about to burst. I can feel it."

Preacher raised a finger. "That's suicide you're describing. God said— "

"Not now," Penney said softly.

Cohen put his hand on Griswold's shoulder. "We can help you, sir. We should have already."

Spencer said, "I think—"

Penney spoke again, but not softly. "Shut up."

Griswold spoke with fear about what he was proposing, and frustration that the men did not seem to understand. "Damnit, don't you hear me? I want to live no less than any of you. And I'm sure the hell not suicidal. But if I don't go out there today, I'll drop dead on the trail on another day soon, and you'll have to delay this God-forsaken trip to bury me. Or I'll take a gun and blow my brains out, and then the children will see the mess."

With nowhere else to turn, Penney turned to their guide. "Nimrod?"

"This ain't part of guiding."

None of the men wanted to look at Griswold, nor at each other. Penney looked at Spencer with disgust. "Get out of here. You're not fit to be near this man."

Spencer sighed in relief. As he walked past Griswold, he said, "Sir, I just want to say—"

"Git!" Penney demanded in a raspy voice, and Spencer scurried off. Committee members looked at each other and realized there was nothing left to say. They walked away, each one shaking Griswold's hand without comment. Nimrod lingered behind.

"You can change your mind, my friend," he said.

"I don't want to be taken alive."

After an awkward silence, Nimrod said, "I got no words for this. No, sir, I don't, except you're a brave man…a good man."

Preacher said, "I'd like to pray with you, sir."

Griswold looked at far-off hills. "I'm covered there, thank you.

I'd like a few minutes alone, if you don't mind."

Nimrod said, "One last time—" Silence. With resignation, he said, "I'll fetch the Pawnees."

Responding to Nimrod's summons, the Indians walked their horses toward camp, stopping two hundred yards away. Nimrod rode out to meet them. The Pawnees had brought a tribesman who could speak some English.

Nimrod said to the interpreter, "Tell the chief he'll have his justice. The man will step out."

"The guilty one?"

Nimrod skirted the question. "He stepped forward. He asks you for a swift death."

When hearing that, the chief said through the interpreter that tribal law demanded a ceremonial death for the criminal. "He'll get the death of a murderer."

Nimrod said nothing for a long moment. Then he said, "Tell the chief I offer another way."

A cluster of Pawnee braves milled on their horses outside an easy rifle shot from the circled wagons. They had no trust for these white intruders. They were waiting to avenge the death of their tribal sister, the chief's mother.

Henry Griswold returned from his time of solitude. He then gave his wagon, oxen, and what little money he possessed to the widow Flora Dickens for her fatherless children.

Word of the sacrifice Griswold was making dismayed people, most of whom had spoken few words to the quiet ex-teacher. No one approached him because no one knew what to say to such a man. Instead, they stared as though he were a circus oddity. They shook their heads in amazement and wondered why anyone would do such a thing. A few glared at Ed Spencer who stayed close to his wagon with an angry, defensive look. Hannah and her children were nowhere in sight.

Nimrod and Penney walked to where Griswold was staring off in the distance. "They're waiting, Henry," Nimrod said. Then, "It won't happen the way you fear. I give my word." The three men faced the Indians in the distance. Griswold looked toward the horizon, and said in a shaky voice, "It's mighty strange to be facing this." He took a deep breath and exhaled slowly as though bracing his determination. "You know, I never thought of this world without me. It's a brutal place, but I dread leaving it. When I was a child, I once walked past a fresh-dug grave, and I thought how horrible to be in a hole like that for eternity, pitch black and with worms. Now, in a short time, I'll be in there, wasting away." He looked at his hands as though he had never seen them. He shook his head. "Amazing."

Griswold stood and slowly turned a complete circle, looking again at the mountains, the brown earth, and the trees scattered randomly through the landscape as though he had never noticed them. He reached down and picked up a handful of dirt and sifted it through his fingers. He sighed. "How can this be?"

"You're a good man, Henry," Penney said. "A special good man."

Perhaps Griswold heard him, but his thoughts were elsewhere. "Looking back, I'm sorrowful I cared so much for boastful things. There's been much I've done that I'd like to undo. Everyone I was mean to, I regret; one especially, but I never said it to her. I hope she figured it out. I wish I'd been kinder to people who needed it. I wish I'd read the Bible more. I hope God knows I tried, for the most part. I tried to be a good Christian, but not as hard as I could've. I hope the scriptures were right, and he's a forgiving God." He lapsed into silence.

Then, Penney said, "Go with God," and Nimrod embraced Griswold.

The old man took a deep breath and resettled his hat with a shaking hand. He started walking toward the Indians, his arthritic knees moving him forward in pain.

Nimrod lifted his rifle and checked it. He hoped it would not be needed.

The Pawnees became still. The chief reached for a lance from one of his warriors. He walked his horse a few feet ahead and watched Griswold coming toward him. When Griswold was about forty yards distant, the chief screamed a war cry and prodded his horse into a gait, then a gallop, bearing down on the old man who had stopped.

The chief was almost on top of Griswold when he threw the lance into his chest. Griswold's lips formed an "O," and he grabbed the lance with both hands, then fell forward. The lance hit the ground, plunging deeper into his chest. Griswold fell sideways and was still.

The chief again screamed his war cry and was joined by the braves. He rode back to the group and waited. People looked at each other nervously. Their expressions asked—What now?

Nimrod lowered his rifle, and Penney said," Was you going to do with that rifle what I think?"

Nimrod didn't answer. Instead, he said, "Come with me. You need to witness this." As they walked, Nimrod explained his purpose. When they reached Spencer's wagon, Nimrod called him out.

Hannah was standing in the distance with her children held tightly under each arm. All three looked stunned. There had been no attempt among the pioneers to shield children from what had just happened. No point to it; no way to do it, anyway. When Hannah saw Nimrod and Penney walking toward the wagon, she guided her children away, her head down. The children tried to look back but kept walking.

Spencer appeared from inside the wagon bonnet where he had made himself scarce, and said, "What do you want?"

Nimrod said, "I want one of your thoroughbreds, now."

"Like hell you're going to get my horse."

Spittle leaked from Nimrod's lips in his fury. "You dirty dog. You drygulching son of a bitch. A good man is dead because of you while you skulked in hiding. Now you get down here or, by God, I'll pull you down."

Spencer looked to Penney for help. The captain said, "You ain't a dirty dog, you're a lawn-shitting cur. Get down right now and do as he says, or I swear to God I'll grab that bullwhip and whip you down."

Suddenly contrite, Spencer climbed down and turned the reins of the beautiful horse over to Nimrod without comment.

Nimrod mounted Bub and led the horse out to the chief and

handed the reins to him. He nodded to the chief, and the chief nodded back, turned his horse, and led his warriors away at a gallop, leading his new thoroughbred.

Nimrod watched them go, then turned and went to where Griswold lay. He pulled the lance and tossed it aside. He lifted the body and laid it across Bub's saddle. With head bowed, he walked the mule back to the wagon train.

People converged around the body. The men took their hats off, and some of the women wept.

Nimrod was still furious. He yelled, "Spencer! Get over here." Moments later, Spencer appeared, as docile as a penitent. "Get a shovel. I want a grave dug for this gentleman, and I want it deep."

After supper, and when the kids had been put to bed, the adults sat in reflective silence around a fire listening to the frogs at the riverbank, the mournful hooting of an owl, the sawing of crickets, and the sound of a shovel scraping as Spencer dug a grave for Henry Griswold in the fading light.

The next morning after breakfast, people gathered around the fresh dirt of Griswold's grave. There was no attempt to hide the hump atop it. Cohen took a loose board someone had no use for. He used white bonnet paint to inscribe an epitaph using a thin paintbrush.

Henry Griswold

Springfield, Illinois

About 75 years

Died, July 1845

Sent by God

Preacher read scripture and said a lengthy prayer, then they sang a ragged version of the recently composed hymn, "Nearer, My God to Thee," with Enoch Brister trying to follow with his concertina. As the pioneers silently walked back to their wagons, Preacher said to Nimrod, "A regular grave like that, you know it's going to be despoiled by Indians or wolves."

Nimrod agreed. "Like as not that's bound to happen, anyway. But at least the gentleman will have a Christian funeral and a dignified grave for a few days. That's more'n some people I know deserve."

CHAPTER NINETEEN

The main excitement was the appearance of Flora in her new riding outfit. She had inherited her late husband's riding horse, but it came with a man's saddle; difficult to ride in a full-length dress.

All eyes in the camp swiveled in shock when she appeared in her late husband's long trousers modified to fit her. Over them, she wore a dress cut down to just above knee length. Flora did not realize, of course, that she predated Amelia Bloomer's well-publicized adoption of the same "revolution" a half-decade later.

The reaction was outrage from a few of the more conservative pioneers. Many women and some men grinned and said, "About time," or "Makes sense." The most severe comment made to her was by Preacher, who said it was "not ladylike" to display female "limbs" in public.

"Well," she said, "what did you think I walk on, stilts?"

In the following days, Hannah took the lead in encouraging other women by altering some of her own clothing. "This is our chance for sane dress. We need to follow Flora's example," she said. Several did, but the older women declined to do so, but, tellingly, they did not criticize those who did.

The one effort to cause trouble was by Simon Tester, who still felt humiliated by Flora's rejection. He whispered to receptive ears that her actions were those of a loose woman. In fact, he had heard...

It wasn't long before his slander made it to Flora's ears, and she was quick to respond. One evening after supper, when everyone was around the center of the circle, she walked up to Tester, and said in a loud voice, "I've been told you've tried to blacken my good name."

Tester had no answer. He looked around with an I-wish-I-were-elsewhere grin.

She said, "You're a scoundrel. I'll give you the thrashing your mother should have." She lifted a rider's quirt and started to whip him around the head and shoulders. Tester backed up, and she followed him. He balled up his fist, but Penney said in a loud voice, "Don't you hit that woman! You can run, or you can take your medicine, but if you hit her, we'll show you real punishment." Tester turned and made the most graceful exit he could manage.

There were no sad faces watching his disappearing back.

Billy was currying Hambo. At the same time Spencer approached Hannah leading his palomino. He started upbraiding her as she prepared dinner. "Hannah, I forbid you to shorten your dress like the Flora woman. You remind me of a New Orleans whore."

"Well, Ed, I'd have to bow to your experience concerning that."

He changed tack and softened his manner. "My dear, it ain't seemly the way you turn away from me. Other folks ain't blind."

"You're right, Ed. People aren't blind. I think they see a bully and a killer. I think what they see is a wife ashamed of her husband. Take your pretty horse and your popinjay ribbon and ride away from my children and me."

Spencer grabbed her arm. "You won't humiliate me!"

Hannah reached for a hot poker from the fire. "Let go of me or I'll brand you like the animal you are."

Spencer backed off and mounted his horse. He fingered the ribbon with a malicious grin. "This was given me by the most expensive whore in New Orleans. Now, there was a real woman."

Before Hannah turned her back, she said, "Then see if she'll have you back."

Billy continued currying with tears in his eyes.

At the noon break the next day, while people were eating their cold lunch, Aaron Proctor looked around and saw Penney and Cohen talking to Nimrod. He fast-walked over to them, and said,

"You better come quick. There's trouble about to start over at the pimp's wagon."

The men looked at each other quizzically, but then Cohen snapped his fingers, and said, "The Benny Bogle wagon." All of them headed in that direction at a fast pace. When they arrived, they found Ethel Pearl standing in front of the wagon, waving a butcher knife at Benny Bogle. He was standing as far back as he could from her without disappearing into the wagon.

Ethel was a woman large in heft, but not fat. She had a mouth that someone remarked could be heard in Santa Fe against a strong wind.

"Listen, you mouse of a man, you keep your floozies away from my son, Homer, or I'll cut you into a buzzard's meal."

Bogle was a small man who tried to appear debonair, or at least citified, by wearing a black suit with a string tie and paisley waistcoat. The effect was ridiculous in the heat and dirt of the prairie, but staying in character was an ego thing.

"Ma'am, ma'am," he pleaded, "it was a misunderstanding. The lady was just asking some questions about the wagon train, that's all."

"She weren't no lady, and that's not the way it was. It was the young one. Homer, he came home in a state of arousal. I know the way of men. A proposition was made, I just know it. For Lord's sake, Homer's but nineteen."

Bogle tried another tack. "At nineteen, it's a condition could happen in church." He briefly grinned self-satisfaction of his quip.

Ethel drove the knife a quarter-inch into the driver's seat. "Don't you go funnin' me, you, you—flesh peddler!"

He held up both hands in a supplicating manner. "Oh, please, ma'am. I meant no offense. I'll make sure the girls give your son plenty of space if they see him again. Please, please put the knife down."

Cohen walked over to Ethel, making sure he stayed in her sight, and clear of her knife. "Now, Mrs. Pearl, you've made your point. Why don't you go along back to your wagon and let the committee take care of this?"

Ethel huffed off, and Nimrod said to Cohen and Penney, "Let

me talk to him. I've seen men of his pursuits before."

Penney exhaled with relief. "You're welcome to him. Just make sure his doxies don't agitate any more peckers. That could be enough trouble to tear this train apart." Nimrod, with Cohen a curious observer, waited until the area in front of the wagon was clear, then he called out, "Bogle. Benny Bogle. A word, if you please."

Bogle peered out from behind the bonnet. "What you want?"

"Come down here for a talk."

"I don't have to come down for anything or anyone."

Nimrod's tone was not intended to give comfort. "You might want to think it over."

Bogle had a keen ear for a threat. He climbed down and stood before Nimrod. "Whatcha want?"

Nimrod extended his hand, which Bogle, surprised, shook. "Now, Benny, I've been around enough to understand how you do your business. Your kind has been known to give useful service to some men in places where females ain't common. That's why I'm talking to you cordial-like, man-to-man, so to speak. I want for you to understand this ain't where you're welcome to be doing business." He paused, then added, "I'm being gentle about this."

Bogle shrugged in frustration. "I don't have to be told that. These sodbusters ain't got money to spend on my girls. Plus, there ain't no place to work. It's not the girls giving trouble, it's these fellers sniffing around them that's getting their own women agitated."

"Well, you can't hardly blame the ladies. Not many things more fearsome than a hen defending her brood."

Bogle was frustrated. "My idea is to get to Sutter's Fort with these girls. From what a gent in St. Louis told me, I'd have the field to myself for miles around, maybe in the whole territory, except for maybe some señoritas or squaws in business for themselves, I reckon. But speaking about the here and now, Mary and Louise, my oldest—ah, more experienced—girls, they know better than to sashay around men with no money. It just boils them into steam with no safety valve. My problem is with Red."

"Red?"

"That's her stage name, so to speak. She's a redbone. Don't know her real name, for sure. Found her in Paducah. Can't be more'n eighteen. She ain't learned to rein in her charms yet, at least not where there's no market for them."

"Well, sir, unless she does, you'll be forced to leave the train. The men running things around here are skittish about having trouble stirred up. And if'n—if—you got cut loose from the train, you'd find about the Indian bucks that they don't ask, and they don't pay."

Bogle sighed. "People think this is an easy business."

Nimrod said, "Have her come down here; I'll talk to her myself."

Bogle leered. "Talk?"

"Don't insult me, peddler," Nimrod said with a glare.

Answering the summons, Red popped out from behind the bonnet with wide eyes and a big grin. She was what was called a 'redbone' as a person of mixed race, but with a complexion of a reddish hue, and moderately wiry hair. With little effort, she climbed down and stood before Nimrod. "You wanted to see me, kind gentleman?" She wasn't sure if this were business or pleasure or intertwined.

Nimrod stammered. "Well, yes, uh, miss, I been told you enticed a young man of this wagon train. Is that true?"

She looked confused for a moment. "Enticed? Oh, you mean— No, sir. He sidled up to me. I warded him off."

Nimrod regained his ease. "Warded?" He grinned. "When's the last time you 'warded off' a man?"

She saw the humor and laughed. "If I 'warded' too often, I'd have to be a nun, now wouldn't I?"

The grin disappeared. "Well, Red, this ain't no joke. This here is a group of church-goers—for the most part. They don't cotton to how you make a living. And when you get around their menfolk, the women, they get nervous and resentful."

She put hands on hips. "Well then, Mr. Lee. I didn't ask to be here. I'd like to be most any other place. But if a man starts shining me on, what am I supposed to do?"

Nimrod became exasperated. "Damnit, girl, you know what to do. Just pretend he's an ugly old man with no money."

"I'll try, but it ain't easy. It goes a-gin my calling," Red said, and giggled.

"I ain't joking," he warned. "These people won't put up with much."

Walking away, Cohen asked, "What's a redbone?"

"A touch of Negro," Nimrod said.

On the way to where he had Bub staked out to graze, Nimrod heard a scream and turned and ran to the far edge of the camp. He arrived in time to see a coyote running away with what looked like a bundle of cotton in its mouth.

Agnes Patterson was watching the same scene, but crying and blubbering. "That animal, that wolf, came up and snatched my Benjamin." She turned an imploring face toward Nimrod. "Sir, can you help him, my Benjamin?"

Nimrod spoke with compassion because he knew some cunning and hungry coyote had caused a great tragedy in the woman's life. "There's no help for it, Agnes. I'm sorry, but your dog is gone."

Day after day, the train plodded along the south bank of the Platte, rising in elevation, just a foot here and there, but it added up. The grasses were becoming dry and thin. It was suitable forage for the less-finicky oxen. However, the horses showed the effects of a less nutritious diet, even though they weren't doing heavy work.

Spencer kept his mouth shut and avoided contact with other people. Hannah kept the children and herself out of the mainstream of camp life when possible, though no one blamed her for Spencer's behavior.

Hannah seethed with anger and resentment, not sparing herself for bringing him into her life.

When Nimrod casually encountered Hannah, he was surprised at the boldness in her eyes. He didn't understand the reason, but it left him with an undefined hope and a reaction he hoped others wouldn't notice.

Simon Tester, the man who joined the train just before departure, made his presence increasingly hard to ignore. He was judgmental and brash. His cronyism with Zack meant that each fed off the meanness of the other.

※

Penney, Nimrod, and Jackman were sitting on stools outside Penney's wagon, watching the guards take the animals out for grazing.

"I'm thinking we should ease up on the guard shifts. Four hours is a bit much for men who've walked alongside oxen for a whole day in the heat," Penney said, looking at the three men shuffling out with their guns. He waited for a response from Jackman, but the other man's thoughts seemed in another place.

Jackman cleared his throat. "Uh, Captain, I've got an important committee matter to discuss."

That was Nimrod's cue to excuse himself. Penney was silent, anticipating a negative turn to the conversation.

Jackman took a deep breath. "This is awkward, but it needs to be dealt with. Zack, my kin, he came to me this morning after breakfast, all agitated. He, uh, told me he had discharge from his member."

"Member of what?" Penney asked, mystified. Then, it dawned on him, which caused a modest grin. "Sounds like the clap. Tell Zack not to worry. It'll fall off in a week or two."

Jackman frowned. "This is serious, Captain. The family expects me to keep him out of trouble. Zack says he was enticed by that whore named Red down by the river three nights ago."

"She was warned about such as that," Penney said. "What can we do?"

"Expel the whore wagon from the train," Jackman said in frustration.

"That would be a death sentence out here with Indians behind every rock. That doesn't seem to fit the offense," Penney said.

Jackman grimaced and muttered, "I'm beginning to hate this trip."

Penney looked at him with surprise, then frowned. "Well, something's got to be done."

Jackman turned angry. "I can't take much more of this," and stalked off into the night which was Nimrod's cue to return.

"Well, don't that beat all," Penney said. "Something's dogging Abraham besides Zack's ailing pecker. A man don't sour overnight like that with nary a reason."

Nimrod smiled. "We'll find out soon enough, Captain. Ain't no secrets for long in a wagon train."

At the noon break, Nimrod and Penney went to Benny Bogle's wagon. By prearrangement, Nimrod was to do the talking. "

"I don't fancy people such as them," Penney said. "I might get carried away and say something intemperate."

"What?"

"Lose my temper."

"I figured that's what you meant."

Nimrod cupped his hands and helloed. Bogle came to the flap and said, "What do you want?"

"To talk."

"I got nothing to say to you."

Nimrod said, "Well, I do to you, bad enough to come up there and pull you down."

Bogle stared long enough to realize Nimrod was serious, then clambered down. "What's so all-fired important?"

"We got a story about your gal, Red. She's said to have give a young feller in the train the clap."

Bogle bristled. "My girls are clean. That's a lie."

"Would a drippy pecker convince you otherwise? Ask Red to come down here."

"I'll do the talking for her," Bogle said.

"Unless you're the one who gave him the clap, you just stand there and listen."

Bogle called up to the wagon. "Red! Get down here."

Red peered out from behind the bonnet with a big smile. She was wearing a shift that would send any other woman in the train scrambling into concealment. She jumped from the front wheel to the ground and landed right in front of Nimrod.

"Well, if it ain't Daniel Boone."

"Howdy, Red. I hear you been on the job."

"What job?" she said, teasing. "I do this for fun."

"The funning just stopped. You gave a young feller the clap, we're told."

Before Red could respond, "She don't have the clap," Bogle said, acting offended.

Nimrod looked at Bogle as though he were unworthy of a response. "I don't believe you, Bogle. I don't like your kind. You mistreat women. You ain't a gentleman."

"I suppose you are." Bogle snorted and looked around to see if his humor was appreciated.

Nimrod glared at him. "That little bitty gambler's gun I know you got in your pocket, give it to me."

"You ain't going to take my gun. I need it." Bogle closed a hand over his waistcoat pocket, which identified where he held it.

"What do you need it for. To fight off an Indian raid? To turn aside a buffalo stampede? Any purpose you got for such a weapon is not in the best interests of this wagon train. Mr. Penney will give it back to you at the end of the trip."

With an angry look, Bogle removed the small pistol from his pocket and handed it to Penney, who looked under the hammer and removed the percussion cap. "You'll get this back when we see the last of you and your kind," Penney said.

Nimrod indicated the wagon with a toss of his head. "Now get up-top so we can talk to Red."

Defeated, Bogle climbed back into the wagon. Nimrod called after him. "If you even touch that girl, I'll be touching you."

Bogle mouthed something that wasn't clear, which may have been to his benefit.

Nimrod and Penney walked her out of earshot of the wagon, and Nimrod said, "Tell us what happened between you and Zack."

"Zack? Was that his name? Late one evening after supper, I was washing some clothes down by the river. I was by myself, and this Zack fellow came up behind me, and grabbed my arm—" She held up the inside of her forearm to show dark-blue bruises. He covered my mouth and pulled me into the bushes alongside the river and raped me."

"Isn't that what you do for a living?" Penney said.

Red looked at him as she would an insect. He sensed he'd said the wrong thing, so he lowered his head and studied the ground.

"He told his uncle you enticed him, even though he refused to pay you," Nimrod said.

"He lied." She thought for a moment. "That makes no sense. I'm a whore; I ain't a singer in the choir. Why should I lie? And he said he wouldn't pay me? You can wager I ain't about to do business sex with the likes of him for free." She laughed at the idea.

Nimrod and Penney looked at each other for anything else to say. Penney said, "Thank you. You can go back now."

Red's accusation against Zack became a sensitive issue considering he was the nephew of Abraham Jackman, who, of course, was also on the committee. Conveying news to Abraham that Zack was accused of rape was not something Penney rushed to do.

The two men sat on three-legged stools some distance from the wagons. Penney gave the news to Jackman, then waited for a response.

Jackman looked long at Penney. "I'm ashamed to say I believe it. Zack's a bad seed. I brought him along as a favor to my brother. I wish I hadn't, but…Anyway, you fellows do what you have to do."

Concern crept into Penney's voice. "'What do you mean, *you fellows*?' You're one of the fellows, Abraham."

Jackman lowered his head. "I can't be on this committee with a clear mind. My life isn't what it was even a few weeks ago. I've— Never mind."

Penney slapped Jackman on the knee. "I never try to talk a smart man out of something he's thought hard about. You know your mind."

He rose and shook Jackman's hand. "I wish you well, my friend."

The committee was stunned to hear of Jackman's resignation. They decided to call a general meeting and elect a new member. Meanwhile, they had to decide what to do about the accusation against Zack. The occupation of Red, the alleged rape victim, hung heavy over the deliberations.

Masterson said, "It's her word against his—Damn! We need Abraham with his legal knowledge."

Cohen shook his head. "Zack's his kin. It's obvious some sexual congress took place," Cohen glanced at Preacher to make sure he hadn't violated some moral code with his word choice.

"Congress?" Nimrod was confused.

"That means getting together," Masterson said.

Preacher stood up. This was his theater of operations. "We have two sinners seeking justice. No other place can true justice be found than before the throne of our Lord."

"I don't think—" Masterson was interrupted by Preacher, who launched a sermonette about the wages of sin, and how adultery was bound to occur when young people were exposed to the fleshpots of modern society.

Cohen said, "The banks of this river don't seem to be a good place to locate a fleshpot."

Penney said, "Plowing bean fields didn't prepare me for such as this." He looked around, and his eyes settled on Nimrod who was observing in the back. "Nimrod, you've got your own stress, guiding us, and all. I don't mean to drag you into this, but seeing as how you know both of the players—so to speak—do you have any ideas to get us out of this thicket?"

Nimrod looked around to make sure his input was welcomed. He was a hired hand of the committee, and he didn't want to step out of his place. "Well, I reckon if you take this before the whole of the wagon train, they'll commence to arguing, some for the woman, some for Zack. We don't need that kind of spite. Also, Zack would have to admit to the clap, which I'm thinking he's not eager to do."

The others nodded to each other. Nimrod continued, "I haven't talked to Zack. That's not my place. However, the woman answered questions. Her name is Red. I found her words believable. She said Zack forced himself on her. I can't speak for the truth of any of it."

"Don't forget, the woman is a whore," Masterson said.

"I don't see that as mattering," Nimrod said. "Gentlemen don't attack women."

"Well, Zack, that piss ant, he ain't one of those," Penney said dryly.

"Nimrod, you know more than us about how wagon trains react to people problems. What would you recommend?" Cohen asked.

Nimrod rubbed his cheek. "Well, sir, I'm not in the justice

business, but if we put this before the men, I fear most will side with Zack on account of the lady's trade. Some, I'm sure, will side with the woman. I don't know which side the ladies would come down on. And, gents, I don't think we're in need of bitterness between our people. We don't need this adding to the stress we've already got."

"So, where are we?" Cohen said.

Penney said, "How's this for a just solution: Just drop it. The woman gets spared having strange men tearing into her reputation, what there is of it. And Zack has to walk around with a drippy pecker."

Preacher said, "How is that just?"

Penney said, "Maybe it ain't exactly just, but it'll shore amuse the pioneers." The others laughed.

Cohen said, "With that settled, we can get on with the business of getting to California."

"Hear, hear," Masterson said, clapping, and the men walked out chatting with each other.

Penney beckoned with his head for Nimrod to stay. When they were alone, he said, "You got an eye for leadership. You got anyone in mind to take Abraham's place?"

Nimrod hesitated, as though weighing a decision. "Ain't my place as a guide, but you asked, and yes, I do."

Penney's eyebrows were raised by Nimrod's suggestion, but then a nod and smile showed he approved. He took it to the committee, which, to a man, shared Penney's amazement. Preacher alone was opposed. Penney said he would call the entire company together later for a yea or nay.

In the meantime, Penney took the extra measure of asking Ethel Pearl to drive her wagon close behind Bogle's to keep an eye on their goings on.

"Would you be willing?" he asked.

"Willing? They won't sneeze without me knowing it," she said. "They better not make any brazen advances to my son, either. If they do, I'll go after that weasel of a pimp."

CHAPTER TWENTY

The travelers were bored by the hour-by-hour plodding. However, they would have welcomed more boredom if it distanced them from the loud and irrational fury coming from the Horner wagon. Maude berated her husband by the hour for taking them away from Terre Haute and into the wilderness. More than once, they heard her call him a witch.

Although most women in the train would agree with some of Maude's complaints, it was recognized that she was "bedeviled," as one woman described her. Her actions were often bizarre, and it was unnerving to people unexposed to mental illness. And there was gossip as to who was the real witch in that family.

An unexpected benefit of Maude's hysteria was that Indians stayed away instead of visiting the camp looking for handouts, either food or trinkets. They feared she was in the possession of evil spirits. Their views were not a source of dispute among the pioneers.

What all of them didn't understand was that Maude was trapped in the middle of nowhere, surrounded by shouting people, disease, and danger. Given that frightful circumstance, and fragility of her mind, her refuge was to escape into the shelter of her illness.

Billy's donkey, Hambo, was a particular cause of Maude's hysteria. She thought the animal was the Devil's emissary come to control her soul and fly to hell with her on its back. Anytime the donkey would walk through the camp seeking a sugar handout, Maude screamed to keep it away from her. At night, when Hambo was with the herd and brayed, she cried out.

The sun was still asleep when Jackman came up to Penney's tent and hollered for him in a frantic voice. "Shadrach! Shadrach, come out here quick. The Indians got my wife."

Penney was outside within one minute with his pants over his long underwear with suspenders dangling. A crowd gathered in the dawn gloom.

Penney was still blinking the sleep out of his eyes. He said, "Now, hold on there, Abraham. Quiet down. What's this all about?"

Jackman said in an agitated voice, "I woke up early, and she was gone. Davy Owens, too. The Indians must have skulked in here last night and grabbed them. I've searched the whole camp. Two horses and a mule are missing."

Nimrod added, "I walked the camp this morning. No Indian sign."

Aaron asked if anything in the wagon were missing. Jackman said he hadn't yet looked.

Penney hesitated, trying to frame the right words. The task he faced was not easy. "Abraham, I'm sorry to tell you this, but your wife and your hired man ran off on you. That's what happened, it's clear, and I'm sorry for it."

Jackman's head snapped back in shock. "That can't be. I treated her right. She loved me."

Off to the side, Zack was making amusing asides to one of his buddies, but loud enough to be heard by Nimrod.

"I seen it coming. Davy sort of told me what they was going to do. One time, I stood guard while he rutted her like a cow in heat."

Nimrod edged over and whispered to Zack, "Shut your evil mouth, you damned fool."

Zack swung around and knocked Nimrod to the ground. "You won't talk to me that way, bastard, guide of not." He raised his voice so everyone could hear his boast. "I'll hit you so hard there won't be enough left to snore."

Nimrod leaped to his feet, pulled and reversed his revolver, and whipped it across Zack's head, twice. Zack fell to the ground, dazed and with blood streaming down his face and into his ears. "You don't fight fair," he whined.

Nimrod scoffed. "Fight fair? You think this is a schoolyard tussle? You ever touch me again, I'll kill you."

Aaron said loudly to the watchers, "Zack'd last with Nimrod

'bout as long as a pint of whiskey in a four-handed poker game."
The laughter was noticed by Zack and filed away.

The pioneers appreciated gossip as much as any, but having
a hired hand run off with a lawyer's wife was something beyond
the proper and sedate lives they understood. That it happened to
Abraham Jackman, a man they respected, cast a pall of glumness
over the company.

However, coping with the challenge of getting through
a wilderness alongside a sluggish, muddy river, soon pushed
Abraham's domestic troubles out of their minds. He helped quell
the gossip by yoking his oxen and taking his place in line without a
word and carried on as though nothing had happened.

Two days later, following supper, Penney sent two kids around
to summon the adults to a meeting with the committee.

Since the company did not know what was to be discussed,
they gathered with anticipation in the middle of the wagon circle.
Penney spoke of Jackman's resignation, then thanked him for his
service.

Penney cleared his throat, and said, "Seeing as how we have an
open spot on the committee, we have to fill with a two-thirds vote
of all the men. Your committee has given this matter much thought,
and we've discussed it at length." Penney's nervousness gave him a
slight stutter and caused his words to ramble. "After all that talking
about it, we think the person who has shown good judgment, and
the greatest concern for the welfare of this company is— and I'm
mighty proud to give you our recommended candidate—Hannah
Spencer."

There was dead silence at first, then a gabble of voices. Hannah,
in the front row, stood with her mouth agape in shock. Her
husband, a few feet away, had a purple rage on his face.

Penney said, "Now, we gotta vote. All in favor of Hannah
Spencer becoming a committee member, give us a show of hands."
A flurry of male hands shot up. "Now, opposed?" Fewer hands
showed. Cohen and Masterson compared their counts and gave
the result to Penney. "According to our vote, Hannah Spencer is
two votes short of two-thirds. The motion is failed." The crowd
wandered away.

Thirty minutes later, however, Penney sent the same two boys around to summon everybody to another meeting. When they were assembled, Penney said, "We have unfinished business, folks. I turn the floor—" He attempted a lame joke about the "floor" being prairie dirt, which gave him the silly look of failed humor. He recovered by saying, "Uh, Millie Plum wants to say something."

Millie had become known for being outspoken. She moved forward and faced the group standing straight in her modest height. Her stockings were gray with dirt. She wore her hair in a bun held in place by metal combs. Back home, her dress would long since have become rags. Before talking, she wiped her hands in a streaked apron draped across her swollen middle. The wind swirled and made her dress flap.

Though she was short, her bearing was tall. Millie said, "Thank you for coming back. Several—more than several— of us wives been talking about this. We calculated we need to do something, and we stand together on it."

She turned in a slow circle to face everyone. "Most of us— women, I'm talking about— didn't want to come on this so-called adventure, or, as I've sometimes called it, this nightmare. But you all know that, I reckon. I ain't spilling a secret. You men gave us no choice but to leave our homes, our families, our relatives, our churches, and our neighbors, only to spend these months risking our lives and our children's lives to go gallivanting to a place we don't know nothing about, and where we'll for sure be seen as invaders when we get there. I won't mention the misery all this has brought to the lives or our children and ourselves.

"We did this, we turned our lives upside down, just to please you, our husbands. Not many of us are glad we did, that's the God's truth. But we're here and making the best of it."

Her voice became shrill. "However. However! We demand a voice in what all this does to our lives and the lives of our children. We want a vote to choose this member of the committee. We demand a new vote with us having a voice. If you do not—do not!—show us that respect, we will not launder our husband's clothing until the time this expedition, or wild goose chase, or whatever you want to call it, gets to where we're going, wherever in hell that might be, if you'll pardon my language. We also will resist sharing other activities of our marriage, the details of which to be discussed in private."

Millie marched over to the edge of the clearing, and many of the women followed, standing defiant and glaring at their husbands.

Penney walked to the center of the clearing, biting his lip to conceal his mirth. He looked toward the women. "Well, thank you, Millie, and thank you, ladies." He turned back to the men. "Well, gents, do we give the ladies a vote on this vacancy? All in favor, raise your hands." A clear majority of the men raised their hands amidst a fair amount of not unkind laughter.

Penney nodded. "Very well, then. Ladies, if you'll rejoin us, we're about to take another vote on Hannah Spencer as our replacement committee member. All in favor?"

Considerably more than two-thirds raised their hands. Penney said, "So be it. Hannah Spencer is now on our governing committee. Congratulations, Hannah." He took several steps and shook her hand. She was still dazed by the unexpected honor and extended a limp hand to be shaken. Men and women surrounded her with congratulations. Out of the corner of her eye, she saw Ed stalk off. In the same glance, she also saw Nimrod grinning.

After the meeting broke up, Penney, Cohen, Aaron, and Nimrod were chatting in the empty clearing. Ed Spencer stalked toward them with Tester at his heels. He rose to full height and glared at Penney.

"How dare you appoint my wife to any position without asking my permission?"

Penney said, "We have the right to call on anyone in this company to serve as we see fit. Anyways, we appointed her, not you. You wouldn't have gotten any votes. You should be proud she's your wife."

"Being your wife wasn't even held against her," Aaron said with a wicked grin. "We've already had one slave in this outfit, and that's one too many."

"It's all the fault of that agitating Jew bitch," Tester said with a jutted jaw, referring to Clara Cohen.

They all looked at Cohen for a reaction. He was first stunned, then burst into laughter, and turned to Spencer. "We've heard worse insults from men who wouldn't let the likes of you walk their dogs. I'm almost insulted to be insulted by such a rapscallion as you. Your bite is that of a harmless insect, sir."

Penney was starting to steam. "Let me tell you, mister. Hannah is a member of this committee, and if you or anyone else tries to prevent her from attending meetings or doing her duty, you'll deal with this same committee."

Spencer took a step toward the old man but happened to glance at Nimrod. What he saw caused him to turn and walk away, with Tester a step behind, and glancing backward with a pout on his face.

The confrontation ended as a shot came from the back of the train and was followed by a woman screaming. The men with nearby weapons grabbed them, fitted a percussion cap on the nipple, and ran toward the screams. "Indians," one shouted, and others took up the cry.

Nimrod headed toward the rifle report the moment he heard it. When he reached the Jackman wagon, he guessed what had happened. A buzzing group was clustered around. Penney climbed stiffly into the wagon, followed by Nimrod. Inside, Jackman was sprawled against the sideboard, dead, with his rifle next to him. Penney moved up and studied Jackman's face and the round black hole in the forehead. It was bleeding, but the flow slowed to a seep as blood pressure stopped. The two men looked at each other. Nothing to do. Nothing to say. They covered his head and left the wagon.

Folks who had observed wife Susan's humiliating antics with Davy Owens and their subsequent disappearance realized what had happened.

Penney faced the semi-circle of gawkers. "This man died of an accidental gunshot wound. It was an accident." It was all he could do for a friend who was handed a bad deal. "Get Preacher."

Zack was standing nearby, feeling self-important for knowing what no one else knew. "He blew his head off, he did. Damn!"

Nimrod shook his head. "It was an accidental gunshot wound. I've seen it before."

Zack became indignant. "No, it wasn't. I saw—"

Nimrod stepped close and hissed in a low voice heard only by Zack. "You need to think again." Zack saw Nimrod's threatening body language and suddenly saw the light. "Uh, on second thought, I think Mr. Lee is right. Yes, sir, he was cleaning his gun just before it went off."

The mourning for a good man was not made easier by knowing the disliked Zack would take possession of Abraham's property.

Zack was exulting over his windfall when Cohen said, "You have possession, not ownership. If Susan ever returns, this'll be hers."

Zack snarled. "That bitch will get it over my dead body. She betrayed my beloved uncle."

Masterson almost responded, but decided not to. Instead, he said, "That's the law of inheritance, Zack, and you will abide by it."

The next morning at daybreak, Preacher read scripture at the burial of Jackman, and Brister played a hymn on his squeeze box. The livestock were run over the grave. Camp was broken, the oxen yoked, and the wagons lumbered toward the next dozen miles, gradually leaving thoughts of the late lawyer behind.

One evening after sundown, Hannah and several women knelt at the edge of a small brook washing clothes. To take their minds off aching backs and angry-looking hands, the women discussed their childhood years. Ruth Cohen told of growing up in Munich's Jewish quarter. But the stories she related were not of repression, but of family happiness, of love, of the fresh, chill winds blowing in from the Alps. It was a good life.

Just as another woman started to tell her story, Hannah straightened up and stretched her back. "Ladies, excuse me. Has anyone seen my Rachel? She was supposed to bring more soap."

The women shook their heads. One said, "Not for a half-hour, or so."

Hannah sighed. "That child…" She pushed herself to her feet and walked back to camp. She approached the tent, heard muffled sounds, and looked inside. She adjusted her eyes to the dim light. "Sar—"

Her eyes widened, and she stared transfixed. Then she screamed and didn't stop. Neighbors looked up. The men grabbed their guns, and all came running, just in time to hold Hannah back from attacking Spencer with a butcher knife outside the tent.

When the men who gathered learned that Spencer was accused of sexually molesting the girl, several demanded lynching him. Penney, Cohen, and Nimrod arrived in time to wrest Spencer from the men surrounding him. They took him to an area on the far side of the camp where they sat on stools and stared back and forth at Spencer, then at each other. Women who had been standing nearby attempted to comfort Hannah and Rachel.

Within the hour, the committee, minus Hannah, of course, had finished interrogating Spencer as Nimrod looked on. Flora Dickens, Gertie Proctor, and Ruth Cohen, who had talked to Rachel, Billy, and Hannah, were called in to tell what they knew. They were satisfied that molestation had occurred many times over several months.

Spencer, sitting outside the group, attempted to speak. His smirk had turned into a frown, as the seriousness of his situation began to creep up on him.

Penney snapped at him. "You'll get your chance to speak, so sit there and be quiet." Then he turned to the others and spoke of Spencer as though he weren't present.

"Well, then, getting down to it. There's no doubt Spencer did it, had his way with the child." He hesitated as though realizing the meaning of his words. He shook his head in disgust. "This is the most cuss-ed business I was ever in." Masterson said, "This yahoo's not worth piss in a whirlwind."

Cohen said, "Several got there quick when Hannah screamed. The poor little girl, Rachel, has hardly spoken since."

"Make sure to keep his wife away from him. Hannah had a mind to carve him up, I'm told" Penney said.

Preacher harrumphed and said, "What do we do with this man? 'If thine eye offend thee, pluck it—'"

Cohen interrupted. "With all respect, Preacher, this ain't a theological court."

Penney grumbled, "I know what I'd do, but we only do it to bulls, damn it all."

Cohen nodded. "Well, we can't turn him loose to do it again, that's for damned sure."

Spencer sat rigidly on a stool just outside the committee circle. He spat out his words, hoping defiance would save him. "I won't be judged by a damned Jew."

The men ignored the comment. Bigotry was the least of Spencer's troubles.

Penney turned to Spencer with finality in his voice. "Well, what do you have to say for yourself that isn't an insult?"

As the men showed no sign of easing their outrage toward him, Spencer's thoughts locked down out of fear. He couldn't deny the evidence, so he said in a cracked voice the first thing that jumped into his mind: "The girl enticed me."

The men were horrified at Spencer's audacity. It was ridiculous, almost to the level of humorous. Masterson rolled his eyes.

They glared at Spencer. Penney waited for more, but Spencer stared at the ground and could think of nothing else.

Masterson, amazed, mumbled, "Jesus!" He looked at frowning Preacher, and said, "Sorry." He then said, "Why can't we be done with him? Hang him, I mean."

Cohen turned away from Spencer. "Because he didn't kill anyone. This ain't the middle ages."

Penney kept glancing at Spencer to make sure he hadn't run, although he had nowhere to go within five hundred miles. He resumed his stool seat, and said, "Seems to me I recall something in the Bible about casting out, or some such."

Preacher said, "Those were demons."

Masterson pointing to Spencer with his thumb, said, "What for god's sake do you think he is?" He turned back to a frowning Preacher, and shrugged. "Heat of the moment."

Penney was staring at the ground as he listened and thought, then he straightened up. "I've been puzzling on what to do." He turned to Nimrod. "Will you take the prisoner out of earshot? This committee's got to do some opining."

Nimrod motioned for Spencer to precede him, then had him stop about fifty yards distant. For a half-hour, nothing was said, then Spencer, unable to control his hatred, and out of sight of his judges, glared at Nimrod. "You've wanted my wife from day one, haven't you? I saw you casting looks at her."

Nimrod stared at him, not with hatred or disgust, but as though examining a strange insect specie, marveling that such a creature could exist.

Spencer said, "What if I took your fancy pistol away from you? Then I'll bet I'd see you beg."

Nimrod sneered at Spencer. "I'd accept a month in jail to have ten minutes alone with you. I ain't no old squaw picking up buffalo turds. But if the spirit ever moves you to try me, I wouldn't discourage it."

Penney called them back, and said, "I'll make this short, Spencer. We've fought down the urge to string you up, but it was a near thing. There ain't no way you can stay here. Sure as shootin', one of the men with a young daughter might just happen to be nearby when you had an unfortunate accident, you can bet." He looked again at the committee and saw only tight-lipped faces. He again faced Spencer. "We're going to give you a running chance. You'll leave this wagon train with one horse, a week's provision, your rifle, and half your cash. And that'll happen within the hour. Any questions?"

Spencer was aghast. "You are robbers! I've got a sizable sum in my poke."   "That's good to know," Masterson said with a grin.

Cohen said, "I reckon your wife would say whatever you have is not half enough for the abuse she and her children have put up with. And regarding the wagon and livestock, that's all hers. This ain't gonna be argued. Now, let's get this over with." The four committeemen strode toward the Spencer wagon, with Spencer trailing, and Nimrod bringing up the rear to keep an eye on him.

Hannah saw them coming and sent the children to play with friends. She glared at her husband until Penney explained the decision.

When Hannah heard she was going to be given half of Spencer's money, she said, "He's got a fat purse, but I don't know where it's hidden."

Penney rubbed his hands and turned to the others. "Well, boys, we-uns gonna take this wagon apart." After giving Hannah a few minutes to remove unmentionables, the four men started piling the contents on the ground. They looked through the wagon, checked the running gear, the saddlebags of the horse, then rapped on the wood for hidden compartments in the sideboards. As they searched, Spencer sat on the dirt under the glares of the crowd that had drifted over. From time to time, they heard a whoop from the searchers; each one made Spencer wince, and the crowd gave a small cheer.

As they finished, the committee put their heads together, then walked over. Penney smiled as he looked at Spencer in triumph, then spoke to everyone. "This feller can hide things better than his cousin, the packrat. He squirreled away almost five hundred dollars, script and gold."

He spoke to Spencer so everyone could hear. "The ladies put together vittles for a week." He pointed to a pile on the ground. "You can have your clothes, and your rifle unloaded, with powder, lead and caps. Here's your half, two hundred thirty-nine dollars. You get the script money, she gets the gold." He looked over to Aaron who was leading out Spencer's thoroughbred with the pink ribbon tied to the saddle skirt.

Spencer loaded his goods in a bundle and climbed into the saddle as Penney held the bridle. "Now, count yourself lucky you can ride out of here. And if you get a hankering to come back, you don't have to bring a rope, we got plenty of those, and we can find a tree." Penney released the bridle. "Now, git."

Spencer started to protest, but Hannah, standing nearby, picked up a loose length of leather strap and whipped the horse on the rump. Before Spencer could say anything, his horse left the wagon circle on a gallop.

Watching her husband become smaller going back down the trail, Hannah turned to the others with a flushed face and said in words she bit off, "From this day forward, the children and I are not Spencers. We will be called Blanc." She raised her voice emphatically. "Not Spencer. Blanc"

The crowd left with outraged mumbling. The committee members scattered with nothing more to say. They believed what they did was the right thing, but had the discomfort of being unaccustomed judges of another person.

Later, as Penney undertook to change her name on the company roll to Blanc, he studied the spelling she dictated. He looked at her quizzically. "This here name reads 'Blank.'"

Patiently, she said, "It's a French name, pronounced 'blah.'"

Penney's brow furrowed. "Then why'd they spell it like 'blank'?

She shrugged. "I don't know. I just say it the French way."

His forehead knotted in concern. "Foreigners be taking over our American language."

"The English language," she corrected.

"That's what I said."

Nimrod standing nearby, said, "I trapped with many a Frenchie. A strange lot, they are." He quickly added, "No offense, Hannah."

As Penney walked away shaking his head, Nimrod turned to Hannah, and asked, "Can you manage alone? Will you fare all right?"

"I'll be better off," she said. "Much, much better." They locked eyes but said nothing. But heavy between them was wondering and probing, and maybe, just maybe, promise. They parted and went about their business.

For the next several days, the train returned to its plodding progress along the Platte. It was as though Ed Spencer had never been among them. Except for stopping to double or triple teams to drag a wagon out of a crevice, or to repair broken axles or wagon tongues, it was one weary day after another, for both people and beasts. The animals were holding up well, but water and grass had been plentiful. That would change.

Nerves were beginning to fray, and the people were becoming less patient and tolerant. Men who had been sizing up other men settled on an unspoken pecking order, and those who felt stronger started asserting dominance. Violence was just a trip-hammer away.

The children fought boredom as they always do by getting into things, teasing each other, and attempting stunts to impress girls and to outshine other boys. The rowdiest was Roger, the hyperactive twelve-year-old of Earl and Maude Horner. He delighted in causing kids to gasp at his daredevil tricks around moving wagons. Why Roger was rebellious was not a question that would even occur to others. He was just another pest.

Things had been quiet in Benny Bogle's pimp wagon. After the incident with Red and Zack, it was made clear that the Bogle entourage was on a short leash. An emphatic warning had been given that he and his whores could stay in the train so long as they kept quiet and near the wagon, especially after dark. If another of his girls became involved with a man of the company, the Bogle group would be booted out, no matter where they were at the moment.

That arrangement was adhered to, except the outgoing Red, the youngest. She was like a caged white rat found under a couch, and nobody could figure out how it got there.

Despite their disapproval, the folks of the train developed a fondness for the girl whose life story—truthful, or not—brought tears to the eyes of many and resulted in her sharing meals at several campsites. Women opened their hearts to the fallen angel; men, not so much, wary as they were of the watchful eyes of wives.

There was nothing unusual about Red except her likeability. She could tell stories of the underside of life that somehow were courageous rather than depressing, and certainly not condemning of her—and, perhaps, some even true. She had been made from cookie-cutter poverty that stamped out young girls by the dozen in poor urban areas and from farms where thistles were far more common than shoes.

Red formed a strong bond with Gertie Proctor, who was eager for the companionship of a young woman her own age. Red's bubbly personality enlivened evenings after the food was prepared for the next day's breakfast, and the dishes washed and put away.

One evening after supper, Gertie said, "Red, will you fetch me the ladle from the wagon?"

Red did as she was asked, then spoke in muted voice to Gertie.

"Here you are, but Red ain't my name, not my real name. Benny calls it a stage name, but bless me, I don't know why that might be."

Gertie looked up in surprise, then stopped what she was doing and gestured Red to share the log she was sitting on. "What is your real name, then, my dear?"

"You mean my birth name?" I don't got any idea. I never knew my maw. I been told she was a slave, a high-yeller." She chuckled. "I reckon I'd find my daddy up in the big house. I heard she got sold down river. I don't know why." Red looked at Gertie's kind gaze and continued; tears filled her eyes, then they filled Gertie's. "I reckon she'd have give me a name that was gentle, maybe ladylike. A name of fine manners, of pretty words, and pretty dresses. Yes, I think my maw would have done that. I had a dream where she talked to me. I saw her face for the first time. She was a real looker with a soft voice. She said my given name was Verity. I don't tell people 'cause people don't believe in dreams. But that's who I am to me—Verity."

Gertie reached out and took the young woman in her arms and patted her heaving shoulders.

Aaron, too, was fond of Red but was careful how he showed it. Red would sleep under the wagon while the Proctors were nearby in their tent. When it rained, she was allowed in the wagon. Benny was delighted at Red's popularity because he hoped it would increase his chances of staying with the train. He didn't want to lose a young, good-looking whore, but he figured she'd show up again down the line. They always did.

It was hard to not like Red, except for Zack, he of the afflicted appendage. Whenever he saw her, and he seemed to go out of his way to do that, he glared with menace. It was noticed, but people didn't take the implied threat seriously, because Zack himself wasn't taken seriously.

The weather along the Platte turned mid-summer hot, and the humidity also rose and made the temperature meaner. Evenings, however, cooled off some, and if there were a late afternoon shower and a breeze to scatter the mosquitoes, the banks of the Platte could be a thing of song.

It was such an evening with the camp bedded down, and the fires banked that Nimrod chanced upon Hannah, strolling near the edge of the camp.

He tipped his hat and spoke in a soft voice, as though not wishing to disturb the discordant snoring lullaby from the wagons. "Evening, Hannah. Don't wander far."

She smiled. "It's warm tonight. Is it safe to walk down to that cool brook that feeds into the river?"

Nimrod said, "I best escort you; hard to say where the savages will make their mischief, though they might be squiring their squaws down to a similar spring." He pulled back in mild alarm at his words. "I meant nothing ill-mannered."

Hannah laughed. "I'm used to your frontier manner. I've grown fond of it."

The two walked to the brook sheltered by cottonwoods. Without being asked, he removed his deerskin coat and make a place for her against a tree." She sat down and leaned back. "That I trust you to be here like this, sir, is a compliment to you as a gentleman."

"You're as safe as in your own bed." He grimaced, and gave a hang-dog look. "Proper words and me ain't well acquainted."

She said, "The bugs aren't bad down here."

"The water's fast-moving, and there's a breeze. Bugs find that discouraging."

"Well, that's something to be thankful for, I suppose."

"Your spirit seems heavy as a bag of stones, and I appreciate why. He's your husband, after all. I'm sorry for it."

Hannah snorted. "Him? No. I'm well shed of him. I was a fool for letting him into our lives." Hannah started to tear up, and Nimrod started to reach an arm out, then thought better of it.

He said, "Don't whip yourself too hard. You had children to provide for."

Hannah wiped her eyes. "And quite a job of providing I did! I let a monster loose with my daughter. For what he did to her, I can never forgive myself."

Nimrod flipped pebbles into the water as he spoke. "Not to make light of it, but your daughter is here with you. God knows where mine is."

"Where do you hail from?" she asked.

"Kentucky, nigh on the Tennessee line. Not far from the Wilderness Road where Shawnees did for Dan'l Boone's boy, James."

"Do you ever go back?"

"Not since I left. There was some difficulties."

"I won't even ask. I've had enough of those for a while."

Two coyotes across the river started howling. Hannah leaned toward Nimrod. He could feel the softness of her shoulder against his.

"That sound chills me," Hannah said.

Nimrod hoped she wouldn't move. He laughed. "Mr. and Mrs. Coyote would be fairly amused to hear you say that. The missus is saying, 'Them red foxes in the next canyon stopped by today. That prideful bitch was carrying-on about her bushy tail, like she was the only one with a tail. I told her it was almost as pretty as a skunk's. She growled at that. I reckoned they'd never leave.' And then Mr. Coyote, he's saying, 'You got a hankering for jackrabbit tonight?' And she's saying, 'Jackrabbit? Again? Can't you catch a partridge?'"

Hannah was laughing, which is what he hoped for as he continued. "Now, Mr. Coyote, he ain't happy. He says, 'Partridges can fly. I can't. *You* try to catch one sometime. You're never satisfied. That's why I sometimes hunt all night and don't come home.'

"'Who you trying to humbug? You just go out and howl with your worthless friends.'"

Nimrod could sense her mood softening as she teased, "Do you speak coyote?"

"Some. But not the big words."

"You love it out here, don't you?"

"Got no place else to go. It's the onliest place that'll have me."

Hannah moved closer. "Comfort me, Nimrod." She edged into his arms. He held her in a brotherly way. He assumed that was what she wanted. But she slipped into an embrace. He held her like a crystal goblet. If he dropped her, she'd be gone. He felt her breath on his face. He traced his fingers over her cheek with one hand and ran his fingers through her hair with the other. He felt himself grow hard, which was not a first where she was concerned, but this time it wasn't a fantasy. He leaned forward, and her lips met his. He opened his lips, but she didn't. Hannah pulled back and got to her feet.

He looked up. "If I took advantage, I'm sorry,"

Hannah stood up and brushed off her clothes. "Don't be foolish. I called the tune." She sighed harshly to show her self-disgust. "This is not good. I'm still a married woman. I've got children asleep in a tent a stone's throw from here. I lost a grip on myself." She looked down at Nimrod and mellowed as their eyes met. "This shouldn't have happened, but I don't regret it." She started to walk away, then turned back, and laughed. "That acifidity bag, as you call it, around your neck. Could I buy it? I'll pay any price just to give it a decent burial." She disappeared into the shadow of a cottonwood.

On impulse, Nimrod untied the acifidity bag from around his neck and threw it into the stream. He'd take his chances with disease.

When the wagons were moving along the trail at their languid pace, the children enjoyed playing with Hambo. They had been warned that the donkey could be temperamental, so they were cautious around him. They plied him with sugar and stubs of carrots, but he always returned to Billy's side as his home port. At night he would depart to join the livestock when they herded up to graze.

One night, Andrew who was on herd watch woke up the camp by shouting unintelligibly. Making it a cacophony was the braying of Hambo, loud yelping, and the nervous lowing of the cattle.

When they went to investigate, they found in the moonlight a coyote stomped to death. Penney nodded with satisfaction. "Old Hambo is earning his keep."

CHAPTER TWENTY-ONE

As the camp roused at dawn, a teenage boy went to the river to retrieve a wheel that had soaked overnight. Wheels were soaked after a week of travel because the dry air shrank the wood, and the river soak restored them so they would fit tight to the iron rims.

As he wrestled the heavy wheel ashore, he noticed a strange bundle in the water. He laid the wheel on the bank and waded over to it. In the deep grayness of dawn, it looked maybe human, but the clothing was bloused up with air, so he wasn't certain. When he reached the form, the light allowed a good look. It was a woman, a dead woman. He panicked and ran for the camp, yelling what he had seen.

The entire company gathered in a semi-circle on the bank, nudging for position to see the body of Red pulled from the gentle eddy that had kept it pinned to the bank. As two men stretched out the sodden body, people gasped and groaned as they saw the cut across her neck. The savagery of the wound and the cold water had drained the body of blood and turned it gray.

It was as a chill wind had swept across the crowd as they stared at her body. The sight of the violent death caused men to stare and then look away, and women hugged themselves to ward off the gruesome reality. Children were shooed away, but, of course, they didn't leave, just went to a different part of the crowd where they absorbed images that would never leave them.

"A terrible thing. It don't matter what she was," a woman said to her neighbor.

Aaron turned to face the woman. "Don't speak in such a way about the dead," he said in irritation.

The body was given to the women for cleaning and dressing

as the men dug a grave. Instead of one of her gaudy gowns, they chose a simple gray smock. In late morning a brief burial ceremony was conducted by Preacher. Benny Bogle and his two remaining prostitutes joined the muted crowd.

Penney asked Bogle to leave, although the two women could stay.

"You can't do that," Bogle protested. "I cared for the girl."

"You cared for the money she made you. You didn't care a lick for the girl as a child of God." Penney pointed toward the Bogle wagon. "Now, git!"

Preacher read a perfunctory service and never mentioned Red's name. When he finished his last prayer, Gertie spoke up. "This lady's name was Verity. We need to know that. Her name was not Red. It was Verity. She became my friend. Her life was filled with suffering, but she had a warm heart, and she wanted to do good. God could have done something with her. He did with Mary Magdalene."

Right after noon dinner, the committee got off to themselves to discuss the murder. Masterson had been tasked to pull the brief investigation together. The Proctors joined them because of their acquaintance with Red.

Bogle was an obvious candidate for suspicion. The supposition was Red might have been disobedient, and he went into a rage and killed her.

Cohen offered a persuasive counter argument. "I don't know that way of life, but the girl made money for him. Why would he take money out of his own pocket?"

"Bogle bragged that Red was his top earner," Hannah said, her first speak-up as a committee member.

Nimrod said, "Pimps don't kill their girls that act up, they beat them."

That left Zack as the remaining suspect. Masterson said, "The boy who found the body said when he took his wheel down to soak last night, he saw Zack hanging around the river after everyone else had left for bed. When I talked to Zack this morning, he denied knowing anything about the killing, but he was jumpy as grease on a hot skillet. Zack said he slept out by himself last night. He also had scratches on his face. He said they were from scratching bug bites. I asked to see the skinning knife at his side. It had traces of dried blood on it. He said it was from skinning buffalo."

"We haven't killed a buffalo for ten days. A hunter, like Zack claims to be, always keeps his knife clean," Cohen said.

"We got to get back on the trail," Preacher said impatiently. "We know who did it, who killed that girl. Let's hang that roughneck and be done with it."

"We all know he did it, yes, we do, but he's not had a trial," Masterson said. "That would be murder."

"Justice is mine, saith the Lord," Preacher said.

"With all respect, Preacher, you ain't the Lord," Cohen said.

Penney cleared his throat, and the others fell silent. "I've been thinking on this. Where we sit right here is by law called Unorganized Territory of the U.S., which means we're in the wilderness, and there ain't no law here. We are it, and we're a poor excuse for playing God."

Masterson said, "We don't have time to play lawyer games; truth is, we don't know any."

"We all know damned well who did it—Zack. Ain't much we can do about it, though," Penney said.

"You're asking us to overlook murder," Preacher said. "That'd be an injustice."

Penney shook his head in frustration. "I know it galls, but a worse injustice would be to execute a man without a trial. Ain't the American way."

Hannah spoke up in an angry voice. "Red was a nice girl who fell on evil times in her life. Then she was killed by an evil man. We know Zack killed her. Since there's no court to turn to, I see two options: turn him loose, or hang him, and I don't want to see a killer go free."

The men looked at her with raised eyebrows. This kindly mother who tended the sick also had a fire in her against men who victimize women.

Cohen said, "I think we all share your reaction to what this fellow did, Hannah, but as civilized people, I fear our hands are tied."

Penney said, "The resolutions we agreed to back in Independence says we have the power."

Cohen said, "We have the power, but do we have the *right*? Resolutions or no resolutions. Why don't we tell Zack we know he killed the girl, and we're going to watch his every move."

Penney looked around. "I'll bet we all agree with Hannah's feelings, but also with Malachi's thinking, a bitter pill to swallow, such as it is." He scanned the small group to get a visual sense. "Any objection to his plan?" Except for a couple of disgusted shrugs and a grunt, there was no reaction. Even Hannah didn't object. Penney slapped his knees in resignation and stood up. "I guess it's my job to tell him he's wiggled off the hook. I'd rather fight a wildcat than turn that rat loose."

They camped the next evening about fifty yards from a clean, fast brook. After supper and the chores were finished, the camp collapsed in exhausted slumber under the sliver of a moon. Hannah sought out Penney standing outside his wagon and asked if he would give her guard protection while she took a bath in the brook. Penney reached into his wagon for his scattergun and said something to his wife. Together they walked toward the water. He stopped some yards distant.

"Getting protection was right smart, Hannah. Can't never tell what's out there in the dark. I'll be right here. You can be at ease. Ain't many times I'm a gentleman, but I'm prideful this is one. I don't have eyes in the back of my head."

She laughed merrily. "I couldn't ask for a more gallant guardian." She pronounced it "ga-LANT."

Hannah took her towel, fresh clothes, and a bar of soap and went into the darkness to the water. She stripped and slid into the cold, fast-moving brook. She shivered, but the water felt so good she barely minded. She walked to the middle and felt the rough soap scour her skin. She was careful to rinse quickly lest the harshness of it burn her skin. She climbed out and dressed in the one fresh dress she possessed, then rubbed her teeth vigorously with salt. She walked up to thank Penney who was gazing in the opposite direction.

Penney turned and touched his hat brim, and said, "My pleasure, though it makes me feel glum."

"How so?"

He laughed. "It's sad a beautiful woman would feel safe taking a bath with me just a hop and a jump away." He reached his wagon, then turned and said, "Have a good night, Hannah."

"I believe I will."

Nimrod made it a practice to stake his tent a distance away from the circled wagons and closer to the grazing livestock. His purpose was to be alert for disturbances among the animals without the distracting noise of coughing, snoring, and soft conversations coming from the wagons. On a crescent moon night, he was atop a small hill with a stiff breeze that scattered mosquitoes.

It had been years since he experienced a deep sleep. He had developed a subconscious trigger that was like a string on his toe. It made him instantly alert to danger, usually preceded by unexpected movement or sound. Thus, he was aware of the outline of a head poking through the half-open flap. His fingers curled around the butt of his revolver, and he watched, ready to meet any threat.

The voice was low and familiar. "Nimrod? Nimrod, I'm coming in." It was Hannah. She entered on her hands and knees and slid next to him. His thought as he raised himself to an elbow, was the obvious one—What was wrong to bring her here in the middle of the night?

There was a reason; one she believed was not wrong. Even though no one was within twenty yards, she spoke *sotto voce*, in a loud whisper.

"I'm free, Nimrod."

"Free from what?" He was confused. He was a little bit concerned. "Sneaking into a mountain man's tent can be dangerous."

A good-natured pout was in her voice. "I'm free from not being free."

He laughed. "Well, that's a good thing, I reckon. Best I can understand it."

"I'm free in my mind from the stupid sense of virtue that has kept me from you." In the dim light she could see the confusion on his face. "I was married to a bad man, a vicious man. But I wasn't *really* married to him. I've come to realize that."

"You was not married?" He was trying to catch up to her thoughts.

"No, not the way marriage should be. I was a prize Spencer bargained for, and he kept the price low because I had no choice. His price included controlling my life. He treated me like a servant—no, a slave. I never loved him, never respected him, and now I'm glad he's out of my life." She ran her fingers over Nimrod's cheek. "And stupid me, at last I can make room for you."

He couldn't resist pulling her close and running his hand tenderly over her face and through her hair. Then he pulled back. "I don't want to misbehave."

She giggled. "Do you need a formal invitation, you silly goose?"

Because he had to be ready for any emergency, Nimrod always slept dressed. Hannah started to unbutton his linsey-woolsey shirt. "I better not find one of those horrible acifidity bags," she joked.

"I got rid of it just to please you. If I die because of it, I'll come back and haunt you." They helped each other struggle out of clothing in their awkward space. They did so with the urgency of lust, but also with the humor of two mature people not over-awed by what they were doing.

Nimrod muttered, "Are you sure? You know, because—"

She knew he was talking about pregnancy. "I know about those things. Don't worry, but thank you."

They were both ardent lovers, but what each sought was not a sexual frenzy but an escape into togetherness, and out of loneliness. Their lovemaking was languid, and it wasn't until they neared the end that the blood coursed fast, and the breath rasped between tender kisses.

When it was over, she snuggled into his enveloping arms and found contentment. The first gray rays were coming out of the east as she began wrestling with her clothes in the tight tent space. "I have to get back to the children," she said.

He lay on his side and watched her. "If I wake up and find this has been a dream, I'll be fit to be tied." He reached up and caressed her face. "You're as pretty as a speckled pup." She chuckled and moved toward the entrance. He said, "I wanted you. Now, I want you more." She blew him a kiss and was gone.

The most peaceful time on the trail was when they were moving. The stresses of guiding the oxen, avoiding rocks and crevices that could snap an axle, and enduring the sun and insects left no energy for conflict.

That could change in the evening when exhausted, hot, and irritable people had time to ponder what a miserable existence their lives had become. There were a hundred things to fear or be vexed by. Not least of these were fellow travelers they considered unsavory or beneath their station; people who, back home, they had the luxury of avoiding.

A source of tension was the presence of Zack Monroe, whom some believed had gotten away with the murder of Red. In their sympathy, she was transformed from a sassy prostitute to a fun-loving young lady with a big heart. Others who didn't know Zack rallied to his defense. To them, he was a boisterous young fellow who had done nothing except fall prey to Red's depraved charms, and was innocent until proven guilty.

Zack himself didn't play the victim. He swaggered around the camp with a mocking smirk. It was countered by the malevolent glare of Aaron when they passed each other. Knowing that the Proctors had befriended Red made Zack's mockery more pleasurable. Nimrod watched the two and knew from living with rough men what could happen. He mentioned it to Hannah, who said he should do something or say something.

"That's not how it works. It's got to play out. And it will."

Nimrod and Hannah were as circumspect in their public dealings as the memory of their passion could allow. To the casual observer, they were doing business-as-expected between a guide and a member of the governing committee.

However, late at night, when the children were asleep and the neighbors not looking, they managed to slip away with a blanket to wherever prying eyes and hungry mosquitoes were not. Howling coyotes, cicadas, and snorers in the not-too-near wagons were intrusions in the night quiet.

One night, when Hannah believed she was fertile, they were content to "bundle" as she called it. He didn't push her. With faces inches from each other, they whispered secrets of their lives.

Hannah told him of difficult times as she attempted to use her education to make a spot for herself in a man's profession, and of Abel, the man who supported her strivings.

"I had five years of schooling," he said, with just a hint of regret. "What happened to your husband?"

She spoke with sad fondness. "He went to the other side."

Nimrod was confused. "The other si—Oh." After a moment, he understood. "How did he pass on, if I'm not too bold."

"This side became inhospitable." She shifted the subject to him. "Tell me what life was like in Kentucky."

"You'd have to be a sour person not to love Kentucky. It's got green mountains, green fields, and a big share of God-fearing folks. We had a lot of nothing, which mostly meant food. A muskrat was a good Christmas dinner. You can eat most anything if you're hungry enough." He paused in reminisce. "It's easier to look back on it than to live it."

"It appears you liked the people."

"Most."

She was aware of his reticence, but all the more reason to probe. "Tell me about your folks."

"Sharecroppers. Never had nothing. My daddy spent more time with his old friend John Barleycorn than with his own wife and youngins. Least he wasn't mean. My momma loved Jesus 'cause it seemed no one else much loved her back, 'cept us kids, but they don't count for much when her husband would rather drink pop-skull than love her."

"Why did you leave?"

He kissed her nose. "That's a pert little beak you got there."

She felt his hand creeping up her dress. She slapped in play-indignation. "I told you," she scolded. She let him complete his journey as his fingers knew where to go. He gently massaged her. "I warned you not to…" She chuckled lightly as she said it, having no intention of stopping him.

"There's more than one way to skin a cat," he said.

"In a manner of speaking," she added.

It didn't take long. She pulled his face down to hers, and he felt her hot pant on his cheek. Then, she stiffened and shuddered. She put her arms around his neck and hugged him close to her. He responded with rapid kisses over her face from forehead to neck, and especially the lips.

She struggled to a sitting position and pushed him down to where he was looking up at her hovering over him. Quietly, she said, *ceci pour ça.*

"What's that you said?"

"It's French."

"I barely know English. What's it mean?"

"It means 'this for that.'" As she spoke her fingers were busy working on the buttons of his trousers.

He raised his head to kiss her. "The 'that' was special. I'm chomping at the bit for the 'this.'"

Afterwards, they lightly slumbered in each others' arms, until Hannah heard some voices in the distance. She said, "I best be going." She kissed him lightly and crept away.

Hannah finished her chores and saw Rachel leaning against a wagon wheel, lost in thought, and drawing on a slate. "Rachel, darling, do you want to come with mother to hunt for buffalo chips?"

Rachel shrugged. Without a word, she put down the slate and walked barefoot out to join Hannah. Together, they went past the circled wagons and into the nearby prairie, making sure to stay within shouting distance of the camp. While they searched the ground, Hannah studied the pensive face of her daughter. "A penny for your thoughts, sweetheart. Can you tell me?"

Rachel didn't take her eyes off the ground. "Nothing."

Hannah tried to joke. "Well, you know, Rachel, it's impossible to think nothing. Because when you say 'nothing,' you're thinking about 'nothing,' so that's something." She looked for a reaction and got none. She reached out and took her daughter's hand as they walked. "Let me tell you what I know, Honey. I know I failed you." That got Rachel's attention. Hannah continued, "I failed you by not paying attention to what that monster I married was doing to you." Hannah's voice was wistful, almost pleading. "I wanted to give you and Billy security; to make sure there was food on the table. But I now know I failed you by not watching, by being blind to your pain." Hannah stopped and looked down at her daughter. "I—It never occurred to me that there could be such men." Her voice softened. "Please forgive me."

Rachel spoke without taking her eyes off the ground they were searching. "I didn't think you'd believe me. He told me you'd be angry at me. He told me it was my fault, and I didn't want to be blamed and have you stop loving me."

Hannah dropped her basket and brushed away tears. She embraced Rachel, then looked into her face. Rachel had no tears. She should have, Hannah thought. She once would have. Oh, how much this child has hardened her heart!

"Oh, darling, darling. You could never lose my love, even if you did something wrong, and you absolutely did no wrong; no wrong at all. You're the same angel you've always been."

Hannah sensed she shouldn't prolong the stressful conversation. It was a start. However, Rachel wasn't finished. She stopped, and said timidly, as though she were about to say something wrong. "Mother, let me ask you something, and please don't be mad at me."

She stopped and smoothed Rachel's hair. "Why, never! You can ask me anything, sweetheart."

Rachel pulled herself close to Hannah and wrapped her arms around her mother. "Please, let's just be you, and Billy, and me. From now on. Not another man I would be afraid of and who might want to hurt me."

Hannah blinked back a flow of tears and reached down and kissed the top of her daughter's head. "I will never, ever let anyone hurt you again, my darling."

She held Rachel at an admiring arm's length. "I guess we've got enough of these dreadful chips for now. Let's go back, dear." She reached for her daughter's hand. In the other hand she carried a basket of the despised buffalo chips.

Hannah's talk with Rachel caused her a period of deep introspection. It put a sharp edge to her regret about what her daughter had been forced to endure from Ed Spencer. She had brought an evil man into their midst, and the guilt it caused spread over her like a mold. It had been a choice she thought she had to make, but was it? Or was it a matter of insecurity and weakness that led her to choose a man—especially *that* man—over her children? She became ensnared by him only because she herself had stepped into the trap. She resolved to never again make such a mistake.

That, of course, brought Nimrod into her thinking. Was she on the verge of falling for a man who could be another monster to her children? She didn't think Nimrod was that way, but she had reason to be distrustful of her own judgment, especially of this man from another world. Nimrod seemed to be, at times, a thoughtful, sensitive person. He was kind to her children, but they all were, until they got what they wanted.

Nimrod certainly was sexually appealing. Oh, yes. But to put the worst face on it, he was also an uncouth, undereducated, violent man. He could do things that terrified her, no matter that his intentions might be good. Above all, she could never allow another Spencer near her children. The fear caused a maelstrom of worry. She must never hurt her children in that way again.

She knew that, eventually, she might be compelled to choose a man. The wilderness for which she was headed would be dangerous for a single woman and her children. But she would have time to choose a normal, unaggressive man she could control, at least enough to protect her children.

Despite all her calculations and musing, her thoughts always came back to Nimrod. But then she would slam a door on those thoughts. He was little more than a stranger. She dare not risk another mistake. She dare not. But, still, there was something about him…

The difficulties of the trail caused her to put the question aside, but it didn't go far.

CHAPTER TWENTY-TWO

A s Fort Laramie neared, children would ask their eternal question every few hours: "Are we almost there?" The women buzzed to each other as to what shopping might be available. The men hoped to hire craftsmen who could repair a wagon better than they, and, maybe have the opportunity to belly-up to a real bar.

Primitive Fort Laramie seemed like a visit to the county fair. It was a sign of how isolated they were feeling. They were juiced with eagerness for some civilization, even of this sorry kind. After many weeks of staring at the hind ends of oxen, swallowing dust along the prairie, and talking every day to the same few people, they were ready for Fort Laramie, and Fort Laramie was ready for them.

It was a fort only if you wanted to puff-up the term. It wasn't even called by its actual name, which was Fort John. It was a small trading post of adobe walls and a front gate open to all comers. For a reason no one remembered, it was named for an old-time trapper of no other renown, Jacques La Ramée.

The emigrants mixed with traders, mountain men, explorers, and Indians buzzing around the post in a babble of chatter, laughter, and oaths. Blacksmiths pounded on anvils. Oxen bawled while being winched up for reshoeing. Wainwrights hammered repairs to wagons. Gamblers tried to entice emigrants into a row of tented saloons where plenty of help was available to assist them in emptying their pockets. Ladies of the night were open for business at all hours. More than one wagon family was left stranded by the misadventures of a weak-willed and gullible husband.

In the distance, the pioneers could see two parked wagon trains, and fields dotted with a couple hundred teepees sheltering occupants from several tribes. Most were there to trade, some to get drunk, some to beg, and just a few to cause trouble. Regardless of the Indians' motives, to an approaching wagon train of Midwestern flatlanders, their presence rattled nerves.

A group of pioneers stood near Nimrod and looked with concern across the Laramie River at the small forest of tipis. One man looked over with wariness, and asked Nimrod, "How do we treat them?"

"Like people," Nimrod said. "I opine they asked each other the same question about the likes of us."

"It's hard to know what they're thinking," the man said.

"Well, just remember, you're near as strange to them as they are to you. Since furs ain't dear to us anymore, Indians don't have much to trade, but they still want the things they see—blankets, knives, whiskey, guns—to them, we're a general store stingy with credit. They're a war-making people, so they'll want to find out if you got any bark on you. Some of the Indians you see over that-a-way are like the no-accounts you used to see hanging around the billiard parlor back home— shiftless, and always happy to see trouble break out. Don't let them push you, and don't you push them. Leave their women alone, and don't give them likker."

The Laramie River was low for the season, no more than three feet with a firm bottom. After crossing, they found a camping area near the other trains. Once the wagons were parked in their circle, Penney called the pioneers together and stood at their front. At a suggestion from Nimrod, Penney asked the pioneers to salvage any discarded containers that could hold water.

"Why?" a man asked without thinking.

"There are dry days ahead, lots of them," Penney said with a glance at Nimrod, who nodded. Penney continued, "Nimrod, tell us what we got facing us here."

"I know we've been eating dust for weeks, but some of the folks you see over yonder at the fort ain't your friends. They ain't out here in this God-forsaken scrubland for the country air. They aim to come between you and your money. The whiskey is poison; the games are crooked. The women—well, the women ain't here to teach Sunday school." His reference to prostitutes caused many eyes to seek out Zack whose face burned at the attention.

❦

After Hannah's children were asleep, she and Nimrod stole away to a secluded spot in the soft grass along the Laramie River. They made hurried love while being alert for footsteps. You take what's offered. Later, sitting against a big cottonwood, they talked as lovers do, just to hear the voice of the other.

"I hope we didn't put you in a family way by how we carried on," Nimrod said.

"Leave that up to me. I know what I'm doing," Hannah said. "I've wanted to ask you: Why don't you talk about Kentucky, and your life there?"

He pulled blades of grass absently. "It weren't anybody's business."

"Am I anybody?"

He looked into her face. "No, reckon not."

"I'd like to know about your life," she said, hoping to simply sound curious, not probing, which she was.

"We was sharecroppers. I had me five years of schooling and started a sixth. My daddy couldn't leave the corn alone. When I was twelve, as I recall, he fell into the Licking River drunk and drowned."

"Licking River?"

He shrugged. "I didn't name it."

"Sorry. Go on."

"Maw cleaned house for the Embrys up the hill. They let us stay in our shack. My brother and sisters and me, we worked in the fields. It was corn-picking time when he got hisself drowned. That's when I left school."

Her penetrating gaze searched his face. "Something else happened, or you'd still be back there."

He pursed his lips and decided what he wanted to share. "When I was eighteen, I got involved with Hester Embry. She was the daughter of Mr. John Embry, the man who owned our shack and gave us all work."

"Did you love her?"

"I've spent time over the years trying to figure that out, and I'm of the belief I did love her. An eighteen-year-old loves in a different way than a grown man, but uh-huh, I loved her as best I figured out what that was and how to go about it. She said she loved me. I reckon maybe that was so, too. I would've married her." He gave a short laugh. "When a Lee marries an Embry, that'll be the day pigs dance at the wedding.

"At eighteen, though, you spend a lot of time on nonsense thinking. Figuring out what love is at that age is 'bout the same as tracking a weasel in a rock field. All you know for certain sure is you love your hound dog, your rifle, and your horse, if'n you are blessed to have one. Loving a woman confuses a young feller 'cause, love is mixed in with lust. All lust shares with love is four letters, but a young feller ain't learned that yet."

"What was she like, Hester?" Hannah asked.

"Hester was on the pretty side, and she was perky, and—I didn't see it at the time—she was a bit light in the head. Well, maybe more flighty." He stopped for a brief moment to find elusive words. "Not the sort of thing a feller could understand, not at eighteen, but, looking back, it was there, for sure.

"Anyways, her daddy told me to stay away from her, but I didn't. To get her away from riff-raff like me, he threatened to send her away to a fancy school. That's when—"

Hannah heard a catch in his voice.

He spoke fast as though the words were hot to the tongue. "That's when Hester went down to the river and drowned herself."

"Oh, my! And you blamed yourself?"

"I did, but not now, not as much. People don't do that to each other. They do it to theyself."

Hannah could tell from the pain in his voice that his memory still visited the banks of the Licking River, back to when he looked into the brown water to see her face-down, semi-submerged, her long hair floating around her. Hannah sensed his grief and put her hand on his forearm and caressed.

"Her daddy blamed me. Mr. Embry was a decent, honorable man, but he couldn't see straight for his grief. He told me if I left the county for good, he'd let my maw keep her job and the shack. So, I signed on with a flatboat taking hogs to Cincinnati, and then lumber down to New Orleans. I jumped off in St. Louis. A few years back, I ran into a feller in Memphis from back home. He told me maw still had her work and the shack. Mr. Embry kept his word, and so did I. I reckon by now she's gone, but I can't say for sure."

Hannah searched for words, but none came to mind. "Thank you for sharing that."

"I hope you don't think less of me, Nana."

"Who?"

"Nana. My sister was a Hannah. We called her Nana. I loved my sister."

She was pleased with the nickname and reached out and hugged him. Her embrace was warm, but her heart was doubting. The fears of her daughter were too insistent in her mind to ignore. Too much had happened in her life for unrestrained feelings. The wall had too many stones. Even so—Nana. He had made her name into an endearment, and that had brought her to the edge of the bridge. However, things would happen, and he would not speak that name for the rest of the trek.

Nimrod wandered down the dusty wagon tracks that passed for a Fort Laramie road. He welcomed the pounding of the blacksmiths, the bawling of the oxen being winched-up to be re-shod. From the ramshackle saloons, the hoarse laughter of the drunks and the theatrical shrieks of the prostitutes made respectable women hurry their steps as they passed.

Nimrod was chatting with some mountain men at dusk when he glanced at a man riding by in the distance. He froze. His muscles tightened, and his breath caught. Was it Rake Face Marcel? He watched the horseman fade into the gloom. Maybe. It was not the first time Nimrod saw or imagined seeing his blood enemy. He lectured himself to stop seeing things.

Nimrod's shook off the image when he caught sight of a clean-shaven, short man dressed in a buckskin blouse reaching almost to his knees. The faces of both men brightened as they wrung each others' hands.

He said, "Well, I'll be damned and go to hell. Kit Carson his own self. What you doing out here in the middle of nowhere?"

"Howdy, Lee. The middle of nowhere is about the only place that'll have me." Both men laughed. "I'm scouting for Captain Fremont. We're snooping around for the government and calling it surveying."

Nimrod could have guessed that. "I heard we've kicked up a storm with the Mexicans. I'll wager two pelts you're fixin' to set a trap line for California."

Carson nodded without agreeing. We've traveled out that way." He grinned. "Whatever soup's a-cooking, we want the first sip."

"They tell me that back east you got famous, even got books written about you."

"Good thing I don't read right well. I might even believe them."

"Speaking of back east, any news?" Nimrod said.

"A trader from Independence said Andy Jackson died in Nashville a few weeks ago. He was sober when he told it, so I reckon it's true." He sighed with resignation. "Old Hickory hisself. Died in his bed, he did. Seems old age and good whiskey got done what the Lime Juicers and the Red Sticks couldn't."

Nimrod became quiet as he absorbed the crumbling of a pillar. "The old man lived strong, he did."

"Hear tell you're nurse-maiding a wagon train," Carson said with an impish grin. "Ain't that an old man's job?"

Nimrod sighed. "If it ain't, it'll sure as hell turn a feller into one." He took advantage of Carson's experiences with the Fremont expeditions by asking a battery of questions.

"Things is changed along the Humboldt River," Carson said and paused at Nimrod's baffled look. "That's what you knew as the Mary's River east of the Sierra mountains. Captain Fremont changed the name just recent, which he likes to do for everthing he comes across."

"What's a Humboldt?" Nimrod asked.

"A feller. Some sort of explorer; a foreigner."

"What's new out there?" Nimrod asked. "It's been ten-eleven year since I was in them parts with Joe Walker."

"The Diggers been kicking up a fuss," he said, referring to the unflattering label given to Paiutes, a tribe known for digging roots for food. "They shoot arrows into cattle at night, figuring they'll be left behind when the wagons move on. You have to kill a few—Indians, I mean—to get them to stop. But there's a chief name of Wuna Mucca who's a friendly. He can be helpful if you can find him. It's a big territory. If you do, use my name. We was uncommom free with gifts to him. Some now call him Truckee; no idea where that came from, but I guess it stuck. I heard one outfit also give his name to a river that's a way through the mountains."

"My ears are itching, Kit."

"It's at the end of the forty-mile desert. I reckon you'll recollect—"

"Not about to forget it," Nimrod said.

"After you leave the desert, you come to a big meadow. You go through that, until—"

Nimrod interrupted. "I remember. You reach the river you say is called Truckee. It comes down out of the mountains and turns north. Walker and us rode south from that point a good lick and then crossed into California."

Carson said, "The pass you took is too far south for pilgrims. You made it on horseback, wagons would take too long."

Carson then told him of an old mountain man named Caleb Greenwood, known to both of them, whom he had encountered two weeks before as Greenwood was returning east. "Old Greenwood, he's a tough buzzard; he don't quit. We bent many an elbow through the years. Last year, he guided a train to California by a new trail, led by a feller name of Elisha Stephens." Carson recited details of Greenwood's experience to Nimrod who needed no written descriptions. Both men had the broad country in their heads. Landmarks, rivers, and dangers, were memorized as clearly as family names.

Carson leaned forward to make a map in the dirt with a stick. "Greenwood said there's a way acrost the Sierra going straight west to California. It'll make you sweat a bit more, but it's your shortest, and might save you from early winter, but only God knows that. He says you follow the Truckee west-southwest maybe a week, maybe ten days, 'til you're in the mountains. It's a hard haul, but you head up the river 'til you see a lake 'bout three mile long, shape of a cucumber. Can't miss it. Head for it. Then you have to climb a steep rise to the top of the pass. I reckon you could winch wagons up; it can be done if your pilgrims are fit and got some sand in their gizzards but be sure to pray every step of the way. When you get up there, you head south a short bit to a valley. Take that valley west, then follow the ridge above and angle west a few days, depending on the weather. You'll come to a gap that'll take you down to the Bear River. From the top of the pass to the gap, it's about thirty mile, I reckon, but you'll think it's a hundred. Then all that's left is a Sunday walk along that Bear River out of the mountains to Sutter's Fort."

Carson leaned back and reached for his jug, then added a caution: "It'll take a passel of hard work, but you'll make it. You've done worse." He paused, and said, "Provided you don't get trapped by a sneak snow."

Carson passed the jug to Nimrod, who tipped it and drank, then held the jug up admiringly, and said, "This ain't a bad dust-cutter; just don't tell me what's in it." He drank again. "Go on. I can talk and drink at the same time."

Carson laughed. "But, can you think and drink?"

Nimrod sighed and shook his head at some memories. "I'm here to tell you: I made some bad promises when I been corned."

After emptying his store of learning about getting over the Sierra Nevada, Carson threw away his stick. "You done emptied my brain. You're gonna want to know every rabbit hole all the way to California."

Nimrod sipped the jug and nodded his thanks, but had one more question: "You remember Rake Face Marcel?"

"I can't disremember one of the few men uglier than me. I also remember what happened to your wife up on Horse Creek."

Nimrod looked away. "You see anything of him?"

"I hear some from time to time. Nothing to pin-down. I heard Marcel robbed a couple of small trains. Someone will kill him. It always happens that way."

"I hope that someone is me," Nimrod said.

"You got the right."

Nimrod had enough of the topic. "What's this Fremont feller like, Kit?"

Carson studied the question. "Got his good points. A bit prideful, and plenty headstrong. Fools himself into thinking he's a mountain man. If he was smart as he thinks, I'd be out of a job. I just tell him where to go and how to get there, and then let him think it was his idea. But that's fine; keeps me in work." He paused and smiled broadly. "I'm just japing. We get along fine." Carson's face turned to concern. "You're traveling a bit close to Crow country, I reckon."

Nimrod tensed a bit. "A ways south."

Carson nodded. "They've been known to wander. We went through there two year ago. Many Horses asked about you, and not friendly-like."

"I been told."

Carson violated the mountain man code of minding one's own business. "Seems he blames you for what happened to his daughter."

Nimrod changed the subject. "You ever hear of a writer feller name of Hastings? I saw a guide book he wrote. Folks seem curious. You ever crossed his path?"

Carson nodded. "I did, down in Jim Bridger's trading post." He laughed. "He calls it a fort. Old Jim's skilled at bullshit."

"He gets better with practice, I 'spect."

Carson said, "Getting back to this Hastings feller, he's a young lawyer from Ohio. He thinks the folks back there are poorer for his leaving. I met him once, which will satisfy me for a long while. The fool wants to be boss of California. He's a Pied Piper sort of fella— You know that old children's story? His half-cocked ideas could lead folks into something they can't get out of. Hastings claims he knows there's an easier way through the Wasatch Mountains, then south of the salt lake, and across the salt desert. That's country that'll kill better than a bullet. Bridger is giving him the ballyhoo. I'd wager he figures Hastings' scheme would keep people coming Bridger's way so he can sell them overpriced supplies."

Nimrod chuckled. "That's a good way to get trampled, get between Bridger and a dollar."

Carson nodded. "Cutoffs will come, that's for sure. Men who know this country will find shorter ways to get from here to there."

Nimrod said, "Cutoffs can be trouble, depending on who's

making a claim for them. Speaking for myself, I'd never send anyone on a cutoff afore I'd scouted it personal or been damned sure it was true."

"My point being new cutoffs will dry up Bridger's business." Carson squinted at the position of the sun. "Well, sir, speaking of brash, I better track down Captain Fremont afore he takes a notion to get lost again." He gave Nimrod a strong handshake. "Well, mind who rides up on you."

As Nimrod watched Carson walk away, Penney hurried to his side, and said, "I feared it. I feared it. Sure enough, one of our men got swallowed up by them saloons."

Nimrod said, "That's a thing bound to happen."

"It's Asa Grover. He never quit blaming himself for shooting his wife."

Nimrod said, "Let's go."

"This is not a guide's job," Penney said.

"I know the kind of skunks who run these saloons."

The two men walked to the saloon tent where Grover was slumped on the makeshift bar. Nimrod faced the bartender who was looking on without concern. "We're taking this man out. He's addle-brained out of grief, and he best not be drinking."

The bartender laughed and shrugged.

Penney stepped up. "We'll be taking his timepiece with us."

"What you talking about, old man?"

"You know damn well. You was seen lifting it."

"Kiss my ass. The onliest thing I'll be lifting is your scalp, if'n you calling me a thief."

Nimrod reached for a nearby ax and slammed it into a barrel of whiskey, and stood back as the brown liquid gushed out. He was about to swing on another barrel when the bartender raised his arms for him to stop. He pulled Grover's watch from his pocket and extended it to Penney with his left hand.

"All right, no more. Here. Now get the hell out."

"Penney reached for the watch. In the next moment, the bartender swung across the bar at Nimrod with a knife. Nimrod had anticipated the move and dodged. The knife point got stuck in the bar. Nimrod slammed the bartender's head on the plank by his hair, breaking his nose. He took the knife and sliced off the man's ear. The bartender howled and held one hand over his nose and the other over the side of his head. Blood gushed from both places. Nimrod lifted the severed ear on the knifepoint and put it in front of the bartender.

"This won't fit on your head no more, but it can make a sporty necklace, you dry it right. It might remind you to work on your manners." Nimrod heaved Grover over his shoulder and walked out. Penney, following him, took the ax and severed the pole holding up the flap, then watched the front of the tent collapse. "Closed for repairs," he said.

Penney threw the ax aside, and said, "Did you have to do that? I mean, cut off his ear?"

"Yep. I want that drygulcher to know I'm more savage than he is. If he tries to get revenge, which I know has already crossed his mind, I want him thinking he could lose the other damned ear, and maybe more."

"Word will get around about this," Penny said.

"I had that in mind. I want his friends thinking about their own ears."

Hannah had finished bandaging a small cut on a little girl's leg when an older man with a self-confident air walked over from one of the other wagon trains at the fort. He removed his hat and introduced himself as Estes Jones, M.D., late of Columbus, Ohio, and now a physician for a train headed to Oregon.

"Good day, ma'am. I've been told of your healing abilities from a woman in your company I chanced upon." Hannah rose and shook his outstretched hand. He glanced at her ring finger. "Tell me, Mrs. Ah…"

"Spenc—Blanc. Hannah Blanc. Pleased to make your acquaintance, Dr. Jones."

It became apparent he viewed her as a curiosity, but Hannah wasn't offended. She was quite aware of the rarity of her role. However, the opportunity to discuss medical matters was a conversation she prized. "I'm flattered by your visit, doctor."

He leaned against the wagon while she stood with her hand on the girl's head.

"Were you trained at a medical school of my familiarity?" he asked.

"My late husband was a skilled physician, educated at Dartmouth College. I was fortunate to learn at his elbow."

He nodded. "I know doctors who received education in the manner you describe. Where are you licensed?"

Hannah should have anticipated the question. "Uh, I'm not. The Missouri licensing board rejected me. Other doctors believe they erred." She didn't say the reason was her sex. That was for others to say. She could sense Jones' skepticism rising like a drawbridge.

"Well, Mrs.—Ah, Blanc, you say? Is there any advice I can give you? I saw you bandaging the cut on the little girl's leg. That's a useful service you can render in the absence of a regular doctor."

His words stung, but she had inured herself to the words of pompous men. She changed the subject in order to pick his brains. "If I may, I'd like to ask your opinion about the cause of infection. It attacks people from every direction. The more I see it, the more frightening it is."

He cleared his throat and adopted a professorial manner. "The cause of infectious disease is well established. It is miasma. In other words, bad air emanating from rotting organic matter. The details of how this happens are not well known, but the causative nature is agreed upon by the most eminent physicians. That's something you would've learned in medical school."

"I understand what you say, doctor, but I'm confused when I see a person coming down with a disease after being near a patient with the same disease. However, others who keep their distance aren't affected. Or, take surgery. Patients operated on and kept isolated in a room closed to outside atmosphere, often become infected. Or, consider cholera, in our situation. Why is it that people traveling alongside a river, the Platte, for example, often contract cholera, but when they travel away from the river, nothing near as much?" Jones started to interrupt, but Hannah, starved for medical conversation, was on a roll. "Consider this: If one person is infected with a bad cold and, say, is kissed by a healthy person, there's a good chance the infection will be passed on. But if the healthy person avoids the one with a cold, it won't be passed. So, no 'bad air' is involved, but the infection seems to come from the contact. Every mother knows that."

Jones uttered a defensive laugh. "It sounds like you believe there are invisible little beasties carrying infections around to make mischief."

"It seems to me, the answer has to be more complicated than just bad air. I wonder about such things."

The doctor was put off by what he saw as a woman with a pushy manner. "Well, young lady, I've given you the wisdom of the finest medical minds. If you wish more, you'll have to attend medical school." He put on his hat and took a step toward leaving. "I wish you a good day, madam."

Hannah started to make a fire for supper and pushed Jones from her mind.

She was still struggling to get a flame when Cohen rushed up. "Hannah, we need you over at the fort. John Burns is in bad shape."

Hannah told Billy to take over working on the fire and half-ran behind Cohen. When they got to the row of saloons outside the gate, they saw Penney looking down at Burns on his back off to the side with pedestrians taking a curious look then walking on.

Hannah reached down and felt his pulse, then lifted his eyelid and saw a fixed gaze. "He's dead." She smelled the heavy odor of alcohol. "Alcohol poisoning, I'm thinking. Lord knows what they put in those bottles."

Cohen frowned. "Everyone thought he was free of rotgut."

Penney pursed his lips. "A feller might think he's quit on whiskey, but whiskey don't quit on him."

Nimrod watched the rain as he stood just inside the lean-to farrier shop as Bub was being re-shod. He glanced out at the road and saw Rake Face saunter down the street on horseback. He was right! The horseman had been him. Nimrod roared and rushed toward him. He pulled Rake Face from the saddle and began to beat him. Rake Face pulled a knife and took a near-miss swipe at Nimrod's face. Nimrod twisted the knife from his hand and threw it aside. He wanted this to be even more personal than a knife. Nimrod straddled Rake Face and started choking him with deadly intent. His grip tightened as he put all of his hatred into fingers that dug deep into Rake Face's neck. As Rake Face's eyes started to roll back, Nimrod almost sang with joy.

As the men struggled in the dirt, a crowd gathered, as it does at such times. Some men enjoyed the spectacle, but a few assumed these were two drunks fighting, and it was about to get out of hand. Well-intentioned hands pulled Nimrod off and surrounded him.

"Stop this."… "Here now."… "Let's have no violence."… "A couple of drunks."… "This is shameful."

Rake Face took advantage of the confusion to jump on his horse and race away. Nimrod struggled and managed to free himself. He ran to the farrier shop to get his rifle and pursue, but he realized Bub was not ready to ride. He saw Cohen walking his horse down the street and ran to him.

"I need your horse. Quick".

Cohen was bewildered. He dismounted and handed over the reins. "I don't know what you're chasing, but you won't win any races with this old girl."

Nimrod started off in pursuit of Rake Face who had a much faster mount and disappeared into the distance. Nimrod plodded on, trying to follow track in the light rain and fog.

Nimrod gave up the chase and took a short cut to an overview of the trail he guessed Rake Face would take. After a long thirty minutes in the rain, he sighted him. Rake Face was walking his horse as he concentrated on following the trail. Nimrod was atop a hill about a hundred-fifty yards distant. It would be a difficult but doable shot on a moving target. Nimrod felt the wind so he could allow for it. He guessed Rake Face's pace in order to calculate how much to lead him. He was tightening the trigger when Rake Face disappeared into a fog bank. Nimrod swore under his breath, lowered the rifle, and rode away.

Hannah opened her eyes in alarm at the strange sounds her first morning in Fort Laramie. The clatter of hammered metal and the upraised voices of men working made her think of what was feared most—Indians! Still half awake, she crawled past sleeping Rachel and peered out the tent flap. She relaxed when she saw groups of men repairing wagons and shouting instructions back and forth, and bonnet-wearing women leaning over Dutch ovens on tripods hanging above breakfast fires.

Civilization—how quickly it becomes alien, she thought, then smiled and shook Rachel and Billy. Then reached for her own bonnet to start the day.

CHAPTER TWENTY-THREE

Many of Penney's company at Fort Laramie worked at chores. Others wandered among various wagon trains to chat, inquire, and look for rumors and gossip to carry back as morsels to share.

Abruptly, a strange thing happened. The sounds of tools hammering became successively muted in the distance. The silence was like a fog rolling in. People grew silent on a slow wave that flowed toward Hannah. It accompanied a small crowd following a couple carrying a rolled-up carpet.

Hannah's curiosity was answered by a woman in a hushed voice. She said a small girl had died, and the procession was for her burial.

Hannah's interest reflexively turned to the question of contagion, so she asked the woman the cause of the child's death.

The woman shrugged. Like so many on this journey, she just died.

The fresh grave on the edge of the fort grounds was reached, and the people moved into a circle around it. There were several burial mounds nearby in a haphazard graveyard.

The father lay down the rug and opened it to reveal a girl of about three. Her eyes were closed, and her cherubic face and tiny hands were bone white and in repose, as though asleep. Her light brown hair was neatly combed. She wore her white church dress. On her feet were tiny button shoes. On her chest lay a rag doll tucked into her crossed arms. Hannah's mind formed images of her laughing at her daddy's gentle tease, crawling into bed next to mama to escape a bad dream, and jumping in glee at a sugar treat.

After the mother leaned down to give a final kiss, the father carefully wrapped the rug around the girl. When her face was covered, the mother screamed, and two women friends reached out to comfort her. Two men gently placed the small bundle in the grave. The father stood back and put his arm around his wife who buried her face in his shoulder. Her sobs were the outpouring of a broken heart. The father's face had a gray, sick look, and his gaze went from the grave to the horizon. The same horizon that had beguiled him to chance bringing his family into the wilderness.

The emigrants who had gathered looked on with an ill-at-ease sorrow. Mothers had dread on their faces as they thought of their own children.

Together, mother and father would share guilt for taking this innocent child from her safe home into a valley of death: He for insisting on the journey; she for not fighting harder to resist it. Together, they would be haunted by visions of this barren plain, and the small body left beneath it.

The father said, in a broken voice, "Does anybody know some words?"

Preacher stepped forward with his Bible underarm and raised a hand as he prayed for the soul of the little girl and that her parents be comforted by her salvation. He then led them in a ragged, half-hearted singing of the Wesleyan hymn, "Love Divine, All Love Excelling" because he thought it would be familiar to most. Not to unchurched Brister who followed along on his concertina as best he could. It was sung mainly off-key and without the usual verve. Stepping to the head of the grave, Preacher's sermon was a brief and predictable, "Suffer the little children to come unto me..."

As Preacher turned to console the parents, Hannah took a step toward the grave. On a kind impulse, she started singing softly the poem accompanying an old lullaby.

Sleep my child, peace attend thee.
All through the night.
Angels watching ever round thee.
All through the night.
They will let no peril harm thee.
All through the night.
Thou, my love, to heav'n art winging.
Earthly dust from off thee shaken.

Soul immortal shalt thou awaken.
Home through the night.

Hannah could not see through her flooded eyes that others were crying, too, crying for the child now beneath them, and fear for what lay ahead. No one wept harder than Millie Plum, as her heart was full of thoughts of her own baby in a lonely, unmarked grave located in nowhere.

In moments, the people moved on, abandoning the grave to the emptiness of an indifferent, arid prairie. The mother stood and watched as men shoveled dirt on the covering of the girl's body. The mother's lips trembled, and her eyes were wide with disbelief. They were burying her baby. She fingered a weather-faded shawl pulled tight around her shoulders.

There would be no flowers or visitations for this little girl. Her marker was a cross made of spare boards nailed together. It said, "Emily Pierce, age 3. Asleep in Jesus." Soon, the marker would blow away or be used for firewood by some freezing emigrant. That this mama's darling with the ragdoll ever existed would, in the course of time, be forgotten.

The layover at Fort Laramie allowed the women to get out of those accursed wagons and have fresh conversations with women from other trains. Millie Plum, trying to shed her despondency, had the idea of a picnic and inspired other women to elevate it to a "church picnic" party, just like back home.

The women arose at dawn on picnic day, served a brief breakfast, and then set about with their special menu while the men worked on repairs or went to the trading area of the fort. The women, being aware of the saloons in the fort, gave the men stern orders to return for the picnic at two p.m. The women split up the cooking by employing several Dutch ovens, their basic cooking utensil.

The entrée was "spotted pup," consisting of cooked rice placed in a Dutch oven and covered with milk and beaten eggs. Salt, sugar, raisins, and other spices were added and baked until the raisins were soft.

A second dish was "fried apples." The women fried bacon, then removed the bacon and put peeled apples in the grease and cooked it down. It was completed by covering the apples with cream, butter, and crumbled bacon.

For dessert, they decided cakes weren't feasible, so settled instead on cornbread. To make it special, they used buttermilk, and then added the precious crushed seeds of several vanilla beans, and a dash of rose water that one of the women had been saving.

Stools were placed in a circle, and the food was spread out buffet style on the tailgates of three wagons. The women sent children to round-up the men. Most of them came in a hurry, eager for what promised to be a luxurious meal.

Most came. But only most.

A half-dozen husbands didn't show. With Preacher prepared to say grace, and the food dished up, they waited. After a ten-minute wait, Penney walked over to the fort and corralled the men out of bars and led them back to the dinner, although not in a straight line.

In the loud voices of drunkenness, laughing at stupid inanities, the men sat on the stools, and two of them fell off, and laughed uproariously. Emory Plum vomited in the grass. Meantime, Nimrod, who had declined to join the men on their carousing, sat with his hands clasped in a saintly pose.

Millie Plum looked at her husband in fury, tears streaming down her face. With the men looking on with shamed faces, and the women with tight-lipped anger, she berated him in a muted voice, but heard by everyone. "You had to do this, didn't you? You forced me out of our home, away from my folks, buried my baby in the wilderness, and brought me to this horrible place. Then, I try to do something civilized, and you become a drunken sot—I hate you!" Millie threw her plate loaded with food at Emory's head. Of course, it largely missed him and splattered Preacher sitting nearby. Millie rushed away sobbing. Emory watched her go with rice in his hair. The other drunken men looked shame-faced at their plates under their wives withering glares.

Penney tried to defuse the tension by taking a big bite out of the food. He grinned, and said, "This food is special. I'm pleased as a tick on a fat dog."

The next morning, Penney was busy preparing to get the train ready to depart Fort Laramie. He asked Aaron if he'd seen Nimrod.

"I haven't seen Nimrod since last evening, Captain. Want me to go into town for a look-see?"

"I'd be Obliged."

Aaron wandered the streets of the outpost and looked into stores and bars looking for Nimrod. He located him sprawled on a table with a tipped-over bottle at his elbow. The encounter with Rake Face had torn the scab off and made his most painful memory bleed. The wound had slept fitfully, but the incident with Rake Face had inflamed it.

Aaron shook him. Nimrod lifted his head and blinked hard to clear the fog of his hangover.

The captain's looking for you. What you doing here?"

Nimrod struggled to his feet. "Just thinking."

Several splashes of cold water and three cups of coffee restored Nimrod to the land of straight-thinking, though with a few curves.

On the walk to join the wagons lining up to move out, he noticed Ignacio Lopez standing by his wagon set apart from the others. Lopez beckoned to him. When he walked over, Lopez shook his hand and said, "I would like to say goodbye to you, the one man I trust in this company."

"Goodbye? Where you going, señor?"

"There's a freight caravan headed south to Bent's Fort. We're going to join it. It's good terrain with water, so I'm not expecting problems. From there, we'll make our way south to Taos. I told Captain Penney last night."

"Why the change of heart?"

"Well, my friend, war is coming between our two countries. I need to make myself available to mine. Taos is the closest place."

The last hangover veil had lifted from Nimrod's brain. "I'm not too savvy on these things, but I do reckon it's in the air. I guess it's just got to happen."

Lopez agreed. "It's coming. It has been for some time." He chuckled and slapped Nimrod lightly on the shoulder. "You're a good man, amigo."

"*Vaya con dios*, as you Mexicans say."

"He'll stay with you, as well."

"Reckon we can send Zack along with you?"

Lopez whooped with laughter. "I leave him in your care. I softened him up for you."

The committee set the departure for the morning of the fourth day before any more trouble occurred. There was one matter to be disposed of first; literally disposed of. Penney and the committee marched as a delegation to the wagon of pimp Benny Bogle.

Bogle heard them just outside the wagon entrance and poked his head out. "Whatcha all want?"

Penney, never one to draw out a conversation, was even brusque by his standards. "This fort is where you get off. We want you gone."

Bogle protested. "I signed to go to Sutter's Fort. Are you going back on your word?"

"We're unsigning you. You ain't going nowhere with this company. We don't want your kind. Now git."

That being that, the committee walked away. Cohen said, "That was an oration the equal of Pericles, Shadrach."

The captain chuckled. "I ain't made the feller's acquaintance, but I reckon he was a speechifier."

Penney saw Nimrod coming and waited for him. "Where you been last night, hombre? You hankering to keep John Burns company?"

"Sorting things out."

"I seen you talking to Lopez. Not happy to lose him; a good man. We're now down to fourteen wagons."

"It's easy to lose the good ones, Shadrach. Bad ones like Zack stick like glue."

Penney started to walk and beckoned for Nimrod to follow. "We got to have a committee meeting. We'll need you." He led them to a shady area where camp stools had been set up. Waiting for them were Hannah, Cohen, Masterson, and Preacher. Penney got settled and pointed to Masterson. "Ezra, you go ahead."

Masterson nodded. "The North Platte from here on can be

cantankerous, I'm told. Not like the lazy Platte we came up on. The problem is how to get across the damned thing." Preacher cleared his throat at the mild expletive, but he was ignored.

Nimrod took a stick and drew an outline of the river route. "If you know where you're going, it's fordable." He let his words sink in. "In about ten days travel, we'll come to a bend in the river with an island in the middle. The bottom is rock; not much sand to trap the wagons."

"I'm told it's deeper up river where we're going," Masterson said.

Nimrod agreed. "It's deeper 'cause the channel's tighter. The place we're aiming for is an old Indian crossing. General Ashley first crossed there back in twenty-five. Kit Carson, just the other day, told me Fremont's expedition crossed there not more'n a month ago. It should be lower since we're a mite later in the season."

"What's the travel like?" Hannah asked.

"More rocks and hills than you're used to, but we just pick our way along."

The other members looked from Nimrod to Hannah and back. Though the two principles were unaware, the more perceptive people observed the attraction between the two in its nuances. But because they knew the type man Spencer was, they didn't disapprove or gossip about it as they would have back home. They were full-up with gossip about him.

Penney closed the meeting by saying to the committee, "These last days here have stirred up more dust than a Texas twister. We need to get the hell out of this place."

Just before starting the wagons, Penney said, "We're missing the Plums. Anything wrong with their wagon?"

Cohen said, "They're headed back home. Going to wait for an east bound train or army column they can join."

They looked at the Plums standing by their wagon, Emory at one end, Millie at the other. Separated by a gulf far wider than fifteen feet.

Masterson murmured to no one in particular, "That's the end of the bliss in that marriage, I have no doubt."

Hannah answered in the same tone. "They're going back to a lonely house."

Penney clapped his hands, and said, "We-all need to go over and wish them nice folks well." He started toward the Plums, followed by several others.

The North Platte started in the mountains of what would become Colorado and flowed north in a wide loop around the future site of Fort Casper, then down through Fort Laramie, and then east to join the South Platte, and on to the Missouri.

As the oxen trudged along the riverbank, the land changed. The trail became more rocky and hilly, jarring to those riding in the wagons, but not enough to greatly impede progress. Nimrod directed them a few miles off the trail to a place called Oil Mountain known to most mountain men. There they found an oil seepage which they could scoop up, thicken with flour, and refill the grease buckets swinging on the rear axle of all wagons.

Some found it a bit creepy to see the horizon rising into high mountains in all directions except east. The pioneers were flatlanders to whom the peaks were awesome. They were also frightening because they knew those mountains were going to be an intimate part of their future, and perhaps their end.

The elevation crept upward to more than a mile high. The days blew with a wind that never seemed to grow tired. The sun was hotter at that elevation because there was less atmosphere to filter it. The increase of UV exposure made sunburns quick and painful. When the sun went down, the wind became chilly, though it was still summer. At night, chilly turned into cold.

From Fort Laramie north, the wagon train followed inside the river's loop around and then southwest until they came to the crossing place Nimrod had described. There, the North Platte was about one hundred fifty feet wide with a narrow island in the middle. Nimrod walked Bub across and ascertained it had a hard four-foot bottom with a nasty current.

The men checked the caulking of their wagon boxes, and then used ratchet jacks to lift the boxes off the running gear and place six-inch blocks on each corner for extra clearance. They lined up to cross and waited.

Three men on horseback walked their mounts into the current

to form a picket line to keep livestock moving as they swam across. It was the riskiest job on the drive, so it was rotated. One of the riders was Sam Ritter, a nineteen-year-old son of German immigrants.

The oxen and other animals balked at entering the water, but once herded in, they half-walked and half-swam in a milling, bawling jam. Their tendency as they moved was to let the strong current push them downstream. It was the job of the outriders to command them back into line. Sam was the middle rider. When the cluster of cattle was thickest, his horse stumbled into a hole and fell forward, throwing Sam into the water and trampling him. The herd was close behind, and a hundred hooves smashed Sam into the hard bottom.

Sam's mother was watching from the bank and started screaming when she saw her son thrown into the path of the animals. Others started shouting and staring at the place in the river where the body that used to be Sam half-emerged and floated downstream.

When the cattle had passed, Nimrod and two other men rode ahead and pulled the body from the water. As Sam's mother rushed toward them, Nimrod shouted, "Stop her." He didn't want her to see what he had seen.

❦

The train left the North Platte and followed the Sweetwater River, a tributary from the west that twisted across the landscape like an arthritic snake. It would be a welcome source of water all the way to the continental divide called South Pass.

On an otherwise pleasant day, the wagons were moving along the Sweetwater bank when a drover slapped at the back of his neck and cried out in pain and shock. In moments, he was waving his arms and dodging. Others watched in surprise, but then they also started cursing and crying out as they swatted at winged monsters flitting beyond reach. Children began screaming and running as they flailed the air. Hannah shouted, "Get to your wagons and cover your head and arms." The pioneers grabbed cloths or clothing and did as she said. Soon, the bugs had passed on, and someone called "All clear," but people still peered out from their cover to make certain.

They had fallen victim to a swarm of pirate bugs, tiny insects that feed on aphids, mites, and other insects even smaller than they. The worst thing about them was their nasty bite. For some reason, they were inclined to bite humans, though people were not on the bugs' menu.

Preacher said to anyone listening, "This is like Moses' escape from Egypt. Perhaps next are the locusts."

Everyone tried to laugh the attack off while watching to see if the bugs would return, but Maude Horner, who had remained quiet during the Fort Laramie stop, resumed shrieking.

Hannah listened to her screams, then, knowing the woman was in psychic agony, muttered, "Oh, no. Please, God, no."

The train resumed its plodding along the Sweetwater, one hundred fifty miles from the North Platte to the continental divide at South Pass. It was over sagebrush high desert along the river, which would have been called a stream back home. It was as helter-skelter as the route of a cat chasing a mouse. Had the wagons followed the bank, it would have doubled or tripled the miles. Instead, they forded the small river a dozen times to stay on a straight course.

The terrain was on a subtle but steady upward grade. When they reached South Pass, it would be seventy-five-hundred feet. Their sea-level lungs would have to progressively labor harder as the ground sloped ever higher. The days were moderate, but the mid-summer nights could dip into the forties. Grass for the animals was plentiful. Other than the insect attack, these should have been among their easiest miles. Should have been.

Masterson was first to notice the Patterson wagon starting to lag behind. Their oxen were struggling with the weight they were burdened with pulling. It couldn't go on.

At the mid-day break, Penney approached the Patterson wagon and hailed Jasper.

When the old man walked over, Penney told him what had been observed, then said, "Jasper, it's clear you've got to lighten your load." He let that sink in, then said, "That chest of drawers has got to go. It's the same weight as a big man."

Looking with a long face toward the wagon where he knew Agnes was listening, Jasper said, "I can't do that, Captain, I just can't bring myself to do it. That's all mother has remaining of our family and her home. Even her little dog is gone."

Penney scuffed the ground with his toe and studied the pebbles. Finally, he said, "Well, Jasper, I hope you know this is painful for me, but we'll just have to do it ourselves. We can't have the train slowed down by waiting on this wagon."

Agnes' sobs could be heard from inside the wagon. Jasper's own voice wavered as he said, "Well, we'll just put it alongside the trail, so maybe another family can get some use of it."

Penney shook his head. "Afraid not. Anyone else would have the same problem. We'll break it apart for kindling. Wood's scarce in these parts."

Agnes' sobs grew louder, and Penney again expressed his regret and hastened off to recruit men to remove the chest. "I hate this job," he muttered.

❧

Meister cocked the old-fashioned horse pistol and pointed it at Johnny. All pretense of civility toward his bond-servant had vanished. In his other hand he carried handcuffs.

"Lie down, you worthless bastard. I know you had a mind to break your contract and run away back at that fort. The contract gives me the right to lock you down."

Johnny lay down, but with a protest. "I not be trying to run away, boss."

"I'll make sure you don't."

Johnny, in a helpless rage, glared at Meister who cocked the pistol and held it to his head.

"You make one move, and I'll blow your uppity black head off. You may be thinking you're Nat Turner, but be careful, or you'll get what he got. If you run, I'll pay Indians to track you down and bring your scalp back. You'll wear these 'til morning." He didn't explain how he would recruit Indians he didn't know. Meister locked the handcuffs.

Over the next two days, Johnny went about his chores sullenly. Other members of the company watched, suspicious of Meister's mistreatment. Finally, Johnny stumbled on a simple task, and Meister kicked him. "Get your ass up."

From behind, a commanding voice said, "Stop that. He's a free man. You freed him."

Meister whirled and confronted Andrew. "He's bound to me, all legal. I got a right to discipline my worker. Just mind your own business, pervert."

Andrew whirled and knocked him down. Meister jumped to his feet and grabbed an iron bar and held it threateningly aloft.

Penney happened to be nearby, holding his scattergun. He lifted the gun level with Meister. "That there club is going to hit the ground, mister. The question that should interest you is whether your hand will be attached to it."

Meister dropped the club and pointed at Andrew. "He's interfering with my property rights."

Penney said, "I can't change the law and make this man shed of you once and for all, but I can stop you from treating him like a dog."

"He'll run on me."

"For God's sake, there's no place to run," Andrew said with exasperation. He turned to his partner, Martin, for support, but received a glassy-eyed stare in return. The reaction was not lost on Nimrod.

The following morning, Nimrod interrupted his scout to ride to a hilltop and built a fire. He sprinkled water on it, then covered it with a blanket. After giving the smoke time to collect, he pulled the blanket off, releasing a large puff of smoke into the air. He repeated it two more times, then settled back to wait.

After two hours, he saw a group of curious Sioux on horseback watching from a distance. He made sure his fire was out, then mounted Bub and rode toward them.

He was at peace with the Sioux and recognized the band as he rode up, but nevertheless held his right arm aloft to show he carried no weapon. The leader was a chief he had traded with. In halting English, the chief said, "I know you. You Lee."

"You're Chief Sees Buffalo. Your English is better."

"I spent time with your people; more than I want."

Nimrod nodded. "I sometimes feel the same way."

"You want trade?"

"No trade. I bring a gift."

The chief waited.

Nimrod cleared his throat, betraying a touch of nervousness. "The Sioux are brave warriors, but many fall in battle. Sickness kills many. The women wail through the night. I offer you a new warrior—brave, loyal, and strong."

"Who?"

"A young black man. A slave owned by a bad man. I want him free."

"Why not kill bad man?"

"White man law says no."

The chief turned to his warriors, and said in Sioux, "These dogfaces are crazy." They laughed.

Nimrod smiled. "I want you to take him away from our wagons. But you must promise to treat him well."

"What you give me?"

"Give you? I give you a new brave."

Nimrod knew the plains tribes had a continual population-drain problem. They lost people to the new diseases, to perpetual wars with other tribes, and now to the whites.

The chief studied Nimrod's face. "Men in wagon train have guns. Shoot Sioux." He paused and looked over Nimrod's outfit. "I want Hawken rifle."

"This rifle? Never. This is my right arm." He patted his arm.

"No trade." The chief turned his horse, and the Sioux rode away.

The biggest smile in the company belonged to Hannah's son, Billy. He was the proud drover of his mother's wagon, but of greater importance to him, Hambo the donkey had become his fast friend.

Nimrod saw Billy with his hitched walk leading the donkey and slowed down. "Howdy, Trooper. Is that old big ears treating you right?"

Billy turned and greeted Nimrod with a big smile, and scratched Hambo's ear. "This old boy, Hambo here, is right smart. I love him, and he loves me. Mr. Penney said he's become the guard of the whole herd. Ain't no mean coyote going to get close to one of our animals with him on the job. When I get him to California, he's never going to do any work again. I'll just let him get pasture fat."

Nimrod tousled Billy's hair. "It's fine to appreciate an animal; it's dangerous to love it. Most times, it leads to grief. They die afore us—if we're lucky."

Billy pouted. "Nothing's going to happen to this feller. He's my special friend."

The day had been hot, but the miles covered had been gratifying when the train circled for the night. The herd was set out to graze, and the camp was quiet when Meister called over to Johnny. "It's my shift to guard the herd." He groaned and rubbed his stomach. "What was in that stew you made? I've had the trots bad for the last hour."

Johnny frowned his concern to Meister. "Nothing except what I always puts in it." He bit his lip to avoid laughing about the rotten pieces of meat he had added. "You lookin' a bit peaked, master. Why don't you rest a bit, and I'll take the watch."

"You?" The suggestion was novel to him.

"I surely will, master, I surely will. I'll just holler and come running if them savages show up."

"The committee says guards have to be armed."

Johnnythree thought for a moment. "I can carry yourn. It don't have to be loaded."

"Well..." Meister debated with himself, but just then had more gastric pain, and groaned. "Well, I reckon you can carry my Hawken. Unloaded. Be careful with it."

Meister reached over and picked up his rifle and removed the percussion cap. "Here. Don't drop it." He half-fell onto his cot, groaning piteously. Johnny didn't leave until Meister was snoring.

Two hours later, a small party of Sioux horsemen crept near camp. In the previous half-hour, the camp had been alerted, and many of the pioneers had gathered. No one was allowed to go near Meister's tent. Some of the men carried rifles but had been ordered not to shoot.

Meister woke with a start. His senses were filled with the sounds of laughter and cheering. In the background, sang the yip-yip-yip of Indians on the warpath, or at least having fun. He ran outside, and his eyes widened to see Johnny handing up a rifle to an Indian, and then mounting a horse assisted by others.

Meister awoke and ran outside. He started shouting in rage. "They're stealing my slave! Those red bastards are stealing my slave!" A brave on horseback briefly swerved toward Meister. He shook his fist. "Hey, you! Get away from here! He's mine!"

He rushed back under the tent flap and started fumbling with things. "Where's my rifle? Someone stole my goddamn Hawken!" Then he remembered where his rifle had gone.

The Sioux galloped past the camp, headed for the hills. Johnny waved to the pioneers. Many cheered in response. Meister pounded his fist on the wagon. He moaned. "There goes my investment."

Penney, standing nearby, said, "There goes a free man."

Nimrod shook his head in mock sympathy. "Too damned bad. That's the last y'all are gonna see of him. Thieving redskins!"

Plodding along the Sweetwater, they arrived at Independence Rock, a massive slab of granite shaped like a loaf of bread, a mile and a half long and one hundred thirty feet high. It had been named by Nimrod's old friend, Broken Hand Fitzpatrick, because he considered reaching it by the Fourth of July to be the correct pace to make California before snow paralyzed the Sierra Nevada. They were nine days past that holiday.

Many pioneers, led by the youngsters, ran over to the rock to climb the easy incline, and to chisel their names and the date into it. It was one of those futile stabs at immortality with which humans amuse themselves.

There was another wagon train parked nearby, but Nimrod's eye was caught by a pack train a hundred yards away. Curious, he walked over to one of the hands and introduced himself. They chatted for a couple of minutes about the trail, then the man suggested he meet the boss.

"Who might that be?"

"Judge Hastings." He pointed to a slim, tall young man a short distance away. Nimrod walked over and introduced himself, then said, "Judge Hastings?"

Hastings extended his hand. "Landsford W. Hastings at your service."

Nimrod was surprised. "Howdy, Judge. I've heard of you. I didn't know you was a judge. Pretty young for that job," he said, guessing Hastings' age as late-twenties.

"That was back in Ohio. The title follows you."

"Any judges who judged me were old enough to be my daddy," Nimrod said as he appraised the young man.

"I've always acted beyond my age," Hastings said. "A man's got to be in a hurry."

"Speaking of hurry, there's a lot of talk about your new trail through the mountains and south of the Salt Lake. I know those Wasatch canyons; they can swallow up a wagon train. And the Salt Desert, most of it is a bog. You got to slog forty-fifty miles to reach water."

"With all respect, Mr. Lee, you have a negative view of exploration."

Nimrod gave a short laugh. "I've done a bit. Do you have the trail marked out?"

Hastings pawed the gravel with his toe. "Uh, well, that's what this pack trip is about. We're going to Sutter's Fort, then take my route back to Fort Bridger. Then we'll have an exact route."

"Begging your pardon, sir, but how do you call it your 'route' if you ain't even been on it? Mapping a route by pack horse doesn't tell you what wagons can move through. Horses can twist around trees and boulders, and swim rivers. Wagon's can't."

Hastings set his mouth tight. "You seem at ease telling me what to do."

Nimrod struggled to remain civil. "If they name such a cutoff after you someday, you may wish they hadn't." Nimrod softened his tone. Listen to me, friend. I know the territory you got in mind for your trail. You might be able to cut trees, ford fast rivers, and haul wagons up those heights, but it wouldn't leave enough time to get over the California mountains. Speaking of which, do you know what Sierra Nevada means in Spanish?"

"God gave us English. I have no reason to speak a foreign

tongue."

"It means snow-covered, jagged peaks. And you sure as hell would find that out for yourself."

"Your tone is harsh, sir."

Nimrod took a deep breath and softened his voice. "I'm sorry for that. Mr.—Judge—Hastings, you're young and full of piss and vinegar, but you're fixing to bite off something other folks'll have to swallow. Think hard about going off on a half-cocked plan that could kill people."

"I have a vision of developing California into an empire of plenty."

"That'll take a whole heap of sweet talking the Mexicans.... Any ideas who might be the emperor of this make-believe empire?" Nimrod said sharply.

Hastings turned on his heel and walked away. Nimrod watched him go and wondered if any emigrants could be dumb enough to follow such a highbinder.

Nimrod was checking Bub's hooves when Hannah happened by and heard him humming a soft tune. She said, "You're a right good hummer."

He lowered the hoof, and said, "My maw used to hum that around our cabin. It was the onliest song she didn't learn in church. I don't know its name or the words, but when I hum it, it reminds me of her and home."

Hannah took a step forward and said, "Your mother had a deep soul, I can tell. And you also for remembering." She took another step until she was three feet from him, looked into his face, and began to sing.

Believe me, if all those endearing young charms,
Which I gaze on so fondly today,
Were to change by tomorrow, and flee from my arms
Like fairy gifts, fading away;
Thou wouldst still be adored as this moment thou art,
Let thy loveliness fade as it will;
And, around the dear ruin, each wish of my heart
Would entwine itself verdantly still.

Nimrod stared at her as his eyes brimmed. He looked away and said in a quavering voice, "You sing like a bird in a meadow, Hannah." He said the words with a catch in his voice after looking around to hide his emotion.

Hannah beamed and curtsied playfully. "Thank you, kind sir."

"All these years, I never heard the words. I'd be obliged if you'd write them down for me."

"Yes, but can you rea—" Hannah realized she had made a terrible faux pas. "I didn't mean—"

Nimrod flashed a defeated smile, and said, "No offense taken, ma'am."

Hannah hastily excused herself, and as she walked away, she clenched her fists in anger and muttered under her breath, "You damned fool. You DAMNED fool!" It did not escape her attention that in the space of one insulting blunder, she had gone from ma'am, to Hannah, to Nana, then back to ma'am.

Overnight, the heat hit. What had been a pleasant seventy-five degrees when they left Fort Laramie turned into a humid, one-hundred-degree sauna. The men and women shuffled along through sagebrush and along the small river. Over their right shoulder, the high peaks of the Wind River Range provided occasional shade, but then with the slightest change of direction, the shade would withdraw and beckon the merciless sun to return. Back home, such heat would drive people to the refuge of a shade tree and lemonade. On the trail, however, they had no choice but to plod on trying to numb their brains as the miles snailed by.

Except for muttered curses and angry shrieks at laboring oxen, little was said among the trudging pioneers who chose to sulk in silence. It was the little things that grated and drove them into continual irritation and self-accusation for what they had naively dreamt might be an uneventful trip in the company of a kindly mother nature. Oh, they paid for their misjudgment with miseries that marched in lockstep with them: depression that was a mental rash itching and burning right up to the door of madness; a toothache throbbing without stopping; a twisted ankle stabbing with every step; a migraine pounding ceaselessly; diarrhea erupting at the worst times; crying toddlers that wouldn't stop; torn clothes patched with rags, and danger that could emerge from behind every hill.

And the wind. The wind that wouldn't stop. It came down from Canada and gained force through the mountains. It blew off hats and blew out supper fires. They went to sleep with it howling and woke to the same thing.

A few miles after leaving Independence Rock, the awe-struck pioneers passed Devil's Gate, a thirty-foot-wide, quarter-mile-long gap in the middle of a four-hundred-foot cliff. A few days later, after fording the Sweetwater for the ninth time, Nimrod called a halt. Penney rode up and asked why.

"Just about where we be standing is the continental divide—the South Pass." He pointed west. "In yonder direction, water will flow into the Pacific; behind us, it'll run into the Atlantic."

Penney was amazed. "How'd you know that?"

Nimrod didn't take his eyes off the horizon. He shrugged. "I just knowed it."

The South Pass saddle of land on which they stood was perhaps the most important patch in the growth of their country. It was the gateway through the barrier of the Rocky Mountains and made emigration west possible. To the south and west were the lands of the Republic of Mexico. They were about to become invaders.

Penney looked around at the gentle slope of the pass and was amazed. "I expected it to stand out more."

The pass was a gap of about twenty miles in the Rocky Mountains. It would become the open door for hundreds of thousands of emigrants to follow.

"We're about halfway to Sutter's Fort," Nimrod said. "The easiest half is behind us."

That evening, the committee got together to take stock. Manchester sat with a pad and pencil doing computations. When he stopped, Penney said, "What do your celestial readings tell us, Ezra?"

Manchester looked again at his figures, and said, "We're on August 24, and we've come about fifty miles shy of one thousand. Just about half-way to Sutter's Fort. We've averaged twelve and a half miles per day. We're just a few days behind the goal we set back in Independence."

Nimrod said, "I'd druther be a few days ahead. We're about ten days out of Fort Bridger."

"Bridger is a friend of yours, I heard you say," Cohen asked.

Nimrod tipped his head in acknowledgment. "He's a good man to watch your back on a scout, and he's a frolic to drink with, but I'm suspicioning he's in cahoots with a flim-flam man name of Lansford Hastings who's a disaster on the hoof. Bridger is talking-up Hastings on his scheme for a cutoff through the Wasatch Mountains, even though he knows people might die trying it. All because ol' Jim wants wagons to stop at his trading post. I can't abide that. I've been known to lay a bet or two, but I stop short of gambling with peoples' lives."

"You're the guide," Penney said.

CHAPTER TWENTY-FOUR

J ust before a morning get-away, Nimrod rode up to the Proctor wagon where Gertie was standing next to the driver's seat, shaking out a blanket.

"A good morning to you, Gertie. If you don't mind my asking, do you got any of that sucking candy left? What you got at Laramie."

She finished folding the blanket. "I do. Didn't know you had a sweet tooth."

"Reckon I can trouble you for a piece?"

Gertie rummaged in the wagon and came out with a paper bag and gave a wrapped candy to Nimrod." Nimrod said, "Obliged," and rode to Hannah's wagon, where he saw Rachel putting water on the breakfast fire. He walked Bub next to her and extended the candy to her.

"Here's something a young lady might like." Her reaction was to shrink back. "Child, you have to learn to trust," he said gently. She took the candy, and Nimrod mounted Bub and rode away.

The drive to Fort Bridger was level, and they were favored by small streams that were unchallenging to cross. The first to ford was the Big Sandy River, which was big only in comparison to the Little Sandy.

Of course, "unchallenging," extended to the terrain and moderate weather. There was generally enough grass and water to earn the pioneers' gratitude.

The looming obstacle that caused Nimrod to worry was the Green River.

The Green was a nasty river to cross. It rushed out of the Wind River Range and became a deep artery that joined the Colorado River farther south. Unlike other high desert rivers, it was wide, and in mid-summer might flow to a depth of twenty feet. This was no Sweetwater.

Nimrod had feared trying to ford the Green; the possibility of losing livestock, wagons, and even people was quite real. If necessary, they could hollow out three of the cottonwoods on the bank, lash them together to make a raft. The problems were two-fold: It would be time consuming, and whatever they constructed on the fly would be rickety, and thus dangerous.

Nimrod rode the riverbank, hoping some enterprising mountain man had established a ferry. About two miles to the north, he almost shouted with joy. There on the bank was a wooden barge built atop hollowed logs. It was just large enough for one wagon and was on a narrower river width. It wouldn't win a prize for nautical design, but, by golly, it looked like it could make it across the river, a modest prospect which satisfied him.

From a distance, the man standing at the ferry looked familiar. When Nimrod rode up, he recognized him as Two Fingers Pilson, a good fellow and a bad trapper, even bad enough to catch his hand in one. That mishap earned him his nickname. However, he could joke about it, even sober.

"Halloo, Two Fingers," he shouted as he rode up and dismounted, "I thought you was gone back east to play piano."

Pilson shaded his eyes from the sun. "Well, I'll be a bat flying straight out of hell if it ain't Nimrod Lee." He rushed over and extended his left hand to shake Nimrod's. "The onliest piano I ever heard played was in a whorehouse. The gals weren't any good either....What the hell you doin' on my river?"

"I'm nursemaiding a wagon train to California. Thought I'd stop by and give you a little business; keep you from starving."

"I'm just waiting to make my fortune. Been here a month; had a few customers. I figure when California and Oregon join the union, there'll be a lot more."

"You into fortune-telling now?" Nimrod said as he dismounted.

"Ain't no secret we're fixin' to go to war with the Mexes. You know how that's bound to end."

"Yep. With a lot of dead men."

"That's fine, long as most of 'em ain't ours.... Where's your train?"

"Back yonder a piece. Let's talk some business. What'll you charge for about a dozen wagons?"

"Ten dollars a wagon."

"I thought you was going to wait for us to grab California and Oregon before you get rich?"

Pilson made an elaborate show of looking around. "You see any other ferries handy?"

Nimrod said, "I've got wagons filled with sharpshooters wanting to get to California. They's ready to fight them Mexicans you want to go to war with. You want to line your pockets off them, Two-fingers? Does doing that show your love for Uncle Sam and Andy Jackson? You want to skin *them*? I'd appreciate some patriotism here," Nimrod cajoled. "You can give such good Americans a better price than ten dollars."

Pilson became thoughtful. "You know, I remember when I had my little dispute with a wolf trap seven winter ago back in Brown's Hole. You tended my trap line for me. Maybe didn't steal too many pelts."

"Just the best ones," Nimrod said as he looked over at an Indian sitting on a log. "Who's that?"

Pilson turned to look, as though there might be a crowd. "He works for me. Shoshone. He's my brother-in-law, but I ain't sure he considers it an honor."

"So, brother Two-fingers, you was about to say something sentimental."

Pilson cleared his throat. "For the good turn you did me, and for the fighters you're carrying, I'll take the job for five dollars a wagon."

"I consider that a mighty good turn, and patriotic to boot." Nimrod mounted Bub. "First thing tomorrow."

Pilson shook his head in disgust. "I better get drunk so I'll have an excuse for doing this."

Early the next morning, before the wind came up, Penney had the wagons lined-up ready to be ferried across the Green, which was close to flat.

Penney's wagon was first to board. Also on board were several pioneers who would act as herdsmen on the other side. Others moved the cattle up to the bank close behind the ferry. Billy's donkey, Hambo, was brought forward and tied with plenty of slack to the rear of the ferry. As it pulled out into the water, the donkey was coaxed and pushed into the water and swam behind it. Seeing their familiar guard in the water, other livestock didn't balk at being goaded in, also.

When Pilson was being paid, he studied the pioneers, and grumbled to Nimrod, "Don't look like no sharpshooters to me?"

"That's what we want the Mexicans to think."

Having crossed the biggest river obstacle, the pioneers set out to finish the drive to Fort Bridger. It should have been a peaceful trip.

Except for Maude Horner's occasional wailing, things were calm enough, freeing Nimrod to hunt to replenish their dwindling food supply. On the second day, he rode into camp with a fifty-pound buck pronghorn tied to the back of his saddle. Aaron greeted him and helped untie the carcass. "How'd you get this one, Nimrod? On the fly?"

"Aaron, anyone tells you he brought down one of these on the run ain't telling you about the hundred times he came up empty. You got to remember, theys curious critters. You get yourself into a hide, then let them get close to snoop out your mount."

"They ain't afraid of Bub?"

"Mules never shot at 'em."

When the wagons started up after the mid-day break, young Roger Horner ran wild among the moving wagons. He avoided the other children because some of them teased him about Maude—"Your maw's a witch!"... "The devil got aholt of your mama's soul!" He could think of no comeback except to "show them" by daredevil antics that none of them would be brave enough to attempt. One of his favorites was to jump on the wagon tongue of a slow-moving wagon. No one would be watching as the husband of the family would be facing forward driving the oxen, and his wife might be looking for buffalo chips.

On one wagon, he leaped onto the tongue just as the front wheel dipped into a small hole. The wagon jolted and dipped to the left, causing Roger to lose balance. He fell sideways, and the front wheel of the wagon, with its cargo weighing a ton, ran over his lower left leg, breaking both the tibia and fibula. The shattered edge of the fibula punctured the skin, causing a flow of blood. Roger screamed, and the drover halted the oxen, as did the entire train. People came running from the front and the back, including his mother, Maude, who gathered him in her arms, making him scream all the more.

Hannah pushed through the crowd and shouted at Maude, "Let him be! Let him be!" She turned to Earl, and said, "Earl, control your wife. She's going to do more damage." Earl half-guided, half-pulled his wife away and into their own wagon where her screams continued.

Hannah called for Billy to bring their wagon up and lower the back gate. When that was done, she had four men carefully—oh, so cautiously—pick up Roger and lay him on the lowered gate, bracing themselves against his intensified screaming.

Penney called to everyone to circle the wagons. The day's drive was over.

Hannah cut the boy's pant leg off and examined the damage. She wrapped the open wound with a rag, compressing it to stop the bleeding. She then called for a thin, straight board two feet long to serve as a splint, plus more rags cut into strips. She gave Roger water to drink, then lay him back, hoping to calm him.

She asked Nimrod and two other men to hold him steady while she tried to set the bones. Nimrod wiped the sweat from her forehead as she worked. Every attempt to reposition bones caused intense screams from Roger. At last, she leaned back and inhaled a deep breath before placing the splint against his leg and tying it in four places. She was careful not to cut off the blood flow.

She collapsed into Nimrod's arms without caring who noticed. "All we can do now is wait. I believe I got the tibia back in place; the fibula, I hope so."

The question no one wanted to address was where to take the boy to rest. If he went back to his parents' wagon, Maude would, without doubt, act so crazy it would impede his progress. But yet, how could they keep a mother from a child in catastrophic trauma?

They decided the boy's well-being came first, so Roger was moved to Hannah's wagon. Roger was laid on a featherbed mattress with pillows under the leg.

One of the boys from another family volunteered to drive Earl's wagon so he could keep control of Maude.

Penney and the committee, less Hannah, decided they could hold over a day, but would then have to get back on the trail, and just hope the jarring of the springless wagon would do no damage to the boy's condition.

For several days, Roger's pain seemed to abate somewhat. Hannah fed him broth and spoonfuls of stew. She changed the dressing on his open wound and was discouraged by the look of it. She knew such an injury would almost certainly develop an infection, but she kept hoping his young body would have the strength to fight it off, and he would show improvement.

He didn't.

Earl brought Maude to the wagon several times a day. Hannah lifted the bonnet on the wagon's side so she could see her son and reach in to touch him. After just a couple of minutes, however, she would become hysterical, and Earl would have to take her away.

After a week, Hannah could see Roger weakening. His face was without color and feverish, his eyes were dull, and pain did not seem to bother him as much. When she changed his bandage, the smell made her gag. Pus was oozing from the wound. She knew his symptoms were the onset of gangrene. When she mentioned to Earl that the leg might have to come off, Maude overheard and started screaming. Hannah waited for Earl's answer. She could see the fatigue on his face and the hopeless look in his eyes.

"When?"

"We may have already waited too long."

"Have you done this before?"

Hannah expected the question. "My late husband, Abel, was a surgeon. I watched him. He taught me a lot."

He looked at her and groaned. "Where does it end?"

She refused to be offended. "I'm all you have."

Tired and confused, he said, "I leave it up to you."

Hannah said, "That's not enough, Earl. I need a yea or a nay."

Earl sighed and said, "Go ahead and do your operation." He then put his arm around Maude and led her away.

She called Penney over, and Nimrod accompanied him.

"I'm going to have to amputate the boy's leg," she said. "That's the only hope he has."

On a nervous impulse, Penney blurted, "Are you sure you're up to it?" Then, he hastily backtracked. "No offense. I'd rather you cut on me than most doctors I've seen." She could see him calculating. "How much of a delay do you need? I got to think of that."

"As much as you can give."

Penney's expression was despairing. "One day. Two days, if you have to have it."

Hannah said, "I'll need some thin, strong twine; a small poker, red hot; a saw with sharp teeth, and pliers."

"Pliers?"

"Yes," she said, without bothering to explain. "I'll need porous cloth to cover the wound so it can breathe." The men looked at each other blankly. Then, Penney said, "My wife's got a veil she hasn't used for years."

"That'll have to do. I'll operate the first thing in the morning. I can do it on a tailgate, I suppose. Keep his mother away."

Penney said, "Let me get what you need," and hurried off to find the materials she needed."

She thought for a moment. "And I'll need some help." She looked at Nimrod. "Will you help me when I do it?"

"I'll do what I can," he said.

"Also, ask Gertie. I need a woman's nimble fingers. But what I most want is something to ease his pain. It'll be horrible. I guess whiskey will have to do, although I'm sure he'll vomit it back up. What I need most is laudanum, but I don't have it."

"What's that?"

"A liquid solution of opium. It dulls the senses; enough will make a patient unconscious and block pain," she said.

"How's a person look after taking it?"

"Like in a trance. Why"

"I'll be back," he said, and walked to the wagon of Andrew and Martin. He hallooed, and both men came to him. He gave a rushed explanation of Roger Horner's grave condition and the need to ease the pain of the operation.

Nimrod took a stab at what he suspected accounted for Martin's disconnected conduct. He said, "Martin, we need your laudanum."

Martin's eyes showed fright, and he stuttered an answer. "I, I don't know what you're talking about."

Nimrod's look leveled on Martin's face. He saw a man trying to hide something he was ashamed of. He glanced at Andrew for support.

"Andrew," he said. "Please explain to your partner that a young boy is fixing to have his leg cut off, and unless he gets the drug Martin is hiding, his pain will be the fires of hell."

Andrew looked at Nimrod, then at Martin, then back at Nimrod. "Speaking of pain, you have no idea the pain Martin would have if he had to give it up."

"If it's anything like a whiskey habit, he'd get over it and be the better for it."

"Martin?" Andrew asked in a soft voice.

Martin shook his head in desperation. "I can't."

Andrew's voice became harder, demanding. "Martin?"

Martin started sobbing. "I just got enough for me."

Nimrod said, "Martin, I'll make it easy for you. Give it to me or, for the sake of this child, I'll go in your wagon and find it, even if I have to tear it apart."

Martin looked at the demanding Nimrod, then at the expectant Andrew, and went into the wagon and returned with a small three-quarter-full brown bottle. He gave it to Nimrod, then turned and walked away.

Nimrod looked at Andrew, pleased, but also regretful. Andrew returned the look, then lowered his head and said, "Leave us be."

Nimrod went to Hannah's wagon and announced himself. She came out and stepped to the ground using the front wheel as a ladder. She turned to Nimrod, and without a word, he handed her the bottle. Mystified, she looked at the label and gasped with delight. The label read, "Tincture of Laudanum," with a skull and crossbones under the words.

She clasped the bottle to her breast and said with great relief,

"Thank you, Jesus." She turned to Nimrod. "Where on earth did you find this?"

He shrugged in an aw-shucks manner. "Oh, I had the mix'ins in my saddlebag, so I rustled up a batch."

Hannah hugged the small bottle like a child. "This is a gift from heaven," she whispered, thinking of the agony the boy would be spared.

That night, Hannah dug into a chest and brought out Abel's surgery text. She spent the next few hours reading and reviewing, then reviewing again the steps to an amputation. She knew reading and doing were two different things. She had seen Abel perform the operation, but, again, translating what she had seen into what she could do was the challenge.

Hannah reviewed the various procedures used by experienced surgeons to perform amputations. She decided the safest for her was the guillotine method, which was done just as it sounds.

Exhausted by the concentration, but also by the tension, Hannah lay down to sleep. Before she dozed off, she whispered, "Abel, help me, Abel."

In the morning, Hannah had Billy move their wagon about fifty yards outside the circle, then told both children to occupy themselves elsewhere. Nimrod and Cohen moved the boy to the tailgate, careful step after careful step. They were followed by Hannah and Gertie.

Hannah put her face close to Roger's. His breathing was fast and shallow, gasping for air. His pulse was fluttery and weak. His face was gray. He groaned often to the unrelenting pain. Hannah thought: He's weak. Oh, God, he's *very* weak. I hope I'm not too late.

She examined the leg and observed that the discoloration reached to just above his knee and had turned gray with splotches of black blending into red and then pink. The creep of corruption. The smell was nauseating, like the rotten meat it was.

She made a mark with a piece of charcoal just beyond the spot where the pink ended. That was where she would cut.

Nimrod started a fire close-by and used a bellows to intensify it. He placed a small poker in the fire and let it heat. Gertie cut several six-inch lengths of strong thread and put them within easy reach. Hannah opened the bottle of laudanum, and with exquisite care watched twenty drops land into a small glass. "I'd like to give him a few drops more," she said, more to herself, "but I worry about his weak condition." She took a deep breath, and said, "We begin. Malachi, you need to hold his mouth open as I pour this under his tongue. It'll taste awful, and he'll struggle to spit it. You have to hold his mouth shut until he swallows."

Nimrod gave her the butcher knife, saw, and pliers which she had already examined. She said to Gertie, "When the leg comes off, the femoral artery and the vein next to it will gush blood. I need to make haste to tie them off. Be ready to hand me the thread. If I drop or lose one, give me another, fast." She turned to Nimrod. "When the cut is done, I'll take these pliers—" She picked them up and opened and shut them several times. "—and clamp the femoral artery, then I'll hand them to you to keep up the pressure. Gertie will pass me the thread, and I'll tie it off twice, just to be sure. After that, I'll take the pliers and clamp the femoral vein, and we'll do the same thing. We must be fast, but not frantic. Keep in mind all these tools—instruments—and the thread will be slippery with blood, so your concentration must be complete. After I'm finished, Malachi will hand me the hot poker, and I'll seal off the other veins. Malachi, Nimrod, be prepared to hold him down if the laudanum wears off. At the end, I'll cover the wound with the veil Shadrach gave me…. Any questions?" She looked at each one. There were none. "You've all told me you won't faint or vomit at the sight of what you're going to see. I hope that's true."

She looked around and saw three faces grim with readiness at the life-and-death task they were to be a part of. Nimrod winked at her, and she tried to answer with a smile, but it came out only as a crease of her lips.

A moment of tense silence was broken by Cohen, who said, "May I speak a brief prayer? The others fell silent, and Nimrod removed his hat, but Cohen did not.

May the One who blessed our ancestors Abraham, Isaac, and Jacob, Rachel, Rebecca, and Leah, bless and heal the one who is ill: Roger, son of Earl and Maude. May the Holy One, the fount of all blessings, shower abundant mercies upon him, fulfilling his dreams of healing and strengthening him with the power of life. Amen.

Hannah looked at the watch pinned to her lapel. "Very well, it's been thirty minutes." She pinched Roger hard several times to make certain the drug had taken hold. There was no response. She tightened a tourniquet around his thigh, picked up the knife, and looked at its shining ugliness. She elevated the leg with a block of wood and, with a deep breath, began to cut. She forced herself to ignore the spurting blood and concentrate on the knife.

Once she had circled the cut to the bone, she reached for the saw and attacked the femur by inserting it in the cut she had made. All the time, Hannah was muttering words none but she could hear — "Oh, God...Oh, God...Oh, God." She was surprised at how difficult cutting the bone was, but she sawed stronger and faster, and then the leg broke free. She pushed it to the ground and reached for the pliers. She clamped the spurting femoral artery and handed the pliers to Nimrod to hold as Gertie gave her a length of thread. She squeezed the artery hard because of its slipperiness but managed to tie it off. She turned to the femoral vein and did the same. She then reached for the red-hot poker and, using the pliers, started to cauterize the smaller veins. Hannah touched the iron to one vein and smelled a whiff of burning flesh, then turned to the next.

Hannah noticed the blood was barely dripping from the first vein, and then from the others. Out of the corner of her eye, she saw Malachi take two steps back and lean over and vomit.

Roger's blood pressure was gone. Her heart fell. She put down the poker and lifted his eyelid. Fixed. Then the pulse. Gone. The boy was dead. She looked at the body, stunned, not knowing what to do. After taking a deep breath and steadying herself, she managed to say, "Give Gertie and me a few minutes to, uh, to arrange things, then we'll get his father."

When Earl arrived at the wagon, the blood had been washed away, and Roger's body was covered by a sheet Hannah had grabbed from her wagon. The severed leg was gone. A shovel rested against the wheel.

The father lifted the sheet and studied his son's face. He replaced the cloth and looked into the distance with the shredded heart of a man who had been waylaid and robbed of the boy he had lived for. His son lay stretched out dead on a board; his wife was held tight in the closed fist of insanity. The meaning in his life? Over.

Earl turned to Hannah, and in a hollow voice, said, "Maude has a right to see him."

"Not just yet," Hannah said. She asked for the boy's clothes, and then she and Gertie dressed Roger's body in his best outfit, washed his face, combed his hair, and arranged his face in a peaceful manner. She then sent word for Maude to come. They all braced themselves.

When Maude appeared, held by the arm grip of Earl, she stared at Roger's body for a long moment. She was quiet as she approached the body and lifted one eyelid, then the other. She turned to Earl. He could see sanity fighting for space in her mind, and losing. She said, "He's not dead."

As Earl led her away without resistance, he turned and said over his shoulder: "Today."

Penney understood and asked some men to dig a grave. They used the same sheet as a shroud, and lowered Roger's body into the grave and filled it in. Earl and Maude were sent for.

When everyone gathered around, there was no singing, and no music from Enoch Brister. Penney asked Preacher to say words. "Keep it short," he whispered.

When Preacher started speaking, Maude broke free from Earl's arm and dropped on the grave. She started crying, "He's not dead! Roger's not dead!" Preacher continued with his sermon. Maude began to scratch at the dirt. "Get him out of there! Get my boy out of there!"

Hannah muttered, "Oh, dear Jesus, don't let this happen."

Penney whispered to Preacher through gritted teeth: "Amen, damnit, say amen!"

The pioneers didn't drift away after the brief service, they scattered. Earl led Maude away as she continued to scream.

Nimrod noticed Hannah walking toward the river with her head down. He caught up as she sat on the bank. He put his arm around her and just held her. She stared ahead, no tears.

"I failed," she said. "I waited too long because I was afraid to fail, and doing so caused me to fail. What a bitter brew to have to drink."

"I'm just a backwoods roustabout," he said. "I can't say if any doctor did a good job or not. I know as much about doctoring as I know about frog hair. You tried to save the boy's life, but he just died. That's what people do, they just die. That's ordinary, but it ain't simple. Did you not get the job done? I reckon not, but I doubt it could be done. I've seen gangrene before, and that boy was already near dead. Pardon my saying it in such a way.

"Anyways, I know you're a good doctor. I can tell that just like I can figure out if a man is a good schoolteacher, which I regret not knowing much about either. In my business we look for 'tells,' how the grass is bent, if birds have stopped singing, what smells are on the wind....To me, the way you care for folks is a tell. It speaks to your skill and to your heart." He stopped and pondered the subject, looking away, then nodding slowly as a truth occurred to him. "Seems to me, a big part of being a doctor is like anything else— Good ones get the job done, but sometimes they don't. In your case, if you do, people go on living, and they'll have you to thank, or thank God with you in mind. If you fail, I'm certain-sure most would've died anyway. Anyways, if a body tries hard enough, and cares enough, failure ain't going to be a stranger. And if you quit on that account, you'd be cheating the next person who needs you." He stopped talking, uncertain of the value of his words. "I didn't say that good, I reckon."

She kept her gaze on the green water of the river for a long time, then she reached for his hand, but he was gone.

That night, one of the pioneer women came to Penney's wagon. He took one glance, and said, "I can see you're all put out. I reckon I can guess why."

The angry woman shook her head from side to side. "I swear. That mad woman's carryings-on is driving us all crazy ourselves. It frightens the children. It even upsets the animals."

"I understand, ma'am, but you need to give slack, beings she just lost her only child. It might be time to say some prayers for her, and for the boy's soul. Anyways, what would you have me to do?"

The moment he asked the question, she knew there was no

answer. She turned and walked away.

Maude screamed and cried-out far into the night until she fell silent from exhaustion, which allowed the rest of the wagon train to do the same.

The next morning as the camp stirred, Earl Horner went to the captain's wagon, and ignoring Penney's "good morning," he said in a flat voice, "Maude's gone."

The words mystified Penney. "Gone? Gone where?"

Earl raised his hands, then let them fall to his sides. "This morning, she was gone. I don't know where."

"There ain't no place to go. Have you looked around the camp?"

"She's nowhere nearby."

"You're sure?"

"Nowhere."

The committee organized a search party of men on horseback to search the river, its bank, and the surrounding area. They thought the search would be quick and easy; however, they went as far as three miles but found nothing. They returned to the camp at the end of the day with heads downcast in disappointment.

Penney hated what he had to do. He approached the Horner wagon and saw Earl sitting on the wagon seat.

"Earl, I'm real sorry about all this."

Earl nodded and looked toward the horizon.

"You know we have to pull out tomorrow, I reckon.

Earl nodded.

Penney wanted to be anywhere else. He said, "Uh, well, Earl, we have to be off first thing, you know that." He reached up and gave a solid pat to Earl's knee. "You have the prayers of everyone on this train." He walked a few steps, then turned. "And so does Maude; she has our prayers, too." When he received no answer, he trudged back to his own wagon.

The next morning, Penney was up and busied himself organizing the day's march. After breakfast, as the pioneers rounded up and yoked the animals, several noticed the Horner wagon appeared abandoned. They walked up to it and waited for someone to do something. No one moved, afraid of what they would find inside. With trepidation, Nimrod climbed up and pushed the bonnet open. The furniture, tools, and clothing were intact.

Ezra Manchester walked to the other end, and called out, "His horse is gone."

A round of chatter followed the discovery. Cohen said the obvious. "He just up and left everything. He's gone."

"We could hunt for him," Aaron said.

"It's clear he don't want that, and he must have a good lead. There's no reason to do anything," Penney said. "Let's move out. I'll ask one of the boys to drive his oxen and wagon, in case he comes back."

Nimrod said, "He won't."

As the people rejoined their wagons, Penney said to Nimrod, "What in the bejesus is this all about? What you reckon happened to Maude? I mean, *really* happened. And why did Earl sneak off?"

Nimrod said, "We'll never know, and I'm content with that."

Before Nimrod saddled Bub to go forward on a scout, he walked over to Andrew and offered the laudanum bottle back to him. "This is Martin's. Giving it was an act of mercy."

Andrew held up his hand in refusal. "Give it to Hannah."

"But…"

"I've been after Martin to stop that devil's potion for two years. Now, he'll have no choice."

CHAPTER TWENTY-FIVE

F ort Bridger confirmed Kit Carson's assessment that it was a fort only by a generous description. Actually, a trading post, the fort's rickety palisade enclosed several structures hastily built to serve the needs of wagon trains, Indians, and mountain men. It housed a blacksmith who doubled as a farrier, a wagoneer, a saloon, and a store for many overpriced items a needy emigrant could get no other place within a thousand miles. There was a corral holding healthy and rested oxen available for swapping for exhausted animals. All prices were a bow to the law of supply and demand, weighed heavily in favor of supply.

The fort was situated on Black's Fork of the Green River, amidst a surrounding valley that offered lush grass in abundance. Indian tipis dotted the area belonging to various tribes wanting to trade, drink, beg, or just hang out.

Bridger and his partner, Louis Vasquez, built the post two years earlier to capitalize on the known route to Oregon and California. The standard trail required a swing south from South Pass to the location adopted by Bridger. It then looped north and slightly west to Fort Hall, and then southwest to the Humboldt River, which led to the Sierra Nevada several weeks away. However, as traffic increased, guides explored alternate routes, or cutoffs, that threatened to bypass Fort Bridger. The best known, Sublette's Cutoff, drove straight west from South Pass to Fort Hall. To counter it, the partners hoped the cutoff proposed by Hastings would open a trail straight west from their fort, through the Wasatch Mountains, and reduce mileage. By no accident, it would funnel wagon trains past Fort Bridger.

Nimrod always looked forward to encountering Jim Bridger, who was a mountain man of peer respect and had an uproarious sense of humor. He had one blot on his reputation, but it was minimized because he had been a green youngster. Other trappers had not forgotten that twenty years ago, Bridger and another man, John Fitzgerald, were given the job of death-watch over fellow trapper Hugh Glass who had been shredded in a bear attack. Spooked by Indian signs, the pair assumed— perhaps by wishful thinking— that Glass was on the verge of death, so they abandoned him to his fate. However, Glass survived and crawled to civilization, and became a mountain-man legend. Though many believed Bridger went "tail down" in a pinch, it was a subject not mentioned to him.

Nimrod, though, was troubled with the scheme he believed Bridger was currently involved in, and that was on his mind as he walked into the log store inside the fort gate. There stood Bridger, tall and lithe, and smiling.

"Well, I'll be a drunk monkey if it ain't Nimrod Lee, the ol' coon hisself." Bridger walked toward the door and reached out a hand calloused like thorns. "I haven't seen you since the last rondayvoo at Horse Creek—" Bridger stopped in mid-sentence as he remembered what had happened to Magpie there. "Did you ever catch that Rake Face feller?"

"I'm still looking."

"Terrible what he did, terrible."

"Have you seen or heard of him?" Nimrod asked.

"I heard he was about, but not since some two year ago. He slithers around like a snake."

"How's business, Jim?"

"Things are bound to pick up when we take over California. War's a-coming, for sure."

"I ran into a fella at Independence rock who speaks of you with high praise," Nimrod said.

"Who might that wise gentleman be?"

"A young lawyer, name of Hastings. He was telling me about big plans for a cutoff from here to go through the mountains."

Bridger grew wary. "We'll see if it's workable. Maybe not."

Nimrod didn't believe for one moment Bridger's ambivalence about Hasting's scheme. He held his tongue until after they had eaten supper and had a couple of bolts of Bridger's private whiskey, not the trade slop. He waited for a long pause in the conversation, then he mentioned his talk with Hastings at Independence Rock. He noticed the wariness on Bridger's face.

Nimrod's voice grew soft, almost pleading. "Jim, that would mean going down Echo Canyon, through the Weber River Canyon, then over the salt desert and those horrible salt flats, all the way to Pilot Peak. Maybe fifty mile without water. For God's sake, Jim, we've both trapped those mountains. We know the truth of it.

"I told Hastings's packhorses can get through, but he'd play hell taking wagons through those canyons. Of course, he don't listen. People might die 'cause he don't listen."

Bridger's eyes wouldn't settle on Nimrod. "Like I say, it's being talked about."

Nimrod said, "I'm going to speak straight, which you and I always do with each other. I think you're afeared other cutoffs to the west from South Pass will bypass your post, here, so this scheme by Hastings will keep them coming this way."

"You're speaking worrisome, Nimrod."

Nimrod shook his head and exhaled deeply to show frustration. "Old friend, I'm not going to beat my gums to a stubborn old coot like you. I just ask you to remember these pilgrims trust us with their lives."

Bridger's face hardened. "I spent twenty-two years ruining my health trapping beaver in freezing water and dodging arrows at the same time. This trading post is all I got. I'm going to fight to keep it. I got to, Lee." The last sentence came out as a plea for sympathy, of fear; unbecoming to a man like him.

Nimrod nodded his understanding, embarrassed for his friend.

"How long you be with us?" Bridger said, eyeing the door.

Nimrod took the cue. His point had been made; the conversation was over. "We need to recruit [rest/feed] the animals in this high grass you got here," he said, "maybe do some wagon fixin', and buy supplies. We'll be gone in two-three days." Nimrod shook hands and walked out. He had done what he could. His mood was low because he was certain if Hastings' cutoff became a reality, people would die.

His premonition would come to pass the following year. At the time he was appealing to Bridger, back in Springfield, Illinois, plans for a large wagon train bound for California were coming together for the next spring. The leaders of the venture were two prosperous farmers named George and Jacob Donner, and a businessman named James Reed. They had read Lansford Hasting's book with interest, and with tragic results.

When she heard the scream, Hannah looked up from the meal she was preparing and realized it came from the Proctor wagon. She dropped the ladle and hurried toward it.

When Hannah arrived, Gertie was crying and frantically trying to quiet her baby by rocking him in her arms and patting his back. Little Caleb's body was in the grip of convulsion. His arms and legs twitched spasmodically; his cough was hacking and rasping and could be likened to the bark of a dog; his nose ran in a ribbon of mucus. Worse, his face was red with fever. Aaron was standing outside the wagon feeling worthless and waiting to be told what to do.

Gertie was terrified. She knew that being an infant was the most dangerous thing that could happen to a human. At that time, almost two-thirds of all deaths in the United States happened to children under age five. And of all infants, only two-thirds reached that age. Gertie didn't know the statistics, but she knew the reality.

"Oh, Hannah, help me. My baby is dying," she pleaded. Hannah put the back of her hand on the baby's forehead, then on the cheek, and on the chest. Her experience indicated the baby's temperature was very high, and she knew it was serious. She quickly took inventory of the baby's symptoms: cough, high fever, runny nose, and shortness of breath. The baby's seizure stopped, but Hannah knew it could start again.

When Gertie told her it started with a cold, Hannah was close to certain that the illness was the croup. She told Gertie to gently bathe Caleb with a cool cloth and wait for her to return. She climbed down from the wagon and instructed Aaron to start a fire and keep a quart of water on boil and to fetch a half-cup of sugar. Hannah went to the riverbank where she had recognized a black willow tree. She cut two slim branches and quickly shaved the bark off. She cut the pieces of inner bark into small sections and returned to the Proctor wagon.

She was stunned to see Dr. Estes Jones, the physician with whom she'd had a testy encounter at Fort Laramie. He was standing outside the wagon talking to Gertie who was holding a crying-coughing baby. Hannah handed the bark pieces to Aaron and told him to boil them. Hannah took a deep breath to settle her nerves and brace herself for the confrontation she knew was coming.

Hannah gave a clipped hello to Jones which was returned in the same manner. She said to Gertie, "I'm almost ready to proceed. You can take the baby back inside while I finish preparations."

Gertie was confused. She looked at Hannah and then at Jones. She knew she was going to be in the middle of a battle, and she hated it. "Uh, Hannah, maybe you should talk to Dr. Jones first."

By way of explaining his presence, Jones said his wagon train was parked nearby, and he was told his services might be needed.

Hannah said, "That was thoughtful of you, doctor." She looked into his face with an icy smile, and said, "I would welcome your opinion, doctor."

Hannah's attitude was not lost on him. "Well, madam, Mrs.?…

"Blanc. Associate of the late Dr. Abel Blanc of St. Louis."

"I assume you mean nurse. What treatment do you propose?"

Hannah ignored the intended insult. "Willow bark to bring down the temperature, which is the greatest danger of croup."

He snort-laughed. "That's a treatment you must have learned from the savages."

"If you mean the Indians, yes, I believe they use it also. But willow bark has been used for this purpose in Europe for centuries."

He elevated his face and looked down his spectacles at her and sniffed. "Folk remedies, so-called, are things doctors are educated to ignore."

What Hannah had learned from observation, but couldn't frame scientifically, is that willow bark contains salicylate which in its active form becomes salicylic acid and is closely related to aspirin of a later day.

"And you, sir," she said. "What would your treatment be?"

Jones' eyes flashed at the indignity of being quizzed by a mere nurse. "Well, in brief, and in terms I trust you can understand, I would recommend a small amount of bleeding, and one dram of ipecac to void the body of poisons, repeated every three hours. Perhaps a small dose of calomel, depending on the child's progress." He spoke to Aaron, ignoring Gertie and Hannah. "My prescriptive advice is based on the recommendations of the New England Medical Society."

"And what would be your fee?" Hannah asked.

Jones glared at Hannah. "I consider that a private matter to be discussed with the father."

Hannah said, "I especially question the value of ipecac as an expectorant. There is no value in making the baby throw up. He could throw up and breathe-in the vomit and die, especially during a convulsion. Calomel, also, contains mercury which science has increasingly questioned as safe. And giving it to a baby? I wouldn't."

Jones turned red, and his face puffed up. "Well, I never!" He turned to Aaron, and said, "I hope you will not regret rejecting my advice, sir." He turned stiffly, like a palace guard, and marched off.

Aaron shrugged and turned back to his fire. Gertie had a worried look.

Hannah sent Aaron to Flora's wagon to borrow a small tin bath she had seen. When Aaron returned, she stirred the sugar into the boiling pot that contained the willow bark. She sent Aaron to fetch a pail of water, then took the mixture off the fire. She put the bath in the shade of the wagon where there was a breeze, and had Gertie rest the baby in its water. She then soaked a piece of linen into the willow bark mixture and fashioned the end into her best version of a woman's nipple. She took the sweet mixture of bark water and offered it to Caleb. The baby eagerly started sucking on the "sugar teat."

Hannah stood up and faced the anxious parents. "I've had plenty of experience with croup," she said. "The greatest danger is high fever. That's what caused the convulsions. The bark water should gradually bring the fever down, and the croup should heal in a few days. Repeat this every hour or so throughout the day."

Gertie embraced Hannah with words of thanks, and Aaron awkwardly patted her on the shoulder, but with a worried smile.

The next morning, Hannah went to check on her patient. As she approached the Proctor tent, all was quiet. She pulled the flap slightly aside and looked in. She saw Aaron asleep with his back to Gertie who was slumbering peacefully with a sound-asleep baby in her arms.

Hannah backed away with a smile and wiped her welled-up eyes. She turned and went back to her morning chores.

Nimrod was discussing with Penney where to pasture the animals when Penney glanced over the guide's shoulder. His eyes got big, and he stared for a long moment, then he said, "Well, knock me down and steal my teeth." Nimrod turned around and also saw Susan Jackman working outside the post store. The two men walked over. She turned, and with equal shock faced two men she didn't want to see.

"Hello, Susan," Penney said in a neutral voice.

She glanced up. "Hello," she said, averting her eyes in embarrassment.

"I've got some news for you," he said. She turned toward him, halfway. "Your husband is dead." No reason to give hand-holding words to this woman.

Her head snapped back. "What? What happened?

"You happened," he said evenly.

Tears flooded her eyes. "That's unfair....What happened to Abraham?"

"He shot hisself over grief," he said.

She sighed and looked away. Penney was reminded of the reaction to expect when a favorite pet dies, not a husband who kills himself over you.

Nimrod grew uneasy over Penney's stridency. He asked, "Where's Davy Owens?"

The mention of Owens caused her tears to turn into loud weeping. "He left. He just left me all alone. He lied to me. Mr. Bridger gave me a job and a place to sleep."

The two men didn't react to her distress, which was obviously more for being jilted than becoming a widow. Penney asked Susan to follow them and led her to her late husband's wagon where they found Zack lounging. Penney said, "Susan here is claiming her inheritance. Get your stuff out of her wagon."

Zack was joined by Tester, and they both started sputtering. "Uncle Abraham told me if anything happened to him, the wagon would belong to me."

Penney scoffed. "Now it's Uncle Abraham, is it? Well, he's not here, but his widow is. He put irony on the word widow. This wagon and team are hers now."

Zack was caught off guard and looked aghast. "You—you mean?"

Penney turned to Nimrod. "Something wrong with my English?"

Nimrod gave a half shrug, "Clear to me."

Penney turned back to Zack. "I'm going to tell Bridger you got no claim to this wagon or what's in it."

Susan interrupted. "He can have it."

"What?" Penney said.

"I don't want it. I plan to return back east. I'll find my own way."

"I'm sure you will," Nimrod said, and regretted saying it the moment the words came out.

Penney turned his attention to Tester standing next to Zack. "This fort's as far as you go. We want you out of here, lickity split. From now on, you ain't a part of this wagon train."

Tester turned to Zack for support, but Zack had gotten what he wanted, so he just shrugged in sympathy toward Tester.

That evening, however, Jasper Patterson came to Penney with a request. "Captain," the old man said awkwardly, "Agnes and I, we've struggled to keep up—"

"You've been valuable members of the company," Penney said.

"Well, I thank you for that, captain, but the days are becoming more wearisome. I heard you were giving the boot to Simon Tester."

"Yes-sirree-Bob," Penney said.

"Well, Captain, I'd like you to reconsider. We know Tester's not the prize a girl would take home to show mother, but he seems to be a good worker, and we could sure use him. We'd vouch for his vittles and his conduct."

"The deed is already done, Jasper."

"Well, sir, a deed can be undone if it's to help two old folks in their seventies who could sure use him."

"You seem to be doing fine," Penney said.

Jasper hesitated, then looked away. "My ticker's been acting up some."

Knowing the man's pride, Penney realized "some" meant "a lot." He squeezed the old man's shoulder. "I'll go talk to him, Jasper. But he's going to be on a short string, you can bet. He's a scalawag."

Later, when Penney told the others Tester would be staying, Flora said, "Well, if the Pattersons need him, fine. But keep him away from me."

Cohen grinned. "From what I heard, I don't think that's going to be a problem, Flora."

Penney said, "I'm going to keep my eye on him, you bet."

The next progress on the trail would take them north along the Bear River to Fort Hall; then make a loop back south along the Snake River; then over the Raft River. They would thereby enter Mexican territory as they proceeded south to the Humboldt River, which was their westward route to the Sierra Nevada Mountains. The Humboldt had until the previous year been called the Mary's River. It was the seventh name given the river by a succession of explorers, each one hoping, and failing, to memorialize his impact on the land.

In state names given later, the route would extend from Fort Bridger in southwestern Wyoming, north into southern Idaho, then south to eastern Nevada, then west to the mountains and California beyond.

The committee and Nimrod discussed the way forward. Nimrod drew on his personal experience, and Ezra Masterson merged it with known celestial navigation data plus his own readings.

"We've come 1,200 miles from Independence, round about," Masterson said. "We're about two months from the mountains. I calculate we should reach the foot of those mountains around the first of October. That should put us ahead of the snows."

"Snows don't arrive on a set schedule," Cohen said.

"They're as predictable as a woman," Penney said with a chuckle that ended with a gulp when he saw Hannah's glare by a side glance.

"Nimrod, tell us about Fort Hall," Penney said.

"It's a pretty poor excuse for a trading post. It's run by Hudson's Bay Company. A feller can buy supplies there if he's willing to pay their price. They'll empty your pockets unless theys gone and got religion or you're able to Jew them down."

Masterson gave a quick glance at Cohen who rolled his eyes, but he knew Nimrod meant nothing insulting by repeating language people around him used every day.

"Fort Hall is where wagons sort out to go southwest to California or northwest to Oregon," Nimrod continued, unaware of his ethnic/religious gaffe.

CHAPTER TWENTY-SIX

The ten days to Fort Hall should have been uneventful, but as usual, Zack Monroe got in the way. On the morning of the second day Aaron Proctor was leading his oxen and horse out to graze when Zack Monroe stepped in front of him. Aaron smelled liquor, and said, "Get out of my way. You're drunk."

Zack was still smarting from his humiliating clash with Flora Dickens and welcomed a confrontation with a smaller man. "Do you miss your redbone whore?" he said. "I had her, and she weren't worth the price." He laughed at his joke and looked around to see if others shared his mirth, and saw they were alone.

Proctor said through clenched teeth, "You're a swine. You dare defile the name of the woman you murdered."

Zack roared in anger and swung on Aaron who fell backwards with Zack on top in an instant. Zack hit Aaron several times in the face with both hands, making blood gush from his nose and a cut above his eye. Aaron could feel the larger man's weight, see the rage in his eyes and smell his foul breath. In desperation, he fumbled for his knife in its scabbard. Pulling it free, he thrust upward. The knife sliced into Zack's abdomen and severed the aorta. There was no turning back from that.

Zack first looked down at Aaron and grunted. He felt the knife's pressure, but no pain. He knew something had gone wrong but didn't know what. In confusion and disbelief, he stared into Aaron's face from a few inches above. His mouth opened and closed, fish like. Then, as the blood pumped into his body cavity, he was flooded with pain as violated nerves protested. He cried out in surprise as well as pain. With a shudder, he collapsed his weight atop Aaron.

Aaron frantically pushed Zack off and onto his back. He scrambled to his feet and looked around and then down in shock.

Zack was no longer a dangerous, mean assailant. Aaron stood looking at the man he had just knifed. He looked at the bloody knife in his hand, and let it slip through his fingers.

Zack became a person Aaron had never seen before. His eyes were still focused, but without object. His expression asked "Why?" but not of Aaron, perhaps of God. His heart was still pumping, but into a chasm. His muscles no longer cared. His breathing became shallow and irregular. He made a rattle sound of half moan-half cough because he could no longer clear his throat. His pupils enlarged and lost focus. His heart ran out of blood to pump. His bladder opened and a dark stain spread over the ground beneath him. His hands stopped clutching the dirt and froze into claws. Zack's eyelids lost muscle control and fell to half open. His expression turned from confusion and terror to a placid indifference. His body form went from human to mannequin. Zack was no longer there.

Others heard the commotion and rushed to the scene. There they saw Aaron standing alone in shock with a bloody knife at his feet. They all stared down at what used to be someone they knew. No one said anything for a long moment, then Zack's friend, Simon Tester, pointed at Aaron, and in a screech, said, "He killed him. He murdered an unarmed man in cold blood. I saw it. Proctor insulted Zack, and when he protested, Proctor attacked him, and when they were on the ground, he pulled his knife and murdered Zack in cold blood." He turned to face the group, and shouted, "Hang him!"

Murmurs in the crowd grew in intensity as Tester's version gained support. After all, Aaron was armed, and Zack was not.

When it happened, Nimrod had his back turned and was cleaning Bub's hoof. He turned as he heard the shouts, then turned and rushed to the scene. Hannah saw Nimrod running in that direction and followed.

Penney and Masterson rushed to the area and took in the situation. Penney was flustered but directed two men to watch Aaron to make certain he didn't run, although to where wasn't established.

After people calmed down, Penney called a meeting of all the pioneers to consider the crisis. He started the comments by saying, "Well, now the fat's in the fire." He mused aloud for a few moments. "I can maybe see an argument of self-defense."

Preacher said, "Blood has been spilled. The Bible doesn't cut any slack. An eye for an eye, it says."

Cohen, listening to Preacher, muttered to himself, "I'm glad that would-be pharisee isn't a Jew."

Tester nodded enthusiastically toward Preacher. "I heard Proctor threaten Zack a while back, so I knew he had a grudge building. Then, today, with my own eyes I saw him attack Zack with his knife already out. He's a stone-cold killer, Proctor is." Tester and Meister kept the crowd stirred up and made it difficult for the committee members to think, and for voices supporting Aaron to be heard.

Gertie Proctor at the edge of the group holding her baby, cried out, "He is not, he's a good man." She began sobbing as Ruth Cohen took the baby from her arms."

Penney frowned. "That Zack feller needed killing, and I don't mind saying it."

Masterson countered, "Zack was unarmed, that much is clear. You don't kill a man over a fist fight."

Cohen tried to sort things out. "Was it premeditated, or an impulse, or self-defense?"

Penney flashed exasperation. "Malachi, this ain't the U-nited States Su-preme Court. A man's dead and he shouldn't be. That's what we're dealing with here."

"Aaron Proctor has a wife and baby," Hannah reminded everyone.

In a brief moment of silence, the reticent Aaron Percival spoke softly, but loud enough to be heard: "But he killed him, Proctor did. Because someone insults you doesn't mean you kill him."

Nodding toward Percival, Martin Grover, who weeks before had accidentally shot his wife, shouted, "Killing is killing,"

"You should know a thing or two about that," Meister snickered in an aside loud enough to be heard by all. With a roar, Grover lunged for Meister who took cover behind a wagon as a bevy of hands groped to hold Grover back.

Penney shouted. "All right, damnit! Enough of that. This is

supposed to be a serious meeting. A man's life is at stake."

Hearing that, Gertie screamed, and Aaron hugged her with a stricken look on his face.

Penney waited for the tumult to subside, then said, "I'm going to ask Aaron to tell his side of the story." He turned toward Aaron and waited.

Aaron's breath was heavy, his breath was quivering, and his eyes darted with disbelief across the rows of people he thought were his friends. He saw people who met his gaze, then looked away; he saw people who looked at him with hatred; he saw a few who smiled encouragement; some had eyes glittering, thrilled at the life and death drama unfolding.

The atmosphere was a Roman forum, fueled by the angry frustration of their grueling, frightful journey. Some of the pioneers, the loud ones, smelled blood in the air, and shivered with the excitement of it. Others, those whose voices should have propped up Aaron, were stunned into quiet. Those who tried to defend Aaron were shouted down.

Aaron started, "You all know I'm not an evil man, and I'm not violent by nature. I killed a bully in self-defense. Zack was drunk and was squeezing my throat. I could see in his eyes that he was set on killing me. I did what I had to do to defend myself. I'm sorry as all get-out that it happened, but it did. I had no choice." His voice broke as he pleaded, "You've got to believe me. It was no murder."

Aaron's description of the fight was rambling and disjointed. He spoke like a man in shock and terror.

Penney asked him if he had witnesses. Aaron shook his head. "Weren't no one around."

Tester interrupted with a shout. "He's a liar! I was no more than ten feet away. I saw it all. They was tussling—that's all it was, a tussle—when he grabbed his knife and stabbed Zack." Tester pantomimed a stab thrust. "Poor Zack just laid there. I heard him say, 'Aaron, why'd you do that? Why'd you kill me? Then, Zack sighed, and his spirit passed." Tester lowered his head priest-like. "May he rest in Jesus."

Penney listened, then said to Tester, "Did anyone witness what you claim you saw?"

Uriah Meister stepped forward. "I'll vouch for what Brother Tester saw."

Brother Tester, my ass, Nimrod thought, but pushed back the urge to say it.

Gertie screamed, "You lie, you black-hearted devils. My husband is a good man."

There followed an hour's back-and-forth discussion. Several times Aaron tried to interrupt to rebut what was said, but Penney said, "You had your say, Aaron."

At one point, Hannah moved over to Nimrod in the back, and said, "Can't you do something?"

Nimrod shook his head. "I didn't see nothing." He shrugged. "I'm hired help."

Hannah gave him a frustrated, disappointed look and moved away. Penney held up his hand for quiet. "Folks we've got to come to a decision. We're the law for nigh on a thousand miles, just us. Justice has dropped into our laps. I wish it hadn't." He directed two men to accompany Aaron and Gertie to the other side of the clearing.

The pioneers argued back and forth for an hour, sometimes agreeing, sometimes not, but at the end, a narrow, grudging consensus was reached.

Penney said, "Well, we can't put it off. Let's bring Proctor over here."

The guards returned with Aaron. Penney decided to spare Gertie the scene and asked the women to take Gertie back to her wagon.

With jangled nerves, Penney cleared his throat with a trembling fist and forced himself to look at Aaron. "I'm dreadful sorry to tell you this, but we've decided--all of us, almost--that what happened out there this morning was a crime. It was a terrible crime. We have to call it murder."

Aaron protested. "You know I didn't mean to do it. I was defending myself. He insulted the memory of a friend."

"A whore, you mean," Tester said with a laugh-snort.

"A man should be more careful picking his friends," Meister added.

"There's your motive, Captain," Grover said, as though he had solved the riddle.

"What's your motive, Grover?" Cohen said in a raised voice.

"Shut up, all of you," Penney demanded, his tension spilling out.

Aaron shook his head in disbelief. "I should have the chance to defend myself against this, like any man."

Penney almost choking on the words he had to utter. "You're going to have to die for what you did, son. I hate the words I just spoke. I surely do. We decided we owe a debt to the dead man, though he was an ugly human being. We got to follow God's law of an eye for an eye. There's no other way around it. There just ain't."

Preacher said, affirming with a solemn nod, "That's in the Book."

Aaron's lip quivered. He looked around at the faces. They all averted their eyes except Nimrod. Aaron glared at Penney, and then at those nearby. "You have no right. You're not the law." Seeing no sympathy to that, he said, "I have a new-born child and a wife who needs me. Surely, you know that."

"We ain't got a regular court, I allow," Penney said. "That being true, we got no choice but to be the law in these parts. We got to do justice as we see it. The dead man has a right to it."

Aaron hung his head in disbelief and took a long moment to gather himself. He looked around for support but saw none. He took a deep, nervous breath, then said, "I can see there's no arguing left, and I'm not going to beg."

"Wouldn't do any good, son."

Cohen said, with tears in his eyes, "We're going to give you an hour with your family, then send them back to your wagon." Aaron nodded numbly, in shock, but no longer in denial. Cohen said softly to the men guarding Aaron, "Take him to his wagon, and bring his gun back."

Nimrod had said nothing, but then he spoke up. "Can't you give the man a chance? There's water and a friendly Flathead village maybe half a day north. I've traded fair with them."

Masterson said, "We're past that...I read somewhere that you hold up a wagon tongue for a tree..."

Nimrod interrupted. "There'd be no drop. He'd strangle. If'n you're looking for a memory to wake you in the middle of the night, that'll do it."

Preacher said, "There are no trees around here."

"A firing squad?" Masterson asked.

"Are you going to be the first to volunteer, Ezra? That'd be an exciting nightmare, for God's sake," Cohen said in exasperation.

Penney looked at Nimrod with a shamefaced glance. "Will you do it?"

Preacher said, "That makes sense. He's had the most exper—"

"Shut your mouth," Penney snapped.

Nimrod did not disguise his annoyance. "I got to get out of here. I'm going out to dig a grave."

An hour later, the men guarding Aaron brought him back to the circle where the committee waited. Gertie was told to stay in the wagon. Preacher extended his hand to Aaron which was ignored. "I offer you the solace of prayer," he said.

Angrily, Flora said, "Damn it! For God's sake!"

Preacher looked at her and sighed, "Do not curse, sister."

"I'll talk any damned way I like," she hissed through clenched teeth. "I don't think he sees you as the way to God."

Nimrod stepped forward and was given Aaron's rifle. No one wanted to own the gun used in an execution. He quietly said to Aaron, "Come with me, friend." They walked out of the camp with no restraint on Aaron. At the edge, close to the wagon with his wife and baby inside, Aaron hesitated and turned toward it. "Be strong," Nimrod said. "Those bastards are watching." They continued walking.

Aaron said in a pleading voice, "Was there—is there— no other way?"

"They argued it out," Nimrod replied, dodging the question.

Aaron said, "I'm sorry it has to be you."

"Put your mind on more important things."

They walked toward the grave that Nimrod had prepared. A few of the company followed at a distance. Nimrod wheeled and shouted, "Get the hell out of here!" and watched with disgust as they scurried away.

The two men reached the grave. Aaron almost buckled when he saw the hole in the ground. Nimrod motioned him to its lip.

"Sit on the edge there, Aaron."

"Will you take care of my family?"

"They'll be looked after."

"Will you tell them I didn't mean to kill him?"

"They already know that." Shame was beginning to spread over Nimrod's spirit like mold, but he gritted his teeth in determination.

"I'd like to pray."

"Take as long as you need."

"Nimrod stood by as Aaron bowed his head and moved his lips silently. When Aaron said, "Amen," Nimrod leveled the gun at the back of his head. His hands had never before shook holding a gun.

The entire company was gathered around Penney's wagon as though at a funeral, which was appropriate. Doubt was already creeping along the ground like a low fog. They flinched at the sharp report of a rifle. An anguished scream came from the Proctor wagon.

The pioneers looked at each with mixed expressions of shame, guilt, and sadness, either real or feigned. Only Tester and Meister had no expression, and that was because they suppressed smiles. In the distance they could head the faint scraping of Nimrod's shovel on dirt and gravel.

The company made haste to move, hoping to put the execution behind them. Though it was mid-afternoon, they wanted to get away from the tragedy they had been a part of. Though two graves were left behind, the memory traveled with them. Already, some were having doubts, and a few deep remorse.

A few minutes later, Nimrod walked slump-shouldered back into camp to a host of questioning eyes. Masterson took a step forward. "How?—" he asked.

Nimrod threw the shovel down in disgust. "Don't ask. Don't ever ask." He mounted Bub.

"Are you all right?" Hannah asked.

"I need to be alone for a spell," he said, and rode off.

As the wagons pulled out, Hannah took Gertie and her baby to the grave. She supported Gertie's weight on her shoulder as the heartbroken young mother sobbed. Hannah left her alone for long minutes. David Percival who had been assigned to drive her oxen waited a distance away.

Gertie didn't leave her wagon that day or the next. When she did emerge, she avoided the others, and they did the same to her. Hannah, Flora, and Ruth alone entered the wagon. No one else dared try.

Shame swept through the company like a virus. Nimrod, having returned, stayed to himself. Over the next few days most of the outrage or grief over the killings subsided to be replaced by regret or shame for the most part. Even most advocates of execution lowered their heads and stayed silent, troubled by their bloodlust, though a few of the agitators smiled. Most had come to realize they had condemned a good man for defending himself against a bad man. But dead was dead. They had acted in a mob-fever in passing a judgment they were unequipped to make. Guilt was the fruit of impulse.

People kept glancing at the wagon in which Gertie stayed apart with her grief and bitterness.

Those who opposed or had misgivings about the execution started to look with anger at the others who had urged or countenanced it. They, in turn, became resentful at the blame thrown at them.

Penney called the committee together to find a way to keep the volatile mood from tearing the company apart. They decided that Preacher would lead a prayer service to assuage the growing sense of having done wrong.

The service was quiet with words of regret from those who had not spoken up against the sentence, and sideward glances from those who had pushed for it. The prayers were shorter than usual, and two attempts to sing hymns went unfinished as the ragged singing ebbed to silence. The meeting didn't set minds at ease, but it seemed to tamp down the dread. Gertie did not attend.

The following week the travel was slower than usual. Things seemed off balance. Assignments were forgotten or ignored. Fires were left unattended. There were angry recriminations over two steers that wandered off or were stolen. Pioneers glared at others who were on the opposite side of the Aaron Proctor judgment. Nimrod, as the executioner, was viewed with awe, or regret, or accusation at his deed. No one thanked him or scorned him to his face. Nimrod stayed to himself, and several times disappeared for long hours. The company assumed he was dealing with grief or guilt, or maybe both.

On the eighth morning after the execution, the women quietly cleaned up after breakfast, the men busied themselves cursing the oxen as they wrestled the yokes in place. Suddenly, at the sound of hoofs, every face turned to the trail behind them to see the outline of riders approaching at a gallop. Apprehension fell over camp. The men reached for guns as all stared with wild, disbelieving eyes as the shapes took form. Riding into camp at the front was Nimrod. Right behind were a half-dozen Indians. They stopped short and milled at the edge of the camp. Suddenly a man came to the front. It was Aaron Proctor on an Indian pony holding his own rifle.

The muttering started low and fearful. The Catholics crossed themselves. But when the people realized they weren't viewing an apparition, voices became louder and filled the air with questions and exclamations.

Penney muttered, "Well, knock me down and steal my teeth!"

All eyes were wide and riveted on Aaron. But what they saw was not a man pleading for his life. Before them was not a quivering lip, but a set jaw. They saw a man who would now not go willingly, but a man who would defy you to come take him. They saw a man who felt wronged by them, and perhaps, maybe, he would forgive.

Nimrod spoke above the sounds of the horses and the buzzing of the pioneers. "These here Flatheads are my friends who wanted to come and thank y'all for the two beeves. They honored their new friend, Aaron here, with a pony." He gestured with a friendly wave to the Indians who turned and galloped off with happy screams.

Gertie peeked out from her wagon's bonnet and screamed hysterically as she hurried down the two steps and rushed to her husband. She grabbed his boot and held on, crying so hard her breathing came in gasps. He reached down and embraced her.

Penney walked to the middle, pushed his hat back, exhaled, and said, "Well, I'll be a son of a bitch." He shook his head in wonderment and slowly repeated his words, punching them out one at a time— "Yes, sir. I will be one hell-fired son of a bitch."

Aaron dismounted, and with his arm around Gertie's shoulders, walked back to the wagon to get their baby. He held his rifle in his other hand. He would not be giving it up.

Standing nearby was Meister. He looked up at Nimrod still atop Bub, and said, "You're a liar and a thief, mister."

Nimrod looked down on Meister. "I reckon you could argue that, but I ain't no executioner, and you can say those words just once, Meister."

It was obvious to everyone that Nimrod had staged a fake execution and hidden Aaron in the nearby Indian village until feelings had simmered down.

Nimrod surveyed the crowd. The look on his face made the others uneasy. He held up his hand for silence, and when he got it, he spoke in a loud voice with a hard look directed at Tester and Meister. "I ain't nothing but a hired hand here, but I'll say this just one time— It's over!"

Later in the day, Penney got Nimrod aside, and said, "What you did, saving Aaron and all, is going to keep many a dark thought out of my head over what we almost did. Some feel the same way. Some don't." Penney mournfully shook his head. "I failed to know how to handle such a thing as happened. How does a crowd of good folks turn into a lynch mob? And it beats all that I was one of them."

At supper, Hannah said to Nimrod: "That was a wonderful thing you did." She shook her head in wonderment. "Who would have thought of doing such a thing?" She paused, tilted her head, and her lips pursed. "Your life certainly travels a windy road."

A week after Aaron's return, Hannah told Penney she had picked up strands of talk that some of the company were considering splitting off for Oregon.

Penney nodded. "I've heard same. Let's keep it quiet and see what happens."

What happened was rumors, and rumors about rumors. A quiet division started to open between California and Oregon. There was growing concern that Mexicans would prevent their entry into California.

Aaron and Gertie pretty much stayed to themselves. Even so, the togetherness glue of the company was weakening over his presence. The stares and glares cast in their direction slowly dissipated and the veneer of civility returned. However, in some, the belief in his guilt simply went underground. The talk didn't go beyond grumbling, but grumbling is always the start.

CHAPTER TWENTY-SEVEN

Aware of how cold nighttime deserts and mountain passes could be, Nimrod asked the women to start modifying warm dresses into pantaloons to stay warm, especially if they had to travel through snow when they reached the high mountains.

A few of the women protested at the indignity of such a thing. Cohen realized the common sense of what Nimrod suggested. He laughed, and said, "Do you ladies know what an up-draft is? Well, imagine it, and then unlimber your needles and thread."

As their children frolicked, Flora and Hannah were relaxing and sewing. They were altering Ed's trousers for Hannah to wear under outer garments in mountain weather.

"How are you and Nimrod getting on?" Flora asked and glanced sideways at Hannah.

Hannah lowered her needle. "What do you mean?" she asked cautiously.

Flora laughed. "Hannah, dear Hannah, don't you think the members of this company have eyes? The only entertainments we have are snooping and gossiping."

Hannah resumed sewing. "Oh, we're just friends. I find him interesting, and a bit amusing."

Flora laughed merrily.

Hannah said, "What's funny?"

"You are."

Hannah smiled and shrugged. "Well, queen busy-bee, I confess he and I've had some spirited conversations."

This time Flora's laugh was full-throated. "Is that what they're calling it now, 'conversations'?"

Hannah stopped sewing and leaned against a wagon wheel.

"Oh, Flora, what happened to me? I had a good husband and a happy life and did good things for people. Then, out of the blue, I lost him, and then I had no choice but to marry a snake because I had children to feed." She waved her free hand at the snow-peaked mountains. "Now, here I am, in the middle of a God-forsaken wilderness, with heat wilting every muscle in my body, bugs eating me alive, and death ready to grab me every mile."

"Life is what happened, Hannah. It happens to all of us. It just does."

Hannah looked up from her needles as she reminded herself of Flora's widowhood. "Oh, what am I saying? You're the one with a right to complain."

Flora nodded thoughtfully. "I try not to, complain, that is. But you know all that; you're a widow, too. I think of my marriage every night when the children are asleep and I'm all alone. I cry myself to sleep sometimes. But when I wake up to the lives I've been left with, I remind myself that William wanted to take us to a place of sunshine and new beginnings. That was his dream. Now, the dream has to be mine. The children and I are on our way to the place of sunshine William wanted for us."

"You're stronger than I, Flora. I can't seem to overcome the dread I feel about what will go wrong next. I can't let the 'wrong' thing be a man."

Flora said, "I know this sounds preachy, but look on the bright side. You're leaving behind those stuffy old men doctors who held you back. You're going to a frontier where doctors are going to be so scarce no one will notice you're wearing skirts—at least for the doctor part." She winked. "And men will be about ten to one in our favor. California can be your land of opportunity."

Hannah grimaced. "It's too damned bad—pardon my language—too bad we need men at all. But that's a woman's lot."

Flora said, "Maybe that'll change one day." Then she laughed, "Meantime, our advantage is they need us more."

Hannah didn't laugh. "Need us for what? That's what frightens me."

Flora said, "The need is one for the other, both ways. We're in a barbarous wilderness. We need what a man gives us, food on the table, and protection. A man such as Nimrod."

Hannah cupped her chin and studied the ground a long moment. She turned to Flora. "I'm going to be honest with you. I'm afraid of his violence. He can be a kind man if things are going right, but the grim reaper seems to follow him around like a faithful dog. I worry that if a man sheds blood over and over again, even in a good cause, does that eventually turn him into that person altogether? I can't afford another horrible marriage."

Flora nodded her understanding. "Maybe he does, too, hate violence. Maybe for the life he's lived, that's the only way to survive."

Hannah shook her head at the puzzle. "I swear, I don't know what to make of it. He scares me, not physically, but in the kind of life he might drag the children and me into. They need a stable, Christian life." Hannah hesitated, "but I confess, he's also—"

Flora teased by pursing her lips, and in a low voice, said, "Oooooooh...?"

Hannah blushed and said, "Oh, you know what I mean."

Flora finished her last stitch and stood up. She reached down and patted Hannah's arm. "You can't live your life defensively, my dear. Be guided by your brain but listen to your heart."

Hannah sputtered out one word— "Men!"

"A-*men*," Flora said over peals of laughter, which Hannah joined after she thought about it a moment.

The warriors were unmoving statues a few yards off the edge of the trail. They were three, mounted on smaller, nimble Indian ponies. They held weapons, but not in a threatening way, and stared straight ahead.

It was Cohen who first saw them, but as they came into view of other wagons, the entire column came to a halt.

Three of the committee—Penney, Cohen, and Hannah—gathered at the front and waited for Nimrod who was the best at sorting out the ways of Indians. When Nimrod rode up and looked at the three men waiting, he said, "Crows. I'll handle this," and rode to the men. As others of the company gathered, they watched Nimrod confer with the three, and waited. Finally, he broke away and returned to the group.

"What's going on?" Penney asked.

"They want me to go with them," he said matter-of-factly.

"Why?" Flora asked.

"Unfinished business." He talked to the group, but his eyes were on Hannah.

"You told them you couldn't, I assume," Cohen said. It was more of a plea than a statement.

"I have to go," Nimrod said, as both looked at the waiting Crow warriors.

"You're going to leave us alone out here?" Aaron asked in a disbelieving voice.

"If I didn't go, you wouldn't be safe."

Penny interjected. "Back in Independence, he warned this could happen. This ain't no desertion."

"Wait three days at Fort Hall. If I don't return by then, go on." He turned to Penney. "Shadrach, take care of my things." He removed his weapons and handed them to Penney. "I've told you everything I know to get through. Remember, buy a few extra cattle, any kind of vegetables, and all the water containers you can find."

"You'll need these," Penney argued as he took the revolver and rifle.

"If I needed them, they wouldn't do me much good. I'm not going there to fight. I hope to see you soon."

Penney shook Nimrod's hand with both of his. "You're a hard dog to keep on the porch."

Nimrod turned to Hannah and searched her face. He saw nothing.

Her words were a veiled accusation. She said, "So, you're going off to get killed." It was a statement, not a question.

Baffled and hurt, Nimrod mounted Bub and rode off with the warriors. Hannah's hand went to her throat.

CHAPTER TWENTY-EIGHT

The wagon train rolled into Fort Hall at the beginning of September, two weeks beyond Fort Bridger. It was a run-down fur trading post on the Snake River built ten years previously but fell short of its builders' hopes. Consequently, it fell into the hands of the Hudson's Bay Company. With the westbound wagon train traffic soon to increase many fold, it would grow into an important waystation, but until then, it was a sorry site.

Gaggles of curious Indians watched the pioneers arrive and camp close to the walled "fort," which was never intended to have a military purpose. Instead, its use was meant for the Indian trade. However, the Hudson's Bay Company had the foresight to see its future as a waystation for wagon trains.

The pioneers set about repairing wagons, reshoeing and doctoring animals, shopping the sparse retail wares available, and just enjoying a few rare hours of doing nothing. After breakfast on the first morning, Penney called a meeting to discuss routine matters.

Just as the meeting was about to break up, Ezra Masterson stood. "I need to speak, Captain." Penney warily nodded assent.

Masterson nervously cleared his throat once, then twice. He looked at Penney, then scanned the curious pioneers sitting on their camp chairs. "Captain, folks, I've got some news you may not like to hear." He paused, and a sudden hush fell on the group.

"Go on, Ezra," Penney said.

"Well, some of us have been talking about what's before us, and we're mighty concerned about a war with Mexico. We're not coming all this way to get shot at. We also hear from some mountain men that the route ahead to California is over deserts where there's no water, and mountains high enough to swallow up people without a trace."

He took a deep breath. "Well, Preacher and I talked to the Dayton party that just came in yesterday. Theirs is a large train headed to Oregon. Their leaders welcomed us."

Masterson let the news sink in, then said, "We're farmers, most of us, and the soil's good up there. Everyone says that. We've just decided we'd rather deal with Brits who speak our tongue than Mexicans who might want to shoot us.

"The reverend here has a hankering to do missionary work. He feels moved by the spirit to join some missionaries up in Oregon country in converting Indians." He looked at Preacher, who nodded.

Masterson hesitated, then spoke in a rush. "I've also got to say folks— and I mean no unkindness or disrespect by this— I've got to say some mighty bad things have happened to this company, things we'd just as soon put behind us."

Preacher interjected, "I've never seen God's displeasure made so clear."

Penney ignored Preacher's comment. He realized, as did they all, that the bitterness lingering from the Zack Monroe killing was pushing the separation. He saw no point in getting into it. "Who's going with you, Ezra?"

"There's been some quiet talk, Shadrach, but we don't know for sure." He let his gaze wander among the pioneers. "If anyone wants to join us, please stand up."

The men of several families glanced at one another, then stood, reluctant to call attention to themselves. Some had discomfort on their faces, but also determination. Some glared with narrow eyes at Aaron. Enoch Brister was among them. Except for his music, his leaving would not be noticed.

The ones remaining seated were the Penneys, Hannah, the Cohens, the Proctors, the Pattersons, Simon Tester, Flora Dickens, and Andrew Banks and Martin Carter. Uriah Meister, still smarting from the loss of Johnny, fidgeted, then jumped to his feet. Masterson looked at Meister, and said, "You stay." Penney put his hand out in a halting gesture. "He wants to go, you take him."

Masterson shook his head with a grimace.

Penney took a Liberty Head one-cent coin out of his pocket and held it toward Masterson. "Call it to see who wins the choice."

Masterson chuckled at such a gamble. "Heads."

Penney flipped the copper coin in the air and caught it in his palm. Both men looked down at the head of Lady Liberty surrounded by thirteen stars.

Masterson grinned as Penney frowned, then sighed and looked at Meister. "OK, you're for California," he said, using a new fad expression that had worked its way west from Boston.

Meister mustered the indignation to say, "I'm not a piece of property."

Penney said, "You mean like Johnny?" Penney and Masterson smiled at the irony.

Masterson turned his back on Meister and said to Penney, "How about Nimrod?"

Penney said, "If he ever comes back, he can decide for himself. He can catch up to y'alls if he wants. I've got his pack mule and some belongings in my wagon."

With the lines drawn and with nothing left to say, there was an awkward silence among the group. Penney relieved the tension as he said, "We wish you folks well, Ezra. You'll be a wise leader." He surveyed those standing. "God go with you."

The time had come to say goodbye. All of the pioneers looked at each other, not knowing what to say except to mutter awkward farewells. The Oregon-bound families shook hands with listless grips, then with nothing left to say, awkwardly walked away to move their wagons to the Dayton train. Eight wagons would remain.

As the Oregon group prepared to leave, Wiley Percival, who would be going, hung back and looked for Alice Dickens, who was staying. He saw her at the far edge of the group crying into a handkerchief. He ran over and said, "Goodbye, Alice. I love you." He kissed her on the cheek. "Someday soon I'll find you, and I'll marry you. Wait for me, won't you, please?"

"I will. I promise," she said, and waved her handkerchief as he ran away.

One never forgets a first love, no matter how innocent. Wiley and Alice would never see each other again, but in later years, each would ponder in passing moments of nostalgia—I wonder whatever happened to my first love?

The ones still seated looked with uncertainty at Penney. Gertie asked in a tense voice, "What'll we do for a guide?"

Penney said, "I 'spect Nimrod to ride in any day now. If he don't, he gave me directions. We'll make it," he said and tried to sound confident.

Penney stood, brushed himself off, and said, "Let's get busy, folks. We've got a lot to do and a long way to go."

The Dayton train departed the following morning. As their wagons rolled out, the remaining pioneers watched their erstwhile companions roll into the distance. There were no waves, nor shouts of good luck, as the stay-behinds turned away and set about their tasks.

Penney delayed departure of his smaller train, determined to wait a few days in the event Nimrod returned.

The next day, a few miles down the trail, a single wagon in the Dayton train pulled out of line and turned around.

After an hour of silent riding, the three Crows led Nimrod to an isolated glen in the Caribou Mountains where a small band of Crow warriors waited. Because they were in the territory of the bannocks and Shoshoni, the group opted for a discreet presence. They were neither a war party nor a hunting party. However, their intrusion into the area of other tribes could still be dangerous. They were here on a mission. Nimrod was the mission. Looking around, he saw a pink ribbon attached to the bridle of one of the horses. Nearby, he saw a palomino, much larger than an Indian pony, tied to a tree.

Nimrod dismounted. On the edge of the clearing tied to a post was Rake Face Marcel. Nimrod turned away and was face to face with Many Horses, the chief who had been his father-in-law. Neither man spoke, just stared. At last, Many Horses gestured, and Nimrod followed him to a private space. Many Horses voice was even and deep. His eyes were searching. He did not smile. He spoke in educated, fluent Crow. Nimrod understood most of his words, but his responses tended to be clumsy and a hesitant search of his limited vocabulary.

"Why did you not return and tell me yourself of my daughter's death instead of sending the black man with your gifts? Did you think that would satisfy me on the loss of my daughter?"

Nimrod looked into the other man's eyes and didn't hesitate. "Guilt, some fear. Me broke word to you."

"You were weak. You let a woman lead you on a rope like an untrained puppy. You did her work. You never beat her. If you were strong with her, she would not have demanded to go."

"Magpie could make man weak."

Many Horses' look was scornful. "Magpie was an Indian woman. You tried to make her a white woman. That turned her head."

Nimrod said, "Me daughter, Wildflower. Is she well? Does she ask about me?"

Many Horses waved the question away. "Wildflower is well.... The black man, Beckwourth, said Magpie was killed by the man Rake Face. Beckwourth is your friend and a known liar, but he only lies to make himself big, not to hide truth."

Nimrod pushed aside Many Horses' words. "Me daughter.She speak me? What look like?"

"She has blue eyes. When she turns a certain way, you can be seen in her face." He looked at Nimrod and read his thoughts. "No, you are not in her thoughts, not that she speaks of."

"But, why—"

Many Horses waved away Nimrod's words. "This man, Rake Face, he did not come to us. We bought him from the Nez Perce; four good horses he cost. He says you got drunk and killed my daughter."

"He lie."

"Those were his words. Many of my people believe him. He is a generous trader, but he is also said to be a bad man who hurts women. We could have tortured him, but torture is good only for satisfaction or ceremony. It does not give you the truth, but what the man thinks you want to hear."

"You know I not kill Magpie."

"I know my daughter is dead, and you ran. If I thought this Rake Face was honorable, you would be dead by now. But you were kind to Magpie. I saw that for myself. I was angry you broke your word, but all men sometimes do that."

"Thank you for trust."

"I have not mentioned trust. I do not know you except from our village. I never saw you drunk and with your friends who kill often. People change from whiskey. We see it. Perhaps you did. I came here to find the truth."

"How did you know—"

"People talk. This is our home. We know who has come into it."

"I would never hurt Magpie."

Many Horses studied him without expression. "We have our laws. The people have claimed the right to put you both to the test. Truth is brave. Lying is weak. We shall see...."

Many Horses walked back to the clearing with Nimrod following. Sitting in plain sight was a deerskin bag that moved constantly as though something inside was trying to escape. Nimrod knew what it was.

He head-gestured toward Rake Face and looked at Many Horses who nodded.

Nimrod walked to where Rake Face was tied and stood close to him and stared, as though looking at a rare species. Rake Face stared back scornfully. His clothes were torn, and several cuts on his face were crusted with blood. Nimrod finally faced the man who had raped and murdered his wife.

Over his years of pursuit, Nimrod had muttered to himself all the things he would say to Rake Face. He would damn him to hell, and relish telling him he was about to die as a rapist and murderer.

But the words did not come. They were not large enough. They would not undo the evil act, nor would they ease the guilt that would forever visit Nimrod's dreams. The chase had gone on too long. The sharp edges of his rage had rounded off. He did not have more to give.

They stood eye to eye, and Nimrod said—nothing.

Rake Face's face was filled with hate, and he said—nothing.

Nimrod turned away.

He was taken to a post a few feet from the one to which Rake Face was bound. He was told to remove his shoes. A warrior advanced with a rope to tie him, but Nimrod motioned him away. The warrior turned to Many Horses who nodded. Nimrod would stand firm.

Many Horses turned and addressed his warriors who had gathered around. "My brothers, we know these two men tell different stories about the death of my daughter, your sister. One is telling the truth, the other lies. We believe the one with a clean heart will be strong, and the liar weak. Our friend, the snake, will tell us."

He motioned to a brave who stepped forward with the snake bag. He opened it and out dropped a four-foot, gray-brown, angry, prairie rattler. The brave pinned the rattler's head down with a forked stick, and another brave tied the snake's tail to a smaller stake between the two, but with enough line to reach either Rake Face or Nimrod.

The snake coiled and stared at Nimrod who tensed up. He inhaled deep breaths to control his fear. He knew this snake, knew it was also frightened. He knew it would not ordinarily strike an unthreatening living man or a creature it didn't want to eat. But if it struck in fear, it would give its full venom. Both he and the snake were on untested ground. Nimrod fought back the urge to panic and forced himself to not cringe.

The desperate snake wanted nothing but to escape. Not knowing which way, it turned and crawled toward motionless Nimrod. He studied the reptile as it approached. The neck was narrow but flared out to the shovel-shape of its head. The black eyes were pinned on him. A forked black tongue constantly flicked. Nimrod knew that through the tongue was how the snake learned its surroundings.

The snake rattled its warning. Nimrod shifted a hard look into the eyes of Many Horses, who returned the stare. He then focused on the snake and met its cold, dead eyes with his own. Maybe, just maybe, he could make the snake know he was not its enemy. The snake crawled closer, within inches of his foot. He knew the snake could smell his presence. He did not move. Rake Face squirmed, and then made the mistake of rubbing his foot on the pebbles underneath, which caused the snake to turn toward the vibration. Rake Face stared with eyes bulging in fear, a guttural whine came from his throat. The snake headed for Rake Face who kicked at it in an unthinking panic. It struck. The needle fangs dug into his foot. Rake Face screamed. The snake was pulled back, its job done. Nimrod forced himself to have no reaction.

Many Horses motioned for the snake to be removed. He looked at the writhing form of Rake Face, then at Nimrod who remained expressionless.

The chief believed the snake had given its counsel. It was the Crow way.

Many Horses gave a slight motion to two warriors standing by. The men raised bows and sent arrows thudding into the chest of Rake Face who slumped over in his bonds, twitched, and died.

Nimrod was surprised at how he felt about Rake Face's death. He felt nothing except relief. It was finally over.

Many Horses motioned for Nimrod to follow him and went into the trees where they could talk. "Do you want the scalp?" he asked, motioning back to where Rake Face was slumped.

"No. Let coyotes have. I want daughter, Wildflower."

"No. She will stay with her people."

"She mine. I want her learn."

"Learn what? To drink whiskey? To lie? To steal the lands of other people? No, she is Crow. We will not let her become a half-breed among people who would have her squat in the dirt outside some army fort, of no use except to drunk soldiers."

"She part me."

Many Horses spoke matter-of-factly. "No, she is all herself. And she is all Crow. If you try to take her, you will be killed."

Silence followed as the two men walked to where Bub had been cared for by one of the warriors.

The matter settled, Many Horses became conversational in the Crow tongue. "Where will you go?"

"Me no home. Mountains all me know. Beaver trade gone."

"You should go where you came from."

"That place no more."

Nimrod took Bub's reins and swung into the saddle. Many Horses patted the mule's withers. "Many of our people believe most whites have already passed here, and there can't be many more to come. I fear there are many more. Who is right?"

"You are. Americans are many, as buffalo."

Many Horses' eyes widened. Then he became grim. "The day will come for a war to the death between our peoples, and we will be destroyed." He sighed. "We'll exist nowhere but in the memory of the winds." He stepped back. "If I can't save my people, maybe I can save what remains of my family." He stepped back, and his voice turned hard. "Go. Do not return." Many Horses turned and walked away.

Nimrod felt adrift as he rode at a slow canter out of the camp under the expressionless, watchful eyes of the Crows. With the death of Rake Face, something had been emptied out of him, an emotion that had filled him, toxic though it was. Hate had vacated its space. He had hoped his life would be filled by his daughter, but Many Horses had pushed that door shut.

He could have made it to Fort Hall before nightfall, but he needed to be alone. He spent hours in a solitary camp staring into the flames of a small fire. The red glow made the tears on his cheeks glisten.

CHAPTER TWENTY-NINE

T he pioneers first saw the single wagon returning to Fort Hall when it was about two miles distant. They gathered on a rise at the edge of the clearing to speculate on who it was. As the oxen trudged over the last rise, and people could see who it was. A shout went up: "It's Preacher! It's Preacher!" There was surprise but no joy in the shouts.

There was an immediate buzz of speculation that perhaps the wagon train had been wiped out by Indians, but, no, Preacher would have also been a victim. They thought he might have been expelled; again, no, you wouldn't expel a man of the cloth. It became obvious he was coming back because he wanted to.

Preacher stopped his oxen at the edge of the clearing and walked toward the pioneers. He approached Penney and offered his hand. Penney took it, then said, "What brings you back, Preacher? I figured you to be well on the way to Oregon."

Preacher grinned, embarrassed at his reversal. "Well, it's quite a story." He looked around and saw only faces flat and empty of reaction. They had learned to mainly expect rebuke from him.

Preacher stepped forward and told his story as though in the pulpit on Sunday morning. "Soon after we left here, the holy spirit spoke to me. It was my road to Damascus, as though I was Paul the apostle without his holiness. It told me of my fears of being a stranger in a strange land, amidst people unlike any I'd ever known. It made me suspicious and narrow-minded. The devil argued. Oh, yes, he did. Oh, folks, he did argue! Old Satan, he said I did the right thing in building barriers to protect myself, that judging people would keep me strong and safe. I prayed for strength. I said, 'Get thee behind me, Satan.' Then, praise God! It became clear to me that I should rejoin you and be a shepherd rather than a judge;

to preach the good news of the Gospel, not the judgment of my fears; to redeem myself for my smallness."

Penney stepped over and extended his hand. "Welcome back, Preacher."

As the camp awoke the next morning, Nimrod was already there, wiping down his sweating mule with the saddle on the ground at his feet. The pioneers hurried out of their wagons and tents and gathered around Nimrod as he worked. A brief, scattered cheer of relief went up: They had their guide back. They peppered him with questions, eager to hear of his mysterious adventure. He answered them with grunts and one-syllable evasions.

Penney stepped forward and greeted him with a wide grin. "You shore bring a gleam to these tired old eyes. What happened to you?"

Nimrod smiled, but continued working on Bub. "I got some things took care of."

Penney gave it another try. "And the man who killed your wife?"

"He stopped being a problem."

Penney surrendered. "Glad to have you back."

Nimrod nodded, and looked around, noticing the missing wagons. "Where did all the people go?"

Penney explained the split of the company as Nimrod listened. Off to the side, he noticed Hannah standing nearby, waiting for Penney and the others to move away. Their hard-to-figure relationship had been an open secret for some weeks. She walked away from the group, and he followed.

"So, you came back." It was a statement, not a question.

He nodded without expression.

"Is it finished?"

He shook his head in resignation. "The truth has come out, but is anything ever finished?"

"How about that man, that Rake man?"

"Dead." A frown crossed her face, so he added, "The Crows killed him."

"Did you find your daughter?"

"She weren't there. There ain't much else to say."

"It's not my place to inquire, but—" Hannah said, prodding.

"They won't let her go. She's just someone else I've failed."

Hannah touched his arm, and her voice softened. "Nimrod, she's with the only people she's ever known. Bringing her into this camp would be like dropping her into darkest Africa."

"That's my little girl back there, mine and Maggie's."

"Hannah nodded in sympathy. "And she's safe. Be content with that. I lost a sweet baby daughter, too; six months old she was. Big brown eyes and curled ringlets falling down the side of her face like this." Hannah traced her finger past her ear, and the act gave her a catch in her voice. "I named her Agnes after my grandmother." She was silent for a long moment, not trusting herself to talk.... You learn to live with it."

He forgot his own pain for a moment. "I didn't know that. How?"

Her voice quivered as she faced the memory. "I don't know. She just up and died." Hannah's eyes clouded with tears. "So many, many children die at birth and at such young ages. Maybe someday mothers can give birth and not have to fear taking a nursing infant from her breast and placing it in a casket." She willed her thoughts back to the present and Nimrod. "We come out here to this wilderness that aims to destroy us; we turn these Indians' lives upside down, then we wonder why things don't work out as if we were in a proper town back east. Thinking on all that is not easy for me."

Nimrod wanted to give her comfort; wanted to find the words that would flow his caring into her heart. He couldn't find them. "It ain't supposed to be easy, life ain't," he said, then looked away.

"What is it?" Hannah said, noticing his discomfort.

"Ed Spencer is dead. I saw his horse outside a Crow tipi."

Her question was matter of fact. "How can I know for sure?... Did you?..."

"No. Do you think I kill so easy?"

Nimrod pulled the pink ribbon from his pocket and handed it to her. Hannah fingered it. There was dried blood on it.

"I guess I'm expected to mourn," she said, speaking to herself. Deep in thought, Hannah turned her gaze away from Nimrod.

He reached out and put his hand on her arm. "Hannah..."

Hannah pulled back, but not angrily. "I'm weary of all this death, of this brutal life."

Nimrod moved off without a word.

On Nimrod's urging, Penney pooled funds to buy a few overpriced, scraggly steers and a bushel basket of shriveled-up cabbages, and one of wrinkled apples that housed a few worm families. Penney looked at the apples and lamented, "Back home, we'd feed those to hogs."

"We ain't aiming to bake apple pies," Nimrod said. "Before this is over, we'll all be adding holes to our belts."

The wagon train moved out from Fort Hall after four days with nine wagons. They traveled south along the Snake River, across the Raft River, and into Mexican territory, which, in a matter of short years, was destined to become Nevada Territory. Their goal was the newly renamed Humboldt River, which Nimrod estimated was two weeks distant.

Although their present course was level for the most part and had more than enough water from springs and small creeks, almost fifteen hundred hard miles of grueling travel through dust, flood, insects, disease, and discord had worn them thin. There was neither cure nor balm for the myriad of afflictions wearing down the spirit as much as the body. Neighbor squabbled with neighbor, and married couples bickered over nothing. Sweat dried into stink, and tasteless food never varied. Privacy became an infrequent luxury. Sex was hurried and hushed. Most regretted was the loss of freedom to get away from people. Fights broke out between peaceable farmers on trivial matters; men who had never before raised a fist against neighbor or stranger. Mile after mile, they came across doleful evidence alongside the trail of foolish travelers who had preceded them with overloaded wagons. Strewn about were personal possessions of sentimental or practical value that had been carried all the way from Independence but had to be discarded to reduce weight. Lying in the dust were tables, mirrors, tools, and even a baby's highchair, and other items whose bulk outweighed their value, cherished or otherwise.

Penney noticed Nimrod standing off to the side of the wagons and looking into the hills as they rolled past. He walked by and said, "What do you see up there?"

"Can I see your spyglass, Captain?" He held the glass up to his eye and took a long look.

"What do you see up there?" Penney asked again.

"Strange," Nimrod said, more to himself, and looked again.

"Damn it all, Nimrod, will you tell me what you're looking at?"

Nimrod lowered the glass and turned to Penney. "A camp; small one. Looks deserted. Buzzards circling."

"What's it mean?"

"Buzzards got one thing in mind. Something's dead up there. Judging from the number of birds, more than one something."

"An attack?" Penney said.

"Not likely; the tipis would be burned."

Hannah joined them and stood by but said nothing.

"I've seen the like before; maybe a massacre, but maybe smallpox. I'll ride up to take a look."

Penney shook his head. "Are you crazy? If it's smallpox you could get it."

"I've already had it." He prepared to mount Bub.

"I'll go, too," Hannah said. "I've had the vaccine."

Both men looked at her, then at each other. "If that's what you want," Nimrod said.

"You can have my horse," Penney said as he walked to his wagon to lead it over.

When they had gotten close to the camp, Nimrod scanned the tipis and said, "Nez Perce." Then the breeze shifted, and the smell hit them. It was like a combination of decayed meat and rotten eggs, doused in revolting, sweet perfume. Hannah had to brace herself not to vomit by breathing hard and willing her throat to stay closed. She looked at Nimrod who stared straight ahead. She thought—If you can handle this, then by heaven, so can I.

As they drew closer, she saw a corpse spread across the entrance to a tipi. The body was blue-green and splotched black. On the face were inflamed sores. Smallpox. The signs were clear that others of the village had fled the camp in panic, leaving bodies untended and everything in disarray.

After circling the perimeter of the camp, Hannah said, "I counted six dead."

Nimrod said, "Seven. There's one over there." He pointed to a figure just inside a tipi. Hannah looked and saw a small figure partly hidden. She started to turn away when she thought she saw movement but discounted it. But on intuition, she looked again more closely…Yes, the shadowed figure had moved a leg.

Hannah dismounted and walked over. She saw a girl of about eight with the signs of advanced smallpox. The girl's round black eyes were clouded but pleading as she looked up at Hannah. Her cracked lips opened without sound. Hannah hurried back to her horse and grabbed the canteen. She poured water into her cupped hand and dripped it into the girl's mouth so she wouldn't choke. Nimrod came up and stood beside her. Hannah looked up at him, shaking her head in wonder. "She's alive," she said. "Maybe we can save her."

Nimrod said nothing, just stared at the ground in front of her. She said, "What do you think?" He looked at her with sad eyes and made a small shake of his head.

She didn't know what he meant. Did he mean she couldn't be saved? Did he mean they shouldn't try to save her? Did he mean the situation wasn't his to call? She realized he meant the decision would have to be hers. Hannah walked short steps away, and with bowed head and closed eyes, she strained her thinking—What to do? What could she do? She returned to Nimrod, and with tears flooding her eyes, told him there was nothing to be done. She couldn't risk infecting any of the pioneers, including the two children awaiting her return. "Let's leave," she said, and mounted her horse and started back.

After about a quarter mile, she reined the horse in and turned to Nimrod right behind her. "I can't," she said, shaking her head with self-reproach. "I can't leave a child to die without trying to save her." She brushed her eyes clear with the backs of her hands. "I would see her face every night for the rest of my life."

Nimrod said nothing. It was hers to work out.

Hannah released the reins and sat in the saddle as the horse browsed for grass. She bowed her head and rested her chin in a cupped hand and let the tears flow. She made her brain sweat, searching for a way to help the girl....Even if the girl lived, she would be contagious for at least ten days until the scabs fell off; there was no wagon space to even try to keep her quarantined on the trail; the other pioneers would be absolutely justified if they rebelled at bringing a smallpox carrier among them.

Hannah exhaled a deep breath of resignation and brushed aside her tears. At last, she vomited, but it wasn't about the smell. She reached down for the reins, and said to Nimrod in a cracked voice, "Let's get back."

They returned to the wagon train where Penney and Flora Dickens walked over to meet them. They listened as Hannah recounted what they had seen.

"Were they all dead?" Flora asked.

"There was nothing we could do," Hannah said.

Nimrod stepped to her side to offer comfort, but Hannah turned and walked away.

That night, as Rachel and Billy slept, Hannah lay in their tent and stared at the canvas ceiling. She felt shame and guilt as tears rolled down and blotted out on her rough pillow as an image of the suffering little girl filled her mind. Why more should she have done?

She also felt sorry for herself as her thoughts swung to the men in her life; a husband who abandoned her through suicide instead of turning to her; of another who abused her daughter in the most evil way; and now, a strange man, capable of tenderness, but who also served the angel of death. Which man is he?

Her self-pity turned to anger as she demanded of herself—Am I weak, or a fool, or both? What is it about me that leads me to such men? She left the questions unanswered as she nodded off to restless sleep. Waiting to enter her dreams were the brown eyes of a small Indian girl looking up at her with a plea for life on her smallpox-ravaged face.

CHAPTER THIRTY

They reached the headwaters of the Humboldt River at the springs that would, in time, become a town named Wells. The desert heat of September was at its brutal worst, especially for the sixteen adults, four children, and a baby who had traveled from the green fields of home to this smelly, arid sea of dust and sand.

The Humboldt wasn't much of a river, certainly not like the broad, deep rivers back east. It had a peculiar smell and the bitter taste of alkali. There were no cheers among the sixteen adults and their children grouped on the bank. It was of no comfort to be told they were in the possibly hostile country of Mexico. In front of them was a faint trail of wheel ruts in the sandy dirt stretching over the horizon and deeper into the unknown.

"This is it? This is a river?" Flora scoffed. "It's like a creek, and it smells."

Nimrod laughed and said, "Look all around, Flora, everywhere else. What don't you see?—water! Before we reach the mountains, you'll sing hallelujah over the taste of this river's water."

"That might be a stretch for me. I don't think I could get that thirsty," Aaron said. Nimrod's grin had a just-wait edge to it.

The Humboldt was narrow and shallow, but its water was life-giving, horrible though it tasted. Its alkali content often gave diarrhea or gastric misery to both pioneers and animals. The alkali was embedded in the land because the river flowed through the Great Basin, an ancient inland sea that left salt deposits which leached into the water. The Great Salt Lake to the east was the most significant example. Right at home was Hambo the donkey because he was a desert animal.

The river wandered through the desert like a confused snake.

The wagoneers were grateful it was level ground, compared to what they were used to, but it required numerous fordings to stay along the riverbanks. The linear distance of the Humboldt was three hundred miles. However, the twisting route meant the channel itself was twice the length. The Humboldt would grow smaller and more bitterly alkaline until it disappeared into an exhausted bog called the Humboldt Sink.

Beyond the sink was a stretch called the Forty Mile Desert. That garden of hell consisted of hot, soft sand and no water. Zero water. Nimrod kept quiet about it for the time being because he knew it would be the most brutal stretch of the entire trail.

A week down the Humboldt, Nimrod's prediction of vulnerability to the Indians came true. Despite two men guarding the herd in shifts, Paiutes snuck close and sank arrows into two steers. Fortunately, the working oxen were untouched.

Aaron and Penney stood looking down in forlorn silence at the wounded steers. Aaron said, "They're sneaky devils. They knew we'd have to leave these animals behind. Damn!" He kicked the dirt. "I couldn't have been ten yards from these animals when they got hit."

Penney said, "Then maybe we should be glad the Diggers ain't cannibals. Good thing we know a thing or two about butchering. Let's carve out the choice cuts, then leave the rest to the Diggers. Let 'em have what they came for. Maybe they'll be satisfied."

"I'll wager the opposite," Aaron said.

Two nights later, Tester was on guard when two Paiutes crept within an arrow's reach of the small herd. Tester saw only the shadows of the men, but took a snap shot which should have hit nothing but sagebrush. Instead, he heard a half-grunt, half-scream. He rushed back to the middle of the wagons shouting, "Indian attack! Indian attack!"

Men and women poured out of the wagons in various stages of dress, each holding a loaded weapon. Penney spread them around the wagons, both for cover and a field of fire. "Don't go off half-cocked and shoot each other," he cautioned.

Nothing happened. After a few minutes, Nimrod volunteered

to reconnoiter. "Don't shoot me," he called out three times and stepped into the dark. There was nothing beyond their perimeter except grazing cattle, and an unmoving form on the ground. Nimrod waited and watched several long moments before he reached down and discovered the Indian's body. He backed away toward the wagons, not taking his eyes off the darkness beyond.

The next night, Nimrod suggested to Penney to tell the guards to fire over the heads of any Indians sneaking in to shoot arrows into cattle. The next morning, they discovered another steer killed with arrows. Meister lashed out at Penney, "You told us not to shoot to kill. Well, look what it got us."

Penney's face reddened, and he started to respond, but Nimrod interrupted to say, "That was my idea. If we start killing them, they'll start killing us. We have to sleep sometime, and there's a lot more of them. We got to understand we're in their territory, and they's got hungry children. We'd do the same, you can bet. I've got it in mind to try something. Wish me luck." There was some muttering at his words, but no objection.

Agnes Patterson sobbed and said, "They're going to kill us all."

Nimrod reassured her and the others. "If they was going to do that, they would've already did it."

Nimrod rode Bub to a small hill about a quarter mile. He didn't know Paiute but could speak some Shoshone, a cousin tribe to the Paiutes. He hoped it would work. He dismounted, cupped his hands, and shouted at the top of his lungs. "Winnemucca. Chief Truckee. Captain Fremont. Kit Carson. *E aisen ne tei* [friend]. He repeated the message, mispronouncing "Wuna Mucca's name," then rode back to the train. He had more hope than optimism.

That night, they lost another steer. They devised a new procedure, which was to stop in the heat of the day to allow the animals to graze and rest, then at night corral them in the circle of wagons with guards posted. Over four days, they lost three more cattle, including two working oxen. On two mornings, they found arrows that were embedded in the sides of wagons or stuck in the ground among the cattle.

On each of the next four days, Nimrod shouted out his plea to the Paiute chief, wherever he might be if he were still alive.

On the fifth day, the pioneers arose with the fading of the gray sky to see a group of about twenty warriors arrayed in a line about two hundred yards distant. They were smaller and darker than the plains Indians, wearing breechclouts and holding weapons. The pioneers gripped their guns and stood frozen, returning the stares.

"Oh, Lord, we're dead," a woman wailed.

"Not yet," Nimrod called out. "If they wanted that, we'd have died in the middle of the night."

After a couple of tense minutes, a man stepped forward accompanied by two younger men who, it was learned, turned out to be his sons. He appeared to be in his late forties, which would make him an old man in Paiute society. He was about five feet, and his wrinkled skin had been blackened by years of exposure to a brutal sun. His eyes were bright, and his mouth smiled. He was unarmed, as were the other two. He was dressed in a feathered headpiece and wore an oversized, faded U.S. cavalry short jacket, the sight of which gave relief to Nimrod. It said the man was familiar with Americans. At least, that's what he hoped. Of course, he could have taken it off a dead soldier; Nimrod was aware of that, too.

Nimrod and Penney walked forward. Without speaking, they gripped forearms in greeting with the small man. Using signing and words from his limited Shoshone, Nimrod forwarded greetings from his friends Fremont and Carson.

Truckee squinted at Nimrod. "I don't know your face, I think."

"I here years ago with Captain Bonneville."

"You were not a chief."

"I young, no chief," Nimrod said. He praised the chief's leadership and said his kindness to Americans had spread far and earned much praise. Though Truckee beamed at the words, he also protested about the warrior who was killed three nights earlier.

Nimrod said he grieved for the man's kinfolk, but owners of cattle have a right to protect it from those who would take it without asking.

Truckee did not press his complaint, but said his people were hungry and had a right to payment for crossing their territory.

"We talk that," Nimrod said.

The chief also said that the wagons scared away game, and the cattle ate the vegetation, the seeds of which were important to the Indians' diet.

"We soon gone," Nimrod reassured him.

Truckee nodded. "Will please people. But your people much to teach us."

During their back and forth, Nimrod noticed the discomfort of the younger son, who was about twenty. When he shifted, Nimrod saw a nasty carbuncle on the man's shoulder, a cluster of smaller boils. It was puffed up, angry red, and spread over his skin to about three inches in diameter. Nimrod knew the pain had to be severe for the young man. In an aside, he spoke to Penney, who nodded and returned to the wagons.

Truckee frowned at the distraction but was reassured when Nimrod turned back to him with a smile and more praise. Within minutes, Penney returned with Hannah, who was carrying a small bag. She walked up to great curiosity from the Paiutes. Hannah went to the side of the young man and examined the enraged mound of erupted skin. She removed a lancet, a small knife. The young man's eyes widened as he backed away. At a sharp word from Truckee, he stopped. Without a word, Hannah gestured for him to sit on the ground. She steadied herself with a hand on his shoulder, and with the other lanced the carbuncle, making sure to pierce all of it, which required multiple cuts.

When she first cut, the young man howled in pain and surprise, then clenched his hands and gritted his teeth until she was finished. As the abscess drained down his back, the man sighed in relief. A bit early, because the pain had not ended, not quite. Hannah opened a small bottle of whiskey and splashed it on the wound to sterilize it. Caught by surprise, the man gave a sharp scream, but caught himself, realizing it was unworthy of a warrior. Hannah then took a long narrow strip of cotton cloth and wrapped the wound. Finished, she stepped back to see his reaction. The man stood, flexed his shoulders, and beamed in gratitude at the relief she had given.

Truckee asked if Hannah were for sale. Nimrod bit his tongue to avoid a smile and translated it to Hannah. He asked with a straight face, "How much should I ask for?"

Hannah was taken aback, but then saw the humor of it, and said, "Tell him the price would be too high. I would be a troublesome wife."

"Too late. I already sold you," Nimrod teased.

Nimrod turned back to Truckee and asked if he would accompany the wagon train to the edge of the Forty Mile Desert and guarantee safe passage. He then asked Penney to summon Cohen.

Truckee paused with reluctance. "It is far; much to do here," he signed. Meanwhile, Cohen had arrived and stood nearby. He had an object in his hand by prior arrangement. Nimrod reached out and was handed the French officer's curved cavalry saber, Cohen's souvenir from the Waterloo battlefield. Nimrod pulled the saber from its engraved brass scabbard and held it flat with both hands in front of Truckee. The saber had a filigree basket handle, and the blade glittered in the sun. Truckee's eyes reflected great envy. He had never seen such a thing but knew it was a symbol of great power, as well as a weapon. Nimrod handed the saber back to Cohen.

He signed to Truckee, "If guide to dry desert, this sword yours."

"No gift?" Truckee signed.

Nimrod replied the same way. "It is pay for service. You gift two steers." With that, Penney separated two steers from the dwindling herd and drove them toward Truckee's waiting people.

"They feast tonight," Truckee nodded with a smile, then said in mixed Shoshoni and signage, "I send sons guide you." Beyond that, no one would bother them, He said. He also would send runners ahead to give safe passage.

"When sons return, they have sword," Nimrod promised.

"I trust," Truckee said. The men again gripped forearms as Hannah stood in the background. Truckee's two sons squatted at the edge of the camp, watching and waiting. Penney had food and water sent to them.

After Truckee departed, Nimrod thanked Cohen for giving up his saber. Cohen laughed. "You're welcome. That fancy saber was the second best thing I got out of Waterloo."

Nimrod bit. "What was the first?"

"Me."

❦

The train plodded along the winding river day after day. Their fatigue was like a clock running down. Clothes were tattered with patches atop patches. Most people walked barefoot to save the shredded remains of shoes held together with rawhide strings and pieces of leather cut to fit atop the soles. Everyone tried to hold back a half-way decent pair to wear in the mountain snow they feared would be in their near future. Snow had become the ghost of their future.

Food was running low, as were the steers purchased at Fort Hall. Also, the dried vegetables Nimrod had urged to be purchased were beginning to run out. As the supply dwindled, the fear of scurvy mounted. They took advantage of wild onions along the riverbank, but they were not plentiful.

Nimrod rode back from a scout and called out to the women, "Bring those baskets over yonder. I've found us some buffalo berries."

"What in tarnation are those," Flora asked.

"The Paiutes call them *wea pu wi*. You won't forget 'em," Nimrod said, laughing. "This time of year, they're so sour they'll make you pucker like a thirsty fish. But they'll help keep the scurvy devil away."

The closer they got to the mouth of the Humboldt, the more plentiful the berries became. Nimrod said the berries could save them from scurvy since the Paiutes ate them, and they didn't have scurvy.

The animals were more worrisome. The oxen lost a couple of hundred pounds each, which meant they pulled slower with more struggling. Alongside the trail were the rotting carcasses of animals that had died in their yokes. The sight was a chilling reminder of what could happen to theirs. They tried to give the oxen more rest in the middle of the day and longer grazing time on the scrub grass along the river.

There had been no buffalo chips for many days since those beasts had more sense than try to forage on a dry plain. The substitute for fuel was sagebrush, which burned hot, but briefly, making a decent cooking fire impossible. As a result, much of the meat was eaten half raw.

Peoples' tempers were short, but because of low energy, conflicts were brief and were left at nasty words. Mosquitoes traveled in clouds and were so tormenting their victims would sometimes weep. The animals switched tails and suffered.

And graves, oh, yes. Grave markers appeared every few miles like warning signs. Some had doleful inscriptions expressing the anguish of those who had to go on. Occasionally, graves became chilling sights on the side of the trail. Nimrod carried a shovel, but sometimes didn't see them in time to cover. Coyotes would dig up remains to gnaw on bones. Indians did the same to steal clothing. In one nightmarish scene, a rotting corpse was left half-hanging out of a robbed grave. Mothers tried futilely to shield children from the sight. Inevitably, nightmares followed.

Penney urged drovers to rotate oxen often to avert exhaustion and called for rest periods every couple of hours or whenever an area with good grass was found.

Billy drove the oxen pulling Hannah's wagon. On the trail, Hambo would trot alongside him, though the donkey would occasionally wander among the wagons, perhaps looking for a dog to stomp or a sugar handout, then he would trot back to his preferred position. Being a herd animal, Hambo's natural position was with grazing livestock, which he would join every night. However, on the trail, the herd was moving, which is what Hambo did at Billy's side.

Billy kept up a chatter to the lead, or nigh, ox. He would never use a whip on the animals, just a rod to tap directions on the nigh ox and give orders in a loud but even voice. He never had to repeat a command more than twice. When he saw an appealing patch of grass in the distance, he would run ahead and gather an armful. When the team caught up, he'd feed it a handful at a time to Hambo while saying encouraging words he claimed the donkey could understand.

After setting up camp in the evening, Billy would lead the donkey to the grazing herd and leave him there for the night. In the morning, when Billy went with the other boys to bring the cattle in, Hambo would be waiting for him. Occasionally, a loud and sharp bray would be heard by the sleeping pioneers, but they quickly realized it was Hambo warning a hungry coyote to look elsewhere for a meal. If the warning was followed by a sharp yelp, it meant the coyote had not moved fast enough.

Watching Billy currying his donkey, Hannah grumbled to Nimrod, but with a smile. "If Billy gets any friendlier with that beast, he'll be sleeping in the tent with us,"

Nimrod laughed gently. "Every boy needs a dog."

As they were camped in the evening beneath the shadow of what would become Winnemucca Mountain, Agnes Patterson rushed over to where Hannah and Penney were standing. "Come quick, please," she said in a keening voice. "I think my Jasper is dead." The two rushed to her wagon with Agnes trailing and trying to keep up. After clamoring into the small space, Hannah checked his pulse and lifted his eyelid to see a fixed pupil. She turned to Penney and said in a soft whisper, "Yes."

Hannah climbed out of the wagon and put her arm around Agnes' shoulders. She needed to say nothing. Penney joined them and said kind words to Agnes. After a few moments as Agnes composed herself, he said, "What happened here, Agnes? Can you tell us?"

"I was returning from the ladies' area when I saw Simon Tester jump out of the wagon. He had Jasper's money belt. I called out to him, but he ignored me and rode off on Jasper's mare."

"Which way, Agnes?"

She pointed with a shaky finger. "The way we came."

Several pioneers had joined them to find out what the fuss was about. Nimrod was among them. From the edge of the camp, Truckee's two sons sat back on their haunches and observed the strange carryings-on of these white people.

Nimrod listened but said nothing. Penney explained to the others what had happened. Hannah, when asked, said she suspected heart failure, but couldn't be certain. Agnes nodded and said doctors back home said he had a weak heart. Agnes wrung her hands and said to no one in particular, "What am I to do? I lost my dear husband. I'm all alone in this terrible wilderness. All we had in the world was in his money bag, nigh on a thousand dollars gold coin."

Cohen said, "We can sort it all out later. Right now, the welfare of Agnes is our concern. I think some of you ladies should spend the evening with her in other quarters. Tomorrow, we can arrange services for this good man who was a friend to all."

A bed was made for Agnes in one of the less crowded wagons, and the women took turns keeping her company. In the morning, they would wash Jasper's body, and the men would dig a grave. Penney guided Agnes away from putting a marker in the ground since it would soon blow away, and would attract grave robbers.

Just as streaks of light lifted the gray of dawn, Nimrod was preparing Bub for the long ride to pursue Tester. Hannah came out of her tent and said in a hushed voice, "What are you doing?"

"I aim to get Agnes' money back. It's all she has."

"And how about Simon Tester."

He stopped cinching Bub's saddle and looked at her. He knew what this was about. "I ain't thought much about him."

"Will you kill him?"

His tone was defensive. "I hope not to since I'm not an executioner. I'd take no pleasure in it. But it might come down to his choice."

"Well, be careful," she said as she walked away, but her guarded reserve was obvious to him.

Nimrod watched her go, then returned to his task when Cohen approached, pulling a suspender over one shoulder. He didn't have to ask what Nimrod was up to. "You reckon you'll find him?"

"He'll stay on the trail we've been on 'cause he don't know nothing else. Fellers like that, they always make the mistake of pushing a horse too hard. The horse will slow down and then give out unless it gets rest. That's when I'll catch him."

"And then?"

"That'll be up to him. All I want is to get back that old lady's money. The rest is wait-and-see." He climbed into the saddle. "Y'all keep moving, Malachi. I'll catch up." He grinned. "If I'm able."

Cohen smiled. "You didn't say 'if'n.'"

"Well, then, I can't let all your educatin' go to waste, now can I?"

Cohen slapped Bub's rump, and Nimrod turned to his task and headed back down the trail they had covered the day before.

Nimrod rode as on a Sunday outing. He alternated Bub between a canter and trot, and let the mule set his own pace. Every hour, he would dismount and water the mule in the Humboldt and walk him for a few minutes. That night, he let Bub graze on the riverbank, then hobbled him in a small grove of cottonwoods, so if any Paiutes wanted to unleash arrows at Bub, they would have to get close. Nimrod figured they might see the danger to that. He put Bub's saddle blanket under a nearby tree. He sat against the tree trunk and dozed in the half-way manner of a man who was accustomed to being aware that danger could spring on him at any moment. It was programmed into his brain.

He woke just before first light, ate a slice of bread and chunk of dried beef, then was back on the trail at the same pace. It wasn't long before he saw the horse Tester had stolen standing loose and trying to walk with a severe limp. "Prairie dog hole," he assumed, a familiar danger on that ground.

He looked for Tester but didn't see him. A shot and the nearby singing of a bullet made him duck, and he jumped to move Bub behind a rock outcrop. Even the inept Tester could get lucky.

Nimrod spotted Tester by the gunpowder smoke in a thicket of reeds near the river. It would have been a doable shot for Nimrod, but he leaned back and waited.

"I didn't kill the old man," Tester shouted. The ragged sound of panic was in his voice. "You can have the money. I'll just wait for another wagon train, and I won't bother anyone back there again." His tone had changed to bargaining. Still, Nimrod waited in silence. Tester must have known another wagon train might not pass by for a week, or maybe not at all. He would also know Paiutes would arrive before that. Desperation was in his voice. He started to plead. "I'll surrender if you can promise they won't hang me," he shouted, trying to bargain. Again, no response. Tester's plea became more urgent, then turned to anger. "Why won't you answer me, Lee? What happens if I give myself up?"

Silence.

"They wouldn't hang me for an accident, would they? I didn't kill the old man. He attacked me when I was looking for a tool in the wagon....Answer me, damn you!"

Silence.

A long ten minutes of strained silence later, Nimrod heard another shot and saw the gun smoke coming from Tester's hiding place. He waited several minutes more, then crept forward, going from cover to cover with his own rifle pointed at the thicket. He raised his head to see Tester's rifle lying in the dirt beyond Tester's curled fingers. Nimrod recognized the sprawl of death. He walked up to Tester—dead, a suicide by a bullet hole in his temple.

Nimrod checked the horse and saw it had a broken leg. He removed the saddle and saddlebags, then put his pistol next to the horse's temple and fired. He stepped back as the animal collapsed. He made sure the Patterson money was in the bags, then mounted Bub. He looked down on the dead man without expression, then rode away.

The next evening, Nimrod had already ridden into the camp center as his presence was noticed. He dismounted, removed the saddle, and Tester's rifle and gave them to Penney. Just then, he saw Agnes Patterson beside her wagon, watching. She had grown frailer overnight, it seemed. The wrenching death of Jasper and the ensuing sense of abandonment worked on her spirit like a file on wood. Nimrod walked over with a group following him and said as he handed her the money pouch. "I believe this belongs to you, Agnes."

Agnes opened the pouch with shaking hands and saw the cluster of gold coins. Tears formed in her eyes, and she reached up and hugged him. "You're a gift from God." Men watching coughed to hide emotion, and women smiled with wet eyes.

He walked a short distance away and was followed by Penney, Hannah, and Cohen. The three had become de facto leaders since the break-up of the larger company. Preacher had excused himself. "What happened to Tester?" Penney asked.

Hannah was more direct. "Did you kill him?" Her expression

said she did not want it to be true.

He reacted to Hannah as though stung. "His horse went lame. He had to decide between coming back here or facing the Diggers. He took the easy way. He shot himself." Nimrod turned and led Bub away, leaving the others looking at his back.

CHAPTER THIRTY-ONE

The wagon train crept along the river for eleven more days, enduring the mosquitoes, sweating in the everyday heat, and shivering in the high-desert cold of the night. Sunburns piled atop sunburns. They built resentments toward their companions just because they were handy. Everyone grew thin, and some seemed wasted. The alkali river water caused diarrhea that drained the energy out of both humans and beasts. The oxen moved slower and with greater effort. In response, furniture and other personal items that held almost religious ties to the homes and families left behind were thrown out with tears and curses.

The front axle on Flora's wagon snapped, dragging her wagon to a halt against a rock alongside the trail. Flora's shoulders slumped as she stared at it, crumpled in the dirt with her belongings spilled out, and the confused oxen bellowing. She knew there was no replacement, and no one among the small group had the tools or skill to repair it.

Flora felt like crying, but damned if she were going to allow herself. Hannah came to her rescue, and Flora removed her most important possessions and two children and crowded into Hannah's wagon.

Flora allowed tears to flow as she discarded the few saved possessions that had been of value to her late husband, and of her own childhood. The wagon was cannibalized for parts. Andrew needed a wheel; Cohen, an axle; and Meister wanted to replace a bonnet because of a long rip.

Wood that had been the wagon was chopped for campfires. Her worn-down oxen were given to those with animals that had died or were lame or sick.

The small caravan moved on. More was falling apart, more

things than axles. As they pulled out, Flora looked back at the skeleton of her discarded running gear and thought it must have some symbolism, but an ominous one.

The pioneers regretted giving the fishing net to the Oregon group because, to their astonishment, the smelly river was home to plentiful fish. Using hook and line, they caught the occasional crappie, bass, channel catfish, and a few cutthroat trout. To their frustration, successful fishing took time, which they did not have. Nimrod shot two beaver and a raccoon to contribute variety to the diet, though no one said they enjoyed the strange taste.

Agnes Patterson declined by the day. Her body and spirit were drifting away without the anchor of her lifelong companion and the home they had left behind. The rough jarring of the wagon was cruel to her weakened body, but she did not complain, neither did she show interest in what was happening around her.

On the mid-day rest in the second week since Jasper Patterson died, Flora fast-walked to Hannah, and said, "You should come. Agnes is in a bad way." Not wanting to alert others, the two women moved without haste to Agnes' wagon. The old woman was lying on a featherbed on the floor of the wagon. She didn't seem in pain; in fact, her face was placid, and she had a small, kind smile. Hannah crept on her knees in the tight space with Flora on the other side and took Agnes' hand. Agnes, in turn, covered Hannah's hand with her own. "You're such a good woman," she said. "You must never stop giving comfort to others because you do it so well. You're needed." She turned to Flora and handed her the heavy leather bag containing her life savings. "Please give this to Nimrod Lee. He's the one who put himself in danger to bring it back to me. He's a good man, a strong man who has to do difficult things. He'll use it well."

Neither woman knew what to say. Agnes thanked them for coming, and said, "Now, if you dears will excuse me, there are many fond memories I want to revisit in this time." She closed her eyes. "I won't be long."

Agnes was buried the next morning in a small cottonwood grove on a rise near the river. No marker was placed. Preacher read from the Bible and said a prayer for the resurrection of the dead, then finished by saying, "She was a good woman. She loved her husband, and she had nothing but goodwill for all people. God rest her soul. Amen."

Flora left Hannah's wagon and took possession of Agnes' wagon and oxen. In the frank reality of the wilderness, Agnes' meager possessions were divided or laid along the trail in the possibility some stranger might make use of them.

When Flora gave Nimrod the money pouch, he stared with mouth agape at her, then at the money as though it were the Rosetta Stone. At first, Flora wasn't sure he understood it was a gift, but then he said, "No one has ever given me anything."

The Humboldt River, at last, trickled to a stop. The dwindling water was diffused over a marshy area called a sink. Over time it had become a swamp with deep, clinging mud in its middle. One creature that lived comfortably in the muck was the mosquito.

After the evening meal, the thirteen adults and their five children sat on camp chairs around a smoky fire and glumly watched it fail to keep the mosquitoes at bay. The children occupied themselves as children manage to do. Truckee's two sons sat a distance and watched. The pioneers slapped at the hated insects and turned to what was next.

Penney pointed to the west where an unbroken plain of dirt, sand, and stunted sagebrush stretched unbroken to the horizon. "This river is turning into a puddle like Nimrod said it would." He studied the land ahead. "I think we're on the edge of hell, is what I think." As the groans died down, he turned to Nimrod. "Tell us how best to get across this ugly stretch?"

Nimrod shook his head slowly and regretfully. "This is the by-God real desert. Forty miles of hard rock, soft sand, and no water."

Penney said, "We'll carry all the water we can."

"That's for certain sure, but never enough," Nimrod said. This is the part of the trail you'll always remember, but want to forget." He looked to the western sky. "What'll you reckon be the date today?"

Penney said, "I'd have to look, but it's getting on toward the end of September." He noticed Nimrod examining the sky. "You still worried about snow in the mountains?"

Nimrod nodded, deep in thought. "Yessir, I'm still worried about snow in the mountains."

After the morning meal, the pioneers were mingling toward the camp center. Penney broke off a long conversation with Nimrod and turned to the others. "Get rid of anything that's not a tool, or clothing, or can't be et or drunk. Weight means survival."

A man points to a rocking chair visible from the back of his wagon. "That was my grandmother's chair. My mama nursed me in it. I'd sooner stay behind myself than dump that. Others nodded support.

Nimrod rose, and the others grew quiet. "What you're seeing in front of us is four days of traveling through hot sun, soft sand, and dry land. Some have taken to call it the Forty-Mile Desert, which sounds mighty close to right. I can guarandamntee we'll get thirsty. We're going to get mighty thirsty." He waited for the sounds of dismay to die down. "This desert is why I axed you to collect them empty jugs and bottles. Fill anything and everthing that holds water. There ain't much forage hereabouts, but cut what you can and carry it along. We'll most likely lose some ox, so change them out from time to time as you see the need." He elected not to say they might lose some people, too.

Romantics rhapsodize about the desert as a beautiful, living thing. They have not stood in the sundown chill at the edge of a mournful, empty horizon of dirt and sand that offered not forage nor water nor hope. The pioneers looked at the bleakness and saw death, and when they looked closer, it was their own.

The next morning at dawn, before the heat had arrived, and one could move without breaking into a sweat, the wagons lined up, ready to enter the forbidding distance. Penney beckoned the sons of Truckee from their usual place on the edge of the camp. He handed them each a meal of dried beef and then beckoned for Cohen to present them with his French saber. The elder son accepted the saber with a grin and bow. No words were needed. The two Paiutes disappeared into the mist.

After eating, the pioneers drifted to where Penney was talking with Nimrod, Cohen, and others of the company. They had the same question: Where do we go next?

"Well, how about California?" Penney joked, but no one laughed. He became serious and turned to Nimrod, nodding his head in the direction of the desert. "What's out there?"

Nimrod said in a flat voice, "Nothing."

Ruth Cohen said, "I'm not worried about nothing. I'm worried about something."

"Sand. That's your something, Ruth. Sand." Nimrod stood up and gestured to the empty plain to the west. "What you see out there is the Forty-Mile Desert. Once you get in it, forty'll seem like four hundred. There's nary a drop of water until we reach what they're calling Truckee's River. Toward the end, the sand will be ankle deep. Pulling through it will kill some of our ox, sure as shooting." He shook his head in sympathy. "That's going to twist the innards of some of you because you'll have to lighten your load."

"Why are you telling us this?" Andrew said.

"I don't want you to be surprised."

"What do you mean, lighten our load?" Gertie asked.

"Just like I said, missus. The ox may not make it, as it is. You need to help them along by dumping what you can. Most important, keep food, clothes, tools, and guns."

The response to his words was an unhappy murmur. Martin Carter said, "Maybe we won't have to throw things out." His voice trailed off. "I mean, maybe,"

Nimrod shrugged. "Like a feller once said to me, 'If wishes was horses, beggars would ride.'"

"How long to get across, you figger?" Penney asked.

"Three days, maybe. Four days, likely." He peered closely at Penney, who looked peaked. "You okay, Captain?"

"Just a bit of a dizzy spell."

He looked at Penney with concern but said nothing. One didn't openly question the fitness of such a man. A few people discarded items, but they were of low weight and thrown away with groans. They filled every possible container with alkaline water.

❦

Deep thirst came for a visit on the first day, but on the second, it went to work. As the sun emerged over the eastern mountains behind, the wagons had already been two hours on the move over the sandy crust. The people were given just a pint of water that morning; the animals, nothing. At day's end, each ox and horse would be given a half-gallon. To a working animal, it was but a teaspoon.

It didn't take the heat long to catch up to the sun in the cloudless sky. Together, sun and heat, were brutal. It squeezed energy out of the body, dulled the mind, and withered the spirit. For the animals, it added tormenting thirst, an agony they had no choice but to accept. Muscles that had served human masters for millennia started to fail at the task, and the wagons slowed from two miles per hour down to a creaking one.

Great thirst is not pain, it's an urgency, a desperation that treats the body like a twisted rag. It so torments the mind that nothing else exists; not love, not hate, not God, not…anything. You would sell your soul for water, and if that were insufficient, you might be tempted to offer your firstborn.

At first, the body complains of thirst by a yearning for a drink, then the mouth dries, and swallowing becomes difficult, then the whole being pleads for water as sweating continues to empty the body of what it cries out for.

The day crept to one p.m., and the sun was at its most brutal at one-hundred-one degrees. Lizards took shelter under sagebrush, but for anything larger, there was no escaping. The small column plodded with dragging feet over the sand-crust like sleepwalkers. The animals shuffled along with heads down.

The pioneers fantasized about water. Clara recreated in her mind the driving rain of the storm on the Big Blue. She tried to recreate in her mind what it felt like to have the cold drops smash into her face, driven by a howling wind.

Children didn't have enough experience to fantasize. They just suffered. They tried to cry, but there was nothing to make tears, so they whimpered.

Cohen tried to remember what water tasted like, and how it felt to be splashed by it. He couldn't, but he didn't stop trying. He tried to pass the time by imagining how he would draw the scene of their struggles.

Flora kept a worried eye on her teenage daughter, Alice. The girl had developed diarrhea and severe headaches, so Flora ordered her into the wagon, even though there was an urgent effort to reduce wagon weight. Clara Penney happened by and heard Alice crying in the wagon. She walked over and extended her own cup to Flora.

Flora looked at her with gratitude mixed with concern. "Are you sure? You need water, too."

Clara smiled through cracked lips and pointed to Alice. She took a tiny sip and handed the rest to Flora who took it, and said through cracked lips, "Bless you."

Most pioneers started the next day barefoot to save shoes for the rocky mountain passes they knew were ahead. However, the sun hyper-heated the sand to the extent it became unbearable underfoot.

Dehydration cuts off the ventilation system for man and beast. Sweat cools the core temperature of the body. The lack of sweat kills. Cattle don't sweat. They keep cool by breathing out heat, but if water is not ingested, body heat overwhelms their system.

The pioneers had to stop midday to rest and give themselves and the animals small amounts of water. It didn't do much good, but it was something.

Oh, and how the oxen suffered. At four p.m., an ox in the Proctor team fell and couldn't get up. They removed its yoke and put in one of the remaining steers. The new animal was not trained, but it would have to go along with the other oxen and at least do some pulling.

The downed animal was shot and butchered for choice cuts before moving on. Nimrod looked over his shoulder at the carcass already being fed upon with vultures darting in and out between snarling coyotes.

That won't be their last meal from this wagon train, Nimrod thought.

The meat from the butchered oxen was put over small fires, but was taken off half raw before they had to move on. The beef was repulsive at first, but the distaste decreased as the hunger increased.

They stopped again in the late afternoon for two hours because the oxen were starting to balk. They gave the animals a half-gallon of water and each other a pint.

Gertie tried to nurse baby Caleb and realized she had nothing to offer but a few drops of milk. She opened the baby's diaper and felt. Dry. His last urine was three hours previous. His eyes were sunken, and his body was listless. She cried out for Aaron to fetch Hannah, who came running.

Hannah felt the beginning of a fever on the baby's forehead, and said, "This baby needs water. He needs water bad.

Hannah thought of Nimrod. She shouted as loud as she could, and he came running. "This baby needs water badly. Please, please find some. Hurry."

Nimrod went to Cohen who doled out the water. "Malachi, Gertie's baby needs water, bad."

"There's not enough to go around. What am I to do?" Cohen said with anguish in his voice.

"Malachi, I'll tell you what you can't do: You can't let the baby die."

Cohen shook his head in self-disgust. "Yes. Of course. Forgive me." He doled out a pint and thrust it toward Nimrod."

Meister happened to be standing nearby and overheard the transaction. "Wait a minute! You can't play favorites with that water. We agreed that—"

Nimrod said, "I'm going to pretend you're not standing here. That'll save me the trouble of running you off." With that, he turned and hurried back to the Proctor wagon.

Gertie reached for the water, and said, "Oh, thank you, Jesus."

"And Nimrod," Hannah said with a smile.

The pioneers picked at their rations in a half-stupor. When thirst becomes desperate, hunger is crowded out. The animals wouldn't graze at all on the scrawny weeds. When Penney called for everyone to prepare to go on, there was a low groan from most; not a groan of anger, but of despair, which is far more troubling. Preacher began reciting.

The Lord is my shepherd, I shall not want.

He maketh me to lie down in green pastures; he leadeth me beside the still waters.

Yea, though I walk through the valley of the shadow of death, I will fear no evil, for thou art with me; thy rod and thy staff, they comfort me....

As they listened, Penney turned to Nimrod, and said, "Me, I'd favor one of them green pastures."

Nimrod said, with a wisp of a smile through parched lips, "I'll trade you a green pasture for some still waters."

Hannah returned to her wagon to hear Rachel sobbing inside. Hannah held her daughter's head in her lap and smoothed her hair. It was then she noticed Rachel was weeping, but with dry eyes. The body had no water to spare for tears.

Hannah didn't know what to say. How, she asked herself, do I redeem myself for causing the trauma she suffered at the hands of an evil man, and for bringing her to this awful place? Instead, she pulled her daughter close and held her until the sobbing faded into soft breathing, then the girl reached up and returned the hug.

Late afternoon, when the low sun in the west had leveled its beam at the people like a cannon barrel, Penney felt dizzy and had trouble walking straight.

Just keep going, he told himself. It'll pass.

But it didn't. In a moment, his vision went black, and he pitched face-down on the sand. Everything stopped as the pioneers rushed forward to circle their leader as though staring down at him might have therapeutic value.

Hannah rushed up, pushed through between Cohen and Aaron, and said, "Pick him up and carry him to their wagon. Put him down on the shady side." When Penney was placed where she directed, Hannah said, "Bring water."

Meister again protested what he saw as the unfair use of water. "We don't have much left. Some of that is mine."

Hannah glared at him and said in a growl, "Water, damn it. Bring it." Meister backed away, and Flora brought a cupful. Hannah leaned over Penney and poured a small amount through his lips. She dipped a corner of her apron in the water and patted his forehead with it. By that time, Clara had come running and kneeled down beside her husband's head. She could say nothing, but she caressed his cheeks with a look of both love and dread.

In a couple of minutes, Penney opened his eyes and oriented his gaze to the faces surrounding him. He forced a smile, and said, "Well, folks, now you all know the truth of it: I ain't no spring chicken. I just had a little spell. I'll be back at it directly." He tried to struggle to his feet, but Clara pushed him down, and Hannah told him he was done for the day.

Cohen suggested they would stop for the day to allow Penney time to rest, and to hope rest was all he needed. He also knew their defense against thirst was to not sweat, human or beast. However, the desert wasn't about to show mercy.

Penney overheard Cohen, and said in a croaking voice, "Go on. Damnit, go on." He was helped into his wagon as the train plodded on for another hour before stopping. He pulled himself up to the driver's bench, and then slumped against the back rest with exhaustion. Someone handed Penney a ladle of water which he smelled before tasting. "Well, it ain't much, but it's wet." He made a face and handed the empty cup to Flora. "Just let me out of that God—" He reflexively looked at Preacher. "out of that consarned wagon. I ain't suited to ride in a bone-breaker like— like—" He couldn't think of a comparison.

Nimrod furnished one. "—Like an old bull who don't have the sense to know he ain't a calf no more."

Penney looked at the bleak landscape. "This God-forsaken place ain't a fit place to bury a rat." He couldn't visualize five or six years into the future when the land they were crossing would be paved with scores of graves of gold-rushers and the bleached bones of hundreds of horses and oxen.

It didn't take Penney more than a few hours to recuperate enough to leave the wagon, but he would tire quickly. He could only walk a little, and then would have to ride. He called Cohen over, and said, "Malachi, you better take over. I don't seem to have the get-up-and-go to boss this outfit." He laughed. "But I'll always have enough piss and vinegar to criticize."

Again, the pioneers ate their distasteful, slim dinner with the acceptance that it didn't have to taste good to keep them alive. Once again, the animals ate not at all. The men and women gathered around Cohen, to whom they gave unspoken acceptance of his leadership. As the stress of their danger grew, decisions became more democratic. Women claimed a stronger voice with no objection. Social convention gave way to necessity.

If anyone slept that night, it was with a feverish nightmare about water, followed by a fervent prayer for water. A prayer unanswered.

The following day, the train struggled along at a listless ten miles per day. The heat, thirst, and suffering marked their faces as they listened to the children's weeping and pleading for water. The side of the trail was littered with bed headboards, rocking chairs, books, and memorabilia from their own and earlier trains. Each keepsake tore the hearts of those who threw them out.

More haunting were the few graves scratched out of the ground by pioneers who went before. They were just a few yards off the trail. Some had scrawled markers, but there was no way of knowing how many were anonymous under the sand.

Children pleaded for water. Animals dropped in their yokes. Two wagons fell apart and were cannibalized. The remains were left by the roadside.

The next day was over soft sand that grabbed like thick mud at hooves, wheels, and shoes. The hard going intensified demands on oxen that had little remaining to give. Several refused to go on despite the whip and prod. They were shot to spare them dying of thirst or being torn apart by predators. As time allowed, steaks were cut off, hastily fried, and eaten near raw.

Two more wagons had to be abandoned so teams could be strengthened to aid remaining weak oxen. Remaining baggage was restricted to food, clothing, bedding, tents, and necessary light tools. An inventory of who owned what was scrawled on a pad by Cohen. Pioneers were told by Penney to keep their money and jewelry on their persons.

Preacher had become a different person; rather, he had become the person he rediscovered within himself. He walked from wagon to wagon, giving encouragement, saying prayers with those who asked, listening to people's fears, encouraging them, and telling doubters that God was watching over them. He even gave his water ration one afternoon to one of the children crying tearless in the

throes of the agony of thirst. Watching him minister, Penney joked
to Cohen, "You know, I sort of miss the old Preacher. It's more
interesting to dislike a man than to admire him."

The caravan snail-paced on in silence except for the squeal of
ungreased axles and the snorts of laboring oxen. Cohen walked in
a shuffle-step trance. He could think of nothing but water, so he
tried not to think at all. His body demanded water—Please! Please!
I'm dying! Give me water! He prayed silently. He couldn't have
water, and he couldn't stop the pleading.

As he struggled to keep pace alongside his plodding oxen,
Andrew tried to spit the nasty taste out of his dry mouth. He
puckered and tried to suction up saliva. There was none. His eyes
were dry and felt like sand was under the lids. His head pounded,
and energy drained from his body. Weeping would have to be done
without tears. Even the loose bowels from alkali water dried up.
Diarrhea is mainly water.

Andrew was one of several who had slid from moderate to
severe dehydration. His condition was not far from being too far.
The body can tolerate astonishing abuse, but it draws the line at
lack of water. Water is life. Its absence is death.

The suffering was most intense on the children. They had no
understanding of why their parents could not help them. The
sobbing pleas from the young ones caused more anguish in the
parents than the thirst itself.

As they inched along, one slow wheel-turn after another, there
were no friends, no enemies, no lovers. There were no dreams, no
ambitions, no memories, no hunger. Only desperation for water.

It was mid-afternoon. The animals were on the edge of
collapse. They stood dumb in their yokes and suffered. Cohen,
who had taken charge of the water, gave each pioneer a half-cup
of warm alkali water from the one remaining container. To each,
it was the psalmist's waters of Babylon. They governed their haste
by handling the tin cup like fine crystal lest a drop fall in the sand.
Their drying-out organs had a momentary revival, but it teased
more than helped.

CHAPTER THIRTY-TWO

As they pushed the oxen and themselves onward for another hour, finally— a blessed 'finally'—the animals perked up; their pace increased, and their lowing became louder. Nimrod shouted, "River ahead. Unyoke the ox. Fast."

"Why, for God's sake?" Meister shouted in confusion.

"The animals smell water. You can't stop them. They'll go out of control."

The pioneers came alive with a jolt and ran to free the frenzied oxen of their yokes while avoiding slashing horns. The animals took off to the west at a dead run for the river a mile distant. Nimrod struggled to hold Bub back. He shouted to Aaron, "Get mounted. We can't let them drink too much. Hurry." With that, he prodded Bub into a fast canter and followed.

When Aaron arrived at the riverbank, Nimrod was already shooing and prodding the oxen away from the water. Together, they kept them back; then, after a half-hour, let them return to drink. The second time, the oxen weren't so frantic and retreated themselves when they were full and turned to grass growing nearby.

As that happened, the pioneers stumbled out of the desert and threw themselves down at the river's edge to scoop water into their mouths. After several minutes, Hannah rolled onto her back in the dust, and whispered, "Oh, thank you, dear Lord."

Gertie, holding baby Caleb, had trailed the others. Aaron filled a jug, mounted, and hurried back to meet her. Before she would take a drink, she soaked a rag from her pocket and repeatedly squeezed the water into her baby's mouth.

As the pioneers relaxed on the riverbank, they started to think of things other than misery, including what lay in front of them. They studied the western horizon, and when cloud cover parted, a terrifying sight appeared. High above them in the vague distance rose the Sierra Nevada, the mountains of snow.

The distant skyline was dominated by dark peaks. Preacher said they reminded him of the teeth of a crosscut saw, cold and sharp.

The earlier mountains flanking the valleys they had gone through were ignored in the throes of their struggle. But these! These monsters on the horizon were their enemies. Backbreaking granite ascents in their path were reminders of the threat of snow and ice that could bury them in frozen graves.

"Oh, my God," Gertie said in an awed, scared voice as she looked up at the gray mountains. She tightened the grip on her baby.

Preacher's voice rang above the stunned reactions of the others:

Fear thou not; for I am with thee: be not dismayed; for I am thy God: I will strengthen thee; yea, I will help thee; yea, I will uphold thee with the right hand of my righteousness.

"Amen," said Cohen. "Thus saith the prophet Isaiah."

The pioneers continued to stare at what lay in their path, then turned away.

"Now, what?" The next morning, Martin spoke the question on the minds of the other pioneers. He raised his eyes to the peaks in the distance as Nimrod considered the question.

"Well, I ain't been past here, but I talked to fellers I trust who know the lay of the land. I reckon they gave me a pretty clear picture. We follow this river west-southwest nigh on eight days 'til we reach Truckee's Lake. There's where you'll put feeling into your prayers. We have to climb a steep pass that'll take us to the summit. That climb will make all of us hanker for a corncob pipe and a warm fire by the hearth."

Cohen shook his head in admiration. "Just listening to you talk—you know this country for a fact, even the parts you haven't seen. You seem to be acquainted with every tree and rock."

Nimrod nodded his thanks at the compliment. "I been told I got a feel for getting where I want to be. One feller called me a mountain goat." He laughed and looked discreetly at Hannah. "I reckon he weren't talking about the smell."

Cohen followed up. "And the mountain men who don't have such a feel, what happened to them when the beaver trade died?"

"Some went back down the Missouri. Some married into tribes. Some are in the bone orchard."

The pioneers entered the month of October as the calendar crept faster. They did not stop to admire the gold tint of the poplar tree leaves and the nip in the night air.

Truckee's River was not what they had hoped. It started out with pleasant days through a verdant meadow that one day would hold the casinos of Reno. However, as it started the climb into the mountains, it became a narrow river of frigid mountain run-off rushing crazily over a rocky bed hemmed in by high banks. It almost made them forget the desert they had recently escaped. Memory is short, and misery once past can seem almost nostalgic.

Because of the narrowness of the canyon and the twists and turns of the river, they had to cross time and again. At times, they had to drive down the middle of the stream with the fast current tugging at their legs. Fortunately, they were at the end of the dry season, and the river was at its most shallow.

Noticed by everyone was the diminishing strength of Shadrach Penney. Since his collapse in mid-desert, his steps were slower, even tentative. He spent more time in his wagon. The raspiness of his voice had always been there but had seemed more tied to age than to vulnerability. Gradually, and without objections, Hannah edged into leadership alongside Cohen. She was the one who often suggested the evening stopping place, the one to inquire of everyone's health, and to encourage everyone's spirit.

To his credit, Cohen was secure enough to partner with a woman. Both relied on Nimrod's advice, and often conferred with Penney.

She said to Nimrod, "Do you think I'm too bossy?"

"Do you?"

"I'm asking your opinion."

He grinned and lifted his hat. "I'm just the hired help, ma'am. Just get us where we're going."

His response pleased her. Leadership gave her a warm, satisfying feeling of power. It was similar to suffering patients looking at her with trust, knowing she cared and would do her best.

Her assertiveness was viewed with acceptance by Nimrod, encouragement by Cohen and Flora, and resentment by Meister. The others didn't much care.

Pushing wagons over rocks and prodding the remaining oxen to labor in knee-high water was misery. They were out of the desert, but not out of danger. Suffering had not retreated.

In yet another narrow canyon passage, the pioneers were forced into the water to wade until the banks widened.

The wagon of Andrew and Martin was bringing up the rear when a submerged rock snapped the front axle, overturning it with a crash. The contents spilled into the water causing women to shriek and men to swear as their keepsakes and tools submerged or floated away. People hastened to save what they could while men freed the oxen.

Nimrod said, "Well, let's get this thing turned over, but it don't look good." The men attached two yoke of oxen at right angles to heave it back on its wheels.

Cohen looked up from what he was doing. "Has anyone seen Ruth?" he shouted above the roar of the water.

"She was near the far bank a few minutes ago," Flora said. Cohen nodded and went back to work. Suddenly, he saw many sheets of paper floating downstream. He uttered an anguished shriek. "My God! Andrew was looking at my drawings. They were in that wagon."

The overturned wagon responded to the straining oxen and creaked back to its wheels with a crash. Andrew went to the far side to inspect it and glanced down. He uttered a scream that frightened the others who watched him reach down into the rushing water. Strange sounds were coming from his throat.

When the others reached him, a cascade of screams and sobbing erupted. Gertie, standing on the narrow bank, called out, "What is it? What is it?"

In moments, two men walked out of the water carrying Ruth Cohen. She had been wedged between rocks under the surface by the overturned wagon.

They laid her on the ledge of the bank. Her face was calm with her wet hair spread over the ground. She was unmarked except for a forehead cut. Cohen rushed over and lay down beside her. He made frantic attempts to breathe air into her lungs. After a long two minutes, Hannah put hands on his shoulders and guided him to his feet.

"It's no use, dear friend," she said, and reached down to close Ruth's eyes. The others were benumbed.

Malachi just stood there. No tears, no oaths, no groans. He looked down at Ruth and then at the trees, and then the sky, and then back to Ruth. As the shock wore off, Cohen's stricken face took on the deep ravages of grief. He sat beside her body and cradled her head in his lap. The others moved away out of respect for his mourning. He forgot the drawings that had floated away.

Hannah directed three men to dig a deep grave in a pleasant grove a distance away. After two hours, Hannah went to Cohen and, with her hand on his shoulder, said, "We don't know all the customs, Malachi, but we'll prepare her with dignity." Cohen looked up without expression, then nodded and walked away to be by himself. The women washed Ruth's body, fixed her hair, and dressed her in the best dress of hers they could find. A clean white cloth was placed over her face. At sundown, they carried Ruth's body to the burial site located on a grassy flat between towering pine trees. They lowered the body to the bottom. They stood around and looked down into the grave, then at her widower. Preacher read passages from the Old Testament. Malachi reached down for a handful of dirt and dropped it onto the body. Each of the women dropped an orange-red alpine lily, picked from a bed Clara had noticed near the river.

Malachi recited the kaddish, the Hebrew mourner's prayer, in English, so his friends could follow along. His voice wavered, but he pressed on:

"...*Blessed and praised, glorified and exalted, extolled and honored, adored and lauded be the name of the Holy One, blessed be He, beyond all the blessings and hymns, praises and consolations that are ever spoken in the world; and say, Amen.*"

As he closed the prayer, Malachi turned to the others. "Ruth was a good woman, an upright woman, and a wise woman who loved God, her children, and this husband who did nothing better than to love her in return." He paused, then added, "When you're a Jew in central Europe, you begin every sunrise knowing grief may be your lot at sunset. Ruth wanted this new land as much as I, and now she is buried in it, and so shall I be. Thank you, my friends."

The losses incurred on traveling from Fort Hall left them with two wagons, nine oxen, two mules, one horse, and one donkey. The struggle up the resisting river went on.

A day later, Nimrod's pack mule slipped on a rock and broke a leg. He unpacked it, then with a regretful pause, removed his revolver and shot it. They then hitched two oxen to the carcass and dragged it to the bank. Nimrod cut steaks from its rump to put on their evening fire, which the pioneers ate glumly, though they were famished after a day with no other food.

The canopy of Jeffrey pines, Douglas firs, and incense cedars blocked sunlight and the warmth it could have offered. The huge trees and their shadows gave the flatlanders a claustrophobic sense of being entombed.

Each night the weary oxen pulled the wagons out of the stream. They found a flat area where they could build fires and try to dry clothes and wait for teeth to stop chattering. Every day, they blinked back tears and threw out more keepsakes and "indispensable" items that no longer justified the weight. In a week, they had climbed from four thousand feet to six thousand, and the night chill hovered close to freezing. During those few days, three oxen wandered off.

Several times each day, Nimrod studied the sky. Once, Hannah asked what he was looking for. "Something I ain't seen yet. A turn of the weather." he said. "Maybe I won't." After one evening meal of mule meat scraps, she noticed him fashioning something near the fire. He was working with willow branches and long strings of rawhide he had carried in his pack.

"What're you doing?" Hannah asked, curious.

"Making snowshoes."

"Oh," she said, not needing to ask why. "Do you know something the rest of us don't?"

"I hope there's nothing to know," he said, and continued with his task.

On the eighth day after leaving the desert, the pioneers made their way to a rise among a grove of pines. Before them, shimmering in the sun, was Truckee's Lake. It was an elongated, snow-fed body almost three miles long and a half-mile wide. Twenty miles to the southeast was a huge alpine lake later to be named Lake Tahoe. Truckee's Lake was named for the ubiquitous Paiute chief. However, soon after the tragedy of the following winter of 1846, it would forever after be called Donner Lake.

In a quiet moment of rest, Hannah sat down next to Cohen. She said, "Malachi, I know it's not important to you at this time, but I'd like to say I'm sorry your beautiful drawings were lost."

"Thank you," he said, then lowered his head and spoke barely above a mumble, "Those images are in my mind and can be saved. All else is lost."

She put her arm around his shoulder, then left him to his thoughts.

As they made their way to the lake's edge, Penney leaned with weak legs against a wagon. His strength was returning, but he was still unsteady from his collapse. Cohen reached a hand out to support him. Had he done so two weeks ago, Penney would have given him a sharp rebuke.

Penney studied the beautiful lake and shook his head. "If it was anywhere else, I'd like to have a Sunday picnic on a spot like this and throw a line into them waters."

Penney's attempt at pleasantry fell flat for Martin. His eyes darted, he hyperventilated, and moaned and whimpered his despair. "We're all going to die," he shouted in anguish. The mind-twisting effects of his laudanum addiction had never quite left him.

Andrew reached out and kneaded his shoulders. "Relax, relax, relax." The others turned their gaze to the west, and the cliff a mile beyond the head of the lake.

"Is that where we have to go?" Cohen asked.

Nimrod said, "If'n—if" you're asking if we got to climb yonder little-bitty hill, the answer is 'yep.' You best wear your walking shoes."

"I've got a baby. How do we get up there?" Gertie asked, studying the escarpment rising high above.

Nimrod sought to reassure, so he flashed a brave smile. "Things look different from a distance. By my eyeballing, this cliff yonder is maybe a thousand feet, give or take a hundred. It's what we have to climb to get to the top of the pass. Everthing else hereabouts is like a brick wall." He swept the forbidding mountains with his arm, then again pointed toward the cliff. "Yonder, I can see there's enough of a slant to allow footholds if you step in the right places. We can get the animals up to the heights if we push them. Kit Carson told me about a train guided by a feller I know, old Caleb Greenwood. He's a man don't get lost. Greenwood made it through to Sutter's Fort in the snow, just last year. Even took a few wagons, but they was fresh and had the ox to do it. We don't."

"Just a minute," Flora said. "Do I understand we're not going to take these two wagons up?"

Nimrod pursed his lips and nodded confirmation of her question. "These here ox ain't got enough left to do it."

Penney spoke up. "Nimrod's right. I been working oxen my whole life. These critters is spent."

Nimrod looked each individual in the face. "We gonna walk out, folks. We got no choice. It'll be a pleasant hike in the trees."

"Sounds like a hard road to travel," Aaron said.

"If you live to a hundred, you ain't never going to travel a harder one."

There was a rumbling of shock, fear, and anger. "We can't leave those wagons. I'll lose the few things I've been able to save," Meister said in angry disbelief.

"There ain't nothing in them wagons you can't replace. The onliest thing you can't replace is your life," Nimrod said, glaring at Meister. "Of course, you can stay and guard your wagon, but it'll be a long winter."

Hannah felt empowered to gain control of the conversation. "Nimrod, what happens to the wagons?"

"We can park them a short ways off in that pine grove. Folks can take a few valuables, money, jewelry, and a couple of light keepsakes—light. I say again, they have to be light. You cover what's left with a wagon bonnet, with branches on top; fir be best."

"What else?" Gertie asked.

"Warm clothes, shoes, and what little food you got. Bring firearms and shot. Bring Lucifer matches, all you have. And if you have flint, steel, and dry tinder, bring those. I'll show you how to make knapsacks out of blankets."

Nimrod had made certain that shoes were collected and saved from all of the abandoned wagons. He had them distributed according to fit, but made sure everyone had extra shoes.

Hannah turned to Cohen. "Malachi, do you have anything to say?"

Cohen shook his head no, content to let Hannah keep the lead.

"How about the wagons? Won't Indians plunder them?" Aaron asked.

"Not much they'll be able to use if they even find them. Indians ain't planning on planting a crop. You can haul them wagons out come spring when the snow melts and the ground dries, if you're of a mind."

Hannah was aware he said "you" instead of "we."

Preacher took solace that the western side would be on a moderate downgrade, according to what Nimrod had earlier told them. "That's a relief. Once we get up there, sounds like it'll be a walk-out on a down slope, gradual like."

Nimrod said, "Walking downhill can tucker you out same as uphill."

Preacher scoffed. That's hogwash, Nimrod. I've walked up, and I've walked down. Down is better."

Nimrod shrugged. His smile was thin, but he obviously enjoyed the give and take. He liked this version of Preacher much better. "Well, 'gradual' in an Iowa cornfield is one kind of gradual; these here mountains have a different kind of gradual. The ground is rough with ravines and boulders. You can fall a long ways. Rocks that'll break an axle have an easy time with a leg. It's downhill, I grant you, but it ain't a Sunday stroll."

Hannah said, "How long to Sutter's Fort? We're almost out of meat, except for the few fish we've been able to catch. Vegetables have been gone for almost a week. Soon, I fear we'll lose the strength and will to go on."

"Once we work our way down to the foothills, Sutter's will be four, maybe five days," Nimrod said.

And between here and the foothills?" Aaron asked.

"I can't tell you that," Nimrod said. "A week, maybe less, maybe longer. Depends."

"Depends on what?" Martin asked, suspicious.

"On what kind of mood old man mountain is in."

Nimrod called over to Aaron. "Pick out the weakest ox, take it beyond those first trees and shoot it. Take good cuts and cook them on an open fire, best you can. Get someone to help you."

In front of everyone, Hannah squared her jaw, and said, "Shouldn't you have talked to me or Malachi before giving orders?"

Nimrod cocked his head and squinted in thought, then looked into her face. "Yes, ma'am, I reckon I should. I got to remember to respect leadership."

Hannah studied him with narrowed eyes to detect sarcasm. She saw none. She smiled and said, "Thank you."

Meister asked, "How many times you been over this route?"

"I been to where Truckee's River turned north. Not a lick beyond. I'm going by what I learned from men who know. Back in thirty-four, we went south to a pass Joe Walker found, and crossed into California."

"Damnit to hell!" Meister shouted. "Now we find out we got a guide who doesn't know where he's going."

Nimrod stared at him, but he said nothing.

Penney sat up and coughed. The others turned to him. "Stop your damned whining. Did y'all expect a road map? This man knows what he's doing." He leaned back out of breath.

As they talked, a cold drizzle started, and quickly accelerated into a steady light rain. The dark sky of mid-afternoon did not auger well for what might be coming.

Hannah could see Nimrod had said his piece. "All right, folks, let's get under shelter and see how dry we can stay."

Darkness fell like a weight, and the rain turned to sleet. To escape the stinging ice pellets, adults and children took refuge in the two remaining wagons. They huddled where they could find space. The animals were staked under trees.

Hannah went rigid to feel Meister's head leaning against her outer thigh, and she edged over to the extent she could. As the night wore on, she gave a mental shrug and ignored Meister and tried to sleep.

None of them paid attention to who was at their side or feet. The main concern was to avoid the leaks of the worn wagon bonnets, and the sharp edges of equipment surrounding them. The air was filled with flatulence gases, snoring, hacking coughs of those fighting colds, the fussing and crying of children, mutterings during nightmares, and adults grousing at others crowding them. A few soft prayers were drowned out.

Spirits were dragged down by pioneers lamenting their fate. Survival was all they wanted and muttered prayers for. They were brain-dead as to why they were here in this harsh, dangerous place.

Toward midnight, the sound deadened, and the pioneers fell into shallow slumber. All except Nimrod. For him, there was nothing comforting about the quiet that replaced the rain. He put his hand outside the bonnet in expectation of what fell into it. The soft touch of snow.

CHAPTER THIRTY-THREE

October 1845

T he pass they had to reach rose one thousand feet to a notch shouldered by mountains. It was the beginning of what later would be called Donner Pass. The angle up was about forty-five degrees of uneven surface. It could be climbed in good weather with some difficulty by both people and livestock.

The Sierra Nevada range that dared their entry was a steep ascent from the east. However, headed west along the pass, it sloped steadily down from the heights, through foothills, to the vast Central Valley of California. The elevation went from seven thousand feet down to sea level at Sutter's Fort. None of it was a stroll.

The pass stretched thirty miles to a cut in the western ridge that led out of the mountains and would be called Emigrant Gap. It would be a very long thirty miles.

The pass was generally flat, but that's an overly benign description. The trail was pitted with sudden ravines that threatened a dangerous fall. There were rocks like minefields, and tree roots that reached up to trip unwary hikers.

The trees were majestic and varied. Most difficult for the pioneers was the manzanita bush, which grew in mini-forests and had spiky brown branches waist to chest high that opposed their passage with painful jabs. Worst, though, were mountain winds that never quit blowing, and never quit punishing by turning cold days frigid, and nights agonizing.

Snow was a roll of the dice for anyone who traveled those mountains from autumn through spring. The Sierra Nevada was capable of dumping more than seventy feet in a single season. Snow, accompanied by deep cold, could occur even before the leaves finished turning. The weather liked to surprise, but even more, to terrify.

When dawn had finished its slow creep into the sky, the pioneers awoke and looked out. What they saw sent a chill through them that cut deeper than the cold. It was a chill of dread. The green and brown of the day before was replaced by snow, a four-inch sheet of white covering all they could see. Even worse, it was powder snow, the worst kind for what they had to do. It would swallow every step, offering no resistance for a foothold. Trudging through it was worse than walking through water; water parted, but powder fought back. They knew it threatened their lives.

They gathered in a small circle over the crackling fire Nimrod had started, standing with arms folded and rubbing their upper arms with downcast faces. They stamped the snow without reason. It wasn't going away. They dressed in whatever warm clothes they found that could fit or come close. Nimrod reminded them to bring every shoe they owned, even if it didn't have a mate. The women were grateful they had followed Flora's example and converted their warmest dress to pants-like bloomers, convention be damned.

"My God," Meister grumbled, "it's October! Whoever heard of snow in October?"

Nimrod's laugh did not hide his misgivings. "This is just practice. Things could get serious. These mountains, they don't start snowing to tease people. Most times, they mean it."

He cut his laugh short. "This might be just a small taste of what is coming. We've got to climb to the top of yonder pass while the snow's thin." He pointed to the crest of the cliff facing them. "The wind will blow off most of this so the ground and rocks will be clear, but in deeper snow, we'd never make our way up."

"Maybe God will be on our side—finally," Cohen said.

His statement was followed by silence. For the days since his wife was killed, Cohen had kept to himself and tended to avoid the others. They respected his privacy and directed reassuring smiles in his direction.

Aaron turned to Hannah. "Is he in good fettle?"

"He's trying to heal," she said, "and up here, he has to do it fast. He's a strong man. Just let him be."

Using blanket knapsacks, the pioneers packed what meat they had left and made sure their Lucifer matches and gunpowder were well protected. They had two horses, a donkey, and a mule. Five oxen remained.

The snow flurries had stopped, so Nimrod said, "We best go."

Nimrod helped Gertie and her baby onto Bub's saddle because the mule would be sure-footed. Aaron and Cohen would walk alongside to stabilize her. Then Nimrod told the others that the children would have to walk to the top.

Cohen protested. "The children should ride. It's not seemly that they wouldn't."

Nimrod said, "The children will scamper up. They'll be waiting for us at the top."

Preacher insisted on saying a prayer before Nimrod started the climb. Some of the others, who in the past had rolled their eyes at his devotionals, decided to become better acquainted with their maker.

At the base of the cliff, three oxen balked and would not start the ascent. After coaxing and goading the animals without result, Aaron led them off the side and shot all three. Reacting to the flinches the gunshots caused, Cohen reminded that the shots were mercy killings.

Penney said, "Shame to see good beef go to waste."

"No time," Aaron said, returning.

Andrew led Aaron's horse over to Penney, and said, "Here's your mount, Captain."

Penney was aghast. "My mount? He gestured toward the women and children. "I'll be goddamned-go-to-hell if I'll ride while they walk." He ignored Preacher's disapproving look.

"What about my wife?" Penney demanded.

"If you stop yammering, we'll put her up behind you. This is a big horse. It can handle both of you.

Penney shook his head in despair at the humiliation. "There ain't no how I'll ride this here horse while women and children walk. No, sir! Ain't no how."

Andrew's patience snapped. "There's no time for this. You're a sick man. You can't make it up there. Get in the damned saddle, or we'll tie you in, I swear."

Hambo the donkey and the most obedient ox were loaded with the group's baggage. Once started, Hambo and the two remaining oxen proved to be adept climbers. Next came Gertie on Bub with her baby clutched tightly. Aaron and Cohen walked beside to support her in the saddle and control Bub. Penney with Clara behind came next atop Aaron's horse, protesting in mumbles. The remaining people, and children brought up the rear.

Hannah watched her children scamper ahead and was thankful they were not struggling as was she. She would take a half-dozen steps, then lean against one of the boulders strewn across the cliff, then grab a Manzanita branch to pull herself the next few feet. Though the midday temperature was barely above freezing, the sweat dripped between her breasts and down her face, stinging her eyes. Her muscles burned with the fire of extreme exertion, brought on by the elevation, and the limits of her overworked body. Her legs cramped, and her breath was a rasp. She stopped looking at the cliff top because to see her slow progress would only discourage her. "Dear Jesus," she muttered, "let this end."

About halfway up, Rachel, who was the slowest of the children, slipped and slid backward about five feet. Nimrod was alert for such a thing. He went back down the cliff walking sideways to use his boots as a brake. When he reached Rachel, she opened her arms, and he supported her to the top while Hannah watched from above.

When all reached the summit, the sweat dried and left them at the mercy of the wind-chill. "That's a good day's work," Nimrod said with good cheer. You're all genu-ine mountain folk now. That's about the hardest work you'll do 'tween here and the moment you shake old John Sutter's hand."

Evenings fall abruptly in the mountains because of the light-blocking of the peaks. Nimrod chose a campsite for wind blockage in a cedar grove. He and Aaron gathered logs for a fire platform. He used flint and steel to save matches, and with much blowing and grumbling, they built a roaring fire after first making sure they were not beneath snow on branches that, loosened by the heat, could fall on the fire.

Nimrod sent everyone out to look for fir branches with needles on them. The branches were spread a couple of feet deep to form a bed atop the snow. That would be their bed for the night.

Andrew brought the pack with the food and prepared to portion it out. Nimrod stopped him, pointed at Gertie, and said, "Hold on. The woman with the baby eats first on account of she's eating for two. She gets double." He looked at Hannah in case his order was out of line. She smiled assent.

Each person in the group was given a conservative share of the half-cooked meat. It was a paltry amount considering each had burned about five thousand calories climbing the cliff and setting up camp. Without knife or plate, each pioneer ripped into the meat with blood dripping down the chin. Hunger can compromise etiquette, but famishment is a glutton.

The next day, the group kept stumbling to the west along the ridge. The trail was of their making as they sought the most level ground with the fewest impediments that went in the right direction. Toward sunset, they came to a clearing that made them all stop and shade their eyes from the setting sun.

They were looking with gratitude at what one day would be Summit Valley, a flat area about four miles long and half as wide. The valley was covered by tall grass not yet killed by frost. To their left was a brook of clear, cold water. It bubbled toward a narrow, foaming river in the distance that rushed down the mountain on a long trip to the Pacific.

Aaron hobbled the animals, though they showed no interest in going away from the grass they had so long been denied. Hambo was left loose. The children gathered dead wood to build a big fire around which they could wrap themselves in damp blankets, and pity their lives for the misery and danger they knew would rejoin them the next day. Hannah and Flora bookended their four children for what warmth they could give. Gertie was given an extra blanket for her baby. Little Caleb cried for much of the night out of hunger because Gertie had only drops of milk to give. The pioneers would fall asleep with thoughts of the homes they left months ago, and the meals they had been without for almost two days.

When Aaron's shift for guarding livestock came around, he stood and wrapped his blankets around his shoulders and checked his rifle. In minutes, he dozed off from exhaustion. After an hour, he abruptly snapped awake and checked on the animals. To his horror, he realized that one of the oxen was missing. He called Nimrod over, and they were joined by Andrew and Penney who hobbled to join them. They looked in a wide perimeter. And, yes, the animal had wandered off and was not to be found.

Penney said in half-disgust, half-trepidation, "Well, we're down to one ox. I'd take him to bed with me if I could, just to keep him safe."

That night it got cold. Really cold. The children whimpered with suffering from hunger and the cold. It cut to the hearts of the adults who blamed themselves for bringing their children to such a hell hole. They at least understood why they were freezing atop mountains; all the children knew was their suffering. Everyone edged as close to the fire as they dared. The coughs of colds and bronchitis sounded like a chorus. The harsh sound of struggling for breath came from where Penney lay.

A shrill scream cut the night air and woke half the company. Martin bolted upright, and said in a quavering voice, "What's that?"

Nimrod laughed. "That's a painter. Probably a Mrs. Painter telling off her feller for trying to sneak into the den late. Don't worry; not close, and they got tastier things than us to eat."

"You mean a mountain lion?" Andrew asked.

"If you like," Nimrod said and rolled over.

Flora raised her voice, but to no one person. "First chance I get, I'm going to write back home and tell them to stay right there."

"In an easy chair just in front of a warm fire," Hannah added.

"And eating a big beefsteak with potatoes and gravy, and polishing it off with apple pie," Martin said.

"Just out of the oven, with fresh cream on top," Gertie said.

All the while, Nimrod was looking at the sky. He saw no stars, and he knew what that meant.

At dawn the next day, everyone was wide awake, even the children. There was no breakfast, so everyone wandered off for a moment of privacy. Gertie and her baby mounted the more sure-footed Bub, and Penney and Clara rode Aaron's horse. As had come to be expected, he protested loudly. Hambo would carry two children, and periodically switch off with the other two. The remaining ox was loaded with what was left of their meager stores and equipment. Meister complained of rheumatism in his legs, but Nimrod told him the best treatment was walking. The pioneers were all urged to keep their blankets as open as possible so they could dry.

The group shuffled along the valley only as fast as the slowest, and those were the children who struggled along as though walking in thick mud. Penney kept looking back from his hunched over perch on the horse, and the humiliation and guilt of riding while children walked was an ache in his heart. They rested for five minutes every half hour, and it was all Hannah could do to rouse them to continue. At noon, she cut the dwindling piece of meat into equal measures and passed them out. Gertie was given a double portion.

On the trail again, the silence that settled over them was broken by a sharp cry. Everyone recoiled in alarm, then looked back to see Andrew running to the edge of a gully where a patch of trail had collapsed. About ten feet below, Martin lay sprawled against a sharp edge of a boulder. Nimrod, Hannah, and Andrew scrambled down a gentler incline to his side.

"Are you okay?" Andrew asked.

"I—I don't know. I feel strange," Martin said fearfully. He reached down and touched his legs. I can't feel anything in my legs." Panic started to set in. "Oh, Jesus, I can't move my legs." He turned to Hannah. "Can you help me? You've got to help me."

Hannah asked Nimrod for his skinning knife. Martin recoiled as he saw it. "What are you going to do?" He asked with a quavering voice.

"Don't worry," she said. "I want to test something." She rolled up his pant leg to the calf. She used the point to prick the leg. "Did you feel that?" she asked, watching his face for a reaction.

"Uh, no. I didn't feel it." He didn't know what it meant except it had to be bad.

Hannah pricked both legs more forcefully in several places. "Did you feel any of that?"

Martin looked at her with eyes wide with apprehension. He shook his head no.

Next, she went to a nearby stunted pine and snapped off an icicle and walked back. She put the ice against his leg and asked if he felt it. Again, he shook his head.

"Try to move your legs, Martin." The strain on his face was evident, but after a long moment, he relaxed the effort and again gave a baleful head shake. Hannah said, "Excuse me," and walked a short distance away after motioning to Nimrod to follow.

"He's paraplegic," she said. "The fall ruptured his spine."

"What's that mean?" he asked, in fear of the answer.

"It means he can't walk."

"For how long?"

"Maybe—likely forever—actually, forever."

The two quickly brainstormed for ways Martin could continue on the trek but shook their heads over every idea. "Oh, lord, there's got to be a way," she said.

"There ain't. There just ain't. He can't stay on a horse, even tied on. I could rig an Indian travois, I suppose, but being dragged over these rocks would kill him." Nimrod kicked at a root. "There just ain't no way."

Hannah nodded in resignation. "I'll tell him. It's my job." She took a step toward Martin and Andrew, and Nimrod started to follow. She looked back. "Wait here."

Nimrod leaned against a boulder as the others watched from above as Hannah sat on the ground next to Martin and put her hand in his. Nimrod saw the shock on the faces of Martin and Andrew. There were no tears, just looks of agony. After a few questions, they saw acceptance by both men. Nimrod knew much was due to their trust in Hannah.

After about ten minutes, Hannah stood and returned to Nimrod. She looked at him and shook her head with a sadness that required no words. She scanned the huddle on the trail above and motioned for Preacher to come down.

Nimrod went to Martin. He crouched and squeezed his shoulder, then shook his hand. "I'm proud to share this trail with you. You're a good man."

Martin nodded absently. His thoughts were elsewhere.

Hannah first talked with Preacher who hastened to be with

Martin. Hannah then went to her pack and removed a brown bottle and followed Preacher. When she returned, Nimrod asked her what she had done. "Laudanum," she said. "For Martin."

In about ten minutes, Preacher returned. Fifteen minutes later, Andrew also came up from where he left his companion. His face was stricken as he forced out the words: "Martin is dreaming now. He's peaceful." He took a deep breath and gathered himself. "He told me to get on to California."

As they reached the end of the valley, they could make out east-west ridges to the north. Nimrod traced them in the air with his arm. "Yonder is where we're headed," he said.

"How far until we're out of these blasted mountains?" Preacher asked, coming perilously close to swearing.

"From what the boys who been through here told me, I reckon 'bout fifteen to twenty mile. It'll be up and down, but generally down."

Cohen said, "I learned the hard way in Blucher's Prussian army—may they all rot in hell—that walking down is almost as much work as walking up."

Flora repeated Preacher's question. "How long before we get out of these mountains?" She looked at her shivering children wrapped in damp blankets. "Please tell us it won't be much longer," she said with a plea in her voice.

Nimrod rubbed his beard and looked into the distance. "Depends."

"Depends on what?" Meister asked with an edge.

Nimrod glanced skyward. "Up there."

They all looked upward at dark, dense stratus clouds forming high above. No one had to say the word—snow.

"Please, God," Gertie said quietly.

The next day they headed for a stream that meandered west. "Yonder be the Yuba River, just where Kit said. Yuba's an Indian word, I'm told. We need to follow it a ways."

Meister snapped, "What's 'a ways'?"

Nimrod said, "A ways is a ways."

"How far is that?" Fear was in his voice.

Nimrod gave Meister a challenging look, then said evenly, "Til I say stop."

Standing a dozen feet away, Hannah heard the exchange and walked away, smiling.

Meister noticed her mockery and turned to the others for support. "We've been betrayed, people. We're lost in a dangerous wilderness. We trusted these people." He pointed to Nimrod and Hannah. "We need new leadership."

"Why don't you go and find a way out, then come back and get us?" Penney mocked from a boulder he was resting against. The others responded with strained laughter as Meister stalked away.

The snow didn't fall, but the clouds remained. The following day was the easiest yet. The going was rough, but level with only a few dips, and they were cheered as they watched the yards march by. In an outburst of unwarranted enthusiasm, Aaron sang out, "Next stop Sutter's Fort," and the others cheered.

Nimrod looked at Hannah with a tired grin. It had a two-fold meaning: He was happy for the enthusiasm, and he was amused at the wishful credulity.

After making camp that night, and finally succeeding in starting a fire and keeping it going, Nimrod went to check the perimeter. He walked by Andrew sitting on a rock by himself with head bowed. He stopped and said, "How-do, Andrew. Ain't it a bit chilly sitting on a rock?"

Banks hurriedly brushed a tear off his cheek. "Just thinking to myself. Passing the time a little."

Nimrod looked off in the same direction of Andrew's gaze. "Losing someone close ain't an easy load to tote. I can speak for that; most folks can."

Andrew said, "The pain is like a toothache of the heart. I loved the man. I loved Martin."

"It's the love, and the loss of it that hurts. It'd be easier if you hated him. Then you wouldn't be hurting."

"Oh, God, no. The love I had was wonderful."

Nimrod started to walk away, but looked over his shoulder, and said, "Then be grateful for the pain."

The next morning, Hannah noticed Nimrod staring into the distance. He beckoned her to follow to the edge of the clearing, and also called for Cohen to join them.

He pointed, and said in a low voice, "Yonder across the river, a ways more'n a half-mile into that thicket, there's a griz—" He noticed their blank looks. "A grizzly bear. He's hungry and getting ready for winter. He's out looking for food, real serious like."

"Just what are you saying?" Cohen asked with rising concern.

Hannah said, "I know what he's saying." Then, looking Nimrod in the face, she said, "Are we in danger?"

"Yes." He let the word sink in. "I don't know what Old Ephraim over there has in mind, but he knows we're here. If this was a month ago, he'd go on his way, but this be fattening-up time. He's thinking about winter starvation, and game be scarce. He wants to go on living, same as us."

The others had gathered around. A child nearby whimpered, and Gertie scolded Nimrod, "Shame on you for frightening the children."

Nimrod didn't take his eyes off the thicket, but said, "Ain't got no time for parlor games. We got to know what we're maybe up against."

"What can we do?" Hannah said, her voice rising as she thought of her two children and the others.

"Say nary a word, and keep the folks moving."

For the next hour, Nimrod hung back and kept his eyes on the distance. When the pioneers stopped to eat their few bites of half-raw beef, he rejoined them and quietly told what was happening. He tried to speak conversationally, to avoid panic. He said the bear was working its way in their direction, but not necessarily after them. Maybe, but not necessarily.

"We need to move," Cohen said in a strained voice.

"We have to have food and rest to keep going, at least a little," Nimrod said.

"I thought they ate berries and things," Flora said with a quiver in her voice.

Nimrod said, "We don't want to be the 'things,' They eat whatever they have a mind to."

Two of the children started to cry, and Gertie groaned as she held her baby tighter. The others looked wide-eyed at each other, but saw only the same look in response.

Meister's face was flushed, and his eyes darted about in fear. He shouted at Nimrod with a quaking voice. "Damn you, Lee. You knew there were killer bears here, but you guided us here, anyway, instead of a safe route. Our blood will be on your hands."

Hannah noticed his scare words were upsetting the others. "Shut up, Meister," she said. The venom in her words made him pause in surprise, then back away.

Nimrod ignored him and, with a quick explanation to Cohen and Hannah, he instructed that the cargo be switched from the back of the remaining ox onto Hambo.

"Wha-what are you going to do?" Flora asked as she stared at him with an arm around each of her children.

"Offer a bargain, and hope Old Ephraim will be satisfied with it."

"Can't we just keep going and lose him?" Gertie asked.

"Lose him?" Nimrod said. "You might as well try to catch a weasel asleep, as to confuse a griz."

The others gathered around, primed to panic. He told them to keep moving and to load every gun. "If he comes and you have to shoot him, let him get close. You get one shot only."

A groan in unison went up from the others.

The others needed no urging to get to their feet and keep moving west. Nimrod let them get out of sight, then took his revolver and shot the ox in the brain. As the animal crumpled, he hoped it would satisfy the bear.

Nimrod caught up to the others, but looked back as much as forward. He saw nothing, and the others, noticing his relief, sighed as tension drained. As they walked, he joined Hannah and Cohen. Nimrod removed a heavy leather bag from inside his shirt and handed it to her.

She hefted the bag. "What's this?"

"It's the money Agnes Patterson gave me. Well over a thousand dollars, gold coin. I want you and your younguns to have it."

Her mouth dropped. "But she gave it to you."

"And I'm giving it to you."

Hannah looked back on the trail, and her eyes widened in intuition. "You're going after the bear. That's what you have in mind!"

"I hope I don't have to. I truly do."

She held the bag up. "I'll hold it for you."

"No. It's yours, bear or no bear. And I wanted Malachi to witness me saying that. Now, you two git."

Nimrod turned away, and Hannah and Cohen rejoined the others. As they walked, Cohen said, "A better man than we know. God be with him."

Hannah nodded.

As the others disappeared down the trail, Nimrod quickly loaded Penney's scattergun with four balls atop a double charge of black powder and put a fresh load in his Hawken. Nimrod took cover behind a large pine and watched and waited. He knew if the bear were tracking the group, the scent would lead him along this route. Nimrod was fully aware he likely would die trying to stop the huge predator. Images flashed in his mind of victims of bear attacks he had seen in the mountains: slashed faces, gutted torsos, and horror in dead eyes. He snorted a nervous half-laugh. At least he wouldn't have to listen to any more campfire tales about killing a grizzly with one shot or with a knife. He also knew there was no hiding from the bear if it were nearby and on the hunt. A grizzly could smell many times better than a bloodhound.

After twenty minutes, Nimrod in a shaky moment almost started back to the group who were now well down the trail, but as he stepped out from behind the tree, the shock that hit him was electric.

One moment, the trail had been clear and quiet. The next moment, the dark bulk of the grizzly emerged from a manzanita thicket and stared at Nimrod from about two hundred yards. He judged it to be about one thousand pounds. There was no retreat. The bear could outrun a racehorse over such a distance. Nimrod flashed on recollections of having seen a dead grizzly's long teeth, but more frightening were the four-inch, curved claws. They reminded him of a longshoreman's baling hooks. One swipe and he would be gutted.

Nimrod quickly moved behind the tree and took a deep breath, which failed to soothe his nerves. He gripped the smooth walnut of his Hawken. He trusted his rifle, but it was not purposed for an animal this size. He knew its lead ball a half-inch in diameter would stand little chance to score a kill with one shot, and yet he also knew one shot was all he would get.

The bear shambled toward Nimrod. It smashed through brush, sniffing the air as it came. Its grunts sounded like a rutting bull. Nimrod braced his rifle against the pine bark and kept the scattergun propped by his knee. He hoped the bear would turn enough so the broad side of its leg would be exposed. He knew his ball would likely get buried in a non-lethal part of the vast body, and a headshot might not penetrate the skull. But if he could break the bear's leg, the animal couldn't charge.

He took deep, steadying breaths. He swiped at the sweat dripping into his eyes. His legs grew weak, and his arm trembled slightly, though he knew it had to be rock steady.

At one hundred yards, the bear turned at an angle that gave Nimrod the shot he wanted, but the bear kept moving, and he would not chance a miss for his only shot. He kept following the bear down the sights of the rifle until at eighty yards, the bear stopped to test the air. By long habit, he became steady as he aimed.

"Turn, please, please," he pleaded under his breath, and as he wished, the bear closed to fifty yards, and, again, stopped and turned to an angle.

Nimrod sighted on the knee, held his breath, and gently squeezed the trigger. The gun kicked, and black smoke surrounded his head. He looked over the barrel to see the bear on the ground. But as the bear recovered from the shock, Nimrod's stiffened in fear as he realized his shot had hit the bear, but its legs were intact and moving fast toward him.

He dropped the rifle and grabbed the scattergun. He had to wait until the bear was almost on him, and he had to hit the face, otherwise, the balls would spread and lose effect.

At twenty feet, Nimrod pulled the trigger. The heavy load's

recoil felt like a hammer against his shoulder, but the pain was not felt as the bear slammed into the tree, knocking him backward. He unsheathed his knife and ran back several yards, not knowing what he would be facing, and how long he might live.

The slugs had torn away most of the bear's face. It rolled twice on the ground with a bellow of thunder. Nimrod stood and stared, realizing he was at the bear's mercy. Nimrod could see blood coming from a wound in its side where his bullet had hit, but he was stunned to see that the bear's nose, jaw, and one eye had been blown away.

Nimrod gripped his knife and waited. The bear rose to its seven-foot height, flailed the air and continued to bellow. Then, the grievously wounded animal turned and ran into a thicket. Nimrod heard it crashing in the distance.

Nimrod reloaded his guns with shaking hands, then he stared into the thicket until he was satisfied the bear was gone for good. Nimrod didn't exult. He regretted such a noble creature would have a miserable death, perhaps to be killed in his weakened condition by other bears in a bear-eat-bear existence.

I swear, I must be getting old, he thought.

CHAPTER THIRTY-FOUR

ndrew was the first to see him approaching. A moment later, the others looked up, and to a person, shouted their joy that it was Nimrod and not the bear. Hannah led the others in rushing up to him. She threw her arms about him, and he felt the softness of her hair against his chest. Before Nimrod could react, the others converged in a babble of happy voices and back-slaps from all angles.

They would not be food for a hungry bear.

"We heard the shots and that awful roar and figured the worst, for sure," Andrew said.

Nimrod's smile was weak. His legs were still trembling, and he was not used to being a hero. "I'd be obliged for a taste of something near as strong as Old Ephraim's breath."

A small jug was thrust into his hands, which he took, moved to a small boulder, and sat down to wait for the shaking of his hands to stop. A few feet away, Penney rested against the trunk of a large cedar. He watched Nimrod take a swig, then lower the jug, close his eyes, and take a deep breath to chase away the fear he'd felt facing a bear almost certain to kill him.

"I'd give a Continental dollar to been there to give cover when you did what you did. You're a handful for any beast, four-legged, two, or no-legged. I ain't done much better than to hire you." Penney chuckled in a gently mocking way. "And I got you cheap."

"I could have used you back there," Nimrod said.

"Watch it, Lee. You can go to hell for lying, same as for lusting." His face showed resignation. "Reckon I wouldn't be much good. That old bear would've died laughing, he'd seen me next to you."

Nimrod said, with chiding humor, "Ah, an old goat like you'll outlive us all."

Penney rubbed his chin. "I'm getting closer to learning the great secret, I am. I worry about Clara. What's to happen to her?" He and Nimrod both became silent and didn't look at each other, avoiding a question for which there was no answer.

Nimrod left Penney with a pat on the knee and went to take care of Bub. As he curried the mule, Hannah approached from the side, and said, "We, all of us, me especially, are so grateful for your courage. You're a hero, a man Homer would bow down to."

Curious, Nimrod said, "Homer who?"

"A man from long ago who told stories of giants such as you."

Nimrod was pleased with the compliment but ill at ease at showing his ignorance. As a diversion, he looked skyward. "I don't like them clouds up there. We've been lucky so far."

"You look worried," she said.

"When this mountain weather turns, it'll kill you faster'n smallpox."

"Then we better be on our way," Hannah said, slightly peeved her compliment seemed to fall flat. She started to walk away, then turned. "If you have a change of heart, I'll return your generous gift, now that you're back."

Nimrod turned away from his mule. "Hannah, that money weren't nothing about the bear. I been thinking of a way to give that to your family since Miz Patterson honored me with it. I opine the Trooper and Rachel would use it better'n me spending it on fandangos."

"What's that?"

"Uh, that's how Mexicans kick up their heels." He rambled nervously. "At least in Taos; other places, too, I reckon."

Hannah was suddenly the one ill at ease. "Oh, well, I thank you again."

The two looked at each awkwardly for a long moment, then Hannah said, "I best get things moving," and walked away.

On her way back to Rachel and Billy, Hannah passed Meister. She stopped and turned back. "Mr. Meister, a moment, if you please." His face was a question as he looked at her. There was starch in her voice to cover her nervousness. "I feel the need to say you've been a bad influence on the spirits of this company. I would be grateful if, in the future, you would be either more positive or be quiet."

Disbelief showed on his face that this woman should dare to order him around. "Lady, er, madam, just why do you think you're the boss of this group, or what's left of it?"

Her eyes narrowed. "That's exactly who I am, sir—the boss of this group. I was being courteous, but let me rephrase it in words more understandable to you: Stop dragging down the spirits of these people with your nasty comments, or there will be consequences."

"Ha! Just what could you do to me, little lady?"

Hannah's face flushed with anger. "We can find something suitably unpleasant for you."

"I don't believe you."

"Very well, I'll start by withholding your share of meat the next time you put a damper on our spirits."

"Damned if I'll stand still for that."

Hannah said nothing, but let her eyes slide to the left. Meister followed her gaze and found himself looking at Nimrod, still grooming Bub.

The group traipsed along, stopping briefly at times for the animals to feed on patches of weeds. Nimrod scouted ahead. Penney rode Aaron's horse with Clara behind, and him grumbling about having two old ladies on one horse. Hannah noticed his legs were swollen. Gertie and the baby rode Bub, and the others walked behind. Hambo, loaded down with tools and supplies, was led by Billy.

In late afternoon, the wind picked up, and the first snowflakes swirled around them. But that was just the beginning. In minutes, the flakes were bigger and wetter. The wind became a knife through thin clothing. The temperature dropped, making each breath felt all the way to the bottom of the lungs. Nimrod spoke in an urgent, loud voice to pronounce a word with the hollow ring of doom.

"Blizzard."

Nimrod hurried to Hannah and Cohen and urged them to stop early and make camp. Hannah noticed Nimrod was limping, but she didn't have a chance to ask why. They selected a small grove of pines for shelter and tied the animals to trees that gave them protection from the wind. Nimrod found the ten-foot stump of a dead pine and took turns with Andrew chopping it down. He then started it on fire with a pile of kindling underneath. He asked Hannah to send the others to find small logs, dead wood, and fir boughs to make a sleeping pad a half-foot or so off the ground, as well as fuel for the fire.

Nimrod said to Cohen, "Break out some food for everyone."

Cohen looked at him, mystified. "Now? We don't have much time, and we don't have much food."

"They'll need it to get through this night. Food in the belly means fuel; fuel means body heat." Cohen ran to his food stash to see what he could come up with.

When the sun disappeared, the temperature started down and didn't stop. From having survived many such storms, Nimrod guessed it had plunged close to zero. He instructed everyone to get near the fire, take off their shoes and vigorously rub their feet, and then hug their footwear close to their chests through the night. Their beds were on fir boughs they had collected. They covered themselves with every blanket and scrap of cloth they had, then they spread a wagon bonnet over all to block the wind and help keep their clothes dry. Nimrod told them to sleep in a tight embrace while also massaging each other's arms and back, and keep their feet to the fire, which the men took turns maintaining.

The critical warmth was body heat. Flora and Hannah hugged their children as tightly as they could. The children whimpered and shivered, making the mothers feel guilt as much as cold. Nimrod was on the outside of Hannah and pressed his body close. Hannah said softly through chattering teeth, "Oh, God! My poor children! How have I gotten them into this?"

Just inches from her face, Nimrod said, "Blame don't do no good. Getting furious does. Get mad about this, Hannah; mad enough to fight back."

Hannah turned her face half-way back toward him, "Don't you ever get scared? Don't you ever cry?"

"Scared? A week don't go by that I don't. Cry? Only when no one can see me."

Lying close, Nimrod felt the rhythm of Hannah's breathing slow as she dozed off. He forced himself to stay awake. He kept his boots on to feed the fire and make certain it didn't go out. His thoughts turned bleak as he thought about the plight they were in and turned the gloom on himself. He said to Hannah, barely above a whisper, "Your fears about me are true. This wilderness is hard, and a man has to be hard, or he gets et by something that's harder. But hard is not good in your gentleness. I wisht it weren't so, but I don't measure up. I finally learnt that." He waited for her response, but none came.

The snow piled up around them and on top of them. The wind continued to howl. They shivered and hunkered down in their thin, smelly clothes and listened to the wind as it shrieked through tree limbs and heightened the punishment of the cold. What the pioneers suffered was not what could be called pain, not like being hit with a stick. It was, well, hard to explain. It wasn't a burn because it didn't make them scream in agony. It wasn't fear, because there was nothing to see. It was misery: misery of a terrible, inescapable, pervasive kind. There was no defense. Its intent was to break their spirits and make them want to surrender. And it took no prisoners. Their minds surrendered to a dark numbness. Stupor was the only relief.

The cold was most cruel to the children. Gertie's baby was held as close as she could clasp it to share her body warmth. The weeping of the children was heard by all and tormented them in their helplessness. There was nothing the mothers could do except wrap them in blankets as near to the fire as safety allowed and to ask God's forgiveness for bringing them to hell on earth.

Nimrod looked often at the sky, hoping to see stars. But when he saw only a black sky, he knew what it meant: More snow. He looked at the branches above outlined by a quarter-crescent moon, and saw they had grown heavy with accumulated snow. He stared at the branches and hoped the trees didn't also want to destroy them. He hoped in vain.

Deep into the night, they heard a loud thump, and peered over the edge of the bonnet to see—nothing. The waxing crescent moon

came out to give him a shaft of light to see that a large mass of snow
had fallen from a branch above and smothered the fire. All they
could do was snuggle deeper and pray.

At first light, Hannah awoke to see Nimrod remove his boots
and balefully examine his feet. He winced as he struggled to put
one back on. Hannah examined the other, then looked at his face,
and said, "You're in pain."

"It ain't nothing but the cold."

She said, "These boots are too thin."

He chuckled wryly, and said, "My others gave out, and I don't
see any warmer ones for sale."

When the pioneers finally straggled out of their thrown-
together camp, they stumbled into a foot of powder snow. Twelve
inches may sound trivial, but for weakened adults and children, it's
a wall.

They were a dejected group as they huddled and faced the hated
trail, but they made no effort to start. Penney watched and realized
lost hope and exhaustion had beaten them down. He raised his
voice. "Back home, we had a saying: 'Root, hog, or die.' What that
means is pretty simple—You quit, you die." In stages, he painfully
raised himself to standing. "Well, I ain't ready to die, least not
today, and not because of a little pile of snow."

Nimrod went to the front and said, "I figure California is just
down the road a piece." He went first on his snowshoes for the
exhausting task of breaking trail, and also to be alert if the snow
covered up danger on the trail. Nimrod kept looking back to a
wary eye on Hambo carrying the baggage. The donkey was head
down and listless. The cold, for which he was not born to endure,
was beating him down. The pioneers struggled along single file in
the path broken by Nimrod and the animals.

Leg muscles became instruments of torture. Even in temperature
no higher than twenty degrees, everyone's clothing was soaked with
sweat that would chill them when they stopped for the night. The
children brought up the rear to gain the advantage of the tromped
snow on the trail. Cohen followed the children to keep them going.

Hannah, walking ahead of Preacher, fell into a snowbank, and he pulled her to her feet. "I can't keep going...but, somehow, I have to. Please, God. Let me," she said in a pleading voice.

Preacher said, "Hannah, God's answer is for you to ask yourself how much you love your children and the people you will heal in years to come." She struggled back onto the trail, ignoring Preacher's helping hand because that would be a sign of her weakness, and she dared not acknowledge it.

Flora saw that the children were falling too far behind, so she went back to help Cohen egg them on. She clapped her hands and managed a cheerful voice to say, "Right foot...left foot...right foot... See, kids, a game, just like recess at school." It didn't help much.

After their noon break, as Nimrod was urging them to their feet, Flora said, "Please, can we rest a while longer? The children are exhausted and cold."

Nimrod touched her on the shoulder. "Keep moving, ma'am. You stop, you die."

That night, they made another fire and a bed of fir branches. However, it turned even colder, and their struggle was to stay alive. Billy and Rachel were shivering uncontrollably. In the middle of the night, Hannah had her arms around Rachel and shrieked. "She's stopped breathing! Please, oh please, God, help me!" Nimrod threw off his blanket and removed his shirt. "Take her shirt off. To the skin. Be quick!" Hannah stripped Rachel's garment. Aaron grabbed her and pressed Rachel's skin against his own. He told Hannah to cover them with every blanket handy. He rubbed Rachel's back as vigorously as he could under the covering. Finally, Rachel stirred and moaned.

"Oh, thank God," Hannah said, and took the girl in her arms. She was too much in shock to thank Nimrod, but he didn't need it.

The next morning, Nimrod reached his breakpoint. He stayed wrapped in his blanket and spoke quietly to Hannah. "My feet got frostbite. They hurt too much to walk. I can't go on."

Hannah said, "Let me look at them." She gasped to see that his toes were bone white as they showed through ragged stockings. She wanted to say how bad they looked, but she knew it was not the moment for discouraging talk.

He moaned. "My boots'll never go back on.... It's gonna be up to you to keep people going."

Hannah became wide-eyed at the preposterous suggestion. "Me? Are you mad? What could I do?" She reached for his feet and vigorously rubbed his toes.

Nimrod groaned before saying, "You're strong. You'll find a way."

"Nimrod, you're the only one who can get us through this hellhole. We'll die without you."

"I'm done."

Hannah saw pink return to his toes. She shook him hard. "Your stockings are no good. Cover your feet with some wool. Massage your feet at noon break, then again at night. Now, put your boots on. You should be all right." She stood up and hovered over him. "Stop feeling sorry for yourself. Get out of that blanket and save these people."

"Don't torment me, woman."

Hannah points to her two sleeping children. "Then get up long enough to tell these children you're going to let them die." Her lips were pressed tight, and her eyes sparked with anger.

Nimrod stared at the children, then at her. Slowly, without comment, he struggled to get into his boots, then lumbered to his feet, wincing and limping.

Nimrod went among the snow-covered mounds of sleepers lying in clumps like hibernating bears. He shook the snow off the wagon bonnet cover that had insulated them a little. Nimrod tensed-up, hoping no one was frozen to death. However, they all sat up in pained stages, first moving an arm, then a leg, then struggling to their feet.

In a loud, cheerful voice, Nimrod said, "All right, all right, rise and shine, folks. I'm going to walk down to Sutter's Fort and get some breakfast. Think I'll have fried eggs and bacon. Eat 'em right next to a big oak fire. How 'bout you, Malachi? What'll you have?"

Cohen sat up. "Eggs, I guess. No bacon."

There was a chorus of mumbled swearing, children whining and fussing, and mothers trying to give comfort that was not to be found. Each waded through the snow to find a private place to squat. The quest for privacy was half-hearted, but no one cared.

"I'm hungry, mama," said Flora's son, Tom. He spoke for every man, woman, and child.

Cohen went to retrieve what remained of the food that was carefully wrapped in the skin of a coon Nimrod had shot weeks before. It was stored in the crook of a tree, out of the wind to keep the meat from freezing.

He cut small slices for each of them, giving a double portion to Gertie. All except Meister. As Hannah had decreed, he was excluded. His loud protests had persisted the previous day, so she made good on her threat. His objections were ignored, except for Cohen, who said, "Uriah, here's what you got to decide: eat or complain. To me, it sounds like an easy choice."

Banks had remained Meister's enemy following their fight weeks ago. He mocked him by saying, "I'll wager right now Johnny is setting down to a breakfast of baked buffalo hump in a warm tipi."

It took just moments to chew and swallow the morsels. They looked longingly at the remaining lump of meat, but it had to be saved, so they turned away with stomachs still empty.

Nimrod noticed Flora giving Tom half her meat. "You're going to need your strength more than the boy needs the meat," he said. He's better off with a hungry stomach than losing a mother who falls along the trail."

Nimrod stood and swiveled his head to make eye contact with everyone who wasn't staring at the ground with wrung-out spirits.

He spoke in a voice loud enough to send out determination. "Do y'all know what's just past yonder peaks?" he said, pointing to mountains to the west. "I'll tell you what: Just over those big hills— that's all they be, just big mounds of rock and dirt. Just a few miles past them is the biggest, greenest valley God ever saw fit to put on this old earth. It's where deer and cattle graze year-round. Birds sing so loud they purt-near hurt your ears. It's freezing up here, but down there, you'll drag your coats along as useless weight."

Preacher admonished gently, "Don't blaspheme, Nimrod."

"The good Lord made that paradise, Preacher, so I reckon he won't mind using his name to tell you about it."

Preacher grinned and nodded to the point.

Andrew said with heavy skepticism, "You wouldn't be funning us just to boost our spirits?"

"It's the promised land, Andrew. You can stay here and wait for spring, but the rest of us is going down *there*!" He pointed theatrically to the west.

Cohen stepped forward, and said, "What Nimrod is saying is we can mope around, complain, lose hope, hang our heads, and just stumble along. However, we can't lose the will to get to California that we started with when it was a dream two thousand miles and five months back. Well, folks, it's just a few miles away now. What we're going through now is just some temporary discomfort."

He saw Meister roll his eyes, and continued, "I know, I know, speeches don't take the frost off your toes, but in a month we'll forget about being miserable. In years to come, we'll have a story of courage and determination that'll be the pride of our lives, and a tribute to our country. So, let's finish the job and look forward to enjoying our new home."

Off to the side, Nimrod quietly turned to Hannah. "I thank you for bracing me."

She smiled modestly. "You are welcome, sir." Her smile said more. It said she was grateful to nurse his weakness.

Nimrod put on his snowshoes and went hunting for any game not already hunkered down in the storm. The pioneers gathered around what was left of a burning stump and waited. They knew not for what. They cast concerned glances at Penney who had clearly weakened in the night. He had laboriously moved to a dry patch of higher ground that Clara had cleared of snow. Cohen asked Hannah for her opinion.

"I don't know, Malachi. He says it's his heart, which seems likely to me. One thing's clear: he's on the downside."

Nimrod returned from his hunt carrying a bundle in his game bag. "Whatcha got, Mr. Lee?" Billy said, running up to him.

Nimrod pulled a dead striped skunk from the bag. Everyone watching backed off out of fear of the odorous creature, even dead. Nimrod playfully held it up and thrust it within a few feet of Alice Dickens. The girl shrieked and ran behind a tree, playing the role of a damsel in distress.

"Am I supposed to eat that thing?" Cohen asked.

Nimrod grinned. "Let's see how hungry you get."

The sun rose, and the wind warmed, causing the snow to start melting. The people rejoiced, but Nimrod looked skyward with a frown. He knew that by nightfall, the snow would freeze and form a crust on top. It would make their progress even tougher.

By early afternoon the snow started to melt. "I can't cotton to this," Preacher said. "Last night, it was a blizzard; today, I've got to worry about a sunburn."

"This time of year, old man winter sometimes has trouble figuring things out. Does he want winter or Indian summer," Nimrod said. "He seems to be arguing with himself."

Because the melting snow had uncovered weeds the animals could feed on, the pioneers decided to camp another night to give the ground more time to dry.

That noon, Nimrod put the two pounds of skunk meat in the coals of the fire and then cut it into portions. For himself, he split and emptied the intestines, and threw them and liver and heart onto the coals.

Flora said, "You're going to eat that nasty stuff?"

Nimrod laughed as he took a bite of liver, and said, "You'll always wonder what you missed."

Cohen grabbed his small piece and invested just a few bites before swallowing it. He announced it as "a starving man's beef tenderloin."

The night again turned bitter cold, but Nimrod told the people to expect that in the mountains, but the next day might be fine. Penney spent a difficult night. His harsh breathing was audible to everyone. Clara fussed around him to keep him covered and feed him small pieces of meat she had softened with her own teeth.

The next morning was colder than the previous day, but the skies were clear. Nimrod awoke with dawn's streaks. He looked around to see Hannah huddled over Penney with Clara at her shoulder, wringing her hands. Penney was lying at the base of a large pine. The snow had been pushed aside, and he rested on a bed of fir boughs. A wadded-up coat was beneath his head. Nimrod quietly walked over. It was obvious by the faces of Hannah and

Clara that Penney was sinking. Finally, Hannah put her ear close to his lips, then looked up and motioned for Nimrod to approach.

Nimrod looked closely at the old man. His lips were blue, and his complexion sallow. He wheezed and coughed weakly. Nimrod could not see under his blankets, but Hannah knew Penney's abdomen and legs were bloated with fluid buildup. Hannah put her arms around Clara's shoulders as the old woman sobbed. All four leaned in to hear Penney's weak words.

He wiggled his finger to draw them closer. He spoke in gasps and looked at Nimrod. "I want a word with this galoot."

Nimrod moved close and sat next to Penney's head. "This is not the best day to sleep in, old-timer."

"I ain't going nowheres today. Least not where you're going. But I reckon I'll get there first." He tried to laugh at his own joke, but the effort caused a spate of coughing.

"I'd like to see you at the head of the column again, being a general nuisance for everybody," Nimrod said.

"I know that, damnit all. But there comes a time when you can't argue yourself forward. My heart's stumbling like a rusty clock…. I've said my goodbyes to my wife, but she wants to stay here. Foolish woman."

"Love can make a person seem foolish. I've seen it."

"Will you see her out?"

"You know I'll try."

Penney tried to raise to an elbow but fell back. "I been watching you hobble around. You're in trouble."

Nimrod said, "We all are."

"If you don't make it, no one else will."

Nimrod gently chucked him on the shoulder. "I ain't yet earned the big money you paid me."

Both men chuckled, then were silent for a long moment.

"Ain't a lot more to say, is there?" Nimrod said.

"We said it all just getting this far. My job's over; yours ain't."

Nimrod said, "When we set foot in California, it'll be your doing."

Penney chuckled. "Next, you're gonna start sobbing."

"You want Preacher?"

Penney shook his head. "No self-respecting God would let that fool influence him."

"I'll come back in the spring and bury you proper."

"You know better. Come the thaw, the wolves'll be quicker. Just let me return to the earth."

Nimrod stood up to leave, but Penney stopped him. "Is California worth it?"

Nimrod thought for a long moment. "It's just a place, Shadrach; depends on how people live in it. It'll be poorer without you."

"You folks best get going. California's just over the next rise."

Nimrod leaned down, and said, "Captain, I'd just like to say—"

Penney shook his head without opening his eyes. "None of that, Lee. You ain't a word man. I know your heart. Now, leave me be. I'm tired." He closed his eyes. They knew he was alive only by the laboring up-and-down of his chest.

Nimrod rose and waited for the others. Hannah reached for Clara, but she lay down next to Penney and cradled his head in her arms. Hannah said, "We must be going, Clara. We'll wait for you in the clearing."

They stood in an open area with the other pioneers. They waited for Clara to say her goodbyes and join them. Clara did not move. When again approached, she shook her head and held tight to her husband. Hannah went over and reached down to help Clara rise. The older woman shrugged her off. Hannah tried again with the same result. Hannah spoke at length to Clara, but with no effect. Finally, she took a blanket and spread it over both of them, leaving only their heads exposed.

Slowly, tiredly, Hannah rose and rejoined the others. "She's staying," she said in a flat voice.

"That can't be," Flora said in astonishment.

"You couldn't talk her into coming?" Preacher said, though the fact was obvious.

"People just don't do that," Andrew said.

"We best be going," Nimrod said. "I'll backtrack in a couple of hours to see if she's changed her mind."

Hannah shook her head. "She won't."

"Just leave them there?" Gertie said, aghast.

"That's what they want," Nimrod said. "It'll be quick."

Hannah said in a scolding voice. "Nimrod!"

Nimrod lowered his eyes into a regretful finger steeple. "Forgive my blunt talk."

Preacher said, "You all go on. I'll catch up." He took a step toward the Penneys, when Meister said, "Is it right to give a Christian blessing to a suicide?"

Preacher glanced back briefly, but ignored Meister.

As they walked away, Hannah glared toward Meister, then in a hissing voice, said to Nimrod, "They stay here to die, and Meister is healthy as a horse."

Nimrod shrugged. "Twernt the first decision of the good Lord I disagreed with."

⚜

A half-hour after Preacher rejoined them, Nimrod kept his word and hurried back to see if perchance Clara had changed her mind. As he reached the two bundled figures, he stole to within a few feet. He could see from Penney's death stare that he was gone. He said, "Clara." He spoke a little louder. "Clara." She didn't move. Her arm was around her dead husband's chest. He could see the slow undulation of her breathing from the back, but she didn't respond. "I'm leaving. Won't you come? We'll take care of you." He waited a long moment, then he quietly removed Penney's boots and hurried to rejoin the others. The tears coursing down his cheeks were lost in his beard.

For the next two days, the small column stumbled along in crusted snow that required punching through with each step to break through. But then the capricious mountain grew bored with tormenting them with cruel weather. As its concession to the group, the temperature edged upward until it reached above freezing, and the sun appeared each day. The snow along the trail gradually reduced to patches, disappearing as fast as it came.

The decline in elevation was gentle, but the terrain along the crest of the pass set punishing traps of half-hidden roots and rocks. The rough ground caused muttered cursing, falling, and aching muscles. Their clothes were torn by struggling through dense patches of manzanita, mountain mahogany, and western thimbleberry.

Granite slabs required detours and sharp rocks pierced thin shoe soles. Streams of snowmelt from rivulets to small creeks required jumping from rock to rock or wading in near-freezing water. The only antidotes for misery available were loud complaining and self-pity.

The knowledge that their leader and his wife were lying back off the trail, probably dead, cast a gloom over their trudging, though nothing was said of it. No one seemed to notice that Aaron was wearing Penney's boots.

They camped that night in a grove of tight pines to ward off the wind. The warm sun had gone down, and the wind came up, carrying cold, but not the bitterness of previous nights.

The food was down to morsels, but Cohen measured and portioned it out, including to Meister, who had decided to be quiet, but used glares to satisfy his animosity. The screaming of a mountain lion frightened everyone, including the animals. However, it was the children's cries of hunger that kept the adults awake and wishing they had no ears.

The next morning, after the animals were gathered, breakfast consisted of a bite of meat and much wishing. No friendly words were spoken as the claws of hunger tightened its grip.

The group's baggage, what was left of it, was loaded onto Hambo. Billy took his halter, intending to walk the donkey to the front.

Except Hambo didn't move. Billy tugged, then coaxed urgently in the animal's ear, but the donkey still didn't move. Billy tried to goad his friend with no success. Others also did, but with the same result.

Finally, Nimrod approached Billy and put his arm over his shoulder and spoke softly. "What your old partner is saying, Trooper, is he's reached the end of his trail."

Billy started crying and pulling on the rope. "C'mon, Hambo, you can do it. We need you, Hambo. I promised you a pasture of clover all your own, and you'd never have to work again when we got to California. We're almost there, Hambo. Please."

Billy walked away a few feet as though he were leaving. Hambo didn't budge.

Nimrod gently guided the boy to a flat rock away from the others. He sat on the rock and held Billy close. "You always told me Hambo is right smart, Trooper. Well, he's showing you he's got a mind of his own. He ain't going to move."

Billy said, between sobs, "I know what'll happen if he doesn't come along."

"Hambo's been a good friend to you, and you to him, but he's suffering because he's where he ain't supposed to be. He ain't built for this cold; he's got no protection. He's come all this way; suffered more than a donkey should have to. But he don't kick, and he don't complain. He just does his job. They say a donkey's stubborn, but that ain't so. He just ain't a puppy wagging his tail to please. He knows his own mind. Now, he's saying he's suffered enough."

"He's my chum, and I love him, and he loves me."

"He's a good worker, and he shines up to you, but don't make him what he ain't. He's an animal that's done his job as best any animal could do. You best let your friend go."

Billy walked over and hugged Hambo tight as his tears rolled onto the donkey's coat. "Nooooo!"

Nimrod hugged the boy, then said, "You're my special friend, and you'll be full grown afore you know it, Trooper, so you got to start thinking like a man. You got to accept the world the way it is. Hambo has said in his own way that he don't want to go on. He's tired and cold, really cold, cold like his kind ain't supposed to be. Nature didn't give him a coat like a horse to stay warm. So, he has to depend on us to do the right thing and protect him from the wolves and mountain lions that would give him an ugly death, for sure."

At those words, Billy's crying intensified.

"You got to stop crying, Trooper, and buck up. Be a young man."

Billy wiped his tears away. "I know you're right, Mr. Nimrod. Like you say, I'll do what a man is expected to do."

Nimrod kneaded the boy's shoulder. "Remember this, Trooper: To be a man, you have to pick up heavy loads and carry them." Billy wiped his tears away and nodded. Nimrod squeezed his shoulders and stood up. "That's a good man. Now, we got to get moving, so go say goodbye to your friend." Billy walked over and hugged Hambo and whispered to the donkey. He then walked over to the others and refused to watch as Andrew and Aaron switched the cargo Hambo was carrying to Aaron's horse. That left two animals.

Hannah watched it all silently.

Nimrod and Cohen hung back as the tiny caravan started down the trail. When the group was out of sight, Nimrod stroked Hambo's cold, thin coat and scratched his ear. Then he ran his sleeve over his watery eyes before he placed his revolver behind the donkey's ear and pulled the trigger. In the distance, Billy heard the report. He flinched but stared straight ahead. Because they had to keep moving to stay ahead of inevitable snowstorms, there was little time for butchering, so Cohen and Nimrod worked fast.

When the group stopped for a noon break, there was no food to silence the growls of empty stomachs. They rested against tree trunks and boulders and looked out at nothing with fixed stares. As they readied to resume the trek, Nimrod and Cohen walked into the clearing leading the packhorse. On its rump, behind the cargo, were bags of meat under which blood seeped down the horse's flank. When it was realized what had just arrived, shouts of joy, and loud prayers of thanks erupted from the pioneers. Flora and Hannah scrambled to start a fire.

The spirits of all turned joyous as they feasted on fresh meat, even Meister, almost. Nimrod took a piece of charred neat over to Billy, and said, "Here you are, Trooper. You need to eat to keep your strength up so you can take care of your mother and sister. It's part of your man's job."

Billy stared at the food, and asked, "Is this Hambo?"

Nimrod nodded. Billy looked at him, then took a bite, then another. Nimrod tousled Billy's hair and moved away, as he made a quick swipe of his eyes.

The next morning was sunny, but with a biting wind. Flora, who came from a place where the weather made sense, said, "The sun's hot, the wind's cold. How are we supposed to figure that?"

Finally, after a meal of more than a few bites, the group started off in the best spirits since they ascended the pass above Truckee's

Lake. For a mile or so, they walked carefully on a narrow path close to a drop-off to the south of about one thousand feet. Abruptly, they emerged from a clump of pines at the edge of a large grassy meadow leveled out and gently rolling downward to the south. It was an area that would be named Carpenter Flat. Andrew looked at it, and said, "That's the way to get out of these mountains. Easy. Like a walk in the park."

Nimrod replied, "That 'park' will lead you on and on, and then into a deep river canyon. I was warned about this. We'd play hell getting out of that gulch." He checked his language, then turned to Hannah. "Scuse me, ma'am." She scoffed. He pointed to the west. "I'm told there's a gap that'll get us out of here a ways ahead."

(A year later, the enticing slope to the south that Andrew had "discovered" would lead a group of the Donner Party to disaster.)

"How do you know so much if you ain't been here?" Meister said. Nimrod shrugged. "By practice, same way you learned to be an asshole." Even Preacher turned away with a grin.

Nimrod continued. "If you stay alive in these mountains, you learn to find out for yourself, or you listen to straight-talkers who know."

Meister tried to rebound by laughing sarcastically. He said, "I'll believe it when you show me. Down this way seems a sensible way. Since you don't know by your own reckoning, I don't see why we should pass up an easy way out."

Nimrod shrugged toward Meister. "Why don't you just go that way? If you're right, I'll be the first to say so. If you ain't, you'll never be seen again. Either way would be a satisfying ending." Nimrod started walking, and the others dutifully followed with Meister continuing to argue, but tagging along. A fog bank enveloped the mountains forcing them to watch the ground carefully. After another two hours, Nimrod approached what appeared to be a cliff drop-off off to the side of a rock outcropping. They approached the lip and looked down to see the beginning of a steep but gradual slope obscured by fog. Nimrod called for a rest, and said, "I got no doubt this is what Kit Carson told me was Emigrant Gap. It's the way out."

As the late morning sun burned off the fog, the pioneers rested against the boulders. Preacher wandered from behind the rocks to the open space by the gap, and suddenly dropped to his knees and raised his arms in thanksgiving.

The others, curious, walked around the rocks and saw stretching far into the distance, a rolling, green valley. It was the great central valley of California. The rains of autumn had overnight turned the vast land from summer brown to glittering emerald.

Preacher stared into the distance. "The saintly John Bunyan said in *Pilgrims' Progress* words that are apt this day: 'We have chosen the roughest road, and it led straight to the hilltop.'"

Nimrod muttered, "And every step was hell." Preacher glanced at him, and Nimrod quickly added, Amen."

For once, Preacher didn't scowl. He grinned.

The tattered group stared with open mouths, too overcome to cheer. California! Right there! Despair was erased as quickly as that brown grass of summer. There had always been a nook in their minds where they harbored a doubt that this moment would ever happen, or that even such a view could exist. But below and beyond, in front of their eyes, lay their future, their hopes and dreams. The land of green fields and endless summer. They had arrived and it was theirs!

Exultant, and feeling redeemed, Nimrod stood back and swept his hand across the horizon. "California! By the great God Jehovah, California!" He pronounced it loudly, but with a catch in his voice for those he had brought.

"That's it, folks. You're looking at it. Right down there in front of you. That's California. And right before you is the Bear Valley, and that's the Bear River. Its waters will end up in the Pacific Ocean. Sutter's Fort is just a whoop and holler away."

Flora laughed happily. "Another Bear River? I hope this one is kinder than the first one."

Nimrod continued. "I ain't much for speechifying, but down below, right down there, that's where you won't have no landlords, and no snow; where your children will pluck fruit from wild trees, and your cattle will grow so fat they'll waddle. Feast your eyes." He stood back, beaming as a ragged cheer finally erupted as they hugged and shook hands.

"I can't believe it. Finally," Gertie said as she wiped her tears and hugged her husband and baby.

"After all this," Hannah said in amazement.

"After all we've sacrificed to get here…" Cohen said with a sad face.

"And the good people we've left behind," Andrew said. Cohen looked at him and nodded at their shared bond of loss.

Aaron looked down at his wife and baby with a wide grin. "You see, Gertie, this is what we wanted. A new life. No sharecropping. This is why we left everything behind, and now we have everything ahead."

Gertie nodded with a reserved smile. The idea of good fortune had become remote to her. "God willing."

Andrew said, "It's a blessing we made it this far, but if someone back home was to write me and say he was coming over this same route, I'd write back and say—Stay home."

"This is a moment of thanksgiving and praise to the almighty Jehovah," Preacher said and fell to his knees. He started a lengthy prayer of thanks, and one by one, they dropped to their knees, even Meister, though reluctantly. Those who had suffered the most and lost loved ones also prayed, but not so fervently.

Descending to Bear Valley required some deft footwork, but they gradually made their way down the slope, slipping and sliding in places, and getting very muddy. Gertie carried her baby with her husband and Andrew bracing her on either side.

"How far you reckon we got to go afore we shake hands with General Sutter?" Andrew asked.

"He goes by captain, I'm told, unless he already promoted hisself," Nimrod said. He explained the Bear River flowed west into the *El Rio de las Plumas,* or, River of the Feathers. They would follow the Feather River south to the larger *Rio de los Sacramentos,* or, River of the Blessed Sacrament, which would lead them straight to Fort Sutter.

After all they had been through, all the sickness, clamoring over sharp rocks, the icy rivers, the biting insects, the fear of attack, and the horizon that never seemed to get closer, the hike ahead of them was that longed-for walk in the park. Because the autumn rains had barely started, the streams and rivers were low, and they had no difficulty crossing.

The undulating foothills could be climbed or descended without a handhold or undue strain. The softened wind, the shade of oak trees, and the green grasses, were blessings they yearned for as they tramped the dusty plains and deserts of almost two thousand miles.

However, with the tension to push ahead over dangerous ground now absent, they realized how weak and tired they really were. They started to take rest breaks more often, and grumble about trivial things. They became preoccupied with how they would survive in a new land with little money and no tools.

Nimrod noticed that Alice Dickens had lost her head covering along the way, and in the bright sun the fair skin of her face was turning a bright pink. He went to Bub and removed something from a saddlebag. He called Alice over, and said, "I think you could use this. He handed her a peach-colored sun bonnet with a frilly trim.

She took the bonnet and gratefully put it on. "Oh, thank you. It's so pretty. How did you happen to have this, Mr. Nimrod?"

"It were a keepsake concerning someone else who wore it. But it weren't made for being in a saddlebag. Someone sewed it for a pretty young lady like you, and the one who used to wear it."

With the passing of shared danger, they lost their sense of togetherness. They morphed from a tight group to individuals headed the same direction. The column started to string out, and those in front had to wait impatiently for stragglers who were in no hurry.

Nimrod had little difficulty shooting two deer, and he found wild onions along the banks of the streams they passed. Full stomachs fueled optimism, and their steps lightened as they approached Sutter's Fort.

CHAPTER THIRTY-FIVE

November 1845

They saw it in the distance from atop a hill. The whitewashed adobe of the walls glittered white in the sunlight. It was almost biblical. It was what they had labored for, dreamed about, risked death for, and sometimes didn't believe even existed.

As they looked in an awe-struck cluster, Preacher held up his Bible and proclaimed it the New Jerusalem.

It was Sutter's Fort. Over four hundred feet long and almost two hundred feet wide. It stood on the riverbank like a palace. The walls were nearly three feet thick and eighteen feet high. The fort had been constructed with five years of hard Indian labor. The human toll with which it was built diminished its alabaster visage.

Beyond the high walls lay fields of agrarian poetry. Orchards of fruit trees stood alongside fields of waving grain. Fat cattle kept heads down in the natural grasses unleashed by the seasonal rains.

Spread all around were hard-working Indians picking, hoeing, and herding the bounty of that empire. From a distance, they had the energy of willing, happy workers, but their faces were not discernable from afar. There were no smiles, no joking back and forth, and no singing the songs that had long given their people pleasure. White overseers on horseback watched them as intently as a parade. To those who hated southern slavery, it was an ominous throwback.

Meandering around the grounds were a dozen or so white men as though looking for something to do, but not very hard. Nimrod recognized several as former trappers who had run out of things to trap, and a few apparent loafers.

Gertie's eyes wandered back and forth over the panorama before them, and she said, "Isn't it wonderful how one Christian man with a vision and determination can turn a wilderness into a garden?"

Nimrod looked at the same scene with a frown, and said, suspiciously, "This ain't in Indians' nature. I ain't never known them to do farmer work, at least not without a hard prod."

Standing at the wooden gate to welcome them was the lord of all they had been admiring—or doubting.

Johann Augustus Sutter was a German-born Swiss expatriate of forty-two who claimed to be an ex-Swiss Guard officer of the Vatican, and a successful businessman. He was neither. He was a flim-flam man who had left a trail of false promises and unpaid bills all the way from Europe. Sutter was a jovial man, and not cruel by nature, but if he had to choose between being wealthy and being honorable…well.

In 1839, he convinced Juan Alvarado, the Mexican governor of California, that he could build an empire in the California wilds to the benefit of the Mexican government. He fast-talked himself into a grant of about fifty-thousand acres of wilderness at the confluence of the Sacramento and American rivers. The land was worthless to the Mexicans, and they hoped Sutter's development would forestall possible American immigration that worried them.

Sutter had lost little time in bribing chiefs of the Miwok and Maidu tribes to betray their people and provide workers to build his fort, plant crops, tend his cattle, and serve in his "army." To maintain control, he fed on tribal jealousies to keep them from unifying. In practice, they became his slaves, hundreds of them, and were treated accordingly. Observers related how the Indians were fed in troughs like hogs and locked up at night.

However, mainly what the pioneers saw as they approached was the refuge they had aspired to for five months of danger and exhaustion. Sutter's Fort was the gateway to their promised land. Nothing else mattered.

Sutter greeted the bedraggled nine adults and five children like relatives arriving at Christmas. He was a stout, balding middle-aged dandy of medium height and with a trimmed goatee and mustache. He wore his self-designed uniform that made him resemble a gereralissimo on parade or the lead tenor in an operetta. It was in character for him, but out of place in the wilderness. His welcoming smile pushed everything else into the background.

"*Willkommen,* my friends to *Neuve Helvetica.* Or, as you would say, New Switzerland." His booming German-guttural voice was followed by a grand, encompassing wave of the surroundings.

Aaron asked a silly question that was ignored. "Is this Sutter's Fort?"

Cohen stepped forward. "*Danke, mein herr.*"

Sutter raised his hands in delight, and said, "A countryman! We must talk. Your words are a soft breeze on my ears. The English language has added gray hair to the few I have remaining." He lifted his hat to show a bald head. Everyone laughed.

A gracious host, Sutter swept his hands in a welcoming gesture. "All of you, please come inside. You are my guests."

The inside walls of the fort were lined with shacks and lean-tos filled with craftsmen of all trades—blacksmith, farrier, wainwright, and also Sutter employees selling food, tools, clothing, and sundries, all at fair prices.

Sutter was a combination of a skilled land planner and snake-oil salesman. He hoodwinked the Mexicans out of a large parcel of California. Then Sutter bought from the Russians all the buildings, livestock, and everything else that had been Fort Ross on the Pacific coast. He had "his" Indians move it all about one hundred fifty miles to New Switzerland. He gave the Russians a note for the purchase, and then forgot about paying it.

Sutter invited them all to an area where Indian women served American farm dishes such as beefsteak, ham, beans, rice, and vegetables, but also some of German origin he had introduced, such as *sauerbraten, schnitzel,* and *hasenpfeffer.* No Indian dishes were offered.

Speaking in his guttural accent, Sutter told them candidly that the Mexican government believed they were using him to build a buffer against a feared invasion of American settlers. However, Mexican purposes and his intentions were not identical, he said. He was actively encouraging American immigration.

"I'm fortunate to have the services of an agent working to

persuade settlers to come here instead of Oregon. He's an excellent salesman. You might have met him on your trail, Judge Lansford W. Hastings."

Nimrod raised his eyebrows but said nothing. He was not about to chance a conflict with their host whom they needed much more than he needed them.

The pioneers sat at Sutter's long plank table in his home. The children's eyes widened as Indian servers put in front of them a German chocolate cake heavy with icing. Sutter walked over to a sidebar for a brown bottle and poured two fingers for each of his guests.

"Port from Madeira," he boasted. "Thanks to highly-placed Mexican friends, I have favored access to ships arriving in San Francisco Bay." Nimrod drank the strange, sweet wine as he would a drink in a tavern by bolting it down in one throw-back. Sutter's face showed a flash of indignation at his prize dessert wine being thus mistreated, but he replaced it with a quick smile.

As they listened to Sutter, the pioneers were dumbstruck by his largesse. He would give temporary housing to each family in shacks he had built on his property, and also employment to each man. In the springtime, he would sell to them land and farming equipment on generous terms and assign Indians to help in building houses. He would employ Flora as a schoolteacher, and Hannah would become the solitary doctor for the Sutter empire, replacing one who drank himself to death.

Hannah put down her fork, stunned. A doctor? Me? She looked at Sutter to make certain he was serious. She wanted to ask him to repeat the promise, but his smile and nod looking directly at her confirmed he was.

He said, "I see you are shocked. You needn't be. Your fellow travelers have praised your healing skills. In due time, we will discuss your needs."

There was nothing about a wage for her, medical supplies, and who her patients would be.

No matter. She would be a doctor. It was enough.

Sutter answered the question on everyone's mind: Why?

He stood up at the head of the table, "We have everything

we need here except what is most important: people. Industrious, God-fearing folk who will build New Switzerland into a Christian empire of peace and prosperity."

What he did not reveal was the goal of greatly enlarging his holdings in the vast interior of California. To do that, he needed settlers loyal to him. Mexico had been independent of Spain for a mere quarter-century, and they didn't quite know what to do with the wilderness called California, almost two thousand miles north of Mexico City.

The non-Indian, *Californio* population of California, mainly white Spanish descendants, was not more than ten thousand. Sutter knew if he built up the numbers of ambitious Americans, acquisitive, and often spoiling for a fight, he would have the leverage to demand control of much of northern California from Mexicans who didn't place a high value on it, anyway.

However, Sutter's generosity was so bountiful the pioneers didn't question his motive. Given their condition, they would have made a deal with the devil, a level to which John Sutter did not quite measure.

Nimrod leaned back and watched Sutter dazzle the pioneers who, for the first time, were able to believe, *really* believe, that California might have been a good idea. However, when his eyes met Sutter's, each could see that he was read by the other. Nimrod saw a huckster using the sweat and pain of innocent Indians to further his goal of cheating Mexicans who made the mistake of trusting him.

For his part, when Sutter read Nimrod's face, he saw a hard man who was not easily taken in. It unnerved him, but it also made him want to win Nimrod over, as though it would elevate Sutter in his own eyes if he gained control of a man who might be his moral superior. As the meal broke up and the pioneers began to leave, Sutter intercepted Nimrod at the door and touched him lightly on the arm. "Herr Lee, a word, if I may."

Nimrod nodded and moved a few feet aside with Sutter, who said after the others had left, "Sir, I'm told of your great skill as a hunter and guide. I require such a man. This valley and foothills have game animals that trip over each other." He stopped to chuckle at his humor. "I would be greatly favored if you would agree to be the main hunter of this fort. You would have every resource at your command—skinners, packers, and supporting hunters for dangerous game. I would pay you well, a matter we can most congenially discuss. It would give the Indians more of the meat they prefer and would save my valuable herd from butchering. I would also give you one thousand acres after two years of service."

"That seems uncommonly generous for a man out of the mountains who trapped beaver until there wasn't none. I'm figuring you might be asking more of me."

Sutter was unused to blunt talk, not often using it himself. He gave a short laugh. "You're a man with a keen eye for more than antelope, I can see. I would be foolish to try to sell a lame horse to such a man." He lowered his voice, though no one was within earshot. "Who knows what will happen in this—" He groped for a word. "In this *flüchtig*, world; 'volatile' might be your word. I am successful because I have foresight. Who knows what is going to happen in these times? I would like you on my side."

"I seen several fellers walking around looking like they can shoot a gun. Why not one of them to do your hunting?"

Sutter gave a short, derisive laugh. "Hah! Farmers and brawlers, that's all they are. You can't hitch a grizzly to a plow, or best one in a barroom brawl."

Nimrod was expressionless. "If I sign on to your outfit, I'll hunt your meat, but I won't bring hurt to Indians."

Sutter seemed injured by Nimrod's words. "In time, you will learn civilizing savages can sometimes be a painful process for everyone."

Nimrod hid a frown, but shrugged. "I reckon I'm obliged to say no, General. I've been recruited to join Captain Fremont's outfit at a place called Mission San Jose. They should be camped there 'bout now."

"I'm hoping you'll reconsider. I didn't hear you ask about wages," Sutter said with his version of a persuasive smile.

Then, Nimrod was the one to smile. "You said wages wouldn't be a problem."

Hannah and her children were led by an Indian woman to a one-room cabin with a fireplace, one small window, a table, four straight-back chairs, and two narrow beds. They were frontier beds with rope straps on which lay corn shuck mattresses sewn into thin, narrow bags. On the wall were hooks for clothes. From what they had been through, it was a mansion.

While Rachel and Billy were exploring their new home, Hannah sorted the medicines she had been able to preserve in the trip across the mountains. She looked up to see a radiant Flora in the door. "Welcome to my castle," Hannah said.

Flora whooped with glee and rushed in to hug Hannah. "I never thought a one-room shack would be a castle. I'm thinking of building towers and a moat. After sleeping in the snow and being stalked by a bear, this is Nirvana."

Hannah was probably one of a handful in California who knew the word. She nodded with enthusiasm. "Rachel and Billy can hardly remember sleeping in a real-life bed." She padded the corn shuck mattress and laughed. "Well, almost."

"And we both have jobs. I'm a teacher again, and you're a doctor. The graybeards back east would think the world was going to pot. God bless captain or general or admiral, or whatever-he-is, Sutter."

Flora had gathered gossip she was eager to share. Malachi Cohen was headed for Yerba Buena, wherever that was. Aaron and Gertie accepted Sutter's offer to settle down to farming. Preacher was going to stay and do missionary work among the Indians. Andrew wasn't certain.

"And Meister?" Hannah asked.

"No one bothered to ask," Flora said, and they both laughed.

Hannah's face turned pensive. "When I see how these Indians are treated, I wonder what God has to do with it. Nimrod said they're worked too hard and fed too little. He finds it troubling." She paused to consider her words. "I think I can do some good here."

Flora's face took on an "ah-ha!" expression. "Did I mention Nimrod? No, you did. Your conversation always comes back to

Nimrod. Why is that?"

Hannah ignored the question. "I heard just yesterday Nimrod is going to be a meat hunter for the fort," Hannah said.

"I heard different. Aaron said Nimrod turned Sutter down cold. He's fired-up to join the Fremont outfit with his friend, that Carson fellow. He's riding out in the morning."

Hannah's face became troubled. "Is that true?"

"Aaron talked to him just an hour or two ago."

Hannah grew silent, and Flora turned to leave. "Well, I've got lots to do." She took two steps toward the door, then looked back at Hannah with words both sympathetic and coaxing. "Listen to yourself, my dear. Listen carefully."

CHAPTER THIRTY-SIX

Nimrod's breath steamed in the chill of the late autumn air as he saddled Bub in the emerging rays of dawn. Others in the fort were also stirring. Their voices carried across the empty stable area as they shouted orders and groused about the day ahead. Nimrod's gear and possibles bag were packed on a horse he had bought on credit from Sutter, to be repaid at some distant date. He had only general directions to Mission San Jose, where he would find the Fremont expedition, but he would find it. He always did.

His mood was somber, as though leaving a family, but the emptiness he felt went beyond that. It was for something he had reached for, but never could quite grasp. He sighed. It was no matter, he tried to believe.

He forced his thoughts to the adventure ahead with the Fremont outfit. He heard footsteps and turned quickly. Footsteps were not to be trusted until their owner was known. He saw it was Rachel, with Billy close behind.

"Well, howdy, youngins. Why ain't y'all tucked in and dreaming about lollipops and spotted ponies?"

Rachel said nothing but smiled and extended a hand to him. He took what she offered and was surprised to see a piece of hard candy, similar to the one he had once given her.

He held up the candy to admire it. "This looks near as good as it's going to taste." He put it in his pocket, and said, "First, I want to do some bragging to the other fellers 'bout the pretty girl what gave me such a sweet favor."

Her smile turned sad as she blurted, "Don't go. Stay." She then wheeled and ran off. Billy kicked the dirt, then moved to Bub, rubbed the animal's flank, and said in his best man's voice, "This here mule needs more regular currying."

Nimrod smiled slightly, then said, also seriously, "Then I reckon I'd better see to it." Before Billy could respond, he saw Hannah coming and ran after Rachel in his hobbling gait.

Hannah came up and patted Bub's withers. "Were you going to just up and leave without a how-do-you-do?"

"I ain't one for goodbyes. They don't change how you feel. They just make you sad about it," Nimrod said, not looking at her.

"Are you coming back?"

"A mountain man don't never know where a fresh trail will take him. My business is done hereabouts."

Hannah gestured with her head in the direction the children took. "Those children don't agree." He nodded, but his gaze remained far off. "Look at me, please," she demanded gently.

He turned to face her and sighed deeply, letting his words form. "Hannah, I'm about to climb on this here mule and head west to ride with some mighty rough boys. They's my people. I was going to leave things as is. I figured that's what you wanted. But since you came out here to talk, I got to say, me and you, we need to dig up the roots of this thing between us. Whatever we have to say, we need to say it. Me and you, we've both of us seen what's over the hill and down the river. You ain't some pert lass I'm sparking on a front-porch swing."

She looked off. "I don't know where to start."

"Just start."

She closed her arms and looked toward him, but past him, with tears in her eyes. "I've had heartaches with men. You have with women. Those are hard gaps to get across for both of us."

He nodded, and said, "I have feelings for you, strong feelings. I surely do. But, like I said, we ain't children. We both know jumping into love is like a—like a clove hitch knot: easy to tie, but it can get tangled damn quick—Pardon my rough words."

"I don't know knots, but your meaning is clear. I'm not a schoolgirl."

He said, "After the preacher finishes mumbling, and the cake-eating, and the drinking, and the dancing is over, you got to piece your lives together. I got fears about you and me, we'd be like hitching a mule and ox together. Neither one would cotton to it."

Hannah nodded. "I can't deny your common sense. Two people ill-fitted can have years to be miserable together. But so can two peas in a pod, so to speak. I'll say my words frankly: Out here in this wilderness, a woman needs a man. If she's lucky, *really* lucky, the one she ends up with will be a good one. Luck has not been my friend in the choices I've made. One man took his leave from me. He was a good man, but I was still left alone. Another man abused my children and me. You know that story."

"Yes, ma'am. I saw that. You got a right to be skittish."

"I've learned to look first for the traits I don't care for in a man. I've seen them in you—a few." She hoped he wasn't offended. He wasn't. "But I let that blind me to the good things, and you've got plenty of those." She paused to add weight to her words. "A whole bunch." She filled her voice with force. "I'll tell you on the level, Nimrod Lee, I've come to realize you're like any other creature on this cruel earth: To survive means to adapt. And you've adapted well. But how you've done it, I'm just not used to. Your violence frightens me, but I've seen you take no pleasure in it, and you don't seek it out. You can be a kind man, and you have a sense of rough justice."

"Thank you, ma'am—Hannah. I left off courting you because I thought you was too good for me, and you had came to realize it. Most of the white women I've known seemed to be of that mind, and it made me fidgety toward you, and I shied away. I thought of you everday. Ever single day. I can't disremember what we shared."

She smiled her appreciation. "You don't seem to have a problem seeing me as an equal. That means a whole lot." Her eyes said his reply would be a test.

He laughed ironically. "Ha! No, ma'am, *that* surely ain't a problem, it surely ain't." He shuffled his feet nervously. "The real problem is, there's lots of arguments agin me, I fear."

She put her hand on his arm. "The heart wins those arguments."

He tensed, wondering where this was headed.

"Let's stop talking in circles. I've learned these past months. I've been wallowing in self-pity; too stupid to see what was right in front of me—you."

She paused, but he was out of words. "I've got feelings for you, Mr. Lee, gentleman of Kentucky. Feelings that promise to grow into deep love." She paused, and then her face became an impish grin. "I want what we had that night on the Platte, again and again—There, I've said it! And I hope you don't think I'm brazen for it."

He looked at her with soft eyes as he removed his hat and went down to one knee; he tilted his face to lock eyes and smiles with her. "Nana, will you marry me?"

She smiled and combed his hair with her hands. Oh, that sweet name.

He took a deep breath to steady his emotions. "I'll love you and take your children as my own. I'll help you be a doctor, best I can. I'll put food on the table. I'll protect you and be faithful to you. My maw made me swear to honor women. And on her memory, and because you are dear to me, I will honor you."

She reached down and guided him to his feet, then put her arms around his waist. "My answer is yes. And I will take care of *you.*"

A kiss.

The end

As you say goodbye...

I invite your gaze to my other books.
My webpage is www.freddickey.net.

I'd also like to hear from you. I'm at freddickey1@gmail.com. And if you have a few minutes, kindly leave a review of the book on Amazon and/or Goodreads. You'll have my gratitude for your forthright opinion.

Thank you for reading *Days of Hope, Miles of Misery.*

Be well, and be happy.
Fred Dickey

Here are the links to copy:
https://www.amazon.com/Days-Hope-Miles-Misery-Oregon/dp/1735834106/

https://www.goodreads.com/book/show/55849811-days-of-hope-miles-of-misery

CPSIA information can be obtained
at www.ICGtesting.com
Printed in the USA
LVHW021616090721
692281LV00001B/42